PRAISE FOR BOOK C  T

Winner of the]

Best Fant.

"*Frost Moon* is a choice and fascinating pick that shouldn't be overlooked for fantasy readers."
—*Midwest Book Review*

"Let me warn readers that they are going to be blown away. *Frost Moon* is one of a kind and pure genius. I devoured this book in one night. . . . Definitely worth the loss of sleep because there was no way I was going to stop reading *Frost Moon* once I started."
—*Book Lovers Inc.*

"A dark and gritty Urban Fantasy with rich characters, great hairpin turns . . . and enough tension and danger to keep you on the edge of your seat madly flipping pages to find what happens."
—*Sidhe Vicious Reviews*

"I am hard-pressed to adequately describe the latest book to be shifted in my direction for review. Thank you to the powers-that-be for the opportunity to be one of the first readers captivated by Dakota Frost and her magical tats. Addictive, sassy, sexy, funny, intense, brilliant . . . any and all of these adjectives describe not only the book itself but Anthony Francis's tall, bi-sexual, tattoo-specialist heroine . . . Mr. Francis has delivered not only a sexy and spectacular heroine, but given depth, emotion and memorable personalities to the many faces found in the supporting cast that give life to this paranormal tale."
—*Bitten By Books*

Books by Anthony Francis from Bell Bridge Books

Skindancer Series

Frost Moon

Blood Rock

Liquid Fire

Spectral Iron
(coming 2016)

Stranded
(novella in the *Stranded* anthology)

Jeremiah Willstone and the Clockwork Time Machine
(coming 2015)

SKINDANCER
THE MAGIC CONTINUES

LIQUID FIRE

ANTHONY FRANCIS

BELL BRIDGE BOOKS

This is a work of fiction. Names, characters, places and incidents are either the products of the author's imagination or are used fictitiously. Any resemblance to actual persons (living or dead), events or locations is entirely coincidental.

Bell Bridge Books
PO BOX 300921
Memphis, TN 38130
Print ISBN: 978-1-61194-626-0

Bell Bridge Books is an Imprint of BelleBooks, Inc.

Published in the United States of America.

We at BelleBooks enjoy hearing from readers.
Visit our websites
BelleBooks.com
BellBridgeBooks.com
ImaJinnBooks.com

10 9 8 7 6 5 4 3 2 1

Cover design: Debra Dixon
Interior design: Hank Smith
Photo/Art credits:
Hand/Skull (manipulated) © Maksim Shmeljov | Dreamstime.com
Woman (manipulated) © Dreamerve | Dreamstime.com
Woman (manipulated) © Peter Kim | Dreamstime.com
Background (manipulated) © Unholyvault | Dreamstime.com

:Lflo:01:

DEDICATION

To the people of Greenville, who gave me life.
To the people of Atlanta, who trained my mind and body.
To the people of the Bay, who welcomed me as a kindred spirit.

1. FIRE IS LIFE

"Fire is life," said Jewel Grace. "That's why I want to summon a dragon."

"Do . . . what?" I said, staring at the cute granola chick in the aisle seat beside me as if she were a crazy person. The gypsy-chic Bohemian had caught my eye from the start of our flight out to San Francisco: wry, curvy, curly-haired—and, from the way she surreptitiously checked out not just my tattoos and my Mohawk, but my breasts, a probable lesbian—but for the first two hours, I'd no time for flirting. I'd been preoccupied comforting my newly adopted weretiger daughter on her very first airplane ride. After Cinnamon finally fell asleep, Jewel and I started talking, and she'd seemed sane, until now; but who knew what bad wires lay beneath that mass of copper curls? "I'm sorry, I thought you just said—"

"Fire is my life," said Jewel, stretching out lithe arms, making her intricate leather and chainmail bracers jingle—and making my eyes follow the deft movements of her delicate hands. "I'm a professional fire magician, and I'm traveling the world, trying to summon a dragon."

Jewel caught me looking and smirked—but then her eyes flicked to my bare, tattooed arms, gazing with delicious indecency at my masterwork: a vast tribal dragon, my totem animal, a glorious, colorful, intricate tattoo covering half my body.

Roused by her attention, the Dragon stirred to life, sliding over my skin like magic.

No, not just *like* magic; my tattoos *are* magic.

My name is Dakota Frost, and I'm a Skindancer, a magical tattoo artist. My skin is a living canvas, covered from my shaved temples to my slender toes in a network of magical marks, powered by my beating heart, that project my intentions onto the world when I dance.

Which makes a cramped middle airline seat the worst possible place for six-foot-two me to lose control of a tattoo. The Dragon is a re-inked version of my masterpiece, but it never set right since I was forced to use it in a magical duel before the re-inking was completed.

As I squirmed, *it* squirmed, empowered by the flex of my living canvas. My control was never the best—I quit my Skindancing training after learning to tattoo—and being crammed into an airplane seat made it tricky to keep my unexpectedly animated Dragon from squirming free.

As it slid over me, I became acutely aware that the beige tube around us was shooting through the air at seven hundred miles an hour, that beneath the dark blue carpet lay six miles of down . . . and that in that duel, I'd destroyed a reception hall with the half-finished design.

The last thing I needed was for the full Dragon to bust out at thirty thousand feet.

"Buh," Jewel said, staring slack-mouthed as the tail of my dragon slid over my shoulder. She rubbed her eyes—then held her hand over her face, peering between two fingers. "Oh. My. God. I just said *summon a dragon*—and your tattoo came to life!"

I sighed. I take back what I said: the last thing I needed was to be sitting next to a crazy magician—the kind of woo-woo who just might decide she needed *my* Dragon to summon *her* dragon. It wouldn't have been the first time that a crazy tried to harvest my canvas.

I know calling that "crazy" sounds a little harsh from someone with a living magic tattoo crawling over her skin—but there's magic, and then there's ridiculous. There's a reason they call me the Skeptical Witch—I don't swallow the lore of the magical world whole.

"Sorry, Miss Grace," I said, pouring on my best Southern charm—which, frankly, isn't much, because between a dad on the Force and a mom teaching Special Ed, I ended up closer to military brat than Southern belle. "You didn't summon a dragon—it's just a magic tattoo."

"Oh, boo," she said, leaning, peering at my skin. "But I'd never say *just* magic—"

"Fair enough," I said, "but still . . . dragons went extinct before the dinosaurs."

"Oh, I know," Jewel said, eyes sparkling at me.

"Even the images of dragons we have are a muddle," I said, finding it hard not to smile back. "Our movie-friendly wings and scaly image is largely from Tolkien, and our myths are a bad jumble of folktales and distorted recollections of the creatures called drakes—"

"Oh, I know," she said again, her own smile growing.

"And drakes," I said, "nothing against them, but they're not really—"

"Oh, I know," Jewel said. "Though . . . I do want to see the Drake Cage while I'm here."

That stopped me for a moment. Drakes *are* some of the world's most magical creatures, granted fire and flight by the magical residue of dragons the same way my daughter was granted shapeshifting by the magical residue of . . . well, whatever the werekin precursor was.

Drakes might not be true dragons, but they were spectacular.

"Me too. Missed it on my last trip; my former girlfriend and I were . . . preoccupied," I said, proud I'd smoothly slipped in two little bits of information about my dating availability. I lifted my shoulder slightly. "Still . . . this is as close to a dragon as you're likely to get."

Jewel blinked, then smiled. "Oh, don't say that," she said, reaching out to gently touch the Dragon as it rippled over my skin. I felt a quiet thrill at the unexpected contact, then an electric charge as the tip of the tail accelerated under her fingers, sliding out of sight.

"I was going to say 'don't do that,' " I said, "but I think she likes you."

Jewel looked at me, mouth quirking up into a pleasant wry smile. Her eyes flicked to my arm, tracing the elaborate tattoos that were slowly shifting back into position—green tribal vines shimmering, red roses rippling in bloom, and sparkling in the design, tiny purple jewels.

"Good," she said, turning forward, smile struggling to grow broader, even as she flushed slightly with—was that embarrassment? *How cute!* Then she said, "Not to diss the spirit of your dragon, but when someone says a *thing* likes something, they normally mean *they* like—"

"*Yapping fuckers,*" barked my daughter—loud enough to make Jewel blanch. I gave Jewel a faint smile and turned to comfort Cinnamon, who was leaning against the window, holding her own tail, muttering, "Oh, when do—*fahh!*—when do we *lands?*"

I sighed and smiled, watching my beautiful daughter, my beautiful weretiger daughter, my beautiful, adopted, lycanthropic Tourette's-challenged brainiac teenager suffering through the last stages of an airplane flight, holding her own tail like a stuffed animal.

"It's all right, baby," I said, scratching her blue bandana; she shuddered, gripping her tail tighter, her head snapping a little in her sneezy Tourette's tic; I was *so* glad that I hadn't let her take this trip alone. "The captain announced the landing while you were asleep."

"I'm sorry, Mom," she said. "I didn't mean—*fah!*—to mess up your flirting."

I smiled, a little embarrassed myself now.

Cinnamon and I have the same last name, the same silver collars, and similar magical tattoos, but there the similarities end. I'm a smart aleck; she has Tourette's. I'm tall, leggy, and Mohawked; my adopted daughter is short, wiry, and crams her orange hair under a blue bandana. I dress edgy to stand out; Cinnamon dresses like a schoolgirl to make people overlook her twitching cat ears and flicking banded tail. I chose my intricate tattoos to achieve a whole library of magical effects; Cinnamon's bold tiger tattoos were imposed on her by a backwoods graphomancer to grant partial invisibility—which, paradoxically, makes her stand out more, since when she's *not* invisible, her tiger stripes cover her face.

I don't want to sugarcoat it; in modern America, where practicing magicians have talk shows and full-blooded vampires are hits on cable TV, werekindred still get the shit end of the stick. Cinnamon had been a street cat, warehoused, borderline abused, and I was happy she'd let me adopt her, gratified she'd taken to school so well, and *enormously* proud my little genius won a math prize which included a trip to San Francisco—but there was no way I'd make a vampire-collared werecat with stage fright go through post-9/11 airport security all by herself.

Or, for that matter, let her go into enemy territory alone.

Don't get me wrong, I love San Francisco, and not just because it's a LGBT mecca. It had a warm place in my heart from my first grownup vacation with my first childhood girlfriend, who'd left more than a few warm spots on my bottom at the dungeon of one of its fetish clubs. It held a new fascination for me as one of the few places in the United States that had a dojo for my favorite martial art, the obscure Okinawan karate called Taido. Heck, it might become a new *destination* for me; my childhood friend Jinx was going to move out here when her husband Doug graduated; they were finishing up their honeymoon in San Francisco right now.

But San Francisco was *not* Atlanta. It might not *literally* be enemy territory . . . but there was no magical shield protecting San Francisco like the magical Perimeter of Atlanta. There was no truce between vampires, werekin, and magicians in California like the mystical Compact of Georgia. There was no authority to prosecute rogue magicians in the Bay Area like Atlanta's Magical Security Council—which I myself had created and been roped into leading.

San Francisco was the magical Wild West.

We were flying into a city where magicians and werekin and vampires were at each other's throats . . . and I was a magician, with a weretiger daughter, both wearing the silver collars of the Lady Saffron . . . the Vampire Queen of Little Five Points.

What could possibly go wrong? All I had to do was beat sense into a whole Conclave of truceless magicians, werekin, and vampires who'd been at undeclared war for a century and a half. The Wizarding Guild actually seemed interested in what I was doing with the MSC, so, if I was lucky, they wouldn't kill us; and, if I was very lucky, maybe I'd collect some new allies.

With that little task out of the way, Cinnamon would be free to collect her award—and, if I was very, *very* lucky, *I'd* be free to collect on a *debt.* San Francisco wasn't just the home of the Wizarding Guild; it was also the home of Alex Nicholson, my contact with the Guild, a good friend who had put his life on the line for me . . . and a man who owed me a million bucks.

OK, technically *Alex* didn't owe me that million; he had just inherited the leadership of the Valentine Foundation, which owed me that million for besting its late founder in a magical challenge he thought he couldn't lose—and, therefore, never thought he'd have to pay.

I closed my eyes with a sigh, then opened them to see Cinnamon's long bony fingers gripping the arms of the seat. "Oh, for the love, little girl," I said, putting my hand over hers and rubbing it warmly—then with that hand trapped, I leaned in, free hand poking at her huge ear. "Statistically speaking, it's the safest—my, are you getting ear mites again?"

"Mom!" she said, ducking away as my finger caught the tufts of hair. Cinnamon started swatting at me with her free hand, and as I continued to probe, she tried to get her other hand loose—but while she had more strength, I had more leverage. "Don't pick at it—"

And then the tires met the tarmac, and we were down.

"Mom," she said, as I released her hand after one last squeeze. She half smiled, half glared, holding her hand, ear twitching something fierce. "Meany," she said, screwing her knuckle in her ear; she never used the claws on anything delicate. "Big old meany—"

"Distracted you, didn't I?" I said, leaning back in the seat. I heard a chuckle, and looked over to see Jewel smiling. I smiled back, a little forced, still unsure of whether there was real interest there or she was just an irrepressible flirt. "What?"

"Nothing," she said, covering her smile with her hand.

After crossing the country at seven hundred miles an hour, the plane crossed the tarmac at a crawl. Everyone pulled out their cell phones; even I dug out my smartphone. I called the Lady Saffron, far up in First Class, but she didn't answer. Jewel? She texted like a demon.

Then the arrival bell rang. Quick as a flash, Jewel hopped up and popped open a bin.

"I hate all this 9/11 nonsense," she said, tugging at her jacket repeatedly, trying to pull it out from beneath a heavy, ancient Samsonite someone had jammed in to the overhead at the last minute. "I have to run all my gear through baggage claim—holy cow."

I'd reached out over her head and lifted the Samsonite out of the way so she could free her jacket. Jewel glanced back at me and did a double take—even on large planes, I can usually bump my forehead against the roof if I stand tippy-toe.

Cinnamon made a little yelp, her tail apparently caught in a tangle of our unbuckled seatbelts. As I leaned to help her, a man in the opposite side stood and opened the bin. Soon, the aisle was filled with passengers unloading their bags, with Jewel two rows ahead of us.

I started forward to get her card or figure out how to continue the dragon discussion later, but irate passengers in the row ahead of me hopped up, and Cinnamon tugged at me from behind. With long arms, I scooped down our carry-ons while the row emptied.

When the logjam of passengers in front of us had cleared, Jewel was gone.

We tromped off the plane, wedged past impatient departees, passed rows of seats empty and full, and sailed out into the terminal. All the airports I had visited since I started the Council were starting to blur. All had the same blah décor—here, blue and gray patterned carpet. All tried to spice it with airport art—here, a giant driftwood horse. And all had an army of underpaid staff—here, Latinos and Asians, picking up after us wasteful consumers destroying the atmosphere with our travel.

Soon, I found the stairs to the baggage claim area, where once again I was next to Jewel.

"Surprise, surprise," Jewel said, mouth quirking up a little.

"Fancy meeting you here," I said, pulling Cinnamon's bag off the carousel.

"Fancy that," Jewel replied. A huge black bag, covered with stickers, thudded out of the conveyor and slammed down onto the carousel, and she began wedging her way with a litany of "excuse me's." The bag was passing too fast, so I reached in and pulled it out.

"Here you go," I said. What *was* it about this woman? I couldn't resist trying to help her, trying to show off for her. I tried to steel myself, to play cool, then I caught Jewel staring at the muscles in my arms as I set the bag down. I flexed my bicep and said, "Show's for free."

"Oh, God," she said, putting her hand to her forehead. "Sorry, thanks."

"No need to be sorry," I said, "and anyway, 'sorry' is normally my line."

"Who's your new friend?" asked an impish Southern belle voice from beside us, and I saw Jewel's head jerk aside to see the red-hair-black-dress- bonnet-and-bomber-goggles show that was the Lady Saffron—my ex-girlfriend. She looked Jewel up and down. "A*dor*able."

"I . . . I," Jewel said, eyes widening at Saffron, clearly not sure how to take her.

Saffron was a daywalker, making few concessions to her vampirism beyond the goggles. The dark black cloth made her red hair stand out like fire, but it exposed her face and throat. Most people never guessed that she was the most powerful vampire in the Southeast.

But you couldn't miss her entourage. Darkrose, Saffron's consort, wore a dark, gray-hemmed velvet traveling hood that cloaked her almost completely. Beside her stood Vickman, her sharp-eyed, bearded bodyguard, quietly menacing in his black hat and bulky coat. Collecting the bags was Schultze, Darkrose's human servant, a tall, swarthy, reserved man in an immaculate white suit with black patterned trim that echoed Darkrose's robe. For those in the know, a hooded figure with matching attendant and hovering bodyguard just screamed "vampire."

But I couldn't tell if Jewel could tell. She looked at Saffron's imperious black dress and regal red hair pouring out of her bonnet; then at the black leather catsuit beneath Darkrose's Sith traveling cloak, then back at me, eyes lingering on the steel collar that symbolized I was under Saffron's protection. Jewel raised an eyebrow; I returned the favor. Perhaps this curly-haired granola girl was into more devious forms of alternative culture than just magical firespinning.

Schultze leaned forward and pulled another bag off the carousel. "The last bag, ma'am."

"Thank you, Schultze," Darkrose said wearily. She was upright, but sagging to the point you could barely see her dark features beneath the hood; unlike Saffron, she was not yet a full daywalker and found the day not only dangerous but draining. "All we await now is Nyissa."

"Another of your . . . friends?" Jewel asked, trying to subtly lift her head to peer inside Darkrose's cloak—not looking at her features, but at the collar of her leather catsuit, barely visible beneath the hood of the cloak. "Is she coming on another flight?"

"No, she came on this one with us," I said, smiling. I had been wondering how far we could push this without actually mentioning the word "vampire," and now, I guessed, was it—I pointed at the traveling coffin coming out of the oversized baggage area. "Over there."

"Oh, no, I'm *so* sorry," Jewel said, face falling. Damn it, I hadn't intended to make her think Nyissa was *dead*. But before I could explain, her phone buzzed and she pulled it out. "Hey, my ride is here. Nice meeting you, Mohawk Lady."

"Great meeting you, Granola Girl," I said.

And Jewel walked off, texting into her phone. Far, far down the terminal, I saw a young, short muscular man with spiky hair waving, and Jewel waved back. But rather than running to meet him, she stopped, wavered, dug something out of her bag—and walked back to us.

"I'm sorry," she said. "I hate the whole 'meet someone on the plane, have a nice conversation, then spoil it by passing over a greasy business card' thing. I hate it when some slimy old businessman or lipstick lesbian does it to me. But after our conversation—"

And she handed over, not a business card, but a little postcard, a glossy little flyer for "Fireweaver's Foray" at something called the Crucible. "We're performing tonight," she said, "so this may be too last minute. But it really sounds like something you'd enjoy."

"Thanks," I said, flipping it over. It was in Oakland, which, according to the directions, was on the far side of the San Francisco Bay. Huh—I always thought Oakland was a suburb of Los Angeles. Who knew? "No promises. We have a full schedule, and I don't know if we can."

Jewel smiled, and when she did so her eyes seemed to sparkle. "Great! See you."

And then she strode off, texting into her phone as she went to join her friend.

"Did I not just say I probably wouldn't make it?" I asked, watching her go.

"With your words," Darkrose said, "but not your tone."

"I heard it as 'definitely make it,' " Saffron said. "Very clearly 'definitely'."

"Mohawk and Granola sittin' in a tree," Cinnamon said—then hissed. The last time she'd used that phrase, it had been "Cotie and Cally," and Cally—Calaphase, my ex-boyfriend—wasn't with us anymore. "Sorry, Mom. That was mean."

"S'okay," I said, rubbing her headscarf until it went crooked and she swatted at me. "Have to get over it sometime."

"And tonight's a good night to do it," Saffron said. "We're required to present ourselves to the Vampire Court of San Francisco, but you're not welcome in their territory until invited—and I'm sorry, Cinnamon, that includes you too. You both wear my collar."

"I knew it," Cinnamon said, head snapping aside. "Nothing but trouble—"

"Cinnamon, you're *never* trouble," I fibbed. "Saffron, look . . . Doug and Jinx are staying in San Francisco. Are you seriously telling me that they're safer there than we are because *we're* wearing your collars? I thought these stupid things guaranteed us protection—"

"*In Atlanta*," Saffron said. "But you're not safe in San Francisco until we know that will be honored. That's not just for your protection; it's for ours. You both wear my collar—so to other vampires, you're not just under my protection—you're my minions."

"I am not anybody's 'minion,' " I said.

"But they don't know that," Darkrose said, raising her head, weary, but with an edge to her clipped South African accent. "And one powerful vampire bringing a formidable werekin and a very formidable witch into the territory of another could be considered an act of war."

"You can stay at the airport hotel, or you can go have a night on the town," Saffron said, folding her arms, setting her chin, making the locks of red hair pouring out of her bonnet look like the mane of a red lion. "But you can't join us in San Francisco until you're cleared."

"All right, *fine*, a night on the town," I said, rubbing Cinnamon's headscarf. "Oakland looks like it could be only, what, a thirty minute drive or so? Let's catch some dinner, then go see Jewel spin some fire. After all—wait for it—what's the worst that could happen?"

—&

"On the streets of Oakland?" asked a sharp voice. "You could *die*, Dakota Frost."

2. Shoot the Messenger

Vickman cursed and shoved Darkrose back with one hand, Schultze closing ranks beside him so they shielded her with their bodies from the short, wiry man in the tough biker leathers who had seemingly popped *right into the middle of us.*

Time slowed down. Everything got quiet. The crowd receded, its people blurring, its noise fading, leaving this man at the center. I jerked back into a low karate stance, Cinnamon hissed, claws out, and Saffron . . . just stood there, amused, as if she was invulnerable.

"What the hell—" Vickman said. His voice echoed oddly, and he stiffened, clenching his teeth. Whatever weapons he had were no doubt in the baggage; whereas this guy could have come out off of the streets with an Uzi under his leather jacket. "How did you—"

"An area glamour," I guessed, relaxing slightly, waving my arm through the air. I could feel the slightest tingle of magic, some sparkle of mana that reacted against my tattoos. "Mostly, a silence spell. Surprising how much people rely on sound to draw their attention, isn't it?"

"Surprising," said the wiry little man—five-six, maybe five-seven, his motorcycle jacket open, and his sandy hair tousled, like it had been blown back—"how much people don't listen. Especially when told things like 'Stay away, Dakota Frost.' "

"I beg your pardon," Saffron said, scowling. "I believe we negotiated—"

"Quiet, Scarlett O'Hara," the man said, eyes fixed on me. "This is wizarding business—"

"*Wizarding* business?" I said. "Like, Wizarding Guild? But I'm *working* with you!"

"You think you're working with us?" The man's lip curled. "Just because we assigned a babysitter to your crazy little Council? Nicholson's barely a wizard, and he's not *working* with you, he was supposed to keep *tabs* on you—and he sure as hell doesn't speak for the Guild."

"Dakota," Saffron said, voice warning. "What haven't you told me—"

"Nothing," I said. "Hang on. When I first talked about this trip, there was some flak—"

"Now she remembers," the man said. "You were *specifically banned* from the Bay—"

"We worked that out, first week! The Wizarding Guild even invited me to give a talk—"

"Before they found out you were bringing a *coven of vampires!*" the man said, raising his voice, not two feet from Saffron—and I suddenly realized, *he doesn't know she is a vampire.* He couldn't; as she glared, he ignored her, leaned in, and said to me, "Consider yourself *dis*invited."

Something was amiss. The Guild had cleared my visit. Their leadership seemed to want to know more about the MSC—I was giving a talk at their request. Heck, I had a Guild wizard, Alex Nicholson, not only on my new

Magical Security Council, but on speed dial.

And yet the guy in front of me who claimed to be with the Wizarding Guild had no clue I traveled with vampires that had no need of a coffin. Then I remembered how complicated vampire politics was with its secrets and factions—and suddenly, I got it.

"You're not from *the* Wizarding Guild," I said. "You're from a *faction* within it."

"The only faction you need worry about," the wiry man said. He shot his hand toward the inside of his jacket, then stopped just short, a grin spreading across his face as Vickman convulsed. "May I? I have a present but I wouldn't want to, you know, spook you."

I caught a flash of white inside his biker jacket. While the wiry man's attention was focused on Vickman, I shot my long arm out. The wizard jerked back like he'd been stung, but not fast enough, and my hand came back with a white envelope plucked from his map pocket.

"Fuck me!" he said, raising his fists in what looked like a karate stance—Tae Kwon Do or something Korean-derived. *Huh.* I was actually starting to recognize the subtleties of the different martial arts. *Interesting.*

"I take it I'm to open this?" I asked. The envelope was hand addressed, simply to "Frost." I passed my tattooed palm over it, but the yin-yang didn't absorb any stray magic. "There's no live magic on this, but if it's filled with powdered anthrax or whatever, Vickman—shoot him."

Vickman scowled, nodded, and put his hand inside his jacket, as if there really was a gun in there he'd managed to sneak past security. The wiry little man's eyes bugged and he started to back up, but he found himself penned in between Cinnamon and Saffron.

Fists still raised, the little man made a shrugging move to back them off, and I expected Saffron to show her fangs—but *Cinnamon* reacted first, growling quiet but deep, staring up at him, chin set, never taking her eyes off him for an instant—like a cat in a challenge.

The little man's face went ashen. "Now wait a minute," he said, looking around for help—but everyone was still ignoring us, passing our zone of silence in quiet blurs. And if he popped the bubble and cried for help, the TSA would be all over him, too. "Don't you—"

"You're the one who materialized in the middle of a crowd of Edgeworlders," I said, cautiously cracking the envelope open. "If you wanted to play this nice, you should have waited for us with a sign that said 'Frost' rather than playing stupid wizard tricks."

The man cursed, but relaxed slightly as I pulled out . . . tickets, back to Atlanta. I thumbed through them . . . and found one for almost every member of our party, right down to my daughter: FROST, CINNAMON. Only Nyissa was left out. Disturbing.

"So," he said, folding his arms, not looking at Cinnamon, even though she could take his throat out. "Now you know the score. We told you not to come. You came anyway. So we're giving you an out. Take the tickets, put a leash on your pet tiger—"

"Oh, you did not just say that," I said, as Cinnamon's growl deepened.

"—leave your vamps in their coffins, and fly with them back to your little hick hellhole!"

At "vamps," Saffron chuckled, glancing at Darkrose, and the little man raised an eyebrow, not getting it. I was looking over the tickets; there was indeed a shipping ticket for one coffin, but apparently he didn't know that—or hadn't been told that. Even more disturbing.

"You've been misinformed," I said. "First, my *daughter* doesn't wear a leash. Second, Atlanta is very advanced—its metro is larger than San Francisco and San Jose combined. And third, most of the vampires in our party don't travel in coffins. Only our . . . enforcer."

Saffron dropped her hand on the little man's shoulder, baring her fangs, and a second later, Cinnamon did likewise, half a snarl, half a grin. The man tensed in fear, glancing back and forth between them—and then I heard a pair of clicks behind me, and turned.

Startled travelers were backing up as the latches on the coffin at the loading area opened on their own. Slowly, the lid lifted, lifted by a porcelain-pale arm; then *she* rose, a shag of violet hair over pure white skin, a slender body wrapped in stripes of dark cloth—with a long metal poker carried in her hands, like a riding crop. The Lady Nyissa. My "bodyguard."

Technically, I was Nyissa's vampire "client," gaining her protection in exchange for an act of submission. Saffron, my former girlfriend, had demanded I wear this actual submissive's collar, like, *in public*, to receive her protection . . . and yet had rarely delivered. Nyissa, on the other hand, my former enemy, had only asked for a drop of blood and a quarter . . . and had guarded me *in person* in a vampire court, nearly costing her life.

Where Darkrose and Saffron were daywalkers, and covered themselves in layers and layers of clothes that helped them brave the day, Nyissa was not—and, as a working dominatrix on top of being a vampire, flaunted her body, wearing as little as she could get away with.

Nyissa sashayed up to us, working it, her hips making her flared skirt sway, her body seeming to grind against the negative space between the two vertical stripes of cloth that covered her breasts. Your eyes naturally followed that great white expanse of flesh up from her navel, between her breasts, and then to her throat—where a horrible scar covered what should have been her voice box. I tore my eyes away and glanced at the little wizard, who was mesmerized—first staring openly like at a peep show, then mouth dropping in horror as Nyissa bared her considerable fangs: sharp canines twice as long as a human's—and far more pointed.

A slight hiss escaped Nyissa's mouth; with her too-pale skin and too-violet hair, those silent bared fangs made her seem even more like a life-sized porcelain doll. She raised the poker until it was level with the scars, and the little wizard actually raised a hand as if to ward off a blow. Cruelly, she smiled, even more fearsome than bared fangs—and subtly, she released one hand from the poker and flicked it at me, American Sign Language for, *is there a problem?*

"Not for us," I said aloud—my ASL is still rusty. The little wizard was still staring—not that I blamed him; Nyissa was eye-catching even in this turn as Scarthroat Vampirella—but I snapped my fingers and said, "Hey! Eyes on me. What's your name?"

"Ferguson," he said sharply.

"Well, Ferguson," I said, offering the tickets back to him, "I don't know what you've done to piss off whoever sent you, but they must have known—*should* have known—we had two daywalkers in our party, and they should have told you."

"Shit," Ferguson said, looking around wildly, trying to get a bead on Darkrose and Saffron without ever fully taking his eyes off Nyissa—quite a trick if he'd been able to pull it off, and quite amusing since he couldn't. "Oh, shit shit *shit*—"

"Regardless," I said, "They should have known we can't accept these tickets; you need twenty-four hours notice to ship a vampire encoffined, and we can't leave Nyissa here without getting the permission of the Vampire Court of San Francisco. It would be a death sentence."

Ferguson hesitated, then snatched the tickets back. "Damn it," he said bitterly.

"What is this, amateur hour?" Vickman said. "If they knew all that—"

"Maybe they didn't," Cinnamon said brightly. "Sounds like they hates vampires. But maybe they never gots to ship 'em anywhere. I means, what's the postage? Maybe they—*fahh!*—wants to see if we're easy to spook. Boo! Or maybe they *did* know and gave'm somethin' to trip over."

"Trip over?" Vickman said. "You mean they *wanted* him to fail?"

"Maybe," Cinnamon said, shrugging, as Ferguson seemed to deflate. "S'like a bunt hunt. You sends a young were out hunting for 'bunts' in a place where humans'll probl'y get 'em. At least Fergie had a chance. If he fails, good for who hates him; if he runs us off, even better."

"I don't take it we can get the name of your employer, Mr. Ferguson?" I said.

"Fuck no," Ferguson said, clenching his teeth. "I don't want to get killed."

"How charming. May I then?" I said. I took the tickets back from him, then wrote CALL ME—DAKOTA FROST on the envelope with my number underneath. "Please tell whoever doesn't want us here that we've received their warning, and I want to speak to them."

Ferguson took it back, incredulous. "The Guild doesn't want to talk to you—"

"Your *master* doesn't want the Guild talking to *me*," I said. "But the Guild does. They invited me to the Northern California Practitioner's Conclave tomorrow, to report on my work in the Magical Security Council of Atlanta. If your master is in the Guild . . . he's probably invited."

Ferguson glared. "Frost, look," he said. "He—they want you out of their territory."

"I don't care what *he* wants," I said, jamming my hands in the pockets of my vestcoat. "This is a free country, and I have the right to bring my daughter here and keep her safe. And as far as the wizards who are here . . . well, all I care about is keeping them safe. Tell them that."

Ferguson started to retort, then froze as Saffron's hand tightened on his shoulder. "Tell them one more thing," she said softly in his ear. "See the steel collar around the Lady Frost's neck? And around the little girl's neck? Her name's Cinnamon, by the way. She's not a pet."

Cinnamon tugged at her collar, and I pulled at mine as well—polished stainless steel, with a soft black rubber liner and an elaborate S engraved on the front. Mine was comfortably fitted to my neck. Cinnamon's was far wider, so she could change.

Saffron drew back slightly, at first I thought to make her look imperious; then I realized the angle would make it easier for her to bite. Saffron waited for Ferguson to nod, then said, "That's the sign of the House of Saffron, the Vampire Queen of Atlanta. *My* sign."

And Saffron bared her cruel vampire fangs.

"Oh, *fuck me,*" Ferguson said, flinching away from her, but Saffron held him firm.

"If any harm befalls Dakota or Cinnamon, my wrath will be . . . awesome," she said, oh-so-sweetly, turning up the Southern Belle accent at just the right point to convey ultimate menace. Her fangs were as long as Cinnamon's. "Please deliver that along with Dakota's message."

"Understood," Ferguson said. He was shaking when she released him.

"Sorry," I said.

"What?" Ferguson said, still flinching away from Saffron.

"They really should have told you," I said. "They had to have known. I'm so sorry."

"What?" Ferguson said, backing away, slipping the envelope back into his vest. "What? Fuck you, lady, I-I'm loyal to—to the Guild! He—they would have told me if they'd known! And I can take care of myself!"

And then he zipped his vest up and whirled, and in a blink of magic he was gone.

My jaw dropped. It hadn't been teleportation, exactly—of that I was certain, as I'd become a bit of an expert in that area—but it was a damn impressive combination of accelerated movement combined with some kind of perceptual effect. I squinted, trying to see the traces, then gave up and put my hand to my brow to dispel the sudden magically-induced headache.

"Cool!" Cinnamon said, peering after him; then she, too, put her hand to her forehead and grimaced. "Ouchies—eggbeaters to the noggins—but super cool! Mr. Wizard meets Sonic the Hedgehog. Wind gots to whip him up though—ergo, them riding leathers."

" 'Ergo?' " Vickman asked, smiling. Even the grizzled ex-South African Defense Forces veteran was softening after half a year hanging around Cinnamon, and he reached to tousle her hair. "Since when does a street cat start dropping 'ergo' in polite conversation?"

"Hey! No mocking the me," Cinnamon said, trying to simultaneously swat at him while readjusting her headscarf. "Since my prof stopped asking me to solve problems, and started asking me to prove theorems." She looked at me. "Well, Mom? Do we bails on San Fran?"

I looked at her in shock . . . and then realized everyone was looking at me.

"Ah, hell," I said, leaning back and staring at the ceiling. I was the head of the Magical Security Council. I couldn't lean on Vickman's paranoia or defer to Saffron's authority; ultimately, the decision was on me.

"We cannot force harmony without a common purpose," Darkrose warned. "The truce in Atlanta was reached after wizards and vampires fought the graffiti plague, together. Perhaps the Guild here is simply not ready to accept an emissary allied to their longtime foes—"

"It's a faction," I said. "Not the whole Guild—"

"We could get a hotel at the airport," Saffron said. "We already have rooms for Dakota and Cinnamon; maybe we can expand the reservation. We can call the Vampire Court with our apologies, and leave as soon as we can arrange transport for Nyissa—"

"No," I said firmly. "Look . . . thanks, both of you. Those are good options, but we won't use them unless we have to. We stay. This is precisely the kind of infighting the Board has been successful at stopping in Atlanta. I'm sure we'll have no trouble here either."

"Oh, you had to go jinx it, didn't you?" Saffron murmured.

"So," I said, "should we hunker down in the hotel while you guys go to the Court?"

"*No,*" Vickman said. "I don't want you isolated in some place Fergie and his employer might know about—especially with your bodyguard here confined to her coffin in our hired car while the formalities are worked out in Court. Go to the club."

"The club? Where Jewel's performing? Neither of which we know anything about?"

"Ignorance is correctable," Vickman said, pulling out his phone. "Give me the card."

I extended the card, and Vickman took it, turned it over, and grunted. Then he flipped down his smartphone's keyboard and thumbed rapidly. He pursed his lips, making the white bristles in his salt-and-pepper beard sparkle; then he handed the card back to me.

"Probably. The website checks out and it's been advertised for months," he said. Then Vickman smiled, and his eyes got mischievous, reminding me a bit of a bearded Crocodile Dundee, though I knew I was mixing up my ruins of empire. "And it sounds like fun."

"You hits the Wayback that fast?" Cinnamon asked skeptically, sneezing.

"I have an app for it," Vickman said, showing her the phone, and Cinnamon cooed appreciatively. He pulled it away before she could snatch it, but then he began showing her how the app worked. "Put together by one of the Van Helsings back at the office."

I watched them natter on about scripts and Internet archives for a minute, then shook my head. When I adopted Cinnamon nine months ago, she had been almost illiterate, computer or otherwise. I had been a computer lab tech in college, so I showed her a few things. Now. . . .

"You ever feel stupid, listening to them?" I asked Saffron.

"No," Saffron replied. She was a few signatures away from a Ph.D. in vampirology, but knew no more about computers than I did; our childhood friend Jinx had got that gene. Saffron said, "They do leave me feeling a bit ignorant. Fortunately, ignorance *is* correctable."

"Only with great effort," I said. "All right, can we have a verdict? Safe? Fun?"

"Safe," Vickman said, closing his smartphone keyboard with a click. "Go to the club. It's an unplanned diversion from our agenda, which means you and

Cinnamon will be safer than we are—because no one will expect you to be there. Just . . . please be careful."

"Definitely fun," Cinnamon said, flipping the card over in her hands. She was smiling.

—⁓

"Alright, Cinnamon," I said, smiling back at her. "Ready for a girl's night out?"

3. PERFORMANCE ART

"The Crucible" turned out to be a fire arts center, housed in a huge warehouse space in grid-like streets near the portside of Oakland. The taxi driver missed it on the first pass, and we wormed our way back toward it through cute little row homes. The houses were nice, the streets were clean, and the cars . . . well, somewhat less so. It was an odd juxtaposition.

Just as the last light was fading from the sky, the driver pulled up next to the ticket stand, a converted hot red train caboose sitting on the corner of the Crucible's tiny parking lot. "You just pay for ride," he said, pointing at the meter, which he had stopped when he passed the Crucible. "My mistake. You no pay for the loop around."

"No problem," I said, digging in my wallet, thinking of the man's olive skin, his wiry dark hair; he reminded me of someone. Then it hit me—he looked a lot like a vampire I'd known named Demophage. "By any chance, are you Romanian?"

He leaned back at me, smiled. "Lithuanian," he said. "Grandmother was Romanian."

"Close enough," I said, passing over one-two-*choke!*-three twenties. "Keep the change."

Cinnamon and I hopped out, someone hopped in, and the cab sped off. At first, I'd been worried about taking my underage daughter to a "club," but the Crucible seemed to be open to all ages. The parking lot was filled with a full spectrum of humanity—haughty socialites in evening wear, down-to-earth families with teenaged children, slackers in flannel and dreads, Goths and preppies, and even a few Edgeworlders mixed in with the mundanes.

A young man with wolf ears caught my eye, reminding me of Cinnamon as I'd first seen her in the rough and tumble crowd at the werehouse. Cinnamon saw him too, swatting at him, but he howled at her, and she squealed and ducked behind me, just like she had at the werehouse.

"Is he—" she asked, peeking around my arm as I laughed.

"I dunno," I said, smiling at the boy, who had laughed when Cinnamon had ducked behind me . . . and who looked about Cinnamon's age. "Fantastic makeup if he's a mundane, a pretty heavy change for the new moon if not. Can't you smell him?"

"Too many," she said, as we lost him in the milling crowd. "And too far—"

"You like wolves, don't you? You could go check him out, sniff his butt—"

"Mom!"

And then we found the line for walkups and patiently waited. I mean, *I* patiently waited. After we'd been waiting a while—approximately seventeen seconds—Cinnamon began doing her best Tigger impression, soon hopping even higher than I was tall, so vigorously that her appropriately-themed Tigger backpack bounced on its bungees.

"Are-we-there-yet, are-we-there-yet?" she was saying, and even though she sounded like she was being ironic, I was glad my tough little street cat could have a little childish fun.

"Hey, hey, hey," I said, trying to guide her with my hands so she didn't kill anyone in the line by bouncing on them. "You can see better than me—"

"I can take the next customer!" a blond-haired lady called, opening a new window. Cinnamon and I bolted forward, and the woman grinned as Cinnamon hopped down in front of her, one ear canted beneath her tilted headscarf. "Wow, that's a wonderful costume."

"It's not a costume," I said, rubbing Cinnamon's shoulders, relishing the ticket taker's surprised double take as Cinnamon flicked her ears. "One adult, one child—unless by, some chance, we're on the guest list?"

"Uh, I dunno," the woman said, glancing aside at something inside the caboose. "That would have been at will call—what's the name?"

"Dakota Frost," I said.

"I mean, the performer," she said, taking a clipboard from someone.

"Jewel Grace," I said. "Don't worry about it, it was a long shot—"

"No, no, you're on the list, a last-minute addition," she said, flipping up the clipboard. Then she scowled and peered out past us into the line. "Where's the rest of your party? She put you down for six spots."

I raised an eyebrow—the same number of tickets Ferguson offered us; then I relaxed as I realized it was one slot for every member of our party Jewel had seen walking. Pretty darn observant—but almost certainly a coincidence.

"They couldn't make it," I said. "Unavoidably detained—vampire politics."

The woman's eyes bugged, and Cinnamon sneezed. "Eff, Mom, be cool—"

"Sorry," I said. "Forget I said the 'v' word."

"Not likely, but . . . OK," she said, handing over two tickets nervously. "Enjoy the show. Jewel's an amazing performer, but I guess you know that, if you're a fan—"

"Nope," I said. "Just met her on the plane flight out this afternoon."

"Well," the woman said, leaning forward conspiratorially, "you must have made quite the impression. She used up all her slots—and put you right in front. I can take the next customer!"

"Interesting," I muttered, looking at the tickets.

"Granola and Mohawk," Cinnamon muttered. "At least she's not a vamp."

I squeezed her shoulders again, and then we merged with the press of people walking through the huge sliding doors of the Crucible. It was larger than I'd expected from the outside, with an actual two-story building in the middle of its cavernous warehouse floor. There were welders and glassworkers and fire sculptors doing all kinds of demonstrations, and placards and catalogs and posters detailing an enormous variety of classes.

I'd never seen anything like it.

Cinnamon apparently hadn't either; her head kept whipping back and forth, and I got exhausted trying to follow her as she darted from exhibit to exhibit. But just when my mind was about to pigeonhole her as a cat chasing shiny things, I noticed what was attracting her attention—not the artwork, but the description of the classes. She'd look at the cat's-cradle made of neon or the flower made of fire—and then stop and lean in to read the placards, muttering and dropping f-bombs as she tried to "read the letters before they swims away." Just one more reminder that the little street cat I'd adopted was, unexpectedly, an insatiable learning machine.

"None of 'em are one-days while we're here," Cinnamon said, stopping in front of a poster for the firespinning classes. After squinting at the schedule, she leaned back and pointed at a long-exposure picture of a girl weaving a huge flower of fire with poi—flaming balls on the end of a chain. "I wants to learn to do that. That looks *amazing*."

"It's *more* amazing live," I said. "Maybe Alex could show you while we're here."

"Alex spins fire?" Cinnamon asked. "For real?"

"For real," I said. Alex was more than my contact in the Wizarding Guild—he was a practicing, if covert fire magician, which had to be a hell of a dance for the host of a skeptical TV show. "He can lift himself right off the ground if the wind is right—"

"Alex spins *magic* fire?" Cinnamon asked, eyes wide. "And can *fly*?"

"Yes, but let's say he floats with style," I said. "Heck, for all I know he's here tonight, if not as a performer, maybe in the audience—"

But before I could whip out my smartphone to ask him, an announcer called out that the performance would begin in fifteen minutes, and Cinnamon practically dragged me to our seats, afraid someone would take them from us.

In front of the two story interior building was a row of bleachers opposite a stage framed on either end by welded metal pillars. Between the stage and the bleachers were three rows of floor seating with an excellent view of the stage. I checked our stubs and blinked.

The ticket lady hadn't lied—we were right up front, the best seats in the house.

I was glad Cinnamon wasn't stuck behind someone taller, but as I seated myself, I heard a snort of disgust and turned to see a short elderly lady behind me, wrapped in some expensive fur that almost certainly wasn't fake, scowling up at me and my Mohawk.

To be nice, I offered her one of the four empty seats beside us, but the woman shook her head, holding herself so stiffly her whole body seemed to pivot. I looked over at Cinnamon, and she shrugged. With a grin at the scowling lady and her morbid fashion statement, I switched seats with Cinnamon so as not to be rude—and just as we got settled, the show started.

Twin gouts of fire roared out of either side of the stage, tearing the air with sharp, spitting sounds, like the hisses of hidden dragons. The audience jerked back from the unexpected flash of heat and flare of light—and then the lights fell, leaving us in darkness.

Something creaked. A drumbeat started. The trumpets of fire again flared, striking the welded iron pillars bracketing the stage. Delicate blue-white flames climbed their ornate sides. The pillars squealed, started to turn—and began throwing off drops of burning liquid.

Cinnamon squealed in delight, and I laughed. The pillars were well designed—they spun just fast enough to throw the flaming drops off, but slow enough that the fiery spray of the fuel fell in wide catch-basins at the bottom of each pillar without hitting the audience.

The turning pillars flared brightly, erupting in roiling gouts of flame that climbed up their ridged sides and rolled toward the ceiling in twin rings of fire. As the waves of heat and light faded, two young men became visible on the stage, as if by magic.

Naked to the waist, hair slicked up into spikes, the men prowled to the front of the stage in diaphanous, beaded harem pants tied at the ankles. Each held aloft a black sword; in unison, they struck them against the pillars and the swords ignited, becoming glowing blades of fire.

The beat of the music grew faster as the men whirled their blades in an elaborate dance of fire. At first, it was simple fan-blade spins and fencing thrusts; then it became more exotic, demonstrative, their sweaty bodies moving with the grace of wushu practitioners.

They ranged the stage, then converged, leaping like acrobats, one flying over the other, their blades of fire spinning above and below them like twin helicopters as the pillars too flared. The sharp tang of the fuel nipped at my nostrils as the fiery acrobats flew apart.

Between their parting blades, two taut young women appeared like genies, holding poi—knotted wicks on chains. The men lit the women's poi, spun their own swords out—and seemed to disappear. The pillars dimmed too, leaving the stage lit only by the spinning balls of fire.

The women wove across the stage, bodies slinking back and forth like belly dancers; but over the jingling of their costumes you could clearly hear the spinning balls of flame rushing through the air as the women wove circles and figure eights and flowers around themselves.

At first, they danced together in unison; then they too broke out, ranging the stage as they performed elaborate tricks with the fireballs on their chains—fast, slow, arcs, flowers, spinning the balls so slowly they seemed to hang there—then even stopping them.

My mouth opened as the audience gasped. The two women had made the flaming balls hang above their heads, eerily motionless; then they jerked their poi down, creating elaborate arcs in the air that were not tricks of the camera but real flowing comets of flame.

The men reappeared, each with four poi, which they lit off the women's flames; dark-garbed ninjas appeared and snatched the women's poi away just as their flames were dying, and the women took the extra poi from the men and began a coordinated show.

My eyes tightened; I hadn't expected the flames to run out that fast. Sure enough, as the show progressed, through fire spinning and fire swords and even an amazing piece involving dancers writhing vertically up and down stripes of silk cloth while they twirled fans of fire, it was always broken into short segments, where either the performers or the poi changed.

I heard a curse beside me, and glanced over at Cinnamon. It looked like she was having a blast. Occasionally, her head snapped aside in that rough, sneezy tic that usually preceded an F-bomb; the doctors had warned us that as she went through her teens, her Tourette's Syndrome would get worse before it got better. But tonight, it seemed as if she was definitely spending more time having fun than fighting her own brain, and I was glad.

The four dancers split apart, drawing a moving panorama of flowers and windmills across the stage with fluid fire. The trails kept getting more complex, and I swore *writing* trailed behind the poi, blue-white letters imprinted in the air as the yellow flames passed. Was this fire magic?

My skin prickled. The dancers parted—and Jewel took center stage.

Her curled hair dripped with water. Her curvy body dripped with sweat. Her harem garb was sheer, showing off every juicy curve. Heftier than the others, she wore her weight with perfect confidence, sporting beneath her silks a tight bikini made of knotted rope.

And in her hands she spun two elaborate fans tipped with fire.

Smiling, Jewel danced toward the crowd, nimble feet covered in leather and chainmail spats that mirrored the gauntlets she still wore, seemingly picking each footfall in time with an expert weave and bob of her spinning fans. My skin shivered with her movement.

She paused behind the fans, and in that brief moment I saw their structure, seven metal blades projecting from a central ring, each tipped with a wick of flame, like a cross between a Chinese fan and a menorah. But then I realized Jewel was looking at *me*, and I blushed.

Jewel winked and whirled away, spinning the fans on her fingers by their central rings. Flame blossomed out from the fans, becoming trails of fire, then shimmering, rippling comets, spiraling out to span the stage like a galaxy, their heat seeming to reach to my bones.

The crowd gasped, and then Jewel danced to the back of the stage, facing the crowd, leaning forward, whirling the fans behind her back. The comet tails joined, then spread again into a huge peacock tail rippling behind her. This was fire magic, and the crowd applauded.

Jewel threw one of the fans high into the air, spinning so fast its flames went out, and thrust her hand forward, grabbing two long wands from an assistant as she caught the falling fan behind her back. She flicked her wrist, and chains ending with poi flew out from the tips of the wands. Jewel lit them with her remaining fan, spun it out and passed both of them off . . . then began whirling her poi staffs in a complicated, interweaving pattern.

The wands were unusual, but the performance was pure, traditional fire magic, the kind I had seen Alex do before—bright bursts of flame, rainbow halos, arcing currents. Now there were no showy acrobatics or sexy dances—just Jewel's enormous speed and skill, creating intricate loops of flame, trails of fire intersecting each other in the graphomantic patterns I knew from skindancing, setting off bright flares every time Jewel completed the logic of a design.

A minute passed, then two, then five, as Jewel continued performing more and more elaborate magic; but as more and more time passed, her poi did not go out. My brow furrowed. The duration of the fire itself had to be magic, but no one else here could appreciate it.

Finally, Jewel stepped the edge of the stage, whipping the poi wands around her faster and faster, rising on tiptoe—then rising into the air. At first, she just lifted straight up; then she pushed forward, floating out above the audience in a spinning ball of flame.

I gasped. *Everyone* gasped. But me more than most. Woven through the patterns of fire, a shape was forming. As complex as Jewel's spinning was, the fire itself, even the symbols writ in the fire, were precise mathematical arcs, like a three-dimensional spirograph drawn in flame.

But sparks like stars flared in the magic. Movement like water flowed through the weave. A living thing took form, coiling around Jewel, sinuous, alive, and arrestingly familiar—a dragon, like *my* Dragon, glowing in space above me like a constellation of the Zodiac.

My face lit up in wonder. The whirling of the poi roared above me like the dragon itself had a voice. I felt it calling to me. Tiny droplets of fire sizzled off the balls of flame and curved off in the magic, more artful than particles in a cloud chamber. I felt an irresistible pull.

I stood, clapped—and then *everyone* surged to their feet in a standing ovation.

Cinnamon was hopping, I was clapping, Jewel was hovering, arms whipping around her as she maintained that fantastic sphere of fire—and then she glanced down at me and winked. Cinnamon looked back at me and grinned toothily, and I flushed, embarrassed—and dizzy.

Jewel subtly changed her weave, and the sphere slowly floated backward, the dragon whirling around it once more before dissipating in a sparkle of mana. I felt echoes in my tattoos, felt my own Dragon sliding against my body, felt it coiling around my legs and belly, flooding me with warmth as the magic dissipated—then my face reddened as the tip of its tail gently brushed the upper edge of my vulva. *Like the touch of a lover.*

This was sympathetic magic, *had* to be, tuned to resonate against my marks. I didn't know what kind of knowledge that would take. For Jewel to pull that off so effortlessly—and after such a quick glance at my tattoos—meant she was a formidable magician.

Jewel settled back to the stage, just as the two pillars belched one last brilliant gout of fire to thunderous applause. She bowed, holding her wands behind her; their flame guttered, but only slightly. The wicks hissed angrily inside the towels when dark-garbed assistants put them out.

Jewel straightened; then bent again as the rest of the troupe joined her for a bow.

"Thank you, everyone," she said. "I am the Princess of Fire, and we are the Fireweavers! We thank the Crucible for providing us this wonderful space, as well Monkton Teriano, the artist who forged Jachin and Boaz, the fire pillars you see here on stage. The Crucible is funded in part by donations, so please drop by their stand on the way out. Thank you and good-night!"

"Wow," Cinnamon said. "*Fuck*—I means, wow! That was amAZing—"

"Yeah," I laughed, tousling her hair. As the performers departed, Jewel glanced back, caught my eye—and then she reached that fluid hand out, pointed at me, and unmistakably crooked her finger at me in a come-hither gesture, just as she left the stage.

I stood there, unblinking; then Cinnamon waved her hand in my face.

—℘

"So, Mom," she said, hopping up with a grin. "Gonna use your backstage pass?"

4. Backstage Pass

"I imagined you, before I met you, as an old biddy," Jewel said. The Fireweavers had let us backstage, and we found the Princess of Fire lounging on a long blue bench, half out of her silks, one curvy leg stretched out, letting one of the male fan-dancers carefully unwrap the leather and chainmail spat she had donned for the performance. "A schoolteacher, head full of nonsense from theory of magic classes, inflicting her little classroom rules on the world."

One of the other fire swordsmen, the one they called Zi, turned around, eyebrow raised. "Wait a minute," he said, wiping his sword and wrapping it in a wet towel, alternately looking at me standing there and Cinnamon bouncing around the room. "Who are we talking about?"

"Dakota Frost." Jewel pointed at me. "*That* Dakota Frost."

"*That's* Dakota Frost?" Zi said, doing a double take, and I raised an eyebrow as the man looked me up and down. He was a vaguely Asian firespinner with short-cropped black hair—and looked cleaner cut than I did. "Holy shit. You are . . . not at all what I expected, Ms. Frost."

"You had expectations?" I asked, eyeing Cinnamon as she sniffed at a set of poi. I'd resisted taking her backstage, but then my former wild child began listing all *her* backstage passes, and at band number seven, I gave in. "You know *of* me, but not what I look like?"

"*I* knew what you looked like," the female firespinner called Yolanda said. "Your face was all over the news after that trial thing. Congratulations on beating the rap—"

"Thanks," I said distantly.

"Her face was not all over the news," Jewel said.

"She was on the cover of *Magnolia* magazine!" Yolanda said.

"Nobody outside of the South has ever heard of *Magnolia* magazine," Jewel said. "You may not keep a low profile, Dakota, but you didn't throw up billboards for your little project—and unlike you law enforcement types, we don't keep dossiers on all of our enemies."

"So, I'm your enemy?" I said, mouth quirking up. *She doesn't feel like an enemy.*

"I didn't mean actual enemy," Jewel said crossly.

"Yes, she did," Zi snapped. "People like you keep trying to shut us down—"

"Am I?" I asked. I couldn't keep the smile off my face, whether from needling this guy or from the pleasure of watching Jewel lounging about like a harem queen. "But I've never heard of you guys before tonight—and I'm a friend of quite a few firespinners."

That gave the guy pause. "Well," Zi said, somewhat less certainly, "maybe not shut us down specifically—but Yolanda told us what you're trying to do in Atlanta. She says you're trying to regulate magic, lock it down, make what we did tonight against the law—"

"Why? Did you kill anyone on stage tonight?" I asked, raising my eyebrows. I was performing now, trying to make a point. "Are you *planning* to kill anybody on stage?"

"No," Zi said. But I just kept staring at him, and he realized it was actually a serious question. "What? No! What kind of people do you think we are?"

"I dunno, I've never met you," I said, still mock casual. "I'd say if you didn't hurt anyone, or plan to hurt anyone, that should be enough . . . except, are any of the audience members who were exposed to your magic going to spontaneously combust?"

"No!" the swordsman said.

"No, and it isn't possible," Jewel began. Then she paused and bit her lip. "Well—"

"Unless you screw up?" I asked. "Magic can do wonderful things, like draw art in the air or even make someone fly. But terrible things too . . . just, no one wants to admit it. People think that tattoos can't control your mind, but they can. They think graffiti can't rip you apart or burn you alive, but it can. And they think fire magic is just pretty entertainment, but is it? Can it cause people to spontaneously combust? Cause epileptic seizures? What dangers do *you* know?"

Again, I raised an eyebrow, glancing between the two of them, and they had no answer. "If you don't know . . . I'm collecting safety information and experts you can ask. So you can say, 'yes, I do know our performance won't accidentally set anyone on fire.' "

"You know," Jewel said slowly, "yes, we do know that. Firespinners are actually pretty psychotic about safety. We're certain none of this magic had a pyromantic effect, and it's actually pretty difficult to create self-kindling magic without the right fuel—"

And then the other dancer, who all this time had been working on that same spat on Jewel's ankle, finally undid the clasp. "*There,*" the boy said, carefully pulling it free, "see? Just took a little concentration to get it untangled. No need to rip it off and have it redone—"

"Yeah, yeah, thanks, finally, I'm *freezing,*" Jewel said, hopping up, pulling off the rest of her silk pants with a quick motion and wadding them up into a ball. She threw them into a red bag, then squatted down and dug in her duffel.

I half-covered my face with one hand—she'd unintentionally given me a *great* view of her curvy rump wrapped in that interesting hemp-rope bikini bottom—but then I noticed her legs and back were covered in an interesting flame design, not a tattoo but something I didn't recognize.

But before I could ask, Jewel pulled a pair of jeans out of her bag, which she immediately began worming on, not even bothering to change into normal underwear. When the hem of the jeans passed the rope on her hips, she glanced back at me, half grinning, half embarrassed.

"Sorry," she said, buttoning her jeans, jerking a dark top off the counter behind her, and slipping it on. "It's just we've got a lot of cleanup to do and I've been stuck here like a useless lump while Henri was getting that off."

Jewel turned, pulling on a lumberjack shirt over the top—but I could see she'd sewn flames and beads into the threads of her jeans, and sequins into the shirt. It was a nice blend of femme and flannel. I stood there, staring, as she buttoned up and smiled at me.

"You should say something," Jewel said, grin growing broader.

"Yeah, Mom," Cinnamon said, poking me. "Stop drooling."

I felt my cheeks burn. "I'm—sorry," I said. "Was I staring?"

"I've been thoroughly ogled," Jewel said, looking like she enjoyed it. "Hey, Dakota, thanks for coming backstage, but now we gotta start breaking things down, and I don't want you handling equipment without a waiver. Meet you out back?"

Cinnamon and I returned to our circuit around the interior of the building, wandering through thinning crowds as exhibitors closed up shop. Then we ducked outside, through the thousand hanging wheels and frames of a community bike repair shop, and onto a back loading ramp where, we were assured, the performers would exit.

The air from the bay had turned chilly, and from the back of the big warehouse, Oakland looked dirtier, less inviting. But just beyond the docks and the train tracks, there were the same nice row houses, and the cool air was clean and pleasant.

"So far," I said, "Oakland is not living up to its reputation."

"Yeah," Cinnamon said, bouncing back and forth on the loading ramp. Abruptly, she bent down, tail flicking through the air as she examined a piece of twisted metal, perhaps a discarded bit of sculpture. "No fightin', not borin'!"

"Come here," I said, extending my arms, and she hopped up and fell backward into my arms. I tousled her hair, then straightened her headscarf. "I love you, Cinnamon."

"I loves you too, Mom," she replied, refixing her headscarf the way she apparently wanted it, with one catlike ear popping up askew. "Thank you for letting me come with you tonight. For letting me come out here at all. For giving me a *life.*"

"You aren't going to be left out anymore," I said, wrapping my arms around her upper chest and squeezing as hard as I could; she let me, but I could feel the wiry werekin muscles underneath. "I'll be here, right behind you, at least until you hit college—*Jeez.*"

"Jeez?" she said, staring off into the distance, her tail thwacking my legs.

"We're going to have to find you a college," I said. "Sooner than we think—"

"So long as they knows Goldbach from Goldfrapp, it'll be fine," Cinnamon said.

"I'm not sure *I* know Goldbach from Goldfrapp," I responded. "Both musicians, right?"

Cinnamon snorted. "For the love—"

The door squealed open, and a short, spiky-haired man in a rumpled shirt backed out, ripped arms laden with two milk crates, one precariously stacked atop the other, both filled to the brim with firespinning gear. He was laughing or coughing, backing straight into us, oblivious. Cinnamon sprang out of the way at once, but my coat caught on the railing and I stumbled.

"Watch out," I said, as he kept backing up straight into me. "Hey, hey, *hey*—"

But it was too late. We collided. He lost his balance *and* the crates, and both of us were knocked down the ramp in a tumbled heap of tangled limbs and gear.

"Ow," I said, holding my arm, which I'd dinged on a rail on the way down. Spiky-hair jerked to his feet, and underneath the rumpled shirt I glimpsed a muscle tee packing a *lot* of muscle. Familiar—ah, the other firesword dancer. "What are you, deaf or something?"

The short dancer dusted himself off, then extended a hand with a grin, saying nothing—and I immediately realized my mistake—he *was* deaf. "Oh, I've stepped in it, haven't I?"

"Not yet," Jewel said, standing at the open door, arms folded—with her devilish smile. "Molokii really *can't* hear you. But don't worry, I can translate—"

"You don't have to," I said, as she tapped his shoulder and began signing, a little too fast for rusty old me to follow—I quit signing when Mom died, and had only picked it up again since Nyissa lost her voice—but I got that she told him *exactly* what I said. "Oh, you didn't have to."

Molokii laughed, a rough, odd sound that was almost a cough, and grinned at me. Again, he reached down to help me up, and I took the hand gratefully. He patted my shoulder, smiled again, then flicked his hands at Jewel. Before I could say anything, she translated.

"He says don't worry about it, you didn't know," she said. He flicked his fingers again, and she continued, "And he is sorry, it *is* really inconvenient at times."

"We do use our hearing to draw our attention," I said, my mind churning. But I knew just what I'd done wrong, or at least why I felt guilty. "But I didn't know that, and just because you bumped into me *isn't* a reason for me to mock the disability of a whole group. I'm sorry."

Jewel's eyes lit up at me. "Tell you what," she said, moving her hands in those delicate gestures again. "Help us gather this up and carry it to his car, and all will be forgiven."

And so I got an education on a firespinner's gear. *This* was the bottle of fuel, the white gasoline Jewel favored; *that* was a red snuffing towel, never to be confused with a white safety towel—the former put out the poi, the latter put out the performers, and "never the twain shall meet lest you and your dousee become twin tiki torches." The poi were swords and wands and fans and meteors and monkey's fists and Jewel's specialty, "morningstars," those long wands, tipped with wicks on chains, that had provided such a spectacular finish to her performance.

When we were done, I took one crate, and Molokii took the other, Jewel took his keys, and we lugged all of it to the scraggly alley where he'd parked his car—a battered Mad Max-looking clunker that turned out to be a Toyota Avalon tricked out on the *inside.*

"*Nice* car," I said. "I bet that was a steal—"

"Five hundred bucks, no joke," Jewel said, waving as Molokii drove off, speakers thumping. "Back when we were at Berkeley, Molokii saw it in a junk-yard, fell in love, and paid for it washing dishes one summer. Of course, it was totaled—one side scraped off—but he's good with fire. He welded spare parts on to patchwork together a decent outer shell."

"Why does he need the sound system?" I asked, as we walked Jewel to her car, following a line of trees that seemed to divide the houses and warehouses.

"Maybe he likes the vibration," Cinnamon said, bopping herself in the head with one of Jewel's poi. "He used the bass to keep time. Or, I dunno, if he rides friends in the car."

"That's . . . those are both about right," Jewel said, glancing at Cinnamon, shifting her duffel. "He does like the feel of the bass, and he sold it to some friends in Sunol, who let him drive it when he's in town. You're a smart little girl."

"Yes she is," I said, reaching out and lifting the duffel off Jewel's shoulder so she could get at the cute little sling backpack/purse trapped beneath it. "Need a hand?"

"Thanks," Jewel said, reaching behind herself to ferret for her keys in her sling backpack. She gave me that wry smile again. "You sure are handy to have around. If the car won't start, would you pop the hood for me, look at the engine?"

"Sure thing," I said, trying to suppress a grin. I know I wear leather and ride a motorcycle—OK, OK, a scooter—but I never intentionally try to be butch. But Jewel seemed to like that, so I played it up a bit. "I'd hate for you to get those pretty little hands dirty."

Jewel rolled her eyes, and Cinnamon snorted again.

Then Cinnamon's nostrils flared. Her head jerked to the side. "Fuck, I means, *fuck!*" she barked, voice rising a register, so I knew even before she dropped into a crouch that this wasn't my little street cat struggling with Tourette's; this was real danger. "I smells a lizard!"

I glimpsed movement. My head whipped around, but I missed whatever it was. I dropped Jewel's duffel and whirled to put Cinnamon at my back, and *now* saw a man in a bulky jacket striding toward us on the sidewalk—and another man casually walking on the opposite side of the street suddenly veered toward us. I looked around for an escape route, but saw two more men stepping from the bushes around either side of Jewel's car.

They were like the United Nations of muggers—white, black, Latino, and a fourth man of an Asian race I couldn't identify, all bearing down on us with purposeful intent. Each one was different—tall, short, wide, ripped; each one was the same, in comfortable khakis and baggy black jackets from which they pulled businesslike automatics I guessed were Glocks.

The four men surrounded us with guns raised.

"Aw, hell," I said. "*Now* Oakland is living up to its reputation."

—❧

The lead man snarled, "You should never have come to Oakland, Jewel!"

5. The Streets of Oakland

"Wait, what?" I said. I should have been terrified, but I felt a giddy exhilaration as I realized the four men were all focused on Jewel. "This isn't about me?"

"No," the man snapped, "and keep your yap shut, 'DJ Irene.' "

"What?" I said, laughing openly now. "What in God's name are you talking about?"

"Dakota, please, *be quiet,*" Jewel said, raising her hands. "Daniel, let them go. This doesn't have anything to do with them—"

"This your new squeeze, Jewel?" Daniel asked, flicking the gun at me. I still couldn't nail his race. Not Korean or Chinese . . . maybe . . . I dunno, Eskimo? Polynesian? "Or your *accomplice?* Maybe we should beat the shit out of her and make you watch—"

"Oh, good fucking luck," I said, putting my hands in my pockets, squeezing my fists tight to build up mana in the yin-yangs in my palms. "Why don't you try it?"

"*What* did you say?" Daniel said, pointing the gun at me.

"It translates to, scram while you can, pups," Cinnamon said. "But you aren't getting it."

Daniel swung his gun toward her. I jerked my hand out, murmuring *shield*—Cinnamon was vulnerable to silver bullets, but with enough concentration, my tattoo magic was a barrier to almost anything—but in Daniel's lapse of concentration, Jewel *moved.*

A dazzling flare of flash powder blinded me, I caught a glimpse of shimmering fingers flickering through an intricate pattern, and then a shield blossomed, a patterned bubble of flame as elaborate as any of my tribal designs. And in the brief moment as the shield expanded, driving our assailants back, Jewel reached over her back into her sling purse—and pulled out two wands.

These were not springy and delicate like the ones she had used inside; they were metal, telescoping like combat batons, with flinty nuggets at the end of each chain. She whipped them down, striking the pavement, throwing sparks—and flint became meteors of rainbow fire.

I pushed Cinnamon back behind me, spreading my hands, shielding her from the fiery battle. It was fluid and spectacular, like the performance earlier—but a thousand times faster. Arcs of light whipped out around Jewel and struck two assailants in the chest. Trails of flame crossed and deflected a bullet fired by Daniel. But her wands were generating more than just fire; my eyes widened as I saw, *definitely* this time, magical symbols in the curves of fire. Jewel whirled the batons faster and faster, creating an elaborate loop of magic around her, and for a brief moment, I flashed on a great big ball of string woven from spells written in fire.

I tensed to move—but as soon as the fight started, it was over. The fourth assailant, behind Jewel, drew two long sticks, with crossbars like police tonfas. He struck them against the pavement as she had, and they lit up too, transforming into swords of flame—which he thrust into her ball of magic.

One of her chains looped around it, disrupting the spell she was building. Jewel saw it, spun, and jerked downward, ramming the handle of her other rod into his chin. Her assailant staggered back, and Jewel whipped her poi free, but while she turned, Daniel had drawn two fire swords—and the other two opponents had drawn fire poi as well.

"All right, we wanted to keep magic under wraps," Daniel snarled, catching her poi with his flaming sword as she flailed it behind her to try to re-establish her shield. "But since you don't have sense to keep our secrets from outsiders, neither will we!"

And they fell on her. In moments, they'd caught her poi-staffs in a hopeless tangle and the fourth assailant recovered enough to clock her on the noggin with the butt of his sword. Jewel fell to the street in a little heap, poi falling from her hands as she clutched her head.

"You should have stuck to the shadows like the rest of us," Daniel said, glaring at her. "You were warned repeatedly not to share our secrets with outsiders, and here we see you giving a public performance built around the most sacred spins and fuels of our art!"

"Fire is too beautiful to hide in the shadows. And a summoning *must* be public—"

"Must be in the *open*," Daniel corrected. "Not *public*. I think the Council is crazy to let you go ahead with this plan, but you still have to follow the rules of the Order. You may be the Princess of Fire—but you have *no* right to out all of us. Hold out her hand."

I raised my eyebrow. *Like hell.* I'd seen this movie before. The fire sword was oh-so-close to that delicate, struggling hand being held by two of the other firespinners. I had to talk fast, to distract them before they could burn her—without giving away that I was preparing to strike.

"Hey! Forget about someone?" I said, folding my arms, shimmying my back, shifting one foot backward to stretch the whole length of the tattoos I wanted to activate. I cracked my neck one way, then the other, feeling the magic come alive; it also had the effect of looking like I was trying to intimidate them, which I was. "Or were *you* planning on a public performance?"

I shot my hand out, murmured *fling,* and vine tattoo uncoiled from my skin, whipped out and struck the flaming sword out of his hand. Daniel cursed and held his hand—then his eyes widened, watching the glowing green tendril curl lazily back toward me.

"Tattoo magic," I said loudly, "is more than just pretty pictures, moving on the surface of the skin." I let the vine coil around my arm, but kept it floating, in the air, at the ready. "I think you gentlemen will find it's the most powerful magic there is—so back down."

I watched them closely, motioning for Cinnamon to move farther back. I no longer had enough vines to extend a full shield far beyond my body, but that one was impressive enough, a fluid green neon serpent of leaves that lit up the night as brightly as the poi had.

But apparently it was not impressive enough to deter four determined muggers with guns and magic fire swords. Go figure. Daniel grabbed his still-burning sword and got back to his feet, cursing; I could see I'd actually drawn blood with the thorns on my newer design.

"You know," he said, whirling the sword experimentally, "I *did* know that." I threw myself back into a low stance, shifting my back as if preparing myself for a physical blow. Seeing me crouch, he smiled and said, "But you know what, *skindancer?* Skin *hates* fire."

He whirled the swords and threw a gout of fire at me, a focused version of Jewel's peacock display. But I'd seen that show tonight—and from his move I knew what was coming. And I've dealt with fire before. Last time I'd been burned. This time was different.

The answer, oddly, came from the martial arts. In the art I practice, Taido, you don't expend energy blocking the other guy's punch; you accept that it is coming and change your body axis to move out of the way and counterattack—sort of like Aikido with punches.

So when that rainbow wave of fire came at me, I was ready, not with a block, but with a twist. If I'd thrown mana into a shield, the fire would have built up against it, fed back and burned my skin; but instead, I whipped my vine out, mana hungry, and murmured, "*Quench.*"

The rainbow fire sprayed off me, deflected by a coiling green line that grew brighter as each wave buffeted off it. It was over in less than a second, but at the end of it, that one vine had blossomed into a thicket of mana swirling around me.

"Yeah, skindancers know skin hates fire," I said loudly, quickly crossing my arms in front of me before the others decided to drop Jewel and turn on me. I drew a breath, preparing my body to take in the rush of mana I was about to absorb. "You know what? Skin hates being poked by a needle too. That doesn't mean we can't use it to do magic. Like *this!*"

I whipped my arms apart, retracting the vine all at once. I hunched, grimacing. It was *excruciating* as the mana I'd stolen pooled inside my body, but I rerouted it all to one particular tattoo. Daniel raised his sword, then hesitated, unsure of whether to attack or to defend.

"*Spirit of fire,*" I said, grinning up at him, "*show them the light!*"

"You call your attacks?" he said, both mocking and bewildered—then jerked back, as the back of my precious vestcoat ripped open and the head of my dragon tattoo reared into the air. Dismayed and astounded, he cried, "My God, she's summoning a dragon—"

The rest of the vest's leathers tore away as the wings of the Dragon spread from my shoulders. My left pants leg was ripped to shreds as the Dragon's tail uncoiled. The limbs of the Dragon slid from my sleeves and down the back of my tattered shirt, spreading wide.

"Oh—my—God," Daniel said, standing frozen, eyes filled with awestruck wonder as the Dragon's spreading limbs briefly mirrored my crouched movements. Then he blanched, as the head of the Dragon reared before him, and he flinched back and screamed, "Oh, shiiii—"

"*Raaaaah!*" I screamed—yeah, articulate—and the Dragon roared rainbow fire. All the firespinners scattered, and Jewel threw herself to the pavement. Daniel tried to deflect the flame with an artful move of his sword, but my magic, powered by my living skin and beating heart, was too strong, and he was thrown off his feet and knocked to the pavement beside Jewel.

My new Dragon was surprisingly bloodthirsty, and I felt the desire to not just fight them, but *chase them off.* I advanced, and Daniel kicked back rapidly, cursing as he burned himself with his sword. The other firespinners were recovering, the hefty Latino man drawing his gun—so I stepped over Jewel, drew my arms together and said "*Essence of flame, melt their bullets!*"

The wings of the Dragon curled down around us like a bubble of fire, and the firespinners all ran off—except for the gun wielder, who stood there, his eyes full of wonder. He grinned, shot at the barrier and watched his bullet sizzle, then laughed and ran away, whooping.

"*Not* the reaction I expected," I said, letting the wings of the Dragon spread. Its head twitched back and forth, creating dizzy double images in my eyes. I rubbed my eyes, then opened them again. *The street is clear.* "Not what I expected at all."

"Oh my God," Jewel said, dazed, eyes following Daniel and his cronies as they melted off into the distance. Then she looked down at her right hand and seized it with her left. She began shaking. I knew that feeling. Trembling, she said, "Dakota, you—you *saved* me."

I started to point out that *she'd* defended my *child*—but then Cinnamon spoke up.

"Yeah, Mom does that," Cinnamon whispered, and I looked over at her with alarm. She was really rattled, ears back, tail flicking all over the place. She stepped past us, reached down, picked at a gleaming pebble, then dropped it, cursing; then looked back at me, eyes wide.

"Like I thought. They had silver. Oh, God, Mom, I could have been—"

I opened my arms and she stepped into them, terrified. "It's OK, baby, I got you," I said, squeezing Cinnamon tight, as the wings of the Dragon flapped slowly around us. "It's OK."

Jewel got to her feet and turned toward us—then her jaw dropped.

"Oh my God," she said, staring at the Dragon, then at me, in unadulterated wonder. Her delicate hands flickered to her mouth, then covered her cheeks. "I didn't imagine—that was *real.* I traveled the world trying to do it, but you did it, you really *did it*—you summoned a *dragon*—"

"*No,*" I said, a little more flatly than I intended. I had already gotten a bad read on my skeptometer from Jewel, and I felt the need to step on unnecessary woo-hooery before it got started. "No," I repeated, more gently. "It's just tattoo magic. *My* tattoo, inked by my hand—"

"Oh," she said, deflating a little. "Oh, boo. I even saw it, on the plane."

"Yes. She is very pretty, but she's not real. I can show you the design."

"Still," she said, hand hovering at her lips, then reaching out. "Can I—can I touch it?"

"No," I said, withdrawing the Dragon's claws, letting them merge into my skin. It hurt, surprisingly; I hadn't realized how much mana I'd generated, or absorbed, in that performance. "It's not a good idea for one tattoo to touch two people, especially not this one."

"Oh," Jewel said, crestfallen. Her hands still hovered, and I raised an eyebrow; then she pulled them back. "Sorry. It's hard to resist. I, uh, *really* like dragons."

"Why not, Mom?" Cinnamon asked, sniffling, then holding up her hand. There was a butterfly on the back of her hand—one that once lived on mine. "You let me have this one."

"One small design, transferred from me to you with just the right amount of mana," I said, flapping the Dragon's wings to fan off the excess magic. *I want to fly free.* The wind made my tattered clothes flap, and I drew calming breaths. "This one's *overloaded* with mana, and firmly attached to me. Best case, Jewel would get a sharp sting and curdled ink burning her skin. Worst case, we could both get a nasty magical infection or psychic whiplash. Sorry."

A siren became audible, and Jewel flinched. "Oh, shit, we better scram—"

"Be not afraid," I said gently. "It's just the police. And I get on well with cops."

"Since when?" Cinnamon said.

"Since I spent the last eight months working with them," I replied.

"But we just did magic," Jewel said desperately. "In public!"

—

"It's not illegal," I said, as flashing lights rounded the corner. "Not even in California."

6. Problematic Identifications

And so I learned a few things. First, the cops in California were far more suspicious of magicians than ones in Georgia. Second, even suspicious cops will get over it—just like my Dad taught me, cops respond to "polite, no sudden moves" and a glimpse of a police booster card no matter what state you're in. And third, when Jewel gave her witness statement, her real name wasn't the stage-friendly Jewel Grace . . . but a more normal Jewel Anne *Grass*lin.

"Annie," I said with a smirk, looking over the statement. "Little Orphan Annie—"

"Oh, bite me," she said, embarrassed. "It's a common name—and what's wrong with having a stage name, 'Dakota Frost?' What's *your* real name, anyway?"

"Dakota Caroline Frost," I said, handing the statement back. "Huh. Interesting."

"Interesting?" the officer—Illowsky, according to her uniform—asked. She was thin as a bird with a pleasant, weathered face. At first, she had been skeptical of our outlandish story, but when the man who'd called in the attack from one of the row homes came down to make a statement, that had greased the wheels of her belief. "What's interesting, ma'am?"

"The witness statements," I said. "Different from the ones we use in Georgia, but still recognizable. Thanks, Officer Illowsky—and for the quick response."

"No problem, and it's Susan," Illowsky said, her eyes lighting up a little. The smile quirked again, and she asked, "Why the interest, ma'am?"

"She's a cop," Jewel said. "A magical cop."

"I am *not,*" I said.

"Yes you are," Cinnamon said. "Sort of a magical enforcer."

"No, I-am-not-a-cop-or-enforcer," I said firmly. "I'm just a tattoo artist—"

"Saving my ass? Trying to set up national rules for the use of magic?" Jewel said, folding her arms, her hands seeming to weave through each other as she did so. "You're more than just a tattoo artist. And for that, I am graceful, Dakota Frost. Grateful. Sorry."

Officer Dean, Illowsky's partner, returned from his squad car. He was a tall, gray-haired black man, thinner than Susan, with a young-but-drawn face and a similar perpetual almost-grin. "They've swept the neighborhood now," Dean said. "If they're on foot, we've lost them."

"But," Jewel said, frustrated, "can't you, like, go after them?"

"We did," Dean said, "we swept with three cars, but these guys sound careful. Large group, identical clothes, getaway car hidden out of sight—and if they ditched the hoodies, or hopped in separate cabs, they're gone. And they were all new to you, except this Daniel guy, so—"

"I know our descriptions are sketchy," I said, "but it was just over so fast—"

"Not your fault," Dean said, "but we don't have enough to start a manhunt. We're dealing with an assault with minor scrapes, and a possible illicit-use-of-magic misdemeanor that could easily turn on you. I don't like seeing you targeted, but there's not much more we can do—"

"Unless," Illowsky said to Jewel, "you want to officially ask for more protection. We can run you down to the station, file formal charges against this Daniel fellow, maybe even get started on the paperwork for a formal restraining order—"

"I'd . . . rather not go to the police station tonight," Jewel said.

"Few people want to," Illowsky said, eyes scanning the air. "Your assailants were men, and you're women with a child in tow. It's an abuse of the system, but we can run you by a battered women's shelter, let you stay overnight for some peace of mind."

"No thanks," I said quickly, raising my hands, conscious of my tattered jacket. "And not just because I'd like to get back to my bodyguards—I seriously need a change of clothes."

"And I've got some good people to stay with," Jewel said. "I doubt Daniel knows where they live, and wouldn't take on the whole commune even if he did."

"All right, all right," Dean said. "We're just trying to give you some options. Not everybody gets assaulted every day; sometimes it rattles you. Makes it hard to think."

"Amen to that," I said. "Thank you, Officer Dean, Officer Illowsky."

As the officers drove away, Jewel rubbed her nose at me.

"What?" I asked, thumbing my nose back at her. "Cops have a hard job. Why make it harder than it is, when they're here saving our butts?"

"And what did they do for us?" she asked, putting her hand on her curvy hip.

"Secured the scene, cleared the neighborhood, so we can have this conversation in peace, without worrying that the bad guys are gonna regroup," I said, thinking it through. "Put out their description, so said bad guys have to lay low while we hightail it out of here."

Jewel swallowed and looked around nervously. "OK, you have a point. Look . . . I just got a little freaked again, thinking about them hiding in the bushes somewhere, waiting for the cops to split. Can I give you a ride to your car so we can all get outta here?"

"We took a cab," Cinnamon said.

Jewel stared at her, then me. "Oh, no," she said. "Uh-uh. You're not waiting around here for Daniel and crew to get another crack at you while I drive off in safety, not after you provided the safety. Where am I ferrying you two tonight?"

"I . . . don't know." I laughed, pulling out my smartphone. "We never actually made it to the hotel, so either we're heading to the airport, or . . ." I raised an eyebrow, reading the curious text from Vickman. "Sounds like we have been cleared for . . . a hotel on Cathedral Hill."

"That's . . . a bit of a ride," Jewel said, "but I'll do it gladly, skindancer."

Back on the Bay Bridge, crawling toward downtown San Francisco, I glanced at Jewel.

"So . . ." I said. "You live in a commune?"

"No!" she laughed. "I'm not quite that granola, even if I did go to Berkeley. I'm just staying in a fireweaver's commune while I'm performing in the Bay Area this week. Back in my native Hawai`i, I've got a plush little condo, thank you very much—"

"You're from Hawaii?" I asked, even as I noticed the slight but precise catch in her voice between the last two I's in "Hawaii" that I normally drawled out as *haw-way-yee*. Then, unthinkingly, I said, "You don't look like a native—"

"*Anyone* born in Hawai`i," she said firmly, "is a native Hawai`ian, whether they're from indigenous Polynesian stock, of European descent—or a mix, as I am. And just because one of my ancestors was a Yankee invader doesn't mean I can't embrace Hawai`i as my home."

I *was* a bit embarrassed at having put my foot in my mouth, but Jewel had gotten a little *too* steamed, and I couldn't let that stand. "I'm sorry," I said, and for once Cinnamon didn't correct me. "I misinterpreted what you meant by 'native.' I wasn't trying to offend—"

"I know," she said, a bit embarrassed herself. "You just hit one of my hot buttons. I'm a hard core Hawai`ian activist, but even after *years* in the cause, Daniel and his crew of yahoos want to push me out because . . . well, because I have Western features and red-blond hair."

"That sucks—but I know how that goes," I said. *Daniel is native Hawaiian.* Most interesting; I should have been able to place him. "Some people don't want me to have a say in the raising of Cinnamon, just because I don't turn furry once a month."

Jewel jerked in her seat. "Oh, hey—she's a *real* werewuh—uh, werecat?"

Cinnamon swatted at her, and Jewel laughed. Then her face grew serious.

"Look, I didn't want to talk with the police around," she said. "Fireweaver business is supposed to stay within the Order—but I was serious about trying to summon a dragon, and Daniel's serious about stopping me. You may think that's all New Age nonsense—"

"But he clearly doesn't," I said. "I'll keep that in mind."

We pulled up to the hotel, and Jewel dropped us off in the turnaround. We thanked her and got out, but when I waved goodbye, she rolled down her window.

"Look . . . Dakota Frost," Jewel said, leaning over, staring up at me through the window. "You really did save my life, at least metaphorically. I do think Daniel meant to maim me, and I don't know what I'd do if I couldn't spin. Thank you."

I rubbed the two forefingers of my right hand. I knew what it felt like, the threat of maiming, the fear of losing one's profession. But I didn't want to dump upon her all the trauma of my past, or to spook her even more. Finally I just said, "All part of the service, little lady."

Jewel started to lean back, then paused, wavering there in the car.

"All right," she said nervously. "All right. I can do this."

"Yes?" I said, smiling down at her.

—⁂

Jewel lowered her chin. "This time . . . can I get your number?"

7. No One Mentioned the Fae

The next morning, I dreamed of a beautiful, curvy fireweaver and her delicious smile. The dreams turned hotter as she spun fire, then darker as her blazing poi deflected bullets. Swirling fire coiled around her like a dragon, threatening to burn me alive.

I awoke in a sweat, to find Cinnamon curled atop my bed like a giant cat.

Quietly, I sighed. Predictable. Adorable, but predictable. I'd specifically asked for two beds, but unless I wanted to exile her to her own room, I could count on Cinnamon waking up in the middle of the night and coming to sleep on my bed, by my side, curled atop the covers.

Gingerly, I extracted my arm—dead asleep from her weight—and slipped out of bed. Cinnamon didn't stir—after staying up to go to the Crucible, she'd been absolutely wiped. She had the oddest sleep schedule, crashing as early as seven, but just for a few hours; she'd get up, bookending midnight, then crash again until it was time to get up for school. I brushed my teeth and slipped out the connecting door to Saffron's suite without waking my baby.

Darkrose and Saffron sat around their suite's tiny breakfast table in matching bathrobes, murmuring to each other sweetly. When I closed the door behind me, Darkrose smiled, nodding to Saffron, who lifted her newspaper—apparently, and unsuccessfully, trying to hide her grin.

"So . . ." Saffron said, not looking up from the newspaper, "Jinx and Doug said hello—they left about half an hour ago to catch a morning boat tour of the Bay. I think their honeymoon went . . . quite well." Her mouth quirked. "What about you two . . . did you guys have fun?"

I stared at her, unsure of what to tell her. She'd *so* wanted last night to go well.

"Dakota," Saffron said, putting the paper down. "Oh no. What went wrong?"

"The performance was spectacular," I said, "and I even got to go backstage with Jewel. She's . . . really sweet and I felt like we hit it off. But when we were walking her to her car . . . we were attacked on the streets of Oakland by four guys—with guns and fire swords."

"No," Darkrose said, straightening in her chair.

"Nothing to do with me," I said, "but they were really serious about hurting Jewel."

"What is up with this city?" Saffron asked. "First the airport, then a mugging?" She shook her head. "Initially, I was skeptical, but now I'm glad Nyissa volunteered to be your bodyguard. Hopefully the Vampire Court will release her soon—"

I jerked. I'd entirely forgotten the arrangements Vickman had made—Nyissa's coffin was supposed to be deposited in our room, since she was acting as my bodyguard. But when we'd gotten to the hotel, Cinnamon and I had gone to our *empty* room without a second thought.

"Oh, no," I said. "What . . . what happened? Do they have any demands—"

"They didn't kidnap her," Saffron said. "She's just in the hospital—"

"Oh, *no*," I said, dismayed. "*What happened?*"

But Darkrose, who had been taking a sip of tea, abruptly spluttered it up in a choked-off laugh. As I stood there, astounded, she shook her head at me, smiling in reassurance, then put her cup down and felt at her mouth. "Caught my fang—"

"Dakota, I didn't mean it like that," Saffron said, her face a mix of embarrassment and amusement. "Nyissa will be fine. She's still under my protection. She's undergoing a medical procedure, thanks to the hospitality of the Vampire Court of San Francisco. If all goes well, you'll see her tonight . . . when we introduce you to the Vampire Court."

I stared at her blankly. "I . . . thought we weren't welcome in their Court."

"Until introduced," Saffron corrected. "Which will happen tonight, because the Vampire Court wants to see *you*, in person—a powerful new magician entering their territory, under the protection of not one but two vampire lords, with a third high-ranking vampire in tow."

I stood there, stunned, trying to process all that. Saffron was a power broker who sat on Atlanta's City Council, so it didn't surprise me that the Vampire Court sat up and took notice when she rolled into town with her South African consort.

But Nyissa wasn't just my bodyguard; she was the Vampire Queen of the House Beyond Sleep, a vampire house officially recognized by the Gentry of Atlanta. Few people outside this room knew that the House Beyond Sleep was three vampires running a B&D B&B in east Georgia.

"Jesus," I said, making Darkrose flinch slightly. "One wizard "guarded" by the queens of not one but *two* vampire Houses? This has to look like a full-on invasion. And we can't explain that our forces in Atlanta were decimated by the fires, so this is basically all we have left."

"No, we can't," Vickman said, closing his phone as he entered the room. "And, just in case someone's bright enough to hit a spy store and pick up some long-range listening gear, let's not even *talk* about any of our vulnerabilities while we're here in San Francisco, all right?"

"Damn it," I said. "If it's that dangerous, should we just leave?"

"She can be trained," Vickman said. "But we can't leave Nyissa with the Vampire Court, we can't retrieve her until tonight, and if we're going to stay the day in San Francisco, we have to make at least a token appearance at the Northern California Practitioner's Conclave."

"Great. The vampires won't let us leave," I said, "but the wizards want us gone—"

"Ferguson's faction is the least of our worries," Vickman said, waggling his cell phone. "The leader of the Conclave just contacted me about new 'security concerns,' and we have to tread carefully. We expected vamps, witches, and werewolves . . . but now there will be fae."

"No one mentioned the fae would be there," Darkrose said quickly. "Dakota?"

"First I've heard of it, but relax, the fae aren't *that* bad," I said. In fact, Lord Buckhead, the fae lord of Atlanta, was a close friend. Well, a good friend. Well, he'd kept me out of trouble. Well—"Regardless, I thought the fae didn't usually send a rep to these gatherings."

"That's what we were told," Vickman said tightly. "That's what we agreed to. But the fae have a standing seat in the Conclave, and have chosen to exercise it. No one knows why they're crashing the party; my guess is that they *also* are interested in meeting you, Dakota."

"That's . . . charming," I said. Lord Buckhead *was* a friend, but he could change shape, walk through walls, command the werekindred, and, if legends were true, grant you prosperity—or curse you to ruin. If he was an enemy . . . "I'll put my best foot forward, then."

"That sounds like a great idea—because a fae delegation *will* be at Conclave," Vickman said. "And because the fae will be there—this is very important—we give them *no real names.* We don't want to give them any more power than they already have."

"But . . ." I said helplessly. "But they know *my* name—"

"And Cinnamon's," Vickman said, an ironic smile on his face. "But we only bring vamps who have pseudonyms, and Schultze and I, who operate under *nom de guerres*. Even then, we will do no introductions, and the rest of our party has to stay here."

"Vickman," Saffron said. "I agree with Dakota. This sounds too dangerous—"

Vickman smiled more tightly.

"I'm not saying we can't jump off the train," he said, "but it has left the station."

8. CONCLAVE

Our rental cars crawled up a steep—I mean, stereotypically San Francisco steep—street toward the top of Russian Hill, a densely packed elevation in the City which I remembered from our last visit as the home of the world's steepest and crookedest tourist trap, Lombard Street.

But while many of the side streets were essentially staircases, we didn't see Lombard itself, and eventually pulled into the gated parking lot of a Spanish Mission-style building nestled amidst looming canyons of apartment buildings and three-story homes.

The place was eclectic: the warm brown stone and curved arches of the mission were Spanish, the dark indigo inscription over the door was cryptic Russian, and inside, the mission was thoroughly modern, with cool carpet and wall hangings in blues and greens.

"I am the Warlock," said the tall, genial man who received us in the antechamber. He was pleasant, and kindly, if a bit dated, wearing a three piece suit and sporting a seventies shaggy haircut . . . but I got a peculiar tingle from him, not a spell precisely, but a magical echo in my tattoos, which definitely caught his eye. "Your clan's inkwork lives up to its colorful reputation. Did your security man warn you about our naming protocol . . . Dakota Frost?"

I let out a breath. "Yes, and why you have that protocol, on which note, *my* name—"

"And Cinnamon Frost's name, are well known," the Warlock said. I glared, but he raised his hand. "Don't worry—celebrity is its own shield. Speaking *your* names openly may actually help dispel fae threats . . . but please don't introduce your companions."

"This is ridiculous," I said. "If there's this much danger—"

"There must be an equal or greater reward," the Warlock said, his eye glinting. "You don't know me, Dakota Frost, but *I* invited you, and I promise this isn't a trap. Please trust that I've contrived this peculiar situation for everyone's benefit—"

"I don't see how," I snapped.

"—because our members can be difficult," the Warlock continued smoothly, "and you had *surprising* success dealing with difficult factions back in Atlanta. I think many of us would be grateful if you told us how you did it; please indulge this imposition."

I sighed. "All right," I said, "but I don't have to like this."

The Warlock escorted me, Cinnamon, Saffron, Darkrose, Vickman, and Schultze up to a large conference room with a lopsided figure-eight floor plan that took up most of the upper story of the mission. A ring-shaped mahogany table filled the larger lobe of the room, while behind the ring's podium, in the smaller lobe, an arc of couches sat beneath mammoth glass windows with a spectacular view of the house-encrusted hills of San Francisco and the blues of the Bay.

The Warlock gave me the podium. Saffron and Darkrose sat at my left and right, with Vickman and Schultze standing behind me like black and white pillars. The Warlock made space for himself and Cinnamon next to Saffron; then he raised his hand in a beck.

The oak doors opened, and the Conclave began filing in.

If the muggers had been a walking UN, the Northern California Practitioner's Conclave was a buttoned-down Mos Eisley cantina. Each of them was different: squat, thin, bulky, and petite; European, Asian, Native, and Latino; men, women, straight, and gay; witches, wizards, werekin, and, yes, the fae. Each was the same: dressing conservatively, entering in silence, and regarding me with cold suspicion. Each contingent—wizards, witches, werekin, and even the fae, but no vamps—came in threes, in coordinated outfits. Perhaps this was a sign of some unspoken truce, some way of ensuring that no group had sufficient power to ambush the others.

As the room filled with more and more Edgeworlders, Cinnamon became more and more nervous, and I smiled to reassure her. But I had the podium, and I'd unwisely let the Warlock put himself and Saffron between Cinnamon and me. Now Cinnamon's head-snaps and exhalations became more and more pronounced as she tried to bottle her Tourette's tics. I could see why she was nervous. As the assembling members of the Conclave sized up our party, they all glared . . . and they were still all arriving in threes. With Vickman and Schultze standing behind me like bodyguards, and vamps on my left and right, I started to wonder whether we had broken some rule against bringing larger groups. Surely the Warlock would have told Vickman—

"*Loser freaks,*" Cinnamon snapped, immediately clapping her hands to her mouth. She stood up abruptly, tail switching, then bolted to the observation area behind us. I turned to follow her, but the Warlock rose and extended his hand, gesturing for me to stay where I was.

"I'll sit with her," he said. "You stay. The gang's all here now—and you're on."

I stared after them, dismayed—but while the couch she'd thrown herself on was behind me, Cinnamon wasn't far, or out of earshot. Still . . . I looked at Vickman, who nodded and turned subtly so Cinnamon and the Warlock would be visible in the corner of his eye.

I turned back—and saw the oak doors closing. The last entrants, a trio of probable wizards, were just taking their seats; and their leader, a blond man in a beige suit, who had also been looking at Cinnamon, caught my eye and gestured to me.

"Dakota Frost," he said, taking his seat directly opposite me. His eyes glinted, and, as if in deliberate challenge to the fae, he spoke his name. "Charles Carnes, of the Wizarding Guild. I believe you have something to tell us about why you're visiting San Francisco today."

I stared at him, gathering my thoughts. The Warlock had not set an agenda. Carnes was a crew-cut blond in a stylish banded collar who didn't look like an obvious magician; at first glance, I might have mistaken him for a Baptist preacher—or even a televangelist.

Magic often draws the different; of all the cavalcade of races, minorities, and classes here, he looked the most normal. But, like the power-suited man and woman on his left and right, he had ornate, jeweled rings, discreet, complex earrings—and arcane symbols subtly woven into his clothing. To those in the know, the three of them gave off an unmistakable vibe of "wizard."

Those who are different are drawn to magic because it gives us an edge—an advantage in a world that has dealt us disadvantages. But there's another kind of person drawn to magic, a person who wants more than an edge or an advantage—a person who wants power.

The Warlock might be in charge here. But Carnes was gunning for an angle.

"Actually, I *thought* this meeting was about my work on Atlanta's Magical Security Council," I said. "But, since you asked why I'm in San Francisco, that's simple. I am out here for my daughter. She's a mathematician, and won an award—"

"Is that really why you brought an entire entourage all the way across the country?" Carnes said, surveying Cinnamon and my companions. "It strains credulity to think that you'd cart half of this 'Magical Security Council' out here just for your child's award ceremony."

OK . . . so you're not even going to pretend you're interested in pleasantries. *Fine.*

Part of me was angry. San Francisco was one of the most advanced cities in the world; clearance from *two* different Edgeworld groups shouldn't have been necessary just for a young girl to pick up a math prize. Part of me felt strangely embarrassed, talking to this Conclave of powerful magical creatures as if I was an authority. But the largest part of me was *wary*.

Clearly, Carnes didn't buy the honest truth that I was out here for Cinnamon's award—and by focusing on the MSC and my "entourage," I wondered if he saw this trip as a power play. From the hostile glares around the table, I guessed the others had similar suspicions.

I didn't know how I could reassure them. But I was going to do my best.

"All right, Mr. Carnes," I said. "I've told this story to the Wizarding Guild, but for the benefit of the rest of the Conclave, I'm sure most of you are aware of the wave of arson that hit Atlanta this winter. But you may not know that those arsons were set off by magic."

Stony silence.

"They were caused by a corrupt graffiti magic spell, distributed under false pretenses," I said. "Most of the graffiti writers didn't realize what they were doing, but dozens of people still died, so Georgia set up a Magical Security Council to prevent that kind of abuse—"

"Meaning, *you* set up," Carnes said. "I'm told the MSC is your project."

"I proposed it," I said, "but it was convened by Lord Delancaster, Master of Georgia—"

"*Vampire* Master of Georgia," Carnes said. "And you've met with the vamps out here—"

"No, our *vampires* have met with the vampires out here, because the vampires out here demanded it," I said, "and even then, that was more vampire politics than anything to do with me. Look, Mr. Carnes, the Wizarding Guild is involved in the MSC—"

"Because we demanded it," Carnes said, "but even then, our rep, Nicholson, is—"

"Is barely there, I know—I have the same beef with him," I said. "Look, *I don't care* who's on the MSC's roster. I was almost killed by that graffiti, and some of my friends did die, so we decided—*I* decided—to establish rules for magic so that wouldn't happen again—"

"So you put a *tabu* on your magic," interrupted one of the fae, a kindly-*looking* green-haired matron . . . whose eyes glowed a hostile red. "And now want to inflict it upon us?"

I looked at her warily. A strange glamour was on the creature, making her look like a middle-aged woman in Bohemian dress—but look again, and her eyes shimmered like candles shining through red wine, the gaze of a night predator gleaming beneath a thicket of holly-green hair. She was actually the most sympathetic-looking of her companions, who included a stoic druid boy with oak leaves for hair and a younger fae girl who looked half Cinnamon's age—except for the strands of white hair partially shielding her piercing, hate-filled eyes.

"No," I said at last. "I believe in educating, not banning, enforcing, not eliminating. Yes, people may break the rules, but I don't want to go back to the old days of hidden magic. But I need support, both politically and practically, to find the right balance—"

"So you wish us to help perfect your geas . . . and *then* dance to your tune?" the boy fae said, eyes glowing like twin moons beneath his leafy bangs. "Yet another human shaman trying to seize control of our power, rather than follow ways which have lasted us a millennium."

"I'm not here to convert you to my ways," I said, though to be frank, the more flak they gave me, the more I was convinced that my ways were probably better than whatever they had. "I-am-out-here-for-my-daughter. *Her* itinerary is Berkeley and Stanford, so I wasn't planning to spend much time in San Francisco proper—until you all demanded I come and speak to you."

"Really," said a trim man whose sandy hair and muscular frame made me think were-mountain-cat. "The story *I* heard is we caught you planning to sneak into our territory, but you claim *we* actually invited *you?* Now why would we have wanted you here?"

"The Warlock," I said acidly, "seemed to admire the Council's ability to head off a war brewing between Atlanta's vampire and werekin factions. For my part, I wanted to find out how California's magical community works. What we're trying to do on the Council is entirely new, at least in Atlanta's Edgeworld. The Conclave, in contrast, has been running for a hundred fifty years. I think the point of this meeting was to introduce ourselves to you . . . and to share experiences . . . dealing with these problems . . ."

I trailed off. The Conclave was no longer looking at me; their attention had focused on two ends of the table. Opposite me, Carnes looked worried, and tilted his head at Saffron . . . and then at the youngest of the fae, who was leaning forward, staring at Saffron intently.

I leaned forward on the podium until I could see Saffron. She sat there, head canted, red hair sweeping out from beneath a brown beret she wore at an angle . . . not entirely unlike the angled placement of flowers in the fragile fae's delicate white hair. Saffron wore a long rumpled casual business suit in many layers and buckles, covering her skin almost completely; the fae wore a long rumpled shirt over a short buckled crop top, exposing her porcelain-pale midriff and neck. Their outfits were superficially different, but clearly from the same designer; they could have switched outer layers and headgear in an instant.

And then I felt a prickling spread across the table, like when a vampire tries to roll your mind. I spread my hands out, closing my eyes; the flux of mana was coming from Saffron, and, to a lesser extent, from the little fae. At first, it was just a trickle. Then it became a torrent.

I opened my eyes, to see most of the members of the Conclave frozen, leaning back as far as they could from a shimmering miasma that spread over the table, barely visible except when you moved your eyes. Heat waves seemed to be coming off Saffron as she stared at the girl.

The white-haired girl fae was rocking now, leaning forward; her older, more Bohemian companion speaking in her ear to calm her. But it wasn't working—the little girl flicked her head, moving her hair off her left eye so she could lock gazes with Saffron.

"I could take her," the fae whispered, her blue-white eyes glowing like chips of ice.

9. Standoff

No one moved. No one spoke. No one dared look into the eyes of the girl or Saffron. From where I stood, the mana surging across the table was so strong, I could feel its flux against my skin, feel it try to activate my tattoos. *Oh, the hell with this.*

"*Bulllllshit,*" I said, as loud as I could.

Saffron and the fae jumped, along with the rest of the Conclave. Even the Dragon on my skin twitched as the magic between the would-be combatants surged across the table. But when the Warlock pivoted around, he merely had a genial smile, and pulled out his pocket watch.

"I mean, what the hell?" I said, glaring at Saffron, then the fae. Both were shocked into embarrassment. "The first 'official" meeting of Georgia and California magicians in twenty-five years and y'all are throwing it for a 'who wore the same dress' catfight?"

Saffron jerked. "No, I—"

"You dare mock me," the little fae hissed, turning her glittery eyes on me, the prickly feeling sweeping over my skin, making the Dragon again twitch. *This one is dangerous.* The tiny creature—clearly *not* a "little girl" at all—hissed, "*None* dare mock *Sidhain*—"

"*Eeeeenough!*" I roared, waving my hands through the air to soak up stray mana and slamming them down on the podium, the impact amplified by mana discharging from the yin-yangs in my palms as they hit the wood. The sudden bang rattled the windows, far more showy than I intended—but I had everyone's attention now. "I take back what I said about needing your help. If you don't have the sense to control yourselves in a simple meet-and-greet—"

"*You're* the one shouting," Carnes said, voice quickly becoming calm. "And you're the one without the sense to keep out of a fae power challenge."

"Mr. Carnes," I said, meeting his eyes, matching him calm for calm, "Not only am I not here to interfere with your battles, I'm not here to create new ones. Y'all *didn't* have to invite me. You could have let us come and go in peace, or, if you're really that threatened by a mother chaperoning her daughter as she's picking up a math prize, a simple 'no' would have done. But, despite the warnings that *some* of you passed to me *ex parte*, I spoke to every group at this table before we flew out, and got a yes—"

"If we aren't giving you the welcome you expected," Carnes interjected, leaning forward, steepling his fingers before him, "you could always leave."

I stared at him. He stared back calculatingly.

I cracked my neck, and made a command decision.

"All right," I said. "We can leave. This spat between my companion and Little Miss Flower Child there is the *third* assault we've seen or experienced in the last twenty-four hours, and I have *zero* intention of subjecting my *child* to this kind of danger—"

Carnes winced at the word "child," and opened his mouth—but I kept rolling.

"I had no reason to expect California was still the Wild Wild West, but I forget that not everywhere in the world is as advanced as Atlanta, Georgia, when it comes to magic. When you're ready to do something to protect your visitors, much less your citizens, call me."

I left the podium, and Vickman and Schultze jerked to follow me. Saffron and Darkrose pushed back their chairs. I turned to Cinnamon, standing by the Warlock; she looked stunned and distraught. Well, fine. I'd rather her emotionally crushed than physically attacked.

"Cinnamon," I called—then I softened my voice. "Cinnamon, I'm so sorry, but we have to go. I thought San Francisco was a civilized place. I never meant to bring you to a war zone. I'm very sorry we'll have to miss the ceremony, but they can ship you your award—"

But before Cinnamon could move, the Warlock put his hand gently on her shoulder.

"Do not worry, Dakota Frost. While Cinnamon is in the San Francisco Bay, she is under my protection," the Warlock said, his voice oddly calm. "But as formidable as my protection is . . . still, 243 people were killed in California last year with magic."

That was terrible . . . but still, I felt myself relax. The Warlock had just done more than stick up for me, he'd shown that he understood my two most important values—protecting my daughter, and protecting everyone else from the fate that befell my boyfriend.

The Warlock stepped past Cinnamon and went to the podium, half-sitting against the conference table on one hip, hands folded over his raised knee—relaxed, easy, but with sadness in that genial grin beneath his moustache.

"That means that almost ten percent of all murders are done by magic," he said, voice without bitterness, but pain in his eyes. "More than domestic violence, more than *assault weapons*, and it's getting worse every year as you so-called 'Edgeworlders' spread."

I scowled at the "Edgeworlder" crack. To me, *everyone* who practiced magic was an Edgeworlder, and living in Atlanta, the de facto world capital of the magical Edgeworld, it was easy to forget that most old-school magicians didn't see it that way.

To the old school, there were people who deserved respect because they kept to the old ways, because they kept magic secret . . . and then there were people who were ruining it for everyone else—"playing on the edge, out in the world," the saying originally went.

I folded my arms and stared at him. What did he drag me here for? Not to get assaulted under a banner of truce, clearly, but where was he going with this? Some kind of old-school versus new-school magical lecture? *I* sure wasn't going to take the blame for—

"Thank God it's mostly practitioner-on-practitioner crimes," he said, checking his watch again. "And a fair share of dumb-shit accidents. Still, it's a miracle no outsider has noticed yet—that's all the excuse some witch hunter needs to start a crusade."

"You're telling me," I said. "Back home, one partially-reported magical assault in Atlanta led to the DEI raiding a secret werehouse. Two hundred and fifty people? *Ten percent of all murders?* I'm surprised the DEI hasn't arrested you all on general principles—"

"They've tried that in the past," Carnes said, scowling. "And they're still trying. The DEI *still* conducts witch hunts—technically, of witches who are also criminals, but we have long memories. We remember when the DEI *proudly* called itself America's Inquisition."

I frowned . . . because he was right.

"No one here will risk going public," the Warlock said. "Most practitioners are too private, too vulnerable. They start burning us again, literally or metaphorically, and . . . most of us will have to go hide. We need someone already *in* public to take a public stand."

I clenched my fists. *Damn it.* Yes, I flap my yapper about being the best tattooist in the Southeast, but I had not really set out to become one of the most public magicians in the country. Yet, I now was, and I had no intention of going and hiding, witch hunt or no.

The Warlock was right, and I'd played right into his hands—not a trap, my ass.

"What, precisely, do you think the lesbian mafia here is going to do about reducing practitioner-on-practitioner crime when just their being here stirs up trouble?" Carnes asked. He gestured at the petite fae, Sidhain, who slumped forward again, letting her brittle white hair cover half her face. "I *warned* you about this. This is precisely the kind of mess—"

"This was nothing. Glares were thrown, but no fists or blasts," I said. "We aren't here to start fights, but we'll stand up and stop them. Some goons attacked a friend with *fire magic* on the streets of Oakland last night. If I hadn't been there, they'd have maimed her for life—"

"*You* fought off the goons?" Carnes asked. "All by yourself?"

"Yes," I replied, and as he held my gaze I amplified, "All four of them, all by myself. But *nobody* should be assaulting *anyone* with magic. And if someone does, there are ways to handle it. We defended, but didn't escalate. We called the police—"

"And they didn't arrest you for a magical misdemeanor?" Carnes asked.

"No," I said, "because I have experience dealing with the police—"

"That how you ended up being charged in Atlanta for murder by magic?"

"No, but you see how that worked out," I said, spreading my hands. "I'm still here. But, since you brought it up, that left me willing to stick up for *anyone* using magic in self-defense, whether it's making their case respectfully to the police—or fighting off their attackers."

Carnes shifted in his seat.

"All right," he said. "I agree—people should feel safe here. Your friend shouldn't have been attacked, and I'm glad you were there to defend her. Clearly, we have a lot to work on. But look at it from our perspective. A wizard's perspective. You're a vampire's servant—"

"I am no such thing," I said sharply.

"Troubleshooter, employee, ally, whatever," he said, waving his hand. "I understand the distinctions, but at the end of the day, you brought the head of a new coven of vampires into the Bay, which is already overrun with them. You can't expect us to welcome *more*—"

"Am I not in the room?" Saffron asked, incredulous.

"What?" the wizard asked. "What are you talking about—"

"I think she's offended," I said. Carnes stared at me blankly. The whole daywalking thing was new here. I clarified, "Did you think she was a fae just because she got in a fight with one? This is the Vampire Queen of Little Five Points and her consort."

Carnes froze, staring at them. "Damn it, that little prick didn't give a full report," he muttered to himself, and confirmed that he was probably Ferguson's unnamed boss. Carnes slowly rose from his chair. "I didn't realize—but *how?* You shipped only one coffin—"

"You didn't tell them," I said, suddenly realizing why neither Carnes nor Ferguson had any clue about Saffron. The Warlock just smiled. "You *knew* you had vampire-slash-wizard problems out here in the Bay, and you didn't tell your *own people* about us—"

"It's sometimes easier to ask forgiveness," the Warlock began, "than—"

"Damn it, no," Carnes said. "She can't be a vampire. It's *daylight* now—"

"I'm a daywalker," Saffron said. "Ah, I take it you've heard of the phenomenon—"

"Don't be absurd, of course I've heard of daywalkers. But I also know they're rare," he said, gesturing at Darkrose. "There's only one I know of on the entire West Coast. One of you I could believe, but *two* in Frost's *entourage*—"

"*We* are not in *Frost's* entourage," Saffron said sharply—then her mouth quirked up. She stuck her tongue in her cheek, then nodded. "Perhaps we are. Regardless, that *is* the thesis of my PhD: daywalking is possible for any vampire, if, early on, they adopt a vegetarian diet."

Carnes blanched, his chair falling behind him now. "Oh, fuck me—"

"They rolled your mind yet, Chuck?" the Warlock asked. "Drained your magical blood? If they even *tried* to 'swamp your will with vampiric power,' don't you think someone in this room, even one of your enemies, would have noticed? Would have *done* something?"

Carnes looked at Saffron, then back at the Warlock.

"No, Warlock, but what do you want me to say? We've been at war with the vampires of the City for almost a hundred and twenty five years. What good did you think would come by bringing more vampires into a room filled with wizards, werekin, and fae?"

I sighed. "Let's just start," I said, "by building on what we just did. Vampires met wizards without a battle. Factions had a discussion without declaring war. And two powerful magical creatures got together in the same room and didn't kill each other."

The little fae girl suddenly looked up at me, grinning a white toothy grin that would have done Cinnamon proud. Carnes, for his part, still looked wary, but the ice seemed to be breaking inside. Finally, he sighed, righted his chair, and eased himself back into it.

"I'm starting to believe you did stop a war brewing in Atlanta, Dakota Frost," he said. "To be frank with you, I'm trying to do the same thing here, but as you may have guessed, San Francisco is so much of a powder keg, I'm not sure we can handle any more factions."

"I have no intention of adding my 'faction' to the mix," I said, raising my hands . . . but then something started to eat at me. "But, to be frank with *you*, I'm worried to hear that a war might be brewing out here too. Clearly, you all can at least share the same room—"

"*We're* trained in the proper use of magic," Carnes said. "But magic is out of the hands of the Guilds and in the wild. The Edgeworld started as hippie magicians casting peace spells, love charms, and flowers of power, but now there are rogue adepts doing terrible damage—"

"There are plenty of rogue *old-school* magicians doing damage too," I snapped.

"We know. We still tell of the horror at the fords," the little porcelain fae said. "In the hills of Los Vados, a witch tried to wreak vengeance on a rival and fell to her own spell." Then the fae's façade cracked, and she shuddered. "It was . . . horrible. A big old splattery mess."

"We don't want to shove magic back into the darkness," Carnes said. "My wizarding master is a university magician. But now, textbooks are filled with magic once hidden in cryptic tomes that took years of study to understand—and magic can be horribly abused."

"Out here, there's no law," said a werewolf. "The vamps only protect humans, their *food supply*. The only police the Edgeworld has are the wizards, and when they care to, the fae. But a small-g god rides herd over the packs in Georgia—Buckhead, Lord of the Wild Hunt."

It was true. Buckhead, a stag-headed fae, intervened in werekin battles that went too far. And Christopher Valentine had called Buck a "fading, wannabe god." Personally, I reserve the word "God" for the Big G; I hadn't realized how seriously people took Buckhead's title.

"Werekin combat *is* formalized in Georgia," I admitted cautiously, not wanting to draw Buckhead into a trap like the one the Warlock had made for me. "Staged battles, with betting and rules, like a sport. Maybe you could adopt such contests here, blow off steam—"

"Maybe," the werewolf said. "Maybe you could ask Lord Buckhead to preside."

The fae all became attentive, and the little porcelain fae looked up, bright and hopeful.

Unexpectedly, Carnes spoke. "If you could, it would mean a lot. To all of us."

"I'll . . . ask," I said. "No promises."

"Since she agrees to ask," the Warlock said, "can the Conclave at least agree to bless Dakota Frost's mission in the Bay, to extend her our protection while she sojourns here—"

"And to wish her daughter success at collecting her prize," said Carnes. "So moved."

The Warlock blinked. "Seconded. Speak, all who concur."

"So mote it be," said the little fae girl, and all around the table concurred.

"Excellent," the Warlock said warmly. "Welcome to San Francisco, Dakota Frost."

10. Clearing the Schedule

The meeting adjourned, and the various groups of the Conclave began leaving by threes according to some obviously prearranged order. Each departing group bowed to some groups while snubbing others, and the targets of their bows respected or disrespected the departing groups with equal randomness. Interestingly, the werestags and werewolves were among the most respectful and cordial, the beefy werewolf getting up and muttering something to the

Korean, who smiled. But it was the departure of the Wizarding Guild I was waiting for.

"Mr. Carnes," I called out. He turned, and I raised my hand to my ear in a "call me" gesture. He stiffened, then clenched his teeth. Yep, as I had guessed, Carnes was Ferguson's boss. I said, "The next time you need to talk, do it direct. I think you have my number."

Carnes broke from his companions and came back, looking at Cinnamon and me.

"You *really* came here," he murmured, "just so she could collect a *math prize?*"

Now Cinnamon stiffened, and I clenched my teeth. "Yes," I said. "Yes, we did."

"Then," Carnes said, clearly debating something internally as he looked between the two of us. "Then . . . you should take her to the Exploratorium while you're here. My daughters love math and science too. If she's anything like them, she'll love it."

My lips parted slightly. "Uh," I said. "Thank you, Mr. Carnes. We'll consider it."

"Yeah," Cinnamon said, still stiff, staring at him. "T-thanks, sir."

He nodded to her, then to me, then turned and walked out of the room.

That left us with just the Warlock and the fae. Everyone had bowed to the fae; no one had bowed to us. But when the fae rose, they all bowed in our direction. I spread my hands out; Saffron and Darkrose stood, and we all bowed, quite formally.

The green-haired elder fae stepped forward and bowed, and I noticed that, one-upping the wizards, she had dozens of magical charms and accessories woven all through her outfit, including the red wings of a dead bird slowly moving upon her elaborate hat.

"Thank you for your presentation," she said, eyes gleaming like amber.

"Thank you for your attention," I responded, nodding back.

The little fae girl, Sidhain, did an elaborate curtsy—drawing her right foot back proper, bending gracefully, and ending with her foot daintily out, though the drawing of her skirts didn't quite work with that long flowing shirt-dress—and then she spoke directly to Saffron.

"I'm so sorry," she said, ice-chip eyes all glittery behind the fragile curtain of glass that was her hair, "that we didn't get to play."

Saffron returned the curtsy with equal grace, mirroring the fae girl's skirt-drawing with a similar pull of her coat. "Perhaps another time."

The little fae rose, and flounced out of the room; her two companions followed, and the huge oak doors slowly closed behind them. Then, and only then, did the Warlock let out his breath. I hadn't even noticed he had been holding it.

"*That* was a miscalculation on my part," he said, gesturing toward the door. "I didn't expect the fae would come at all, and if I'd known they were going to bring the Lost Child of the Ford, I would have . . . I don't know. Perhaps called it off."

"That's . . . good to know," I said. I didn't know who the little porcelain girl was, other than a poorly stoppered vial of extremely bad, but I was glad disaster was averted. "Who was she? The Lost Child, Sidhain, they called her?

That sounds vaguely familiar—"

"I believe she appears in some Irish ballads," the Warlock said tightly.

"So she's . . . an ancient fae? But if they've got her, why do they want Lord Buckhead? Couldn't she preside over the—" The Warlock spread his hands, like trying to wave off a plane from landing, and I sighed. "OK, OK. I could see that she's a problem. But . . . Saffron."

Saffron drew in a breath, then sighed. "Yes, Dakota?"

"Grow up," I said.

"Dakota!" Saffron said, raising her hands. "Please. I know I've been a petulant brat to you . . . well, since I became a vampire, and I'm sorry, but *this* time I didn't do anything wrong. You couldn't perceive it, but I was magically assaulted by that *thing*, right here at this table—"

"No, I felt it," I said, sighing. "From you, the sensation was much more powerful, so I assumed you started it. I'm sorry, that was uncharitable—"

"Really," the Warlock said, looking me over. "Sensing an aura is normally a vampire trait—or a wizard skill. Forgive my prying, Ms. Frost, but I didn't see you use a wand, ring, or dowsing rod—and I didn't think you had a magical bloodline."

"I don't, but have y'all actually *looked* at me?" I asked, pulling up my sleeves to show my tattoos. "I'm covered in two square meters of magical circuits. *Of course* I can sense magic. I'd be able to sense magnetic fields too, if I was this filled with iron filings."

"Fascinating," the Warlock said, peering at the tail of my Dragon as she slid up my arm. "Your clan inks really do produce quite extraordinary color, Ms. Frost. I know a professor at Stanford who'd *love* a closer look. He's Carnes's mentor, by the way—"

"Why didn't you tell Carnes about us?" I said sharply. "About our vampires?"

"Carnes is not the head of the Wizarding Guild in San Francisco—*I* am," the Warlock said, just as sharply, though his ire was clearly not directed at me. "He's useful, and his faction is influential, but the details of your security arrangements are *not* his business."

I drew in a breath. I hadn't thought about it like that. Sharing the details of our party with others would have made us more vulnerable—and further complicated the already complicated politics out here. Rather than blindsiding us, the Warlock had tried to do us a favor.

"Thank you," I said. "Sir, about the Guild, I have tried to give Alex a full report—"

"Alex may have been a no-show, but he's kept us informed—and none of that 'sir' stuff. You do not report to me," the Warlock said. "The Guild demanded a seat on the Council because the work you are doing is too important to proceed without oversight—but it's your show."

"Thanks again," I said.

"And don't be too hard on Carnes. His goals aren't really that different from yours," the Warlock said. "In fact, Ms. Frost, I had hoped to introduce you not just to Carnes but to several other magicians—but after that Oakland business, we should wait."

"Really?" I said. "But I wasn't even the target—"

"San Francisco's public officials in charge of the regulation of magic are *very* straitlaced. If there's another assault, the Commissioner might have you taken into protective custody until 'all the commotion dies down.' " The Warlock grimaced. "I'd . . . keep a low profile."

"We'll . . . try to stay out of trouble," I said. "As much as we can, with a meeting with the Vampire Court and two public talks already on our schedule."

"I wish you the best of luck with that, Dakota Frost," the Warlock said. Then he grinned at Cinnamon. "And congratulations, Cinnamon, on your award. You and your mother should be very proud of your accomplishments, and we are glad to have you visit San Francisco."

Soon, as the doors of the mission closed behind us, I sighed in relief.

"That could have gone worse," I said. "And we're free until tonight, yes?"

"Old-school vampires," Darkrose said, with a smile, "do have a constrained schedule."

"Oh, you do so love your daylight," Saffron said, smiling at her.

"Not as much as I love she who gave it back to me," Darkrose said.

"Lovebirds, get a room," I said, unexpectedly happy for them. Not so long ago, I had been consumed with jealousy and bitterness. It felt . . . good, not carrying that around anymore. "Well, an afternoon in San Francisco isn't the worst thing in the world. Preferences?"

"First, we must feed," Saffron said. "If I don't get some Chinese food in me, I'm liable to sink my fangs into the nearest Chinese person. After that"—her smile grew very wicked—"Darkrose and I would like to go . . . shopping."

I blinked. That *so* wasn't my space. "All right," I said. "Any preferences? Chinatown, two birds with one stone? Haight-Ashbury?" I glanced at Saffron's outfit; she had turned her eye to fashion lately. "You aren't suggesting we go shopping in Union Square?"

"Macy's? *Bloomingdale's?*" Darkrose said archly. "I think not."

"*We* were thinking," Saffron said, "of a place we could find . . . something in leather."

11. At Last, My Back Is Complete Again

SOMA is a blasted neighborhood "SOuth of MArket Street" in San Francisco that has some of the best leather shops and nightclubs in the entire world. Saffron and Darkrose had planned a tour of virtually all of SOMA's kinkier shops, starting with the discount Leather Etcetera, heading down Eighth Street to the Mister and Madame S fetish superstore, and continuing on to a variety of boot shops and corsetieres I'd only heard of, looking not just for themselves, but for our mutual friend Jinx—who had given Saffron a list before she and her new husband Doug had left on that boat tour this morning.

Unfortunately, most of the leather shops our vampire friends planned to visit were also sex shops, filled with rare and delightful toys that Saffron and I had eagerly sought out—long ago. But she and I were split, and the very things that had drawn us to those shops were things I thought were not fit for a minor. So, right at the start, I had them drop Cinnamon and me off at their final destination, Stormy Leather, where I had one special purchase in mind.

Leaving Cinnamon outside, I went in, past rows of corsets and vinyl and leather and a woman behind the counter who, shockingly, remembered me after nearly a decade—apparently she didn't get many deathhawked customers my height. I passed racks of buckles and straps—part of a former life. I squeezed down a narrow stair, discovering a steel bondage chair identical to the one Nyissa had used to imprison me when we had been enemies. It was in the clearance leather department, where the ceiling creaked as patrons browsed above, that I finally found what I wanted. When I emerged from the basement to pay, I enjoyed the saleswoman's double take as she said, "Wait . . . isn't that what you bought . . . last time?"

I stepped out into the street wearing a brand-new leather vestcoat—identical to the one that had been my signature before it had been ruined with paint and blood. It was long, barely brushing the ground, and straight, accentuating my height; sleeveless, exposing my arms, but buckled, so I could snap it closed if cold. I'd get interior pockets sewn in back home, but still, it was the best coat I'd ever worn, and cheaper than most, too. Under my arm I held a bag with a second one—the last one on the rack, and quite possibly, the last one like it in the world.

"At last," I said, shimmying my shoulders, feeling the tails of the coat brush against the ramp as I stepped out onto the street, "my back is complete again."

"Didn't you wants to go to the stores with them?" Cinnamon asked, smiling, clicking off her iPod. "Or, I dunno, slip me in? Nothing in there's gonna shock me. Back at the werehouse . . . I probably had more boys than you have."

"That was a different life, for both of us," I said, adjusting my vestcoat. *Like a pair of leather wings.* Cinnamon was right, but I was determined to give her a real childhood, as best I could—and after our little backstage experience watching Jewel get undressed, I was determined to be a little more careful what environments I took her to from now on. "Now, I have all I need right here: a new jacket, and a new daughter, who I'd very much like to spend time with."

We walked up the street. SOMA was nowhere near as "blasted" as I remembered, and we stopped at Harvest Urban Market, a slick health food grocery wedged underneath apartments—a nice retrofitting of mixed-use onto an old office building. I bought an heirloom tomato from the well-stocked produce section and a slice of cheese and a croissant from the deli, Cinnamon got a few hunks of stew meat from the meat counter, and we found a cozy table beneath the plate glass windows on the Eighth Street side and had a little snack as the cars whizzed by.

I pulled a knife from my boot and cut the tomato, carefully slicing it along the grain of the sections so the juice wouldn't spill everywhere. Then I salted the slices and ate them, one by one. Cinnamon watched with amusement, tearing chunks off the meat, wolfing them down, and occasionally grabbing the salt shaker to zing up some of the more chewy bits.

We talked about Cinnamon's "Young Investigator" award. The actual award would be handed out Thursday night at Stanford, at the conference proper, but her sponsor, Professor ZQ, wanted her to give a practice talk at Berkeley first. The request didn't help her nervousness.

When I got down to the last few slices of tomato, I slipped them and the cheese into the croissant, and chowed down. A little tomato splurted out, and Cinnamon laughed a little *too* loudly, head kinking aside—some Tourette's tic bubbling up. Neither of us paid it any mind. Fighting it wouldn't help Cinnamon keep it under control; only medication would, and it didn't work too well on the werekindred. She giggled as I took another bite and lost more juice.

"That Chinese lunch didn't do it for you?"

"Noff so muff," I replied, wiping my chin again. She giggled, and I sighed, just staring at her: the kinky orange hair, the curvy tiger-tattooed cheeks, the kohl hiding the tattoos around her eyes—my *daughter.* "Ah, Cinnamon. Didn't know what I was missing, not being a mother."

Cinnamon laughed again, looking away, a bit embarrassed. Then she got serious. "Mom, why *are* we doin' this? I knows—*fah!*—I knows you. You'd do anything for me, even tellin' me I couldn't come here if it wasn't safe. But when the wizards gave you flak, you didn't back off. What gives? It's like you wanted to take on the whole city."

I stared into the distance. In a way, I *did.*

In that plague of magic graffiti, I'd lost more than just friends—I'd lost my lover, killed by magic right before my eyes. Cinnamon lost a childhood friend, burned alive when their home went up in flames. The MSC was more than just a Hail Mary play—it was a full-on crusade.

And it put my old friend Alex Nicholson right in my crosshairs. The Wizarding Guild had forced me to accept Alex as their representative on the MSC, and he'd served well at first . . . but became surprisingly scarce once the Valentine Foundation's payments had dried up.

That made my blood boil. I wanted to grab Alex Nicholson by the collar and shake him until my money came out. It wasn't just the mortgage or the Prius. It was Cinnamon's school, her college fund, the flexibility to slack off at the shop to spend time with her. *Damn it.*

I set my impromptu sandwich down.

"OK," I said. I was about to lie to my child about my motives. I was a cad. Or . . . was I? There was more to the crusade than just avenging Calaphase and Revy, and more to this trip than shaking down Alex. "You deserve to know. But this stays between us. Sir Leopold—"

"That evil old lich," she said, staring straight at me, her ears folded back. That "evil old lich" was Sir Leopold, the leader of the Gentry, an evil-*looking* vampire who had served as Sherman's lich during the burning of Atlanta. "He was gonna have me killed, wasn't he?"

I stared straight back at her. The lich had reacted badly to her Tourette's; I never had found out exactly what she'd said to him to put her on his shit list. But the lich wasn't the problem; he'd actually started the Vampire Consulates. The problem was his protégé.

"Sir Leopold knew you were involved. But no, the threat was Scara, his enforcer. She goes off the chain, like she did when she staked Nyissa in the throat." Cinnamon squirmed, and I said, "She was ready to go after not just you, but all the werekin; the lich let me do 'this little Security Council thing' to defuse the situation. But some of the stuff we've seen in Council . . . you can't unsee. It's like that story about Lincoln and the squirrel. You don't want to learn the tree in front of your house is rotten, but once you do, you have to cut it down."

"Sure, but . . ." Cinnamon looked away. "Won't things eventually blow over with Scara?"

I let out a breath. "When bad shit used to go down in Atlanta, Scara had to track it down *personally*," I said. "If I just quit, before real procedures are in place that satisfy Scara . . . I'm afraid six months down the road, she's going to take matters back into her own hands."

"So you're stuck with—*fuck!*—stuck with this . . . forever."

"No," I said, shaking my head. "This can't be a one-woman crusade, or eventually it will all fall apart. Maybe it isn't like the tree and Lincoln after all. I'm not trying to cut something down, I'm trying to build something up. But I can't quit until the structure is standing—"

"Well, thank God you haven't been shot in the street," Vickman called through the glass, and we both jumped. He was standing on the Eighth Street sidewalk, making "pshoom, pshoom" motions with his fingers like he was firing six shooters. He cupped his hands and cried, "You'd think that little emotional experience with Jewel would have made you more cautious!"

"Yeah, yeah," I said, finishing my sandwich. Saffron stood behind him in a new corset over a frilly spray of a dress, but Darkrose was so bundled in her traveling cloak that whatever she had bought was hidden, assuming she was even wearing it. "We're coming."

"We desperately need to, as you would put it, 'crash,' " Darkrose said. Saffron opened her mouth in protest, but Darkrose overrode her. "Including you, my Lady Saffron. I insist. I have no intention of going to dinner with the Vampire Court with us all on the brink of exhaustion."

"All right," I said, checking my watch. It was almost three. For a vampire, that had to be like staying up until five in the morning, or worse. Abruptly, I squeezed Cinnamon in a big sideways hug, and she squeezed back. "We can go back to the hotel and plan our next—"

My smartphone rang and, with my free hand, I dug it out—it was Jewel. At first, I cheered up; then I recalled I hadn't felt that way about getting a phone call since Calaphase, and the feeling drained away. I sighed. I hadn't expected that nerve to be so raw.

"Mom, are you all right?" Cinnamon said.

"Yeah," I said, clearing my throat, then hitting the button. "I'm fine. Hello?"

"Hello?" Jewel said uncertainly. "I'm sorry, is . . . is this Dakota Frost?"

"Yeah," I said, trying to perk up. "Yes, this is Dakota. Sorry. Your call . . .

reminded me of something. Never mind—it's good to hear from you. What a nice surprise, Jewel!"

Cinnamon sneezed and cussed, and Saffron put her hand to her mouth.

"Hey," Jewel said, then paused. "This is again last minute, but I, uh . . . oh, hell."

"Yes," I asked, smiling. Maybe smirking. Everyone was grinning at me. "Go on?"

"There's an art show tonight," she said. "Monkton Teriano, the guy who welded the spinning fire pillars at the Crucible, he's having a showing at Liquid, and a whole bunch of fireweavers are going. Afterward, we're going to do a performance at Union Square."

"Wow, firespinning in Union Square!" I said, raising an eyebrow at Cinnamon. "That sounds spectacular. How did you even get a *permit* for that?"

"We *didn't*," Jewel responded.

Both my eyebrows shot up. "Breakin' the law, breakin' the law," I said. "I'd love to see you spin again, but we're booked for dinner tonight—"

"That's all right, Liquid is a nightclub," Jewel said. "Artist reception is from seven till ten, and then we'll walk over to the Square and spin until they chase us away."

The phone was abruptly taken from my hand. "This is the Lady Saffron," Saffron said, ducking as I tried to take it back, "Dakota's friend with the goggles. We would love to see you spin fire, and we plan to be there unless hostile vampires drag us away."

There was a squawk on the phone, simultaneous with one from me as Saffron spun away, listening. She nodded and smiled. "At Liquid, then. All right, I'm going to take Dakota away from you now for some important business, but I will let you say goodbye."

The phone was thrust back into my hand, and I fumbled with it. "Uh, so, I guess I'll see you tonight, then?"

"I hope so, Dakota Frost," Jewel said, and I swore she licked her lips on the phone. "See you tonight, skindancer."

"See *you*, fireweaver," I replied.

"That beats 'Granola and Mohawk' any day," Cinnamon said.

"What the hell?" Vickman said. "What are you playing at, Saffron?"

"Yes, my Lady," Darkrose said. "You know we cannot ditch the Vampire Court—"

"I'm not 'ditching' anyone," Saffron said crossly, adjusting her bomber goggles. "First, I want an excuse, however slim, to bail on this little 'dinner' if things turn nasty. And second . . . my ultimate goal here is not 'ditching' . . . it's more of 'hitching.' "

And she smiled straight at me, pulling her bomber goggles up so I could see her wink.

"Oh, hell," I said. "All right, all right, I know I'm licked. I'll go, I'll go—"

"But first things first," Darkrose said. "We vampires must 'crash'—"

—☙

"And then," Vickman said, "we all try to survive dinner with the Vampire Court."

12. Red Velvet and Leather

With the blessing of the Conclave, I'd felt better—but I wasn't kidding myself. The rest of the trip, Cinnamon's award, even my chance to shake down Alex for my money, all hinged on the approval of a court of magical creatures who were holding my friend Nyissa hostage.

This trip, we took a stretch limo, rather than our rental cars, and that loss of one degree of freedom made me antsy, an apprehension which grew greater as we surged through a chaos of horns and lights toward the stronghold of the Vampire Court of San Francisco.

We pulled in front of the Clift, a forbidding monolith of gray brick and glass, a row of two-story arched windows at its base creating the appearance of a series of pillars. Vickman stepped out briskly, then motioned to Schultze, and then Saffron and Darkrose.

"All right," I said, squeezing Cinnamon's hand. "Last row of the gauntlet!"

"They hits me with sticks," Cinnamon said, "I tears—*fah!*—tears 'em a new one."

The Clift's exterior was grim, but the inside? Oh-so-chic. The featureless two-story gray stone walls looked clean, rather than forbidding, and the weird lights and end tables, not to mention a fantastic oversized ten-foot-tall chair, gave the room a hip Seussical vibe.

But behind Jack the Giant's chair, beyond two smooth stone columns, the calming gray wall rippled up into black, contorted sheets of stone. Fire roared in a pile of stones at its base—and before the fire stood a muscular, weathered man in a business suit of black leather.

Lord Varguson, leader of the Vampire Court of San Francisco.

The Lady Saffron stepped forward, bowing slightly (or was that *stiffly*) in her new red leather corset, and Lord Varguson returned the bow graciously, kissing her hand. I fumed as my ex-girlfriend exchanged court pleasantries like she was a born noble—we'd gone to the same grade school. Vampire nonsense was worse than that of the wizards.

Then Saffron looked back at me, and Varguson's eyes glinted—not a full glow, just red pinpricks—but that, and the leather, standing before the fire, made him look like the Prince of Darkness. But he seemed to beckon to me, and I stepped forward, not looking in his eyes.

He looked me over, then exchanged glances with Saffron, and they both nodded. Without a word, he turned and walked off. Two mammoth bodyguards I hadn't seen detached themselves from the shadows, one following him down a dark passageway, the other guarding its entrance.

"Saffron—" I began, but she shushed me. Then the guard touched his finger to his ear and beckoned to us, and Schultze stepped forward, followed by Saffron and Darkrose. As I passed, I noted the guard's excellent tribal tattoos climbing his neck. "*Nice* linework."

The guard's mouth quirked—he'd checked out my tattoos as well. "You too."

We passed through a dimly lit tunnel of cut black stone into a vast square room hung with red velvet curtains that fell like frozen waterfalls of blood. Everywhere, cut glass and gleaming metal were patterned in subtle harlequins, and the faces of the patrons hovered like ghosts over glass-topped tables illuminated from beneath. We passed a high arch opening on a bar decorated with glowing portraits of uber-chic faux Victorians, and I was struck by one picture, a woman in a cocktail dress staring demurely at her hands—then her eyes moved, looking straight at me.

I shuddered and moved on. A plasma screen. That's what it *obviously* was, in retrospect. And this might be a vampire stronghold, but it wasn't an exclusive enclave—the bar and dining area were filled with hip San Franciscans and T-shirted tourists. Vickman had said that this was a neutral ground where *our* three vampires could meet *their* three vampires in an attempt to avoid unpleasantries, but I hadn't realized that neutral ground meant *in public.*

The guards escorted us to a round table in the inner corner of the restaurant. The table's semicircular booth was so high-backed, it reminded me of the Alice in Wonderland chair in the lobby. From another stone tunnel, three vampires emerged: a Japanese vampire in a staid black business suit, a Middle Eastern vampire in a stark black dress . . . and then, Nyissa, breathtaking in a purple leather dress with deep décolletage and a sparkling choker.

My first reaction was to relax. Nyissa was safe, not a prisoner. But then I really noticed her outfit, and my breath caught as I followed the pale flesh from the choker down between her breasts. Nyissa gave me a cocky smirk, and I reddened a bit; then I shook it off. Her neckline went to her navel, and she knew I was bisexual, so she had to expect I would notice.

"Lord Varguson, Lady Astryia, Lord Kitana," Saffron said, again bowing slightly. "So pleasant to see you again, and our thanks to you for your treatment of Nyissa." Saffron looked at me with a slight smile. "May I introduce to you Dakota Frost . . . leader of our entourage."

In the corner of my eye, I could now see *everyone* was looking at me; apparently, I was now "on." Saffron *had* warned me I'd have to speak, but somehow at a dinner, I hadn't expected the same degree of attention as at the Conclave. But my ex-girlfriend had long since forgiven me for our unnecessarily messy breakup, so Saffron hadn't put me on the spot on purpose. Perhaps this was demanded of me by some unspoken rule of vampire politics—or perhaps the Vampire Court had demanded this of her, giving these magical creatures a chance to probe my motives before they decided to welcome us . . . or to bar us from the Bay entirely.

"Greetings, Lord Varguson, Lady Astryia, Lord Kitana," I said, glancing at each of the vampires: the swarthy, vaguely Spanish-looking leader, the fanged Jewish matron, the grave Japanese revenant, all in staid vampire black. "Thank you for receiving us."

"Thank you for following our protocols," Lord Varguson said, extending his hand to the table. "Let us extend to you our hospitality. We have worked with the staff of Asia de Cuba to ensure the best possible experience for both our vampire and our human guests."

So we all sat around the vast round table, the San Francisco vampires lording it in the semicircular booth like it was a throne, flanked by standing guards;

our vampires sat opposite, flanked by us non-vamps. Cinnamon sat between Saffron and me, putting me uncomfortably close to the grave Lord Kitana; Vickman and Schultze sat on the other side, apparently not uncomfortable sitting next to the curious, yet oddly reserved Lady Astryia.

"So, vampires have met the Wizarding Guild without violence," said Lord Varguson. The swarthy vampire lord raised politely a glass filled with a dark red liquid that was almost certainly not wine. "My congratulations to our daywalking guests."

I stared at that glass. *Oh, shit.* And so, when the waiter reached toward me with that dark, red, unmarked bottle, I hurriedly flipped my glass over. Cinnamon did so as well. Then the waiter reached Saffron, and she raised her hand.

"With all due thanks to our hosts," she said, "I shall have the house Merlot."

The waiter looked at her, befuddled. "I'm . . . not sure to what you refer, my Lady," he said carefully, proffering that dark red bottle for her inspection, even as she leaned back from it. "Your companions have already ordered from the . . . special collection."

"Yes, but again with respect to my hosts," Saffron said, bowing her head deferentially to Lord Varguson, "I shall have the house Merlot. The Merlot. As in the wine. It's made from grapes. I'm sorry, perhaps I am not being clear—*stop.* Please do not pour me blood."

"Oh," the waiter said, withdrawing the bottle. "I'm, uh, sorry, I—"

"So it is true," Lord Varguson said. "You *are* a vegetarian."

"I shall believe it," Lady Astryia said, "when she eats."

"I am looking forward to the menu this evening," Saffron said.

"I as well," Darkrose said. "I too shall have the Merlot, with thanks to our hosts—"

"With thanks to our hosts," Nyissa croaked, "*I* shall drink from the special collection."

I looked up in shock—I had not heard her voice in six months. Saffron had said she'd been in the hospital—and even though Nyissa's striking Vampirella-esque dress exposed her from navel to throat, her neck scars were covered with a wide, sparkling choker.

I had assumed the choker was a fashion statement. I was wrong—it was a bandage.

"And to toast another success," Lord Varguson said. "Nyissa's operation."

"Your surgeons are clearly as skilled as you claimed," Saffron said. "Thank you."

"We are all in your debt," I said. Suddenly, all three vampires of the Court of San Francisco looked at me coldly. Hopefully I was not speaking out of turn—I didn't know the rules of these weird quasi-medieval vampire courts—but this was the twenty-first century, so I forged ahead, "I am *particularly* grateful, as the Lady Nyissa lost her voice in my defense."

Lord Varguson just stared at me. Unlike an ordinary vampire, his dark eyes did not light up with the power of his aura. His features looked young, but there was something nonetheless weathered about him, something that reminded me of Sir Leopold, the lich. Perhaps Varguson was a relic of the conquest of the

New World, like our own Lord Delancaster—another European vampire who, like their human counterparts, came over and made trouble for the natives.

The waiter returned, filled Saffron's and Darkrose's glasses. After the waiter disappeared, Lord Varguson, who had been staring at me the whole time, slowly raised his glass.

"To the Lady Nyissa," he said, "for reminding us that the relationship between vampire and human . . . should be more than just predator and prey."

As he stared, I realized he was talking about Nyissa's relationship to *me*.

"To Nyissa," I said, abruptly raising my water glass to her, grateful to be out of that almost-staring match with Lord Varguson. For a flicker-quick instant, Nyissa was rattled, then regained her "too cool for the room" vampiric composure. I smiled at her. "Thank *you*."

"Thank you," Nyissa said, struggling to keep her expression cool as her voice rasped out. It was sad—her Irish lilt had been exceptionally beautiful, and now she could narrate a horror movie. She raised her blood-filled glass with a wounded smile. "And thanks to my hosts."

And then she drank the entire glass, like she was taking a shot.

"Drink as much as you need," the Lady Astryia said, passing over her glass, from which she had only taken the slightest sip. Astryia sounded Israeli, though as an old-school vampire, she probably predated the state of Israel—but I presumed she was not Orthodox, or she would not be drinking blood—or, hell, I didn't know how being a Jewish vampire "worked," any more than I understood how Saffron could be a Christian vampire. "You must feed to fully heal."

Nyissa took the glass from the "special collection" gratefully and drank it down, more gracefully this time. Lord Varguson watched her carefully, beckoning with his hand to the waiter, then he returned his eyes to me, and I looked away.

"I hope," he said, "this action on our part is an ample demonstration of our good faith."

Saffron nodded, but silently; then she looked at me. Apparently, she'd taken that "entourage" comment by Carnes to heart, and it actually made sense. If she really was out here just for me, and not as a power grab, then it was my responsibility to take the lead.

"Of course, Lord Varguson," I said, looking back at him nervously. "Simply by being open about what you needed to make you feel safe, and by not threatening us, you have shown more grace than others we've met on this trip."

Lord Varguson nodded gravely. Looking off-center in his face, I was impressed by how compact and muscular he was, how much the weathered skin, superficially human, reminded me of boot leather. Even though his eyes did not glow, I felt more aura from him than anyone else here, except Saffron. With that kind of control and power, he would be a fearsome opponent.

"So, tell me, Lady Frost," he said, taking a slow sip, then putting down his glass. "To what do we owe this trip?"

I frowned. Speaking to ancient, powerful creatures who drank blood and read minds made me feel oddly unqualified as the Chair of the Magical Security Council, but I didn't think I could afford to show weakness. I decided to focus on my immediate goals.

"My reasons are simple," I said, smiling at Cinnamon. "My daughter won a prize—"

"Surely you have seen that San Francisco is a hornet's nest—and surely you know that disturbing a hornet's nest can have . . . unfortunate results." Varguson's eyes glittered, tiny sparks of light appearing in them for the first time. "Have you really no other motive for visiting?"

Yes, of course—getting my money for winning a magical challenge last year, I thought, *but I can't tell you that.* And I had no desire to tell these vamps I was trying to keep Cinnamon safe from Scara. But why was I letting them rattle me? The MSC *wasn't* just a game, nor should its principles be limited to Atlanta. I really believed what I had said to the Conclave earlier.

"Many vampires died earlier this year," I said, as clearly as I could, focusing mentally on the reasons that followed from that, and no others. "The Vampire Gentry demanded action. But I can't save the world all by myself. We—the vampires, the werekin, and the wizards of Atlanta—are trying to stop the next magical catastrophe before it kicks off witch hunts in which we'd all suffer. That's a political threat. You can't fight politics like a mortal opponent—not alone."

And then, they listened. Or seemed to listen. Or let me rant. The point is, I spent the rest of the meal articulating the charter of the Council, its problems, my plans, and how we might work together with the Edgeworld of San Francisco. Finally, Saffron raised her hand.

"She is as I described to you, is she not?" she said politely.

"Guileless," Lord Kitana said. It was the first word the Japanese vampire had said all evening, and I was not sure whether it was a compliment or an insult.

I felt my cheeks burn, and took a bite from my plate; my crispy tofu had grown cold. But Cinnamon grinned at me, wolfing down her *second* helping of nearly-raw wagyu beef—whose price had made my eyes water, until Astryia had told us the entire meal was on the house.

"We shall not meet with the wizards of San Francisco," Lord Varguson said. "We shall, however, allow you to do so on our behalf, and in exchange for that invaluable service, we shall allow you free rein to operate within our domain during the duration we have prescribed." He passed a small envelope to Saffron, who slipped it into her corset. Then he said, "And in thanks, now we have something special for you all . . . and not just from the special collection."

Then the waiters brought an absolute bounty of desserts: house-made ice cream in three flavors and Mexican donuts dipped in caramel and several different dessert "liqueurs" that definitely were from the special collection. Cinnamon practically cooed; so did I.

But despite the bounty, I was getting antsy—the hour was getting late. I glanced at Saffron, who nodded and bowed her head again to Lord Varguson.

"Thank you for your warm welcome and your extremely generous hospitality," she said. "But now, if you will excuse us, we have another engagement. An art opening—"

"Really?" Lord Varguson said. Pinpricks sparkled in his eyes, and then on my exposed skin. "You wish to abandon our hospitality?" Varguson said, his icy tone making it seem like we were abandoning them on an ice floe. "In favor of . . . an *art opening?*"

"The invitation," I said, trying to rescue Saffron, "was extended by the local commune of fire magicians, and their visiting guest. It would be unwise to abandon that opportunity."

Lord Varguson's pinpricks settled on me again. They were bright enough now to see their color, little sparks of red in his dark, leathery face. "Local magicians, not part of the Wizarding Guild . . . and yet within their territory," he said. "Most interesting."

"I am aware of them," Lord Kitana said. "They call themselves the Fireweavers, and are largely harmless." His voice was surprisingly forceful, once he used it; he could have been a radio announcer. "Though they usually operate in the East Bay."

"Fire wizards, come to our stronghold, without consulting us, or the Guild," Varguson said. "Even more interesting. We would like to accompany you to this . . . art opening."

I stared back at him, just off-center. Me and my damn mouth. I knew, even without looking, that I should not turn to Saffron or Darkrose for rescue, and they weren't jumping in to volunteer an out either. Come to think of it, there *was* no out: it was a public performance.

—೭

"Wonderful," I said, pulling out my smartphone. "Let me get the address."

13. WINDOW SHOPPING

We had over an hour before Jewel's fire show, so the vampires, to my surprise, suggested we *walk* from Asia de Cuba to Liquid, which was a block or so north-east of Union Square. Cinnamon eagerly agreed, claiming she wanted to "get the feel of the streets."

Before we left, however, Nyissa excused herself . . . to track down our waiter.

"It's nice, no longer being the prettiest girl in the room," Saffron said. The other female vampires glanced at her, Lady Astryia angrily, Lady Darkrose hurt. But they did not contradict her, nor did I; it was just the truth. "It feels good to see someone else get all the attention."

"That may be true," I said, watching Nyissa speak to the waiter, give him her card . . . then kiss his hand, lingeringly. The waiter almost swooned, but I swore I saw fangs glint when her lips pulled away. "But she's not into boys. I don't think it's his affection she's after."

We stepped out into the night air. It was surprisingly cold, worse than I'd expected from our night in Oakland, but neither Cinnamon nor the vampires minded; Lady Astryia even loaned me her cloak. Vickman gave me an odd look, and I suddenly wondered what I'd done wrong.

The hair stood up on the back of my neck. I became acutely aware that I was a normal human—as normal as you can get covered with two square meters of magically tattooed skin—amidst a whole crowd of supernatural creatures who fed on blood.

And I'd stepped out with them onto a dark San Francisco street. Wasn't there some horror movie rule about this? Even my so-called "bodyguard," Nyissa, was one of them. The only humans here were Vickman and Schultze, and if the vamps did something, we were toast.

I shook my head. These were my friends. My *daughter* was a were. I had chosen this life. Picking at it, my real fear was the Vampire Court of San Francisco, insinuating themselves into our evening, insisting they oversee us as we walked through their stronghold.

We had made it through dinner, but . . . these vampires were an untested quantity.

But nothing came of my fears. Lady Astryia and Saffron discussed their respective Vampire Consulates; Vickman muttered with the bulky bodyguard with the well-inked tats. The others were silent, and eventually Cinnamon and I relaxed enough to notice window displays.

We paused in wonder at one closed shop, which displayed carved statues in dozens of materials. Several were of Chinese origin, carved from elephant tusks I hoped were collected before the ban. One was even carved from what was claimed to be a mammoth's tusk.

And then my eyes focused on one ornate dagger, carved in the shape of a tooth. I stared at it curiously. It wasn't a dagger carved in the shape of a tooth—it was a tooth carved in the shape of a dagger. It was huge, jagged, dark, almost translucent—but clearly had once been alive. Yet it wasn't from any animal I recognized. What was it from? A sabertooth? No. Too wide at the base. A T-Rex? No. Too elegant. I felt a shiver ripple through my tattoos. *Was it a—*

"Oh my God," I said, pressing against the glass. "Is that . . ."

"Yes," Lord Kitana said, leaning in next to me. I could see his reflection in the glass, eyes glowing slightly; vampires not having a reflection was a myth, but reflections did give their auras an eerie, distorted feeling that ran shivers up my spine. "Technically, it's not a true tooth, but a papilla or 'tonguehook,' a fact which staggers the imagination, if one has any—"

"My God," I said, again shivering—*this is real.* I let my own tongue glide against the roof of my mouth, then run against my teeth, thinking of the size difference between those teeth and the papillae, the tiny feelers that coated the tongue. "That's just a *papilla?* Unbelievable."

"Yes. I had the item appraised when considering it for my collection. It is genuine."

After some hunting, I finally found the tiny little tag at its base:

FOSSILIZED DRAGON'S TOOTH DAGGER

$350,000

"That's a steal," I said.

"It is indeed," Lord Kitana said.

"Those carvings aren't contemporary," I said.

"No, they are not," he replied. "My appraiser estimated them at ten thousand years."

"It isn't fossilized, is it?"

"No, it is not," he replied. "Desiccated, though. There is no magic in it."

"Still . . . don't they know what they have here?" I said. "It's just in the window—"

"No thief would dare take it from *this* shop—not when *I* am its patron." Lord Kitana chuckled. It was a chilling sound. "No magician would buy it—desiccated dragonbone and dragonhorn can be acquired far more cheaply. No art collector would want it—they do not understand. And no museum would acquire it—they do not believe."

We leaned back from the glass.

"You desire it?" Lord Kitana said.

"Surprisingly . . . very much so," I said. "There are only a handful of nonfossilized dragon relics in the world; the idea of an artwork made from my totem animal is . . . intoxicating."

"One day," Lord Kitana said, smiling at me with something between genuine respect and infinite coldness, "perhaps, if you prove to be the crusader you claim to be, I shall gift it to you, Dakota Frost. If not . . . one day, perhaps, you shall receive it another way."

I swallowed.

"Dakota," Saffron said, concerned. "Isn't . . . that Liquid up ahead?"

"Damn it," Vickman cursed. "This looks bad—"

And then I saw it—a crowd milling outside the very same building that Jewel had described, all pointing and gawking at an ominous blue light in its window.

"Aw, *shit*," I said.

Vickman and one of the human servants scoped out the crowd, inspected the window, then waved us forward. Liquid was embedded in the bottom floor of a narrow four-story building, like a brownstone; but a façade of sheer black marble had been added to the bottom floor, beneath a sign that read **LIQUID: artworks - cocktails - dancing**. But hovering just above the surface of plate window beneath that sign, crackling against—and cracking—the glass, glowed an intricate magical mark four feet in diameter, burning with a blue-white flame.

Arcane symbols spun lazily in five concentric rings around a central mandala of Chinese design that looked, vaguely, like the abstract lines of a dragon. The spinning rings around it were suggestive of a magic circle or a light spell, but I'd never seen anything precisely like it.

Apparently, the patrons and the staff hadn't either—they were still pouring out into the street to inspect it from a cautious distance, or peeking at it nervously from the inside. As we approached, the blue flame began to flicker, then went out at once, leaving the glowing rings of red letters spinning within intricate circles of blue-white light—and the shift of light made the dragon design in the center mandala stand out even more prominently. Now that I saw it more closely, the Chinese design looked more like Chinese *characters*, woven together.

"Aw, man," Cinnamon said. "We just missed the show."

"Agreed," Vickman said, turning from the bartender. "He says this happened minutes ago. They saw someone run up to the window with what looked like a torch or brazier, wave it around like he was doing some kind of performance, and then—blammo!"

"Let me guess," I said, trying to grok the design. "Gone before anyone got outside."

"Right first time," Vickman said grimly. "All the bartender saw was a guy in a jacket and a flaming torch. Let me ask the crowd. Excuse me, ladies and gentlemen—"

"Mom, you needs to take a picture," Cinnamon said. "Before it fades."

I pulled out my smartphone and did so, but it *wasn't* fading. After the flame went out, the design kept rotating, glowing, maintaining its speed and power. I leaned in—there was nothing beneath the design but glass, and it barely scratched the surface, almost like it was a decal.

I wanted to touch it. I reached out toward the central dragon.

"Don't," Vickman said, stepping up beside me. "You'll be burned—"

"No, if it was hot, the air would feel warm," I said, letting my hand hover over it. "And it would already have started to dim as it cooled. Even its magic would begin to fade more quickly, given the logic of this design." And again, I reached toward the glass.

"Dakota, seriously," Saffron said, stepping up on my other side. "You're not going to touch it, are you? Remember *Doctor Who and The Green Death?*"

I hesitated, a wry smile coming to my lips. In the reflection, I could just make out both of them, watching my hand over the surface of the glass. I felt almost no mana . . . but I had to touch it. *I have to know what it is saying.* "Trust me, I know what I'm doing."

"Mom!" Cinnamon said. "At least have a spell ready or somethin'."

"Always the smart one," I said, my hand still hovering over the glass, an eerie, electric attraction. I closed my eyes, thought carefully, then undulated my hand in the air, building up a null intent in my hand, backed by a mana charge in my arm—the magical equivalent of a diode. If I'd crafted the impromptu spell right, I'd get a sense of the spell's intent with almost no mana behind it. "*Spirit of fire . . . give me insight.*"

I pressed my hand through the symbol to the glass, and an electric shock rippled through my tattoos—harmless, but far more intense than I expected. Yet the glass *was* cool to the touch, and even though I could still feel the strangely sharp mana rippling through it, like a live circuit, there was nothing else to the magic—nothing in the glass, no decal on its surface. A light vapor brushed against my fingers as the circles rotated, and the magic slightly curdled in its wake, but that was it. It was a self-sustaining magical design with only a barest whiff of material substance, like a tattooist's *projectia*. If it was designed to achieve a magical effect, I couldn't grok it. *The message was hidden from my sight.* I could feel the glass cracking under its influence, more slowly now; the magic was fading slightly, but still powerful. This was bad.

"It has a power source," I said, withdrawing my hand, watching, as I expected, the central dragon reform and the magic rings return to their orbits. I turned to look at the others. "The last time I saw something with a mysterious power source, nearly half of Atlanta burned."

"What is the intent of this design?" Lord Kitana asked.

I cocked my head at it. "I . . . don't know," I admitted. "Magic isn't always obvious."

"I—I don't know either," Cinnamon said. "I sees light magic, spinning magic, some fire—but I don't know what they adds up to. What's the dragon for? It looks like letterin', but it doesn't seem to be connected to the circuit. And what are those spinny symbols?"

"I don't recognize them," I said. That was also bad; this thing could be a ticking time bomb, spinning down to some countdown embedded in those symbols that we couldn't read . . . or could we? The more I looked, the more familiar the symbols became. "Wait a minute—"

I struggled to remember where I had seen those symbols. *They call to me in some deep, resonant way.* Had I seen them in what I'd been reading? No. In the fireweaver's performance art? Maybe. Then it hit me—I'd seen those symbols *today*. In, of all places, a *tie.*

"*Carnes,*" I said, and explained to Saffron and the crew the mystical symbols I had seen woven through the garments of the Wizarding Guild. "And here I thought that 'die on the streets of Oakland' crap and the attack on Jewel was just coincidence."

And then an addled man with wiry red hair stumbled out of Liquid, eyes wild. All the patrons and staff seemed instantly to defer to him, or at least recognize him. "Oh my God," he said, staring at the rotating symbol. "What the hell? What happened? What is that?"

"A magical mark," I said, jamming my fists in my pockets, cracking my neck to try to release some of the tension in my tattoos. "And who might you be?"

"Monkton Teriano," he said, puffing himself up. "I'm the artist. This is my opening, and I don't appreciate you trying to horn in—"

"We didn't have anything to do with this, Mr. Teriano," I said. "We're friends of Jewel Grace. She asked us to meet her here."

"You just missed her," Teriano said, turning, the hair flaring out over his head, making him look like a clown. He cocked his head at the symbol. "This is fire magic, isn't it?"

"Maybe. Could Jewel have done this on her way out? Like, an ad for your show—"

"What? No!" Teriano said. "It's cracking the glass! Jewel's a firebrand, not a vandal!"

"Aw, shit," I said. "Daniel, or friends of his. Where's Jewel? We have to warn her—"

"They already left," he said, alarmed. "They wanted to set up early—"

—&

"In Union Square," I said. "In front of thousands of tourists."

14. THE BATTLE OF UNION SQUARE

It had been ten years since I had set foot in Union Square. It was as I remembered it—a huge empty box, with a central column rising from a stepped performance space, surrounded by canyon walls of marble, brick and stone plastered with glowing corporate symbols: Macy's and Nieman Marcus, Bloomingdale's and Borders. Behind those neon logos were millions of square feet of shopping space, filled with shiny toys for those running the consumer rat race.

Despite mentioning them to Saffron earlier, I had no interest in what was behind those façades. Most of what I wanted came from more specialized dealers. But that was not true of what had to be tens of thousands of tourists that visit the Square each day, who swarmed to those stores, each often the largest of its kind any individual consumer is likely to have seen. Even the stepped surface of the Square itself is built atop a parking garage, filled with thousands of cars, each with a convenient tank filled to the brim with explosive gasoline.

It was atop this wide expanse that the battle began.

Nyissa and Astryia ran point, almost flying through the streets with Cinnamon just behind. Kitana, Saffron, and Darkrose followed, their servants and bodyguards struggling to keep up. I don't know how *I* kept up, but when we shot into the Square, I was not far behind them.

From the flares of light, the sudden curdling of the crowd, and the spreading reactions, it was clear that there had just been a firespinning demonstration, just now spinning out of control. We ran across the street onto the Square proper, where a policeman was leaning against a giant statue of a heart, chatting up a girl—when he suddenly jerked, whirled, and drew his gun, running with us as we flew over the steps and saw the battle's beginning.

In the center of the Square blossomed an orange bubble of flame, fifty feet wide and growing wider, sending tourists fleeing as it expanded over the wide gray expanse of concrete covering the parking garage itself. Then the giant fiery soap bubble bowed under the pressure of a stream of rainbow fire that shot up the steps of the Square from the street below, impacting the shield in a screeching, squealing shower of incandescent sparks.

Inside the bubble, Jewel whirled a firestaff, desperately trying to maintain the shield as her companion firespinners were stumbling back, regrouping, some trying to regain their footing, others screaming in pain from obvious burns as the safety crew tried to put them out. Then the rainbow stream stopped, just for a moment, and I saw dark-suited figures on the street, dressed like ninjas, each whirling a different weapon tipped with magical flame.

In my frozen moment of assessment, the vampires all had moved. They didn't need me to tell them what to do; they just moved. I still had trouble wrapping my head around the idea that the vampires were the force of law and order on the magical Edgeworld, but here was the proof—six vampires from four continents and two clans acted as one to defend humans from magic.

Varguson and Kitana darted out into the crowds. Astryia and Nyissa flanked the bubble, trying to force the fire ninjas back. Darkrose looped further around, running far faster, trying to come at the fire ninjas from behind. And seemingly from nowhere, Saffron leapt through the air, sailing over the bubble and down upon the ninjas—but then Union Square lit up like Fourth-of-July fireworks as the ninjas fought back with fireballs and fireblasts and artful streams of flame.

Crackling bangs ripped the air. Screams followed. Flares of light assaulted my eyes. Running shapes created chaos. Amidst the colorful sparks, smells like gunpowder and gasoline and burnt hair stung my nostrils. Terrified for my friends, I ran toward the firefight—even vampires are vulnerable to fire. But before I could do anything to help, my tattoos seemed to squirm to life all on their own, struggling for release, making me stumble and nearly fall.

I caught myself on one hand, struggling to bring my magic under control, watching helplessly as Darkrose herself stumbled back and Nyissa dodged a fire bolt. Amidst the crowds and chaos, I couldn't find Lady Astryia or Saffron—and where was Cinnamon? Shit, shit, shit! Frantically, I staggered to my feet, looking around wildly for my daughter, first spotting Lord Kitana, drawing his namesake sword, then finding Vickman, shouting to the other human servants; finally, I caught sight of Lord Varguson standing stock-still, hand out, chanting, tourists fleeing past him in two running, oddly coordinated streams. *But where is Cinnamon?*

I whirled and flinched as a gout of fire roared toward me. Before I had even begun to dodge, a shimmering blur tackled me, slamming into my waist and hauling me to the pavement as the flames blistered over our heads. As we tumbled to a stop against the glittering tiles, the blur resolved into Cinnamon—my little genius, who had disappeared from my sight because she'd very sensibly used her tattoos to turn invisible when the fight started.

"Mom, get down," Cinnamon yelled, a yellow glow flaring across her now-visible face, and we dove behind the tables of a café just as the tongue of fire swept back. We rolled aside as the streamer of flame knocked the tables over and made the chairs clank around wildly on the end of the chain running through their bases. A table slammed into the concrete an inch from my face, and I hunched behind it, clenching and unclenching my hands to try to build up power.

"There it is again! What the fuck *is* that lizard smell?" Cinnamon said, sniffing; then she ducked as another fireball shot over our heads. When it had passed, I started to edge up over the table, and she pulled me back. "Mom, what are you doing? You can't fight all of them!"

"I can sure try," I said, peeking carefully over the table to get a better look.

Now Jewel's firespinners were fighting back, but the fire ninjas were holding their own. I saw one of the dark-garbed figures holding off both Lady Astryia and Nyissa with a firestaff, and another keeping Darkrose and Saffron at bay with looping trails blazing off his fire poi—lazy arcs of rippling fire that were whipping around the square like snakes, flopping out into the crowd, even reaching where we crouched, as it had seconds before in the café.

Thumping music became audible over the snapping of the flames, and I realized it was from a boom box overturned amidst Jewel's group—and then I realized I could hear it because Jewel's fire sphere was faltering. Her firestaff was going out, and even though another spinner tossed her his poi and she caught them without a beat, the sphere contracted, shimmering into almost nonexistence, then flattened again as another gout of fire blasted against it.

Lord Kitana was engaged in a long-distance gun/sword battle with another fire ninja. The ninja was shooting at him with a pistol, and Kitana was deflecting the bullets with flickering speed. Vickman, the cop, and a human servant were all blasting away at the ninja, who whirled his fire sword in an arc that created peacock fans of flame, shielding him from the bullets.

Cinnamon and I ducked down again as a stray bullet ricocheted off the table, then got up in time to see a fire ninja running down on us. He had a strange porcelain mask on, with a odd grilled Chinese design reminiscent of the one we had just seen on Liquid's window—and he had two fire tonfas, which he whirled to create a blast of flame that seared the table. We screamed—then Cinnamon leapt up over the table, claws lashing out, shattering the ninja's mask. Dark cloth protected his face underneath, but still he cursed, falling back, kicking her midsection. Cinnamon slammed back into the table, snarled, and popped back up just as the ninja threw another blast at her.

This time I was ready. I whipped out a tattoo vine in a coiling arc and drew the mana off his flame. But it was harder this time than it had been on the streets of Oakland; even though my vine seemed to gulp the magic down, turning the flames into flickering confetti of light, the magic it absorbed then surged through me, reverberating through my tattoos, collecting into the Dragon, which twisted and shimmied within my skin, struggling to get out.

The ninja stepped forward, then halted as I writhed, spinning his fire off. Then he threw his hand down, creating a bright burst of flame that dazzled me and drove me back. When my eyes recovered, I saw him running away, throwing random blasts of flame at the crowd.

I hunched over, trying to get control of my magic, studying the battle. The fire ninjas had clearly thought this through. Each one was tough on his own, holding off two, three, even four defenders armed with guns or vampire speed; but that wasn't enough. There were at least seven of them all total, four holding off our vampires and guards, two running through the crowd and creating chaos—leaving one with his sole focus on destroying Jewel's shield.

You'd think five fireweavers could fight off one ninja, but the ninja's fire was whiter, brighter, longer lasting; the weavers' poi, in contrast, were already guttering, the dark cores of their wicks showing beneath the flickering glow. From the fire raging over their bags of gear, the ninja's first target must have been their fuel cans, leaving them only the fuel in the wicks they were spinning; unlike their fire, however, his poi seemed to not be going out.

The lead ninja was skilled, fluid, spinning his poi with swift grace, somehow managing to attack and defend at once—creating a personal shield at least as intricate as what Jewel had woven the other night, while still managing to fire blasts of flame at Jewel's diminishing bubble. Jewel was focused entirely on her far larger shield, while the two remaining active spinners in her bubble were firing out streams and sparks with little effect against their foe.

Another gout of fire sailed overhead, and I wrenched in pain as the Dragon struggled again to get loose. I concentrated, starting a slow dance to try to bring it to heel. It twisted and resisted my attempts to control it . . . and then, it occurred to me—I didn't have to.

Let me loose . . . and I can deal with the fireweavers.

I spread my arms. The Dragon's wings burst through my jacket. I cracked my neck. The Dragon's head coiled up behind me. Then I pushed off with my feet, and the Dragon's tail slid out through a rip in my slacks, propelling me up into the night sky.

I can't put out enough power to actually fly—the physics of human-powered flight don't work much better with magic in the mix. But with each beat of the Dragon's wings, she soaked up ambient mana from the fire battle—growing larger and larger, and stronger and stronger.

The Dragon emerged fully from my back, a vast half-Chinese, half-European artwork of glowing fire, gripping my shoulders in her foreclaws as her wings flapped powerfully upward and her tail spiraled below. *Free again.* We rose through the canyon of the Square, past the top of the central column. I rested there in her claws, eyes closed, feeling the Dragon soak up the powerful, hot, intoxicating magic of the fire ninja's weapons; seeing the battle below through the Dragon's eyes as she surged higher and higher. We stopped rising as the magic began to fade, and the Dragon's wings beat faster, trying to drain every last ember of mana from the air.

Here, I could see the whole battle rage. My friends and our new allies still battled the four ninjas down at the bottom of the square. At the top corner, Lord Varguson stood, eyes glowing, still chanting, tourists flowing out of the Square at his direction. And with no more tourists left to chase, the two hellions had abandoned the crowd and joined the first fire ninja, assaulting Jewel's shield. From here, Jewel's dying bubble looked like a fiery little snow globe, which someone was poking at with tiny little roman candles.

Then I saw the solution, and murmured, "*Spirit of fire, give them your strength.*"

The Dragon and I sank downward, her wings beating faster and faster as she absorbed more mana, her tail coiling in an arc like my vines had earlier—but not to steal power; to *lend* it. The tail of the Dragon coiled around Jewel's ball in a lazy helix, brightening it, reinforcing it, making the bubble gleam and surge with renewed vigor.

The lead ninja looked up and screamed, whipping the poi around quickly to throw a blast at me. Without me even consciously directing it, the Dragon spread her wings wide, then swept them downward, sucking all the mana from his blast, redirecting it into a torrent of air that tore through the plaza, shattering windows and snuffing out half the fires all at once. Mana still surging through her, the Dragon raised her head and screamed, burning fire into the sky.

The ninja shook his fists, clocking himself with a poi as it swung wide. Then he spun, whipping the poi faster and faster, performing an intricate, extended maneuver that blasted a blue-white ring of flame toward the glass façade of Macy's. The curling fire ring impacted and roiled outward—and then the ninja followed the ring with new coils of fire, slamming into the already churning magic, leaving a giant disc of filigreed blue-green fire crackling against the windows—with an elaborate coiled Chinese-flavored dragon looping at its center.

"Oh, my," I murmured.

I closed my eyes again, almost without wanting to, seeing the shimmering dragon ring through *my* Dragon's eyes. Even more of the logic of the design was visible through its eyes than my own, and I marveled at what the Dragon showed me, even though I didn't understand it yet.

Then my perception expanded, seemed to double, like I was seeing Union Square from two different angles, one from where I was, one watching myself from a vantage point spinning round the Square, a tiny person cradled in a vast glowing dragon flapping its wings in a torrent of wind and magic. From this view, I could see that the wind from his wings was starting to shatter and crack the façades of the hotels and shops in the Square. Fear gripped me—the expanded view and extent of the destruction meant I was losing control of my magic.

I spread my arms, sighed, let myself go limp. The Dragon felt my calm, began to relax, and her wings beat more slowly. The double vision faded, my single vantage point began to sink down into the Square, and the Dragon's vision began to fade altogether. I opened my eyes, seeing the vast spinning symbol, with a stylized dragon at its center, crackling against the surface of Macy's—the fire was going out, leaving only that blue-green glow, as at Liquid.

The magic bubble beneath me sucked at the Dragon's magic hungrily, and we began to fall, faster and faster. *I need more magic to land safely.* I broke the connection to the bubble and focused, drawing my hands and legs through a complicated, sinuous move that Arcturus had taught me, re-energizing the Dragon with my own magic. Our rate of descent slowed, slowed, and then stopped, just as my feet touched the tiles of Union Square.

I fell to my hands and knees, letting the Dragon slowly dissipate mana through each beat of her wings. Chairs and tables and debris were still being swept away by her wings, but I kept it under control, slowly lessening her magic until she began, reluctantly, to merge with my skin.

I raised my head and saw Jewel, Saffron, and Lord Kitana staring down at me in awe as the Dragon merged with my kneeling form. The other fireweavers, vampires, and human guards were approaching as well, even the policeman who had joined us in the battle. In fear, I looked around until I found Cinnamon, visible just beyond the beat of the Dragon's wings. Only Lord Varguson was missing; I would make sure that we accounted for him before it was all over.

The Dragon's arms and legs merged into me, its tail began to coil back around my leg, and, with difficulty, I stood, using the last few beats of his wings to steady me. Standing once again, I glanced around the Square. It was trashed, debris was everywhere, store windows were shattered, and a massive magical mark still defaced the front of Macy's . . . but there were no bodies on the deck. Many people were injured, but no one had died.

And San Francisco's vampires? They were no longer an untested quantity; they'd fought alongside us without a second thought. This had been a literal trial by fire . . . and I found that these creatures I had feared had become people that I trusted.

"Victory, my friends," I said, glancing over my shoulder. The back of my new vestcoat was split, but unlike previous adventures with tattoo magic and clothing, the splits were clean, and the jacket had miraculously held together.

"I'm going to get slits cut in this damn thing."

Lord Kitana stepped forward, eyes calculating, sheathed sword in his hand.

"It will take time to make the arrangements," he said, slipping the sword into his coat. "But I shall be true to my word."

"What?" I asked, feeling myself at last beginning to relax.

"The dagger," he said. "I shall have it delivered to the Consulate on your behalf."

15. I Get On Good With the Police

"Clear those windows," I said to the officers, pointing at Macy's, where people were curiously inspecting from within the vast circular dragon symbol that still flickered against its façade. The mark was enormous—the slowly rotating perimeter symbols looked larger than the people watching them. "It looks pretty, but it's a mammoth magical mark of unknown power. If you can't evacuate, I want at least a thirty foot cordon in front of and behind that glass."

Within moments of the end of the battle, a swarm of police cars had descended upon Union Square, filling even its cavernous space with flashing blue and red lights. With the help of the beat officer who had been first on the scene, Jack Targan, we were able to get quick control of the chaos and channel the first responders into putting out the fires and helping the wounded rather than running around with guns looking for bad guys.

"Dark clothes, face masks—but of course, they may have ditched them," I said, calling after a group of officers who were going to spread up the street. "Most of them were male, but it's hard to be sure. Consider armed and extremely!"

Ambulances and fire trucks were now arriving, and Officer Targan and I met with the first of the paramedics, pointing out the injured, especially a group of burn victims we were helping in a makeshift first aid station near the ruins of the café.

"And keep a close watch on *anyone* with burns," I said. "There's always that chance someone may burst into flames as a result of a spell. Well, actually, it is hard to accidentally create a self-combusting mark, but we take no chances—this was magic fire."

"Magic . . . fire," the paramedic said, eyes widening with disbelief . . . or fear.

"Aaarg. Don't you see that?" I said, pointing at the still-glowing circular mark covering the façade of Macy's. Even now, fifteen minutes later, the central dragon coiled slowly within its mandala, and the five rings of bright letters inexorably orbited it. "That ain't neon."

While Cinnamon and Darkrose and our guards had tended the wounded,

Saffron and Nyissa had circuited the Square, trying to "detect confederates" of the fire ninjas. Of the San Francisco vampires, Lord Varguson and his servants were long gone—apparently he did not "do" public appearances. But Lord Kitana and Lady Astryia remained; she as the representative of the Vampire Consulates of San Francisco, and he with some undefined relationship with the police which generated instant and immense respect, enabling him to help us quell the chaos and lending implicit authority to Officer Targan and me.

But that situation did not last long. The poor fireweavers, who had been assaulted mere moments after their performance began, now sat huddled in a circle in the center of the Square while firemen and paramedics examined them, surrounded by police unsure of whether to arrest them. Just as Targan and I were going to clear it up, a slender bald man in a "Rockstar" T-shirt strode through the crowd, a badge hanging down over his shirt, stalking forward with an authority that had "Detective" written all over it.

"Who's the officer in charge?" he asked sharply.

Officer Targan looked at me. I pointed back at him.

"I believe you are now, sir," Officer Targan said nervously. "I was first on the scene—"

"What happened here?" he asked, glancing up at the huge glowing symbol, then at the overturned tables and shattered glass. "Reports were someone set off some 'dragon fireworks' and broke some windows, but this looks like a full scale terrorist attack—"

"I believe I can explain," Lady Astryia said smoothly, stepping up beside us.

"Lady Astryia, always good to see you," the bald man said, nodding.

"Good to see you as well, Detective Brookstone," she responded. "Yes, there was a terrorist attack. These young people were performing in the Square, and were attacked by fire magicians. My companions and I were nearby, and responded. The 'dragon fireworks' were spells set off by one of my companions, which rechanneled the offensive magic into a shield that prevented the loss of any life. I'm sorry for the damage, but as it was in self-defense, I must insist that the immunity of the Vampire Consulates be extended to *all* of my companions—"

"Don't tell me *all* these people are under your protection," Brookstone said, pointing at the firespinners. "Because I am going to take names, and if a single one of them is not on the official list, I can assure you even *you*, ma'am, can be brought up on charges—"

"Of course," Lady Astryia said delicately. "I did not mean to imply a blanket immunity for the entire crowd. I must *insist*, however, that vampiric immunity be granted to the Georgia delegation of the Unified Vampire Consulates, as per California law—"

"That won't be necessary," I said. "Detective Brookstone, *I* set off the 'dragon spell.' I did it defending these people and the crowd. I'm happy to answer all of your questions. If you feel the need to arrest me after my report, I'll go quietly, and take my chances that you and the DA will sort it out, or that I'll be exonerated in the courts. I have *nothing* to hide."

Lady Astryia stared at me, then bowed. "I defer to your wisdom, Lady Frost."

"Guileless," Lord Kitana said.

Brookstone turned to me. "Thank you, ma'am," he said quietly.

"Dad's a cop," I said. "Ask your questions."

Fortunately, Officer Targan saw enough to get me out of a "we have to charge you with *something*" situation. But, even though the spinners were clearly the victims, it was looking like they were not going to be so lucky. At best, they'd be slapped with creating a public disturbance, and at worst, a California magical "misdemeanor"—which, I gathered, had *huge* fines.

"Brookstone, look," I said quietly. "Could I show you something?" I asked, crooking my finger. We walked over to a pile of confiscated spinner's gear. "This is a safety towel, used to put out a performer. This is a dousing towel for the wicks, fireproof and dampened. This is a portable fire extinguisher. These people take fire safety very seriously—"

"And how do you know their gear so well?" he asked.

"One of them tripped over me yesterday, and I had to help clean it all up," I said. "And before you go any further down that road, that was at a *licensed* performance. I'd never participate in an illicit performance, no matter how entertaining they are to watch."

He raised a skeptical eyebrow at me, but I pressed on.

"Look, at most, this is a misdemeanor, and if you'd seen them performing you'd have watched a few minutes yourself. But *that*"—I pointed to the sizzling ring covering the front of Macy's—"is a real threat, and a real crime. At least vandalism, possibly a death threat."

Brookstone stared at it, then nodded.

"Don't charge them, but don't sweep this under," I said. "Take this seriously. That young lady has been assaulted twice in the last twenty-four hours, here and in Oakland. And when you're done? I need those witness statements, photographs, the whole shmear."

"*You* need?" he said. "I thought you said you weren't a cop?"

"I'm chair of the Magical Security Council of Georgia." I said.

"So," he said, eyes tightening a bit, "your jurisdiction in California—"

"Is still to be determined," I said, and Brookstone got even more skeptical. "Six months ago, there *was* no MSC. I'm here on a, well, call it a fact-finding mission, but this just became an investigation. Both of these were magical assaults, so I'd like to pull in the DEI—"

"Oh, good fucking luck," Brookstone said. "I don't know how things work back in Georgia, ma'am, but you've got to pull teeth to get the Department of Extraordinary Investigations to show up in California."

"I have a contact," I said. "His jurisdiction's also East Coast, but I can almost guarantee I can get this started—if you'd like the help and I'm not stepping on your investigation. I'm not here to wrestle over jurisdiction. You tell me to back off—and I back off."

Brookstone stared at me, then pulled out a piece of paper. "I'm going to give you my star," he said, writing a number. "That identifies me with the department, and this is my cell. I'm not going to lie to you, Ms. Frost, there is no way we can sweep this under. The performers need to come down to the station, but I'll do my best to keep them out of jail."

"Thank you," I said.

"Don't mention it. Really. I'll contact Oakland PD. You got a case number—"

"I do," I said, pulling out my smartphone and entering his number. "And the officers that took it down. Mind if I get your picture?" He stared at me, and I took it, adding his surprised face to the contact; then I thumbed through to my notes from the previous night. "Here."

"I want your phone," he said, staring at it in his hand. "This is new?"

"If you need something, buy the best or make do without," I said.

"Apparently," he said, copying my notes. "All right, Ms. Frost. I'll contact this Officer . . . Illowsky, and if your story checks out . . . oh, hell, go ahead, you can call the DEI. But no offense, ma'am, I hope you're just bullshitting me to get your friends out of a charge."

I took my phone back from him. "Oh, wouldn't that be a nice world?"

He stared back over his shoulder at Macy's, where the vast magical mark still glowed, faded but flickering with cold fire. The Chinese-lettered dragon at its center shimmered, almost as if it was trying to break free of its spinning, symbolic prison. "Sure would, ma'am."

It *did* take jurisdictional wrestling to decide what "the station" was, as the attack had spilled out into the Central, Southern, and Tenderloin police districts. Ultimately, the police took us to the Southern district's Field Operations building, a massive block of concrete in SOMA, not three blocks from our shopping sojourn earlier that day. After they finished with me, we waited on the firespinners out on the steps on Bryant Street.

It was pushing one in the morning when the spinners came out, looking bedraggled and whipped. Brookstone followed Jewel out, giving her a lecture about performing magic in public in California. He pointed at me, said something firm, then went back inside.

"Did I hear that cop right?" asked Jewel's friend Zi, staring back at the building, running his hand through his close-cropped hair. He looked incredulous, staring between Jewel and me. "Did *Frost* here pull strings to get us a get-out-of-jail-free pass?"

"I guess so," I joked.

"You *saved* me," Jewel said. She had actually started crying when Brookstone had been lecturing her, and the glitter and mascara on her face had run, not unflatteringly. "*Again.*"

"All part of the service," I said, putting my hands on her shoulders and giving her a gentle squeeze. "Are you all right?"

She nodded, gulped, looked back over her shoulder at police station.

"All right, then," I said. "Now. Listen to me. *Cancel* whatever you've already planned for your trip to San Francisco. You don't have to hide under a rock, but . . . do something different. Your schedule is your key for your opponents to get to you."

Jewel nodded. Over her shoulder, Vickman nodded in curt approval.

"That goes for all of you," I said, looking at the rest of the fireweavers. "Mix it up. If you were going to practice on Thursday, do it on Wednesday. If you were meeting for lunch, do it for dinner. If you were going to a protest, volunteer in a soup kitchen instead. I don't care. Just don't be where anyone expects you to be—and don't go anywhere alone. Got it?"

"I'm sure not sticking around," Zi said. "I'm going back to Salinas until it blows over—"

"I can stay with some friends in Sunol," one of the female dancers said. "Or—"

"Discuss that later," I said. "Just in case one of the black pajama squad is devious enough to hit a spy store and spring for some long-range listening gear, stop detailing your plans when you're standing in a public street. Catch a cab, *then* figure out a destination—"

"Can—can I go with you?" Jewel said, swallowing, looking right at me.

"Oh, uh," I began, cheeks coloring. I stole a quick glance at Vickman, who appeared to be suppressing a frown, but I couldn't depend on him; this was all on me. "I cannot guarantee it will be safer. Actually, I can guarantee based on past experience it will *not* be safer."

"I-I don't care," Jewel said. "There were *five* of us, and they went after us anyway." She must have seen some hesitation in my face, because she held up her hands. "I'm not trying to impose. I can sleep on a *cot* if I have to. Just . . . I'm very scared."

"All right," I said gently. "We can work something out."

—

Cinnamon snorted. "You've gone and done it again, Mom. Picked up another stray."

16. To Our Fortress on Cathedral Hill

I don't know why Cathedral Hill is called that; I never saw a cathedral near our hotel. I do know why we called the Cathedral Hill Hotel our "fortress": its parking garage was gated and underground, its formidable entrance was closed and guarded at night, and its looming ramparts gave it a castle-like feeling. Also, Vickman made a deal with the hotel to get a linked set of suites with "extra security," and each night, we went through elaborate procedures to keep us safe.

In the lobby, we paused for drinks at the bar while Schultze went up and checked out the suites; about five minutes later, Vickman's phone rang, he stepped out of earshot and exchanged a few terse words, and then cleared us to go to our rooms.

Waiting for us upstairs were friends from Atlanta I hadn't seen in a while—Jinx and Doug, Skye "Jinx" Anderson being Saffron's and my oldest friend, and Doug Suleiman being Jinx's new husband. Doug was in fuzzy flannel pajamas and a bathrobe, but Jinx was still dressed to the nines in Gothic Lolita finery—black and white, corset and lace, gloves and bonnet.

You'd think he'd just turned in earlier than her, but I knew better. They were both a bit flushed, and as Doug guided her round the corner, Jinx surreptitiously adjusted her suspiciously rumpled dress. You didn't need a playbook to realize that Doug dug every inch of her outfit, but you'd need some inside info to know that if you pulled back Doug's bathrobe and pajamas, you'd most likely see straps of black leather crossing his muscular chest. They were perfectly matched for each other. I smiled, but kept my observations to myself—the last thing they needed after their honeymoon was for Cinnamon to start calling them "Goth Girl and Dog Boy."

Jinx tapped her way up with her spirit cane. "Dakota, Cinnamon," she said, giving us a slightly formal nod warmed by a sly, impish smile. Then she abruptly canted her head. "And well, *hello.* Who is your wonderfully-perfumed companion, Dakota?"

"Hey, Jinx, I'm *so* glad we finally got to see you after all this *mess,*" I said, shepherding forward Jewel, who still seemed rattled. "And . . . Skye 'Jinx' Anderson, my oldest friend, please meet Jewel Anne Grasslin, my newest one."

Jinx took Jewel's extended hand and held it delicately; then she raised her other hand to her dark glasses and pulled them down. Jewel drew a sharp breath; Jinx's eyes were blue and milky, like two geodes covered with black snowflakes. Jinx leaned forward, still holding Jewel's hand, as much for the feeling of the bracer under her thumb as to pin her target there, I think; then she rocked her head back and forth, trying to catch Jewel from every angle.

"Oh, *my,*" she said, releasing Jewel's hand. "You must be *such* a beautiful woman."

Jewel's mouth fell open, as she realized Jinx really couldn't see more than a blur.

"That she is," I said, squeezing Jewel's shoulder, and she glanced back and smiled.

"Beautiful, delicate skin, and a wonderful scent," Jinx said, pushing her glasses up. "Well, at least I can appreciate two of those properly. It is my *very* great pleasure to meet you, Jewel Anne Grasslin. You always have such interesting friends, Dakota."

"That she does," Jewel said.

We convened in Saffron and Darkrose's suite, the largest, to powwow. Carnes wanted me out of town, maybe, Daniel wanted Jewel shut down, definitely, and mysterious "fire ninjas," associated with one or both of them, or possibly neither, had assaulted Jewel and left mysterious messages that were a threat, a warning, or, based on our experiences in Atlanta earlier this year, possibly a part of a larger spell whose ultimate outcome was unlikely to be good.

"Have you ever seen anything like those symbols before, Jewel?" I asked.

"No," she said, glancing away. "Oh, damn it, I won't lie, they're fireweaver signs—a specific kind of sign fireweavers use to communicate. The disc pattern is a standard base used in certain fire magic, and the symbols running through the rings are also used in fire magic—"

"I think we got that," Vickman said. "Tell us something we don't know—"

"I don't know what you have against me, Mr. Vickman," Jewel said, "or maybe I'm just not making myself clear. Yes, they're fire symbols left by fire magicians. I'm saying I recognize those *specific* combinations of rings and spells from secret fireweaving texts."

"What are they used for?" I asked.

"Like I said, they're secret," Jewel said. At my glare, she spread her hands. "Oh, hell, Dakota, they're used for . . . well, *everything*. To light the walls, as a base for more complex spells, and sometimes, well, sometimes just to send a message."

"Can you read the message?" I asked.

"I didn't mean a literal message—more like a warning," Jewel said. "That ring of fire symbols on the outside just looks like jumbled up gibberish. But the symbols on the inside are easy to read. They make it a threat—like pictograms of a severed dragon's head on the bed."

"Ew," I said, flashing on *The Godfather*. But Jewel looked troubled, strangely reticent, and I felt as if she knew more about these symbols than she was telling. "Jewel . . . surely there's more to this than just a fireweaver's version of an offer you can't refuse?"

"I . . . shouldn't say," she said. "It's better not to talk about it. It can give it power—"

"Jewel," I said, chilled. "What else can these fire mandalas be used for?"

"Sometimes," Jewel said, swallowing, "they're used to cast a curse."

I drew a breath. "Curses" were a contentious topic in the magical community. The old school believed in them; modern practitioners often dismissed them as woo-hooery. I was in the latter camp, but accusing someone of woo just led to arguments, so I kept my mouth shut.

Unfortunately, I did not have the psychic ability to deliver that memo silently.

"I thought curses and hexes were largely a myth," Doug said.

"I wouldn't go that far," Jinx said, "but hexes are largely toy spells—"

"And just what kind of magic do you do, Skye 'Jinx' Anderson?" Jewel said.

"I am a graphomancer," Jinx responded coldly. "A *proficient* graphomancer."

"Well that explains . . . wait, how does that work?" Jewel said. "You're blind."

"Mostly, now," Jinx said, even more coldly, "but I wasn't once—and that part of my brain works just fine. And I don't need to be able to see to know that most spells that *purport* to deliver a curse are the magical equivalent of useless fireworks."

Jewel bit her lip. "I've stepped in it, Ms. Anderson, and I'm sorry, that was just plain rude of me," she said. "But my point stands. Graphomancy is the most prosaic of the magical arts. It's the Euclidean geometry of the magic world, all cut and dried points and lines—"

"What you call 'prosaic' is the backbone of most tattoo magic," I said, "and actually, of most of the fire magic we saw tonight. I'm not saying that there are no curses—but most of the time, once you're out of range of a spell . . . you're out of range of the spell."

"Now I see why they call you the skeptical witch," Jewel said, shaking her head. "But how can you possibly be a practitioner thinking like that? After what

I saw tonight, I'd think you'd be the last person to underestimate what can be accomplished by magic—"

"I'm not," I said. Even now, I could still feel my masterwork trying to settle back on my body. "But I do want to set your mind at ease. A real curse generally requires physical contact with the victim, like a potion or a brand or a tattoo—"

"That's the origin of the myth that a spell will turn back on its caster," Jinx said. "Benevolence rituals work to better your own life because you're essentially casting them on yourself. Try to wish ill to another based on the same scheme, and it will hurt you first—"

"You told me," Jewel said, looking at me, "about some giant curse in Atlanta—"

"Generated by a mammoth city-wide network," I said, "of magic graffiti."

"Jewel has a point," Jinx said, canting her head. "It's theoretically possible to achieve a curse-like effect with hair or blood samples and magical resonators, but, still, remote *vodoun* spells have a five-to-ten mile range. To be safe, we could move out of the City proper—"

"Argh. You people," Jewel said, staring around at us. "*Technical practitioners.* You act like magic is some kind of technology, some prosaic little thing you can program up and stamp down and pack into the stores for Christmas—"

"I *don't* think it's that simple," I said, "and I'm not even denying that there are spiritual powers at work in this world. But the sad truth is that most of what people think magic can do is just superstition mixed in with fear, uncertainty, and doubt peddled by magicians."

"Dakota!" Jewel said. "How can you say that? You summoned a *dragon* tonight—"

"I didn't 'summon a dragon,' " I said. Even though I knew the Dragon's manifestation had been impressive tonight, I also knew it was important to deconstruct that, so Jewel didn't take it as more impressive than it was. "I energized a tattoo and projected an intention—"

"That's what you *want* to see," Jewel said. "But that's because you're shutting it out. Dakota, I know you claim to be the 'best magical tattooist in the Southeast,' but no matter how good you are, no tattoo is going to deflect a bullet, much less grow into a magical fire-breathing dragon two hundred feet high smashing every window in Union Square!"

"Well," I said, "not *every* window—"

"Pretending you can graph magic with lines on paper misses the point of magic," Jewel said. "Magic is whole, and holy, and you can only see that if you let it in *as a whole*. If you keep trying to break it into pieces, then all you'll get are broken pieces. You'll end up witnessing a . . . a *miracle* like we saw tonight and think it was nothing more than fireworks!"

Everyone was silent.

"So, what *would* a fireweaver say about what we witnessed tonight?" I asked.

"Fireweaver legends say a powerful magician can summon the spirit of a dragon in times of crisis," she said. "You know I've been travelling the *world* trying to summon a dragon—and I could only have *dreamed* of summoning the spirit you did tonight."

My eyes narrowed at her. "Did you weave a summoning into your performance?"

Jewel's mouth opened . . . then she smiled. "I can't share the secrets of the Order with the uninitiated," she said, smile growing into a smirk. "How's that for a non-answer answer? But leaving magic out of it, *all* my performances invoke dragons as spirit animals."

"All right," I said, though, skeptical little me had no idea how a tattoo on my own back that I'd inked myself could be a "spirit of a dragon." "That's how you see your magic—and mine. What about Daniel's? What do fireweaver legends say about those rings of fire?"

Jewel's lip trembled. "That . . . they are the mark of death for those who see it."

"Rings of fire, marks of death," I said, putting my face in my hands. The Dragon stirred uncomfortably on my back; I didn't like how reactive it was becoming, even when inactive. "And a dragon appearing in a time of crisis. Sounds like it fits the legends to a T—"

"Surely you're not giving credence to this," Doug said.

"I'm taking *everything* under advisement," I said. "I'm a scientist, not a skeptic. Well, actually I *am* a skeptic, or more accurately skeptic*al*—oh, hell, I don't have time for another dissertation. We need to pool our knowledge, not fight with each other about theory."

Doug rubbed his face. "No, no, you're right. Sorry, Jewel, I'm not trying to diss you—"

"Me neither," Jewel said. "Sorry. Didn't mean to fight. Kumbaya, or whatever."

"Kumbaya, Lord," I laughed. But my friends were all still worried; we needed to talk in confidence—because we didn't really know Jewel yet. "Jewel, is there anything else we should know? No? OK. Jewel, we'll do what we can to help, but my friends and I have some private business we need to discuss. Schultze can show you to your room."

"All right," she said, standing abruptly. "I—I'm sorry if I was curt," she said. "I really do want to thank all of you for saving my life and the lives of my friends. Clearly, the way you do things works for you. I just . . . want you to understand what I know, and take it seriously."

"We do, fireweaver," I said, smiling. "Go on. I won't be long."

When the door closed behind them, Jinx cocked her head. "How did I end up on the skeptical side of that conversation?" she asked. "I'm starting to sound like you and Doug. But . . . still . . ." She considered, then shook her head. "I'm having trouble seeing fire rings as delivery mechanisms for a curse."

"I agree," Doug said. "Both tattoo and graffiti magic depend on proximity for effect."

"This is fire magic. Maybe it's different," I said, grimacing as the Dragon shifted. "And we've seen distance effects—those graffiti gateways. And werewolves—even deep underground, werewolves can feel the need to change, even if they can't see the moon—"

"That's a 'spell' woven through someone's DNA, triggered by an entire *planetoid*," Doug said. "And those graffiti gateways required an enormously complex matrix to receive power—many layers. Fire magic is a *cast* spell—"

"Only as complicated as a caster can think it," Jinx said, holding her spirit cane up to her chin. "No, that's not why I'm resisting it. My *religion* says hexes turn back on you threefold. My *science*, on the other hand, says hexes rarely work . . . but that doesn't mean they're impossible."

"Agreed," I said. "And Jewel's a fire magician, so sought after, people shipped her out from Hawaii, skilled enough to whip up a fifty-foot fire bubble under fire—and to maintain it while switching poi. We have to take her seriously."

"We do," Vickman said, "but after all these attacks . . . I'm starting to get suspicious."

"You don't think she had a hand in this?" I asked. "She was under attack—"

"I know," Vickman said, "but I feel like she's holding out. I don't trust her."

"You don't trust anyone," I said. "But you know me, trust but—"

"Trust but verify," Doug finished.

—☙

"I was going to say," I said, smiling grimly, "trust but verify, don't trust but verify, who cares whether you trust or not—always verify. You never know where the truth is going to come from; sometimes it just reaches out and bites ya."

17. Memories of a Pockmarked Moon

Pizza finally arrived—after the fight in the Square, I'd become famished. I tore open the box eagerly, then stopped. It was a simple pepperoni pizza—orange, pockmarked with red discs, delicious. But something felt weird. Not, wrong, exactly; oddly, it reminded me of home.

But it was covered with meat, which I tried to avoid eating. I passed the box to Schultze and opened another one, looking for the mushroom one; but this was sausage. Again, looking at the orange disc, I got that weird feeling of home, and this time I nailed it—a memory from my literal home, Stratton, South Carolina, eating pizza with my mother while I read *National Geographic*, comparing the pie to a picture of a pockmarked moon taken by NASA.

That left an unexpected pang. Dad's distaste for my so-called "life-style"—by which he meant tattooing, not bisexualism—left us distant. Mom and I had stayed close. I missed her friendly smile, her slightly slurred voice. I stared at the pizza. I missed my mother—

"Don't hog it, Mom," Cinnamon said, stealing a slice out from beneath me, breaking the spell. I smiled at her. Maybe my mother was gone, but I now had a chance to do for her what Mom had done for me. Then my little ravenous beast said, "So . . . what are we gonna do?"

"Yeah, Frost," Vickman said, gratefully chowing down on a slice, "whaff's the plan?"

"Me?" I said, finding the mushroom in the third box. "Why ask me?"

"You'ff—excuse me. You're in fucking charge," Vickman said, wiping his mouth. "Your daughter, your trip, heck, your fucking Magical Security Council—"

"Maybe I'm in charge, but that's not the question," I said. "You're head of security. First, you tell me whether it's safe to stay, then I figure out what we're going to do. Is it safe to stay?"

"She can be trained," Vickman said. "All right. None of this is directed at us, but at Jewel, all after public performances. If she lays low, she should be safe, and so should we. On the other hand, if you lot are going throw yourselves on grenades the way you did tonight, I'm going to drag you all onto the nearest plane. I'm a bodyguard, not a hero."

"Agreed," I said, finishing my slice and wiping my mouth with a napkin. "If there's another emergency like that, of course we do what we can, but I have no intention of seeking it out. I'm going to get Jewel on a plane back to Hawaii if I can, and then . . ."

"We can go," Cinnamon said. She'd eaten three slices in the time it took me to eat one—but she suddenly became sullen, and didn't raise her head to meet my gaze. "I told you—*fuck*—nothing but trouble. We should go. Before anyone gets hurt. I don't needs that stupid award."

I looked at her in shock. She sounded so *wounded.* I didn't want to just bail, not after we'd been through all this—but then Vickman drew a breath, and I glanced at him, expecting him to nod in agreement. He did look grim, but shook his head, mouthing *stay*.

"Actually," I said, "*I* think we should stay. The Warlock thinks we'll meet more allies out here, and this just proves we *need* them. So, sorry, I have no easy out for your cold feet, Cinnamon. You're still stuck having to collect your big prize."

Cinnamon looked up with a halfhearted grin. "Just when I thought I found an out—"

"I promised you a better life," I said, "but never an easy out."

Then we talked about Carnes. The similarity between the symbols he and his companions wore and the symbols in the fire ninja's alleged curse magic was suggestive, but didn't prove anything—and as threatening as Ferguson's message at the airport had been, and as suspicious as the timing of the Oakland attack had seemed, Carnes himself had seemed to warm to us.

Eventually, we decided the right thing to do was alert the Warlock and Varguson. Darkrose and Nyissa, our two oldest vampires and the most savvy with regards to vampire and wizard politics, came up with a carefully worded message that conveyed what we knew and asked for information without either leveling an accusation or admitting ignorance.

"Regardless, this is a sticky situation," I said. "In case things heat back up, we should get day-of tickets home, and a standing arrangement with the airlines to ship Nyissa's coffin."

"Are there such things as day-of tickets?" Doug asked.

"I have no idea," I said. "But pay enough and we could *charter* a plane."

"Screw that. Call Carnes back," Vickman said. "Maybe those tickets were changeable."

After everyone started heading back to their rooms, I cornered Vickman by the bar in Saffron's suite. "I was expecting you to tell us to bail—"

"You already decided not to bail," Vickman said, surveying the well-stocked liquor selection, which must have cost the vampires a pretty penny. "And I'm backing you up. Like you said, we need allies, and fighting alongside the vampires tonight made us some big ones."

"Thank you," I said. "But . . . we were lucky that Daniel's crew didn't up their game. If they'd had Uzis or high-powered sniper rifles, I'd be dead. So would the fireweavers."

"One grenade could have done them all in before we got there," Vickman said, pouring a Macallan. "That could mean they're more amateur than they appear, that they lack the resources they obviously seemed to have . . . or they're sending a targeted message."

"Or maybe there's more to it than that," I said. "They were specifically targeting Jewel, and she claims to be traveling the world, trying to summon a dragon—"

"Jesus," Vickman said, with a guilty glance at his employers. "Maybe that's why they're so pissed about her performances. Magic is based on intent, so no matter how pretty it looked—"

"Jewel could have been doing *anything* out there," I said.

"Could be those giant magic mandalas are the same—trying to undo whatever she's trying to do, good *or* bad," Vickman said. "If you can't stop the caster . . . stop the spell."

I nodded. "Maybe I should go squeeze Jewel for some more information."

"Uh-huh," Vickman said flatly, folding his arms. "You have fun doing that."

I thought of several witty retorts, then realized how that had sounded.

Vickman smiled as my face reddened. "Have fun tonight, skindancer."

I shut my mouth, nodded, and wished him good-night.

18. SLEEPING WITH OTHERS

Why was I nervous, in a hall well-lit and securely guarded? Why was I worried, after I'd changed out of my ripped shirt and jacket? Why did I have butterflies . . . as my hand hesitated over a simple hotel room door?

After three knocks, Jewel appeared, hair dripping wet, wrapped in a fuzzy Cathedral Hill bathrobe. "Sorry," she said. "I never got to clean up after the performance—"

"No problem, Granola Girl," I said, smiling, though the butterflies did flips.

"I think I preferred fireweaver," Jewel said, smiling back. She hesitated, as if wondering whether to invite me in, then pulled her bathrobe a bit tighter. "Dakota . . . I can't thank you enough. I don't even know how to tell you how impressive your magic is to a fireweaver—"

"You're no slouch yourself," I said. "Creating a shield in the middle of a performance?"

"*All* fireweaver spells are designed to flow between each other," she said, passing one hand over the other delicately. "Ordinary fire*spinning* has spectacular moves, but they dead-end, magically. A fire*weaver* strings their moves together smoothly, one to the other—"

"Sounds like Taido," I said, thinking. "Smoothly moving from offense to defense."

"What?" she asked, leaning on the doorjamb, biting her lip.

"One of the principles of my martial art, fireweaver," I said, rubbing my neck. "Ah, you know, skindancing has a lot of forms we use to generate power, but not all of them 'plug' into each other that easily. I'd love to learn more about how fireweaving works—"

"Well, skindancer," Jewel said, shifting against the doorjamb, dexterous hands tightening her bathrobe sash, "it's complicated. There are seven hundred twenty ways to make the basic moves, and they're like the alphabet—you have to learn the letters before you can spell—"

"I'm willing to learn," I said, trying to keep my eyes on hers. "Seriously, I'm not sure anyone else here understood what you did. You switched poi in the middle of a spell and still kept up your shield. That would be like me keeping up a shield while I swapped out a tattoo—"

"Dakota, I'm glad to hear you're interested," she said—and then her mouth quirked up. "If you want to get started on firespinning, that's great. But fire *magic* isn't just firespinning. It can be quite dangerous. Some of the secrets aren't for the uninitiated."

"Secrets for the initiated?" I said, shaking my head. There was a reason magical tattooists had a newsletter—we progressed by sharing knowledge. "Are those secrets really that important? Your life could be at risk here. Other people are definitely putting their lives at risk—"

"Because I shared secrets," Jewel said. "You heard Daniel back at Oakland. He was as upset about who was seeing my performances as he was about what I was doing. I'm in enough trouble already for doing the things I'm supposedly allowed to do—"

"You're worried about being in trouble?" I asked. "*Seriously?* I thought you were on the vanguard here, what with being willing to die to put on a public performance—"

"Whoa!" Jewel said, raising her hands in a fluid wave that did not . . . *quite* dislodge her bathrobe, dang it. "Who said anything about dying? I was willing to get arrested to thumb my nose at 'the man,' that's it. Before yesterday, no one had even threatened me, not seriously."

"I thought Daniel and you had history—"

"We *started* on the same side," Jewel said. She smirked at my roving eye, jerked her robe tight again—then put her fingers in scare quotes. " 'It's a native Hawai`ian thing, you wouldn't understand.' Seriously, though, the Americans tried to kick us off our sacred land—"

"Wasn't that a long time ago?" I said quietly.

"Yes, no, I mean, recently," Jewel said, hands moving in a fluid corkscrew. "A dustup with Fish and Wildlife over a sacred site and a national park boundary. Daniel wanted to fight—I think that's how he recruited the black pajama brigade—but I took it to court. And 'won.' "

She'd again put her hands up in scare quotes, then shook her head.

"We might as well have let them keep it—by the time we won, they'd ruined it," she said. "I don't know. Maybe Daniel was right. Now he's bitter. He's always talked a tough game, but I never thought he'd go through with actual violence—and it scares the hell out of me."

"Fair enough. Being threatened . . . is pretty fucking scary the first time." I frowned. "Look, Jewel . . . Daniel's already hit you twice without achieving his objective, so he may try again. Vickman and I think you should hop on a plane back to Hawaii, as soon as you can."

"You think I should turn tail and run," she said.

"I think . . . you should consider it," I said. "I mean, I'd fight for the right to tattoo, in theory—but in practice, you have to pick your battles. Is this battle worth your life? Daniel's willing to fight over this, and I'm still not precisely sure what he's fighting for."

"It's . . . complicated," Jewel said.

"Can you uncomplicate it for me?" I asked, frustrated. "I'm not trying to put you to the third degree—you've been through a lot. But Daniel's bad news. If we want to stop him, we need to know what he wants—and you've been really cagey. You claim that symbol is a curse—"

"It *is* a curse," Jewel said defensively.

"OK, you think it's a curse—but what if you're wrong?" I asked, and her brow furrowed. "What if it's a counterspell? You *also* told me you're traveling the world trying to summon a dragon. That *is* the secret Daniel doesn't want you performing in public, isn't it? The spell that summons a dragon? I can see why that's knowledge you'd *both* want to hide. And if that's what you're doing in your performances, Daniel will *never* stop trying to stop you—"

"I-was-*just*-making-art-with-fire," Jewel said. "That's my life. So I use magic—"

"Magic so resonant with my dragon tattoo that it almost activated it at the Crucible? That it almost burst off my back in Union Square?" I said. "Jewel, you're either trying to summon a dragon . . . or your magic is specifically designed to get my personal attention."

Jewel's mouth quirked.

"I'd love to get your personal attention," she said, almost immediately blushing, "but you're being a bit arrogant. I designed those performance spells long before I met you, and . . . if, *if* I was summoning a dragon, I can't see why it would activate a dragon tattoo—"

"And yet it did," I said. "Twice. But the design of the spell is only half the magic—what it does is based on intent. So, if I was on your mind when you cast that spell at the Crucible, that might explain the mystery of why my dragon tattoo became so . . . intimate with its caress."

I smiled wickedly at her, and the flush in her cheeks became like flame. *Called it.*

"That . . . sure is a mystery," she stammered, adjusting the bathrobe again. "But before I give away all our secrets, let me win the battle to show them in public first? I don't really want to hide anything from you, Dakota . . . but I don't want to turn the allies I have against me."

I scowled, then nodded.

"You're so cute when you pout," Jewel said. "I love the shape of your mouth."

"Ready to turn in yet?" Nyissa hissed, *right* over Jewel's shoulder.

"Aaa!" Jewel said, jerking aside. She drew a breath, looking at that trim expanse of pearly white flesh between the dark blue stripes of Nyissa's dress, then quailed as her eyes went up to that coldly perfect face floating in the rain of violet hair. "Ah . . . I . . ."

"I," Nyissa croaked, inspecting the metal poker she carried as her personal intimidation accessory, "have been assigned as your guard, Jewel. We share a connected suite, and while you sleep, I will sit where I can see both doors to your room." She stared straight at me, glaring without glaring; I could swear she was *jealous*. "I will make sure *everyone* stays safe."

"Oh," Jewel said, putting her hand to her throat. I have to admit, I'd been scared myself by that little pop-out-of-nowhere trick, and I'd *known* that Nyissa was in the connecting room because I'd asked her to stay there. Jewel said, "But . . . don't you need to sleep?"

"I slept all day," Nyissa said, tilting her head so her bangs shifted. "It is good to be up."

"Nyissa was our companion traveling in the coffin," I said.

"Oh, my God," Jewel said. "You—you're a vampire!"

Nyissa smiled, oh-so-slowly baring her fangs. "Do not worry, pretty little thing," she croaked, running her tongue over one canine. "I have already fed this evening."

"Don't worry," I said, as Jewel's eyes widened in fear. "Not on a person. Cow's blood."

"I do not think," Nyissa said, "that Asia de Cuba's 'special collection' was cow's blood."

"Oh my God!" Jewel said, backing up. "No, no offense ma'am, but—Dakota! You can't put me in a room with a vampire!"

"You can't get away from it," I said. "Your choices are weretigers or vampires."

"*Regardless,*" Nyissa said, "I do not think Vickman will approve of a stranger staying in the same room as Lady Darkrose and Lady Saffron." She regarded Jewel coldly, twirling the poker in her hands. "Similarly . . . *I* do not approve of her staying with you and Cinnamon."

"Well," I said. "Jewel, listen to me. I trust Nyissa with my life. Absolutely."

Jewel sagged, considering. Then she brightened. "Anyone Dakota trusts absolutely is someone I trust absolutely," she said. "She saved my life, twice, you know that."

"She does that," Nyissa said.

"Sorry I treated you like an 'other,' " Jewel said, and Nyissa and I glanced at each other, befuddled. Jewel explained, "That's the excuse people use when they're scared and want to lash out—their victims aren't people like 'us,' they're the 'other.' You deserved better."

I raised an eyebrow. I was starting to like this woman. Oh, who was I kidding—*starting?*

"Thank you, Jewel Grace," Nyissa said, glancing at me. Then she smiled an odd, knowing, and strangely sad smile. "I will turn down your bed and set up my chair. It's been a while since I curled up with a good novel; this will be relaxing."

Jewel watched her go, then turned back to me, swallowing.

I smiled at her. "You all right?"

"Yes, but—Dakota, vampires!" she said, hand pressed to her breast. "My heart's racing. I know what I said, and I want to be big about it but . . . vampires! Still . . . they're people too, and I guess there isn't a place much safer than with a vampire bodyguard."

"Well," I said, and then stopped. She didn't need a lecture on the limits of vampires or bodyguards, not after her experience. "Well, it's our pleasure. Get some sleep, fireweaver."

"If I can," she said. "I'm still rattled. How can you *sleep* after all that?"

"No choice," I said. "I've got to drive to Berkeley tomorrow morning for a talk."

"Trying to sell the *Berkeley* crowd on your little rules?" Jewel asked, eyebrow raised.

—≈

"Not everything is about me, or magic," I said. "This talk's on math—by Cinnamon."

19. Higher Learning

"Every splittable count," Cinnamon blurted from the lectern, "is the sum of two lonelies."

Cinnamon stood on a short box behind a podium too tall, even given the box's extra height, holding her twitching tail with both hands to keep it still as she faced an auditorium full of students, professors and cameras. If I wasn't her mother, it would have been adorable.

As it was, I *seethed* to see my daughter put on the spot like this. Her remote collaborator on the paper, Professor ZQ, had led me to believe this was an "informal presentation" to his research group at Berkeley—"oh, maybe a dozen people in a conference room."

But when we arrived, we found posters all over Berkeley's campus, directing everyone to a talk by "C.S.F. Frost" on "Stalking Goldbach." My baby almost leapt back into the car when she saw the talk would be in Sibley *Auditorium*, and I thought I'd have a heart attack.

At Sibley, we found three hundred people squeezed into an auditorium meant for two hundred and fifty. The audience that *could* sit had comfy chairs; the rest crowded close around a stage that was little more than a semicircle of wood around a lectern, grievously exposed.

I'd almost stormed off. Cinnamon decided to stay, on the very sensible grounds that the crowd at Stanford would likely be far larger. I couldn't argue with that logic—this was supposed to be a practice talk. And so far . . . she was doing well.

"Splittable and lonelies, that's how I says it," Cinnamon said, clutching her tail more tightly. Before she'd grabbed it, it had been switching back and forth so hard it made the light wood lectern look like a giant metronome. "But you might know it better if I translates it. Counts are one two three, whole numbers; splittable you can cut in two, the evens; and lonelies you can't cut at all, the primes. So every even number is the sum of two primes—Goldbach's Conjecture."

The audience stared in silence. From my post at the side door, I was convinced it was her appearance—with cat ears, fangs, a tail, and exotic tiger stripes, all jammed into a junior-punk fashion plate, Cinnamon was entertaining to look at, no matter what she was saying.

But as Cinnamon stammered through her presentation on "cat's cradle constructions," I could see the audience slowly stop watching the talking tiger and start really listening to the mathematician. But that just made it worse—as it was her voice that was the real problem.

At first, it was just her signature tic, her head flicking aside as she channeled an outburst into a rough blast of air that you could mistake for a sneeze. But the cruel truth of Tourette's is that, the harder a victim fights the outbursts, the harder they become to control—and the disease is at its worst when a child passes through puberty into their early teens. And so, as the sneezy tics became rough cries and barks, interjected at odd points during her sentences, I questioned the wisdom of letting her give this talk, no matter how much Professor ZQ and her teacher Doctor Vladimir back at the Clairmont Academy and even Cinnamon wanted it to happen.

"My cat's cradles, they—*eff!*—generalizes the tilty slants, what I calls the—*fucking*—quaternions," Cinnamon said. We both winced. When the tics turned to cussing, it was a bad sign, but she tried again. "The cradles generalizes the quaternions—*you fucking eggheads*—"

That last one sent a ripple through the auditorium, and Cinnamon flinched, half at her words, half at the reaction. She froze there, hunched over, twisting her head away from the crowd—then blurted, "Fuck! Stop looking at me! Stop looking at me!"

And then Cinnamon shimmered—and disappeared.

The crowd gasped—and I cursed. I should have realized. We all want to disappear sometimes, but Cinnamon literally could—she wore tattoos by the Marquis, a master of two-dimensional magic, and she could evaporate into shimmery distortion, like the Predator.

The lectern jerked, as if she'd bolted from it, and I threw wide my arms, to keep her from fleeing the room. But it turned out that she wasn't running away—she was running to *me*. I gasped as she fell into my arms, thrilled and grateful at the level of trust she'd shown me.

"Oh, God," Cinnamon said, shimmering back to visibility in the circle of my embrace, head buried against my chest, hands bunched up on either side of her face, hiding it from the crowd. "Mom, I thinks of the worst thing to say, and then I gots to say it—"

"It's all right," I said, cradling her, turning her away from the crowd; then I leaned down and kissed her forehead. "I can only imagine how hard this is on you, baby. No one should have to deal with this, but sometimes we gotta put up with stuff that we don't want to."

"I don't wants to go back over there," Cinnamon said, crying. "Fuck! I don't."

"No one's going to make you," I said, disappointed that I'd let it get this far.

"But you thinks I should, don't you?" Her eyes were really wet now, she was snuffling, and I was really steamed. She said, "I means, fuck, Mom, it's bad enough I talks—*eff!*—like a toilet, but I don't wants to call them names! They *hates* me, I *knows* it—"

I bit my lip; Cinnamon had interpreted my disappointment in myself as disappointment in her. I couldn't let that stand . . . but then something mean quirked up in me, not evil precisely, but . . . heartless. I didn't like this new thread in me. But I had to use this to help her.

"They don't hate you, Cinnamon," I said quietly. "But I won't be disappointed if you don't finish your talk—and I certainly won't make you. Still . . . won't you be disappointed in yourself if you come all this way, and run away? And won't you be proud if you finish?"

Cinnamon bit her lip, just like I did—then accidentally drew blood. She laughed, wiping her chin with the back of her tufted hand. I pulled out a handkerchief and wiped her hand down, planning to wash it later; it wasn't good to have werekin blood floating around.

"OK, Mom," Cinnamon said, staring back at the lectern, at the glimpse of the patient but increasingly restless crowd. Then she grabbed her switching tail and pulled it up in front of her, like a snaky teddy bear. "Fuck, I means—I means, I can do this."

And then she went back out there . . . and finished her talk.

Cinnamon cussed again. More than once; I lost count. But she let go of her tail, the podium once again became a werekin metronome, and she lost herself explaining her home-grown theory of numbers—how her "splittables" were even numbers, but her "lonelies" weren't quite primes, and how her "tilty slants" were something new entirely. Then she pulled out her ball of string and showed off her cat's cradle figures, revealing how she'd discovered that her numbered tangles of string mapped onto combinations of primes.

Then she got to that line which had prompted Vladimir to call up Professor ZQ. "So the cradle mappin' is why I wants to know whether the twisty snake folds over itself forever—findin' the zeroes of the Riemann Zeta is—*faah*—the key to cracking the Goldbach Conjecture. I—uh, that's it. That's what they gots me workin' on now. Thanks, I guess."

And then? Thunderous applause and a standing ovation. I thought Cinnamon might wilt—but no, she clearly enjoyed it. The chair of the number theory group said "we only have time for five questions," but Cinnamon replied, "do six, it's a pretty perfect little number," and the crowd inexplicably went wild again. When the questions—far more than six—ground to halt, Cinnamon was mobbed by graduate students, and I watched from a distance with Zlatko Quaeschning, AKA Professor ZQ, a cheery, white-haired German with a walrus moustache who hovered like he was *also* a proud parent.

"Pleased to meet you, Professor," I said, scowling as he shook my hand absently. "When we spoke on the phone, you said this would be a small presentation in a conference room, but when I arrived, I find a packed *auditorium*—"

"We can thank the number theory club," Professor ZQ said, in a thick but surprisingly understandable accent. "When I shared CSF's draft paper with my research group, it spread over like wildfire, first across the department, then on the Internet—"

"You *what?*" I said, stunned. "It *what?*"

"Went viral," Professor ZQ said. He caught my glare. "Mrs. Frost, with something this radical, you have to vet it. Simply stunning work for an amateur. CSF's cradles open entire new avenues of attack. I'm so grateful that Doctor Vladimir shared it with me."

"It's *Miss* Frost," I said coldly, "and I'm not grateful you put my—" and here I lowered my voice, even though Cinnamon was fifty feet away and talking "—my *Tourette's-challenged daughter* in front of a room filled with three hundred people with *no warning!*"

Professor ZQ opened his mouth. "Ah," he said. "Well, Ms. Frost, all of us at Berkeley are adults, and adult language is no barrier. I'm sure most of the people in that hall realized what was going on minutes into CSF's talk. Tourette's is an awful disease, especially in the young."

"Yes," I said, "yes it is."

"One of my graduate students still drops f-bombs from time to time . . . though that might just be a side effect of grad school," Professor ZQ said. "Though that's a bit unusual for coprolalia to persist that long. I suppose CSF was a real terror in her teens—"

"*Cinnamon* is just getting into her teens," I said. "Just how old do you think she is?"

Professor ZQ stared at me, then whirled and looked at Cinnamon.

"When Vlad nominated her for the Young Investigator award, I knew she had to be under twenty-five," Professor ZQ stammered. "Of course, we worked with her, but given her level, I just . . . assumed she was already in college, that she was near finishing, say twenty-one—"

"She wishes," I said. "Lower."

"But those lines around her eyes . . . nineteen?" he said, turning to look at me, looking me up and down. "With a hovering mother? No. But she knows so much math . . . seventeen? No? *Younger?* And she's so small. Ms. Frost, please don't tell me she's *fifteen*—"

"She hasn't even turned fourteen yet," I said. "At least, we don't think she has."

"You think, meaning you don't know, meaning she's adopted, orphaned—and spent time on the streets, out of the system," Professor ZQ said. "A thirteen-year-old genius, struggling with Tourette's . . . and I walked her into a complete ambush. Oh, I'm sorry."

"You didn't know," I said. The man was clearly very smart and sensitive; he wouldn't have let this happen, or would have at least given us a heads up, had he fully known Cinnamon's situation. "Sorry. Maybe my strong words should be for Vlad—"

"Not his fault. He said she was young and I never pressed," Professor ZQ snapped, but his eye acquired a twinkle. "So, Ms. Frost, your daughter's done amazing work, but I'll defer my pitch to have CSF . . . to have *Cinnamon* apply to Berkeley's doctoral mathematics program."

"*Doctoral* program?" I said, laughing. "Let's not get the cart ahead of the horse. She looks older than she is because she came off some hard streets. I *just* got her into school six months ago. Let's let her finish middle school, at *least*, before we start talking PhD—"

"*Middle* school?" Professor ZQ said, eyes bulging. "And here I was thinking she'd skip-graded up into high school. I'm sorry, Ms. Frost, but I take back my 'advanced for an amateur' comment. To progress that far in *six months* is great progress even for a *genius*."

"Yeah, we know that," I said. I turned to watch Cinnamon chatting brightly amidst the graduate students, showing off another of her cat's cradles. They clearly *loved* her, from the top of her cat ears to the tips of her tail. It was *such* a good sign. "But don't get your hopes up."

"But surely, Ms. Frost, given the level of work she's doing—"

"Nine months ago, she was functionally illiterate. She *is* a learning machine, and has made huge strides, but . . . she learns what she wants to in order to solve the problems she's interested in." I scowled. "I still catch her doing assignments in crayon."

"So what?" Professor ZQ said, a twinkle in his eye. "That's probably more fun."

"Ha! Maybe so," I said, "but . . . she's still learning how to be a student. And struggling with severe dyslexia on top of the Tourette's. *And* dealing with being a werekin who can't quite transform all the way back to human. And recovering from . . . well, frankly, child abuse."

Professor ZQ's eyes had widened at the word "werekin," but when I hit "child abuse," his face grew tender. "Oh, my," he said. "I am so sorry."

"Let's not take her childhood away just yet," I said. "She *just* got started on it."

"Hey, Mom!" Cinnamon said, bouncing up to me. "Can I borrow your phone?"

"Don't you have one of your own?" I asked, patting her on the head.

"Yeah, yeah," she said, spinning around, bending back and looking at me upside down, "but I needs the pictures you took last night of the fire circles. I wants to ask the grads a question about how the magic worked."

"All right, all right," I said, pulling my phone out and unlocking it. "One scratch and—"

"Yeah, yeah," she said, scooping it up in her long, bony claws. "More dings on yours than on mine. Back in a bit once we've cracked the case."

"I hope you mean the investigation and not the plastic shell," I said, but she was already bouncing back into the crowd, showing my phone off. I wasn't sure whether the students were more impressed by the pictures, or the phone.

Professor ZQ said. "You saw some stage magic last night?"

"No," I said. "Cinnamon's working with us to help analyze the magic used in that nasty business last night in Union Square."

"The terrorist incident?" the Professor said. "But what . . . how was magic involved in that? I heard it was explosives and a couple of dragon-themed fireworks—"

"Fire magic," I said, shaking my head. "Including two very interesting fire circles."

"You mean, literal magic," the Professor said, clucking. "Surely you're not serious—"

"Did you not see Cinnamon disappear just now?" I asked. I know that the human eye doesn't like to see magic—the changes slip between movements of the eye—but he had to have seen that. "That was literally magic."

"That was an amazing trick," ZQ said, "but we shouldn't call *anything* 'magic.' Ms. Frost, you may not be trained as a scientist, but you seem like a rational person, so—

Oh, not this again. "I *am* a rational person," I said, sliding my arms up so my hands crossed each other, "and I was trained as a scientist, trained to look at evidence, and the evidence says there *is* such a thing as magic—or do you have a better word for *this?*"

I hooked one foot around the other and did a quick 360 degree spin, vestcoat whipping around me in my Michael Jackson move—then threw my arms wide, pouring all the mana built up from my spin into my vine tattoos, which leapt into the air in elaborate, glowing curlicues.

"That is . . . quite an amazing trick," he said, watching the filaments of my shimmering vines curl around each other as I slowly brought my hands back together, "but I would still not say 'magic.' I'm sure there's a rational explanation—"

"Yes," I said, fluidly moving my hands to collapse the vines. "The rational explanation is changes effected to space and matter by intentions expressed through the flux of mana, or, as we quaintly called it at Emory University's Harris School of Magic, *magic.*"

"You can get degrees in many things," Professor ZQ said. "Divinity and chiropractic and even artificial intelligence, if there were such a thing. But just because alchemists can perform quite a few convincing-looking tricks does not mean that the ideas behind it are real."

"No offense, Professor, but you're too educated to be this sheltered," I said. Maybe that was unfair. When Professor ZQ had likely gone to school, the professors who knew magic kept it secret—and tried to publicly discredit it. Still, there *was* a way to prove magic—evidence. I pulled out my wallet on its chain and showed him my picture of Cinnamon at her most Cinnamon. "You can't see your daughter turn into a tiger every month and *not* believe in magic."

"Well," the Professor said, staring at the picture of Cinnamon-the-Tiger and her cute owlish tiger glasses, pawing at a math book, tail switching—then at

Cinnamon-in-the-flesh with *that same tail* thwacking graduate students as she spun and yammered. "Oh my. That tail . . . is remarkable. Forgive my skepticism, but for centuries, man accepted any supernatural explanation for every phenomenon. The scientific method instead demands a mechanism—"

"Just what I demanded of Jewel," I said. ZQ looked at me funny, and I clarified, "You just quoted me talking to a fire magician. I've seen her literally *fly* using magic, but I shut out her ideas because she used different words. *My* magic uses the tools of modern science—the logic of magic is mathematics—but magic *isn't* mathematics. It's a natural phenomenon—"

"Don't you mean 'supernatural?' " ZQ asked, eyes twinkling.

"Bah. *Natural, supernatural.* They're just words," I said. "What I mean is *magic is real.* It works how it works. You have to open your eyes *before* you understand what you see."

ZQ's mouth opened. "So the giant dragon in the Square last night—"

"Was real," I said, feeling my tattoo slither against my skin. My mouth quirked up. *I want to show him.* But that would be a bit too cruel—and I didn't want to ruin yet another coat, not till I could get proper slits cut in it. "Real *magic*, at least, off my back."

ZQ stared at me. "This has been an education, Ms. Frost," he said.

"Mom," Cinnamon said, bouncing up. "I gots it, I gots it!"

"What, Cinnamon?" I said. "What did you get?"

"The marks last night," she said. "I knows why—*fuck*—why the magic looked odd."

"Well, don't keep us in suspense," I said, glancing at the Professor. "Tell us what you learned about those magic circles, Cinnamon, and how you deduced it."

"I deduceded it," she said proudly, "by followin' the logic, just like you and Jinx said. The effect of the spell is accounted for by the lines of the magic. And I accounted for all the parts of the spell completely—*except* for the letters."

"All right," I said slowly, "but doesn't that put us back where we started?"

"No," Cinnamon said. "The spell spins the letters, and lights them, but doesn't connect to their intent. The Euler circuits don't add up—so there's no flux of mana through to the letters' meaning. They're not doin' anything, magic-wise. I means, other than . . . glowin'."

"It's a sign," the Professor said. "What you're saying is, it's a lighted sign."

—✧

"Yes, but it's more than just a sign, it's what's in it," Cinnamon said. "It's a code."

20. Virtually Uncrackable

"Well, it's about time you called me," said Special Agent Philip Davidson, voice rising from the speakers of the rental car as we shot across the San Mateo Bridge toward Burlingame. Philip was my ex-boyfriend, but his deep voice carried a warmth I still shared—a double benefit, since he was my contact in America's mystical spooks bureau, the Department of Extraordinary Investigations. "After your little emotional incident in Oakland, followed by last night—"

"I knew if I didn't call you, you'd call me," I laughed.

"Seeing your name pop up on MIRCwood is one thing," Philip said. "But our job is to prevent crimes and stop disasters, not snoop over the shoulders of every magical person in the country—no matter how much my bosses might like to. What can I do for you, Dakota?"

I filled him in—not that I needed to; thanks to MIRCwood, the DEI's "Magical Incident Report Clearinghouse/Web-Oriented Database," Philip already knew most of what I had to tell him. But when I revealed Cinnamon's insight about the code, Philip had bad news.

"What do you mean, you can't decode it?" I asked. It didn't surprise me that Cinnamon hadn't (yet) picked up codebreaking, nor that Professor ZQ didn't know mathe*magical* codes. But a flat "no" was the last thing I expected from a superspook at the DEI. "Philip—"

"I didn't say *impossible*," Philip said. He'd *already* started looking into the mess in Union Square, and readily agreed to talk to Officer Brookstone in the San Francisco Police Department. But on the code, he was pessimistic. "We'll take a look, but if we can't—"

"Philip, come on," I said. "If anyone can do this, you can. You're the biggest spook I know. Heck, the DEI *specializes* in the study of hidden magic. Surely *someone* at the DEI is an expert in magical codes, that is, assuming you don't have a whole department—"

"We do, but I want to be realistic. First off, we don't even know it's really a code—"

"Hey! No doubtin' the me," Cinnamon said. "*Fuck!* The symbols woven into the spell are cracklin' with mana, but they're cut off from the intent of the spell itself. So their meanin's *everything*. I'll bet someone who gots the counter-spell could read it off in a snap—"

"All right, Cinnamon, I believe you," Philip said. "Who knows? Maybe we'll get lucky, find out they're using a simple substitution cipher. But in my experience, magicians trying to talk in secret use sophisticated ciphers, or worse, mystic codes. It's virtually impossible to—"

"Virtually impossible as in probably can't be done, or as in against procedure?" The more I got involved in the magical Edgeworld, the more cautious he got about what he shared. "This isn't some BS with the National Security Agency, some backdoor you can't admit exists—"

"It exists," Philip said.

That stymied me for a second. "Then—"

"*Virtually* impossible as in very-unlikely-or-at-least-impractical," Philip said. "I'll have our boys and girls look at the message, and I'll also slip it under the door of the NSA—they love a friendly challenge. But deciphering a message can take years or even centuries. Some never get cracked. Even the best expert codebreakers can't just 'crack' an arbitrary cipher, any more than a computer whiz can just 'hack' an arbitrary computer—"

"Or an artist can take a fuzzy image in Photoshop and just press 'enhance,' " I said.

"Exactly," Philip said. "If the message is short enough, there's no way to tell what it is. Sometimes amateurs gaffe and use something that has a known key, but normally, codebreakers need a lot of text to start tackling letter frequencies or looking for patterns—"

"You can't crack it," I said. "because it's a short code?"

"Cipher," Cinnamon corrected. After the talk, she'd dragged me to Moe's bookstore in downtown Berkeley and found a slim Gardner volume on cryptography. She was struggling even though it was written for a junior age level; however, the struggle was with her dyslexia, not her retention. "Jumbled-up letters is a cipher. A code means, like, code words and stuff—doubletalk, secret passwords, little red code books the captain takes down with the ship."

"That's what I meant by mystic codes," Philip said. "They're grimoires of secret words, a kind of hidden language known only to initiates. Good luck if that's what we're dealing with here—they guard those books like demons, and they're usually enciphered as well."

"It doesn't feel like code words," Cinnamon said, a bit uncertainly. "The way the letters all runs together, it feels like normal words all scrambled up, a transposition cipher. But we probably don't gots enough of the cipher to descramble it—"

I shrugged. "So the 'cipher' is short. So what? The longer it is, the more complicated it could be. Somebody explain, in fifty words or less, why we can't crack a short code—*especially* scrambled letters. Me and my dad used to solve Cryptoquotes all the time when I was a kid."

"They wants you to solve it," Cinnamon said, "It isn't so easy when they don't—"

"The intended recipient has the key," Philip said. "The rule for unscrambling."

"But can't you, I dunno, reverse engineer that from the message?"

"OK, let's try one then. What's a cat?" Cinnamon asked. "C-A-T, cat?"

"I dunno," I said, grinning at her hopefully. "A delightfully obscure daughter?"

"Mom! I'm serious," she said. "It's a scramble code. What's CAT stand for?"

I stared ahead, out over the lanes of the bridge. "Uh . . . I don't know. Act?"

"ACT, yeah, that's a good one," Cinnamon said. "But why not TAC, like a tic-tac?"

"Or TCA, part of a longer word?" Philip said. "CTA, some government agency?"

"ATC, maybe somebody's—*fah!*—somebody's initials, like Andrew T. Codebreaker?" Cinnamon said, her switching tail thumping hollowly against the glove box. "Or maybe, by some quirk of the scramble, a CAT is just a CAT."

"The images you sent me looked like sixty character messages from a full alphabet," Philip said. "Assuming it's not something *more* complicated, that's an astronomical number of possible transpositions, billions and billions—"

"Trillions and trillions," Cinnamon said. She shook her head, ears canted. "Sixty factorial is, uh . . . fuck. Lots, even for me. Eight billion . . . trillion trillion trillion . . . trillion trillion *trillion*, and lots and lots of change."

"So, good fucking luck, is what you're telling me," I said.

"Not that it's totally impossible," Philip said. "An agent in the field can't use something arcane. The best ciphers rely on simple rules and some secret that only the agent and his contacts know. For all we know, it's something rock bottom simple—"

Philip's voice cut out briefly as my phone *blooped*, and Cinnamon jumped in.

"Like, scramblin' a message usin' a different Shakespeare sonnet each day of the week," Cinnamon said, as I plucked the phone from its cupholder. She said, "If somebody kept that pattern up for—*hah!*—a month, we'd crack it like pecans on moonsday. With just two—"

"We're screwed," I said, staring at a San Francisco number I didn't recognize.

"Unless we get"—another *bloop*—"more messages," Philip said.

"Or finds the key," Cinnamon finished.

"Figures," I said, flicking the call to voicemail. All I could think of was that symbol—a vaguely Chinese mandala, with a dragon ouroboros, twisted over itself like an infinity symbol, coiling forever at its center. "Dragons are the best at keeping secrets."

"I hate to say this," Philip said, "but I hope it stays a secret."

"What?" Cinnamon said. "But—"

"The messages were part of an organized attack," Philip said. "You said Jewel called it a curse, but I'm guessing *death threat*. Even though more messages might help crack the cipher, I'd rather the ones we have remain enigmas than risk Jewel getting hurt in another attack."

"Agreed," I said.

"On that note, your stunt in Union Square was *spectacular*," Philip said. "I've never seen *projectia* that large, and that's saying something. Hopefully, they will have scared them off—"

"Not likely; they actually seemed more curious than scared when I was deflecting bullets on the streets of Oakland," I said. "Wait a minute. How did you know it was spectacular?"

"Dakota, it's all over YouTube," Philip said. "And it got picked up on FOX and CNN—"

"Damn the Internets," I said. "That's all we need, pictures of the codes everywhere."

"What's the problem with that?"

"Well," I said, "if this is a code . . . who's the message to?"

The car went silent. My smartphone rattled in its cupholder—voicemail arrived. I looked; same number. But who? Not the police, at least not their cells; I'd entered full contacts from everyone I'd spoken to. I put the phone down, unwilling to drop this conversation.

"Well . . ." Cinnamon said, tilting her head. "*Eff*—"

"Jewel," Philip said, filling in what Cinnamon or I would not. "The 'ninjas' don't need it to talk to themselves, so she'd be the logical choice. I've seen this in cults—when members step out of line, enforcers deliver a ritualized warning, understandable only to insiders. The encoded message could be a gruesome threat—a magical equivalent of a horse's head in a bed."

"Ugh. That's essentially what Jewel said the pictograms meant," I said. "As for the code, either she doesn't know or isn't talking. But there are at least three other alternatives—first, it's a message to a confederate elsewhere, like descriptions of the people with Jewel. The last thing we need is an encoded hit list plastered over the news—"

"Mom!" Cinnamon said. "A fire ninja isn't gonna throw down a message and just *hope* the news will pick it up! What if the fire department had doused it, or the police had cordoned off the area? If they wants to send a message, they'd email or text it or something—"

"More likely, a phone call," Philip said. "I agree with Cinnamon, sounds implausible—"

"OK, maybe," I said, "but if Jewel doesn't understand the message, and it isn't plausible it was meant for someone else, that leaves the second possibility. That the 'messages' aren't messages at all, but are part of a larger spell we haven't grokked yet."

"I don't gets how," Cinnamon said. "I went over and over the spell. It's, like, hermetic—"

"I believe you, honey," I said, "based on what *we* know about magic, but . . . what if the fire ninjas know something we don't? And you said a magician might be able to read the message. What if a magician could cast a spell against it, like a lock and key?"

"A magic locker," Cinnamon said. "Holdin' a hidden intent, waitin' to spring it—"

"Oh, great," Philip said. "More unknown magic. What's the third possibility?"

"That Jewel was right the first time," I said. "That it's a curse."

The car went silent again. I shifted in my seat as my Dragon moved against my skin.

"So . . ." I said, "whether it's a curse, a magic locker, or even just a simple message to other bad guys, we don't need images of it splashed all over the news. And if it is part of a larger spell, we *certainly* don't need videos showing copycats how to do it all over YouTube—"

"All right, *all right,*" Philip said. "I'll contact the Oakland and San Francisco police, try to suppress details of the case, but—Dakota. This is America. The attacks have been public. If someone posts a picture to their Flickr accounts, there's nothing we can—"

Philip's voice cut out abruptly as my phone buzzed again, this time with a text message this time. I snagged the phone out of the cupholder, staring at the same San Francisco number I didn't recognize . . . but a phrase that I did: CALL ME—DAKOTA FROST.

The same thing I'd written on that envelope at the airport—and said to *Carnes.*

—

"Philip," I said quietly. "I've got another call. I think I need to take it."

21. Never Out an Edgeworlder

Never out an Edgeworlder—it's a firm rule. But I couldn't just waltz off the phone with Philip "I don't believe in coincidences" Davidson, world's greatest spook. So, without naming the Wizarding Guild, I quickly explained the threat we'd received at the airport.

When I was done, Philip was quiet for a moment.

"All right," he said. "I'll . . . stay in touch, Dakota."

"Thanks, Philip," I said, and hung up. "So . . . Cinnamon. You think he's—"

"—gonna tap your call?" Cinnamon finished. "When *doesn't* he?"

I shook my head. There was not outing Edgeworlders, and then there was letting people get what they deserved. I dialed the text without listening to the voice message. When the phone picked up and the speaker answered, I said, "Hi, I'm returning your call. This is Dakota Frost—"

"—best magical tattooist in the Southeast," Cinnamon finished.

The speaker didn't answer at first. "How rude, Ms. Frost," said an oddly familiar voice. "It isn't polite to put someone on speakerphone without asking."

I cocked my head. "Mr. Carnes," I said. "My apologies, I'm driving."

"I have private matters to discuss with you, Ms. Frost," the wizard said. "If this is a bad time, we can speak again later—"

"No, no, this is a perfect time," I responded. "You're just the person I wanted to speak to, and if you object to my daughter's presence, give it up. She's my closest advisor."

Cinnamon grinned at me.

"Very well, Ms. Frost," Carnes said. "I keep *my* daughters out of the business, but it's your funeral. That was a hell of a calling card you left last night; you now have my undivided—"

"Hang on—what are you calling a calling card?" I asked.

"The giant *dragon* symbol all over Macy's in Union Square."

"Actually, I cast the giant dragon *projectia* that *flew* over the Square while defending my friends from a magical assault," I said. "The giant coded symbol on Macy's façade was left by our assailants, whom *I* assumed were allied with you. Your first message failed, so you—"

"I'm afraid," Carnes interrupted, "I do *not* know what you're talking about."

"Oh, come now," I said. "How did you get this number? I didn't give it to you. You had to get it from the goon you sent to the airport."

"Ferguson is not a goon. The purpose of his visit, as he *should* have stated—"

"He *did*," I said sharply. "We figured out what you were doing with him—"

"What we were doing," Carnes said, "was giving Ferguson a chance to show his mettle, and giving *you* the opportunity to gracefully bow out of your trip—which you were free to decline, as you did. And yes, he did pass along your message to me—"

"Along with *your* thinly veiled threat about my safety on the streets of Oakland," I said, "after which, if you recall, my friend was assaulted on the streets of Oakland. I thought they were unrelated until I saw the magical symbols on *your* tie *billboarded* across Union Square—"

"What? *Jesus*," Carnes said. He was quiet on the phone, but I could hear clicking, as of a web search. Finally, he let his breath out like a hiss; I guessed he'd found a picture. "I hadn't looked closely, but I see the resemblance. Look, Frost . . . we got off on the wrong foot. I didn't order these assaults, and if you didn't instigate those fireworks, then . . . I'm disturbed to see a magical assault in public, much less *Union Square*. My eldest *daughter* shops there—"

"Sorry to hear that. About the proximity, not the shopping. I hope she's OK."

"Yes, she's—that's not the point," Carnes said. "I'm worried about . . ."

"Yes?" I said, after a long pause that drew on to the point I worried about my cell battery.

"Well, frankly, I'm worried about you, Ms. Frost," Carnes said. I blinked—he sounded completely sincere. "I didn't want you here because I was afraid you'd be a disruption, and clearly, I was right. But there are disruptions, and then there are outright attacks—"

"Not everything is about me," I said. "My friend appears to be the target."

"Same one from Oakland?" he asked. "What's her relationship to you?"

"I—" *think she's cute.* My cheeks reddened. "I just met her on the plane in."

"Hell," Carnes said. "She's that fire magician, the Queen of Fire, right?"

"Princess, I think," I said.

"Right," Carnes said. "Alex Nicholson told me about her. I think I've even seen her perform, in Paris, if I recall. So . . . a visitor to the City has suffered two magical attacks. I'm going to take you at your word you weren't responsible, Ms. Frost—"

"And I'll take you at your word that you weren't, Mr. Carnes," I said. "But if this doesn't have anything to do with you and me, then whatever disagreements we have are a distraction. We need to—well, that is, *I* need to focus on Jewel's safety—"

"No, you had it right the first time," Carnes said tightly. "I can't speak for the Guild, but I'm not going to sit by and let magicians get attacked, not in San Francisco, not on *my* watch. *We* need to keep your friend safe. We need to get to the bottom of this. And we need to stop it."

Now the pause was on my end of the line.

"Do I hear you right, Mr. Carnes?" I said, not trusting him for a second. "I'm hearing the kinds of things I was saying at the Conclave, the kinds of things I've been saying to my own Magical Security Council for months. Do I have you on board, Mr. Carnes?"

"Yes," he said even more tightly. "I swear to you, though, if this is some kind of plot—"

"I swear too," I said. "Don't be playing me, as my daughter would say, or I—"

"No, no," Carnes said. "Of course not. On that note . . . did she collect her award?"

"Uh . . . not yet," I said. Carnes kept throwing me—I'd been ready to pigeonhole him as "foe," but he seemed to actually . . . *care*. I told him about the talk. "We thought it was going to be a dozen people in a conference room, and it was three hundred in an auditorium."

"That . . ." Carnes began, with a laugh he quickly suppressed. "That must have been challenging, Cinnamon, isn't it? I know you've got . . . things you struggle with, and it was brave of you to step in front of all those people. Your mother must be very proud of you."

"Thank you, sir," Cinnamon said, oddly muted.

"So, Frost," Carnes said, suddenly serious. "We both know what this is for."

"I take your meaning," I said, looking at Cinnamon. The man had daughters too.

"Make my job easier," he said. "Give the Conclave their quid pro quo. Convince Lord Buckhead to meet the fae. You don't know what that will mean for all of us—"

"First, Carnes," I said, "I do not control Lord Buckhead, so no promises—and no stalling on this problem waiting for his cooperation. If this is a threat, we act on it."

"Look, Frost—"

"It's your jurisdiction," I said, and there was silence on the other end of the line. "It *is* your jurisdiction. All I can do is advise. *You* will tell *me* what to do, unless you want another arrangement." He remained quiet. "*Do* you want another arrangement?"

"Perhaps," he said. "It would make things easier. Let me consult the Guild."

"All right," I said. "And second, Carnes, Lord Buckhead is a friend, and a . . . strategic asset of Atlanta. I'm not asking him to come out here unless we can get assurances of his safety. The last time a wizard wanted to meet Lord Buckhead, it was a trap."

Carnes snorted. "What wizard tried to take on the Lord of the Hunt?"

"Christopher Valentine," I said, "better known as the Mysterious Mirabilus—"

"Mirabilus?" Carnes asked. "The *stage magician?*"

"Only on TV," I said. "Valentine was, in secret, a member of secret skindancing cult and an extremely powerful magician. Lord Buckhead called him the Archmage—"

"Fuck me!" Carnes said. "I've heard of him, a *nasty* piece of work with a huge trail of bodies in his wake. I guess he bit off more than he can chew, taking on a fae god."

"No," I said. "Lord Buckhead tried, but . . . the Archmage planned his attack well. He took him out in under a minute. I had a center stage seat for the whole show."

"The Archmage traditionally kills those he defeats," Carnes asked suspiciously. "How did Lord Buckhead survive? For that matter, how did you?"

"Do you never read the news, Mr. Carnes?" I said. "I defended myself—"

"*You* took on the Archmage and lived? I don't believe it."

"You don't have to take my word for it," I said, pulling the rental to a stop in front of the Valentine Foundation headquarters. "It will be all over TV this fall."

22. Godwin's Law

The Valentine Foundation headquarters was a grey stone structure in the hills south of San Francisco, overlooking a little town called Burlingame. At least, the *signs* said we passed through the "City of Burlingame"; however, climbing the windy road toward the Foundation, I had seen no clear city boundary. Only the odd trees set this place apart—thick, white-trunked, almost like massive birches except for the rich, dark green foliage.

I slammed the door of the rental and stared out over the suburbs and into the Bay. Trees rose through a sea of homes like reeds in a marsh; beyond them hotels and offices, shrunken by perspective, clustered like piles of white toy blocks in a green carpet; and beyond them, washed out by distance, the Bay, mountains and sky stretched across the vista in three stripes of blue. The view was spectacular—Valentine had spared no expense acquiring this land.

Then Cinnamon got out of the car, and my blood boiled. Valentine had deceived us all, and Cinnamon had almost died because of him. How much of this land had been paid for by Valentine's use of real magic to enhance his stage career?

Worse, how much had been paid for by theft from his Edgeworld victims? Valentine had quietly disposed of the real magicians who accepted his Challenge, but it was equally dangerous to have turned him down—most of those who did disappeared after violent robberies.

Even though Valentine himself was gone, I was determined to see his Foundation pay for his crimes in full—to the tune of one million dollars, the one million the Foundation owed me for winning the Valentine Challenge—performing a feat of magic Valentine couldn't replicate by nonmagical means, namely, inking a working magical wristwatch on a willing subject.

Supposedly, the Valentine Foundation itself was innocent. Supposedly, none of the Foundation staff had participated in his crimes. Supposedly, this visit was my last contractual obligation to the Foundation—shooting bumpers for the TV special documenting my defeat of the old coot. And supposedly, after I did that, I'd be free to put the screws to these shmucks.

The only problem?

The head schmuck was Alex Nicholson, who'd nearly lost his life trying to save mine.

"Dakota!" he cried in his familiar voice, and I turned to see Alex descending the steps—trim, blond, muscled, arms thrown wide with easy warmth, smile held wide with more difficulty. "I'm so glad you finally made it out to, ah, to film the trailers—and Cinnamon too! Gimme a hug!"

Charming, with a touch of snake oil. Alex was a bundle of contradictions: magician and fireweaver, clean-cut and tattooed, Valentine's protégé—and nearly his victim. He'd let me ink that magical wristwatch to win the Valentine Challenge—but now was withholding my money as the Valentine Foundation's official gatekeeper. He was a close friend to Jinx and me, but also a near-adversary on the Magical Security Council as the representative for the Wizarding Guild.

Our relationship was officially *complicated.*

"Mom," Cinnamon said, squealing. "The giant Ken doll is crushing me!"

"Oh, give her a squeeze," I said, trying to force a grin. "She's a werekin. She can take it."

"Well, I wouldn't want to break her, but—OK!" Alex said, lifting her again, his glance catching mine, his eyes unexpectedly moist. Cinnamon had almost died from silver poisoning during that nasty business. "Yep, still in one piece, thank goodness!"

Oh great. I'd forgotten he had seen Cinnamon maybe twice in the last six months; because of the show, he hadn't had his face rubbed in our troubles like the rest of us. So we'd be processing this all again. Well, great, we were here to reopen old wounds anyway.

"So," Cinnamon said, as Alex put her down. "Mom says you spins fire. And can fly!"

"I certainly can and do firespin," Alex said, "though I'd call it floating with style."

I grinned—that was how I'd described Jewel's performance at the Crucible. "That's fair," I said; I'd seen Alex do essentially the same trick, though for a far shorter duration, and with considerably less height. Still . . . "But it's far more spectacular than you're letting on—"

"Yeah," Cinnamon said. "Fire magic is *super* awesome. We went to this show at this place called the Crucible or something—"

"I love the Crucible—" Alex began, grinning at me as Cinnamon rolled on.

"—and these guys called the Fireweavers or something ended their show with this super spinny floaty fireball thingy done by this cute fat chick Mom likes called Jewel—"

"*You* saw the Princess of *Fire*?" Alex said, impressed. "What a treat, Cinnamon! Jewel Grace is a real artist. She's definitely old school, but she's got *awesome* technical skill and killer style to go with it. I'd love to pick her brains—"

"I'll see if I can arrange it," I said. At Alex's baffled look, I said, "Jewel's a . . . friend."

"She's Mom's new *giiiirl*friend," Cinnamon said, with a toothy grin.

"She is *not,*" I said testily. "She's . . . just a friend into fire magic."

"You're not kidding," Alex said. "Jewel's more into fire magic than anyone."

Oddly, it disturbed me to learn even Alex knew about Jewel's skill—independent corroboration of her knowledge meant I'd have to consider her ideas about the curse even more closely. And then it struck me—*Alex* was the friend into fire magic I'd known longest.

"Speaking of that," I said, "since you are officially my oldest friend into fire magic, can you teach me about it?"

"What?" Alex said, grinning broadly, a bit too broadly, like he was sucking up to me. "*You* want to be a firespinner? It certainly would go with the whole dragon theme—"

"Well, no," I said, laughing. "I'm just a tattoo artist. I saw some . . . interesting fire magic last night, and I was hoping to pick your brains about how it was done."

"Dakota," he said, reproving but with a touch of the snake oil returning to his voice. "Going from pillar to post? If Jewel didn't feel comfortable telling you, I can't tell you either. It isn't nice to ask a magician to spill his own secrets, much less spoil someone else—"

"Hold on," I said, raising my hand. "First off, we practitioners call you stage magicians illusionists—but I wasn't asking about the secrets of your stage magic. I've seen you do real magic with fire, and that's the kind I'm asking about—"

"Dakota," Alex interrupted, a little more sharply, a little more *honestly*, "yes, I am a fire magician, but . . . our art is not public knowledge. The Order's secrets are passed on only to initiates, and if Princess Jewel didn't see fit to tell you something, I certainly can't."

My eyes narrowed. That was the second time that he'd called Jewel a "princess," and I was starting to think it wasn't just a stage name. That disturbed me, but, on the other hand, I was known in vampire circles as "the Lady Frost," so who was I to talk?

"Well," I said, "while Jewel was not exactly forthcoming, she claimed to be as stumped as I was about that little business in Union Square—"

"Oh, Jesus. Don't tell me *you* cast those dragon spells? You're smirking. Oh, my God. That *was* you. That ginormous dragon *projectia* was *amazing*—and so that was you, *flying?* I know I hover, but I didn't think magically powered human flight was even *possible*—"

Fascinating, how much magic he knew, but still . . . I had a hard time unpursing my lips.

"Well, ah, thank you, Alex," I said, wiping my smile off, "but it's the fire mandala that was a bit more baffling. Cinnamon thinks it was little more than a big lighted sign, but Jewel seemed to think it might be a curse, but she wouldn't say much more than that."

Alex looked like was about to speak, but when I said Jewel wouldn't say more, he folded his arms. "I'm sorry, Dakota," he said uncomfortably. "Jewel was there, and saw it better than I did. If the Princess didn't see fit to tell you, I shouldn't speculate either. I could be censured."

I stared at him. "Princess" *had* to be more than a stage metaphor. Was it a fireweaver rank? Still . . . "Alex, come on. It's the twenty-first century. Magic is out in the open now. We've even worked problems like this on the Council, when you bother to attend, that is—"

"We are in *preproduction* for the new *season,*" Alex said, with a sharp wave of his hand. "I take the MSC seriously, but I was clear to both you and the Wizarding Guild that my actual job comes first. Until the Guild wants to start paying me, like, a *lot*, I am tied up when the show is running." He relaxed a little. "Yes, it is the twenty-first century, but this is fireweaving. This is my art. I swore an oath to keep its secrets, Dakota. You know how it is."

"No," I said, "I don't know how it is. That's why I'm asking—"

"Look," Alex said, frustrated, "surely when you became a skindancer—"

"We don't have "secrets for initiates," we have a newsletter for practitioners," I said. "My old master Arcturus is practically throwing himself at me to pass on his knowledge."

"Maybe so," Alex said, "but still, I have to walk a tightrope already, being a wizard and running a show aimed for skeptics. Hell, we hired Jacob Dauntless because there were things I just can't touch. I thought you, of all people, would understand following the rules."

I pursed my lip. "OK, let me rephrase my life mantra. I follow every good rule."

"And who decides what rules are good? You?" he asked. "That's very relativist—"

"No, it is not, because good is *not* relative," I said. "I don't care what the 'rules' are, at Auschwitz someone needed to stand up and say 'no.' "

Alex let out his breath. "All right, Dakota, you've just Godwined the thread," he said. "I'm not going to discuss this anymore with you—"

"Alex," I said. "I may be computer savvy, but in the end, I am just a tattoo artist. I do not have any idea what you just meant other than 'fuck off.' "

Alex pursed his lip. "To 'Godwin' is to invoke Nazis in otherwise polite conversation."

"We *are* having a polite conversation," I said, "and you're telling me no, because you think the oath you swore is a good one, regardless of whether it's convenient for me. That's OK, Alex, it really is. I didn't come here to bust your chops—"

And then his face fell, and it hit me he knew what was coming—and planned to welsh.

"Oh yeah," I said, slumping my shoulders slightly. "I did."

"Dakota," Alex began, the snake oil creeping back into his voice. "I'm so sorry—"

"S'all right," I said. "Don't take this personally, but where the hell's my money, Alex?"

"Oh, no!" Cinnamon cried, hands going to her mouth. "I knew it, I knew it! There was no way you would—*fahhk!*—would have come all the way out here just for *me*—"

"I did, Cinnamon," I said, grimacing, not meeting her gaze, "but two birds, one stone—"

"I knew this was coming," Alex said, slumping. "You've been dodging the filming for so long, and I wanted to think you were making good, but I knew this was too good to be true—"

"I'm not one to dodge anything," I said, putting my hand on Cinnamon's shoulder. She shrugged me off, but I continued, "As you've noticed, I have a new daughter, and she gets dibs on my time. But I was serious when I said I'd come out to shoot your bumpers—"

"Trailers," Alex said. "Bumpers are for radio—"

"*Whatever*, Alex," I said. "But do *not* talk to me about 'making good' until you cough up what you owe me. You can't welsh on a million bucks—"

"All right, all right!" Alex said, holding up his hands. "Look, Dakota—seriously. I'm just the mouthpiece. I do not write the checks—"

"Latest installment is fifty thousand dollars," I said. "Due May 17."

"I know when it was due," Alex said. "I told them—"

"That was a three month extension," I said. "And a reduction by fifty percent—"

"Dakota," Alex said, "Dakota. The situation at the Foundation has changed since—"

"Alex, we already did this dance. The Foundation agreed to pay up. You *agreed*—"

—

"We did," Alex said. "We did! But we *can't*. The Foundation's going bankrupt."

23. Duct Tape and Baling Wire

Alex's words echoed in my mind—*The Valentine Foundation is going bankrupt*. My mouth fell open; Cinnamon's hands went to her mouth again. I stared at Alex for a long moment, trying to process it. Then everything clicked, and I put my hand to my forehead.

"Oh, Jesus, Alex, don't tell me that," I said. *Of course* the Foundation wasn't going to be able to pay—*I killed its founder*. God knows what that would do to it. Not to mention the half-dozen lawsuits they'd become embroiled in. "I know that you've had hard times—"

"Hard times?" Alex said, with a rough laugh. "The Foundation is going under—"

"How much do you make?" I barked. "What, a quarter million dollars a year?"

"The *show* needs a quarter million dollars by the end of the month *just to pay for the staff*," Alex said. "We quit paying me long before we decided to . . . to defer paying you. Hell, I've been deferring my own salary for three months just to keep the lights on—"

"Jesus," I said, because I believed him. How would I pay for Cinnamon's school now? I stole a glance at her. She looked terrified, and had seized her own tail. She'd been hurt when she realized my ulterior motive—but she was too smart not to connect the dots. "So . . . what now?"

"Well," Alex said. He looked back at the building, then raised his bare wrist, and looked at it. I thought it an odd gesture—and then I realized, *he is looking at the tattoo I inked to check the time.* I felt a sudden thrill—I rarely see my tattoos working on other people.

Alex caught my eye, and despite himself, grinned.

"Yeah, it still works," he said, smile quickly fading. "But nothing else around here does. The Foundation is a mess. We lost most of our endorsements, and we've been hit by half a dozen lawsuits. I've got to warn you, we're re-releasing all the old DVDs just to stay afloat—"

"I don't care if you have to sell the buildings, Alex, you owe me a million dollars. If re-releasing the DVDs will help you pay up, then good," I snapped. He scowled, and I asked, "Not good? Wait—you said warn me. Why? What's dangerous about new releases of old DVDs?"

"Special features," Alex said evasively. "They've cut a deal with one of our directors, and he's doing a whole reality TV thing here, collecting footage for the behind the scenes extras on the DVDs. This time of day, the 'Candid Camera' crew will still be roaming around."

"Oh, Jesus," I said. "Just keep Cinnamon out of it. She's not a show for your cameras."

"Agreed," Alex said quickly. "I'll take you through to the administrative offices—"

"*Thanks*, I guesses," Cinnamon grumbled, glaring at me sidelong. I motioned to Alex, who left to give us a moment, climbing the stairs as I knelt before Cinnamon. Before I could say anything soothing, Cinnamon hissed like a cat and said, "*You should've told me.*"

"Cinnamon, I didn't want you to be hurt—"

"Well color me—*eff*—hurt," she said. "It's red in your crayon box—"

"Now look, young lady," I said, pointing at her. "That's precisely the reaction you have that makes me not want to tell you things. We *are* out here for your award—but I can't fly all this way out here and not at least try to get these losers to cough up our money—"

"I knows, I knows," she said, turning her head aside again, then shaking it. "But . . . I gets so worried. I shouldn't get scared, but no one but you's ever given me a full run of nice. Now this. Mom, what are we gonna do if they don't pay us? Am—am I gonna have to—"

"You are *not,*" I said, "going to have to leave your school. We may lose the house. We may lose the car. But we're not going to lose your future. I may have to do double shifts at the tattoo parlor, or take out a loan, or I don't know. But your tuition is non-negotiable."

Cinnamon sniffed, looking away. Then she looked at me. "Like you and me."

"Like you and me," I said, giving her a big squeeze. "We're non-negotiable."

Cinnamon sighed and shuddered. "All right," she said, looking up at Alex, waiting by the big wooden doors of the Foundation. "Watch out, Mom, the giant Ken doll is up to something. Or he's hidin' something he thinks will hurt us—"

"Charming," I said, rising. "I got the same read. Well . . . shall we? Let's."

The Valentine Foundation blended hip research center, functioning television studio . . . and ratty small business that had seen better days. The lobby was all slate and cherry wood; a brushed-aluminum version of the Foundation's top-hat logo greeted visitors, hanging on a vertical grille of stone backed with a sheet of water lit from behind. Then a figure moved behind the rippling water—it was a window into a conference room, with privacy afforded by the bars of stone and water shimmering down the glass. Chic. Very '70s, but chic.

The vertical grille of stone mirrored the lined façade of the building, and beyond that resemblance, the architect's control over the use of his building disintegrated. Piled boxes were stacked on the receptionist's desk. To the left, signs and equipment indicating a CONFERENCE CENTER were piled up in front of a door now labeled NO GO IN THIS WAY; atop that door now was taped—and I mean, *duct taped*—a sign that said ON THE AIR. To the right, a door was propped open, and Alex took us down a hall lined with coffee-stained psychedelic-patterned carpet and into a breakroom stacked with boxes, where the director who had filmed the challenge was talking to (well, *at,* really) a cameraman adjusting settings on a video camera.

"Shit," Alex said, rubbing his neck. "Weren't we going to use the conference center—"

"Are you serious?" the cameraman asked, in an odd variant of a British accent, without ever taking his pale blue eyes off the settings of his camera; it was the same cameraman too. "Ron and Sunny are screen-testing *Jacob Dauntless* in there. Jacob bloody Dauntless—"

Alex twitched. "Well, Dakota," he said, "I guess we're shooting in here—"

"Just the candids—oh, Dakota Frost! Good to see you yet again," the director said. He was a fidgety, rail-thin African man with intensely dark skin and a wisp of a handshake. "Denis Ekundayo. I shot your follow-up interview."

"I remember," I said. "You two also shot the challenge, if I recall correctly—"

"You do indeed," the cameraman said, still focused on his camera. "David Lloyd-Presse."

"We *were* going to shoot in the conference center until Dauntless agreed to drop in," Ekundayo said, eyeing Cinnamon curiously, "but I thought while we went over the waivers and script, we might leave the camera running and shoot some candid shots—"

"Unfortunately, I have a few ground rules," I said. "First, no cameras."

"What did she say?" Lloyd-Presse asked, turning his head slightly.

"I said, no cameras. My daughter is with me, and she is *not* to be filmed."

"Now wait a moment," Ekundayo said. "How—if we can't film you—"

"Of course I'm here to shoot the trailers," I said, "but appearing on a *reality show* is not in my contract. Even if it was, Cinnamon is not a sideshow. So for now, no candid cameras."

"But it was in my contract," Ekundayo said. "Alex, we agreed. We talked about this—"

"Not to me," I said.

"Relax, both of you," Alex said. "I'm calling Erica. This is her mess, she can explain it. As for Cinnamon, she wasn't involved in the challenge," Alex said. He muttered something sharp into his phone, then put his hand over the receiver. "She should wait in the lobby—"

"She-stays-with-me," I said flatly. "And that means, *no cameras*."

"We sticks together," Cinnamon said. She grinned. "It's non-negotiable."

"David," Ekundayo said, shaking his head. "Turn it off."

"But—" the cameraman said.

"Let it go," Ekundayo said. "She'd have to sign the waiver for her daughter anyway."

"Speaking of, and second," I said, "I'm not signing any new waivers."

"Dakota," Alex began.

"Alex, we're in a dispute," I said, glaring at him. "We've got each other's lawyers on speed dial. You've known I was coming out here forever. You had *six weeks* to send me any forms I needed to sign. I don't sign anything without my lawyers looking at it."

"We don't film anyone without a waiver," Ekundayo said.

"Speak for yourself," Lloyd-Presse said.

"I'll get the original waivers," Alex said, raising his cell phone again. "Erica, bring counsel, and have them pull her whole file. You and me, Denis, watched her sign the waivers together. I promise we've kept everything in order."

"Not for the reality show—"

"I'm not part of the reality show," I said. "You know what? Maybe I would be part of a reality show if it would help the Foundation, even if it had nothing to do with helping you pay up. But not if it's sprung on me like a trap after I flew twenty-five hundred miles."

"And shouldn't it be like a whole 'nother contract or something?" Cinnamon said. "I means, bein' in front of the cameras, it seems natural, but isn't it like workin'?"

"She's right," Alex said. "They're both right, Denis."

Ekundayo wavered, then nodded.

"Dakota, you said a few ground rules," Alex said. "We just heard two. What's three?"

"Oh, that. No script, not when it counts," I said. "Sure, I'll say 'this is the Valentine Challenge' or whatever. But when it comes to my work—I say what I say. You tell me what we're talking about, and ask the questions, but I do not read from a script."

"Look," Ekundayo said. "This is *television*. That is how it works—"

"No, this is how it works," I said. "Jesus may be my God, but my copilot is the truth. I'm a practicing tattoo artist, but I was trained as scientist. Our mission is to accurately represent the world. I take responsibility for *everything* I say, and I will *not* read someone else's words."

Ekundayo let out his breath, long and slow. "OK," he said.

"Feeling your balls effectively busted?" I asked.

He didn't look me in the eye. "You might say that."

"Well, don't worry," I said, giving him a half-smile. "The worst is over."

He shook his head. "Oh, no, it isn't," he said. "You are going to hate this."

A dapper, slender man with a shaggy bowl haircut and a slim briefcase stepped into the room—Felix Meyer, the Foundation's lawyer. His eyes immediately found me, then looked away. We'd grown tired of seeing each other after my long dispute with the Foundation.

Following Felix was an equally slender woman with a dark black ponytail that poured forward over her shoulder like black oil—Erica Browning, chairwoman of the Foundation. We had barely met, but her eyes immediately zeroed in on me and glared. I glared right back.

"Counselor Meyer," I said. "Miss Browning."

"Ms. Frost," Felix Meyer responded, snapping open his briefcase.

"Mr. Ekundayo," Browning said, "I thought Felix already gave you the waivers—"

"I think we're all here to talk about the other bit," Ekundayo said.

"Oh, hell," Browning said, glaring at me, then glancing at Meyer.

"Well," Meyer said, after the briefest pause, "My office is preparing a, a statement—"

"She knows," Alex said. "About the bankruptcy, at least—"

"Damn it, Alex," Browning said. "You can't go airing our dirty laundry—"

"You know, Miss Browning," I said, leaning back in my chair, "when I settled with you earlier this year, it was contingent on you delivering. You welshing on your payments is no different than me welshing on my part of the agreement—"

"Which is what, not suing us?" Browning said. "You put us over a barrel, Ms. Frost. We cut you an advance from your winnings so you could make a down payment on a house. We paid for your legal fees when we should have been suing you for killing *our founder*—"

"Who was a murderous schmuck, but anyway," I said. "You know what, I had forgotten that check, and I've never said thank you. Well, thank you, Miss Browning. You helped me get a nice house—but you agreed to pay the rest on a schedule, and you haven't paid up."

Browning frowned. "Ms. Frost, Alex is right. The Foundation is almost bankrupt. We've been sued. We've lost donors. Valentine himself helped bring in a lot of income in speaking fees. The only thing keeping us going is—"

"I don't care," I said. "Or, you know what, I do care. I don't want to put you guys out of business. I admire the job you're doing of skeptical education. But I lost two teeth and nearly my life in the games Valentine pulled on me, and I still beat him fair and square. *I want my money.*"

Browning shifted uncomfortably. "Well, that brings us back to the show."

I glowered at her. Then, I got it.

"Aha," I said. "That explains all the stalling on my check. You had to re-sell the rights to the show, and are waiting for your next payment from the network—"

"Almost right," Ekundayo said, "but it isn't that simple."

I stared at him. He had an interesting accent. I liked listening to him talk. I had a feeling I wasn't going to like what he had to say.

"*The Exposers,*" Ekundayo said, "was on its *seventh season*. That's ancient in network years—close to two hundred episodes, which are self-contained and interesting and have a lot of replay value. Seven seasons is all a network really needs to syndicate them—"

"And after Valentine was killed," I said, "*The Exposers* got canceled."

"No, even before that, it was nearly canceled," Alex said. "Valentine fought for it, tooth and nail, me too. We lobbied the network hard, brought Denis back on board, had all these specials planned—but then you exposed him for what he really was, and, um—"

An uncomfortable silence spread across the table.

"Anyway," Alex said, "ghoulish as it sounds, all the terrible publicity after his killing makes for great TV. So we've got a hook for the network—but no headliner. By myself, I'm not big enough. We're bringing back Jacob Dauntless, but even he isn't big enough—"

"But *I*," Ekundayo said, "found the angle which finally clinched it."

He smiled grimly, and a growing sense of horror filled me.

"Oh, hell," I said. "What did you do? Spill it."

—

"To sell season eight," Ekundayo said, "we listed *you* as a presenter in our roster."

24. I Said, No Cameras

"Say *what?*" I exploded. Somewhere in the back of my mind was outrage about being asked to profit on all that pain, but all that popped out was, "You owe me a *million dollars*, and want me to *work for it* as your *trained monkey* on TV?"

"Fuck," Cinnamon said.

David Lloyd-Presse's eyes gleamed, and I suddenly saw, concealed under his hand, the red camera light that meant he had been recording this whole conversation.

"Damn it, I said *no cameras*," I snapped, clenching my fist and twirling my hand to uncoil my vines—then snapping them out to hit the OFF button on the camera. The cameraman cursed, jumped back . . . and then lifted the camera with both hands like it was a baby.

"Oh my God," Lloyd-Presse said, looking alternately at the camera, then at the glowing vine retracting into my hand. "Oh my God," he said, hitting REWIND, then PLAY. "Tell me I got that. *Tell me I got that*—"

"Maybe you got it, but you're not going to use it," I snarled, rising.

Lloyd-Presse cradled the camera protectively. "You don't understand. That was an awesome shot, exactly what we need for the promos—"

"I *said*," my voice rising to a shout, "my *daughter* is *not* a *sideshow*—"

"Mom," Cinnamon said, very quietly. "It's OK. Let it go."

She stared up at me, her lower lip set.

I pursed my lips. Then I nodded.

"All of you, get out," I said. "Everyone with a camera. Everyone with a briefcase, or with a bad attitude, or with the bad fucking idea of putting foul-mouthed foul-tempered foul-everything *me* on network fucking TV. I need to talk to Alex."

"Remember," Browning said quickly, "Alex is not authorized to negotiate—"

"No, *you* remember, very clearly, that I signed no fucking waiver that would authorize you to use that footage," I barked. "None at all. And if I find another hidden camera, hidden microphone, or so much as a *court sketch artist* hiding behind a potted plant—"

"Miss Frost—"

"Out! Everybody but Alex out!" I barked, cracking my neck, letting mana run down my skin, making my tattoos glow. I felt the Dragon shift and twist on my back, raring for release. *Let me at them!* But I just shook my head and snapped. "Out! Right the fuck now!"

Browning backed up, backed out the door. Meyer stood as well, wincing, but, oddly, smiling. He and Ekundayo took Lloyd-Presse's arms and gently led him from the room as he muttered, "But don't you see that? I have to get that. We need to film that—"

The door closed behind them, leaving Cinnamon and me alone with Alex.

"Tell me," I growled, "there are no hidden cameras in here."

"No," Alex said. "I'm surprised you let them leave with the film—"

"I was already committing assault. I wasn't upping it to robbery. Alex! Talk!"

Alex rubbed his forehead. "First, do you see why I made *them* tell you?"

"No!" I snapped. Then the ridiculousness of that set in. "Scratch that—yes."

"You're pretty scary," Alex said, "and not only did I not want to tell you . . . I really wanted to see the look on Browning's face when you blew up."

My mouth dropped. "I missed it."

"Priceless," Cinnamon said. "Very most sincerely gobstopped."

"Anyway," Alex said. "Look, this is a huge mess. In case it isn't already clear to you, I do not run the show here. But when it was clear the Foundation was in trouble, I had some ideas, I talked, they listened—and I take full responsibility for the mess that we've gotten you into."

I stared at him. My eyes narrowed. "You take full responsibility . . . meaning, you approve of what Dennis did? Meaning you *approved* the idea? Alex. Alex! Whatever gave you the idea that I'd let you turn me into your trained monkey?"

"Well," Alex said, "the families of the victims are suing the Valentine estate—"

"I know," I snapped. "I was almost party to the suit. I hear they're settling—"

"Yes, I am," Alex said. At my blank look, he clarified, "I wasn't just Valentine's protégé. I'm also his heir, and the executor of the estate. After I found out what he'd done . . . *of course* I settled. It was the only decent thing to do. I'm even trying to set up a fund for the victims—"

"That," I began, then stopped. Alex was Valentine's heir, and it was technically *his* money that he'd given away. And as posh as Valentine's private little empire here was, that had to be a *lot*. "That . . . that's the decent thing to do. Thank you, Alex."

"Oh, don't thank me," Alex said bitterly, "because that's how I screwed you—"

"Alex," I said. "What did you do?"

"Valentine treated the Foundation like his private bank," Alex said. "Leeching off it, then feeding his own money back into it—oh, that's not fair. His salary on *The Exposers* was outrageous, I admit, but he was also the executive producer of the show—"

"Meaning he coughed up the seed money for each new season," I said slowly. "Like Lucas bankrolling the later *Star Wars* films, which gave him total creative control. But you gave that money to the victims. Leaving none for the show. And leaving none for me."

"Dakota," Alex said, "I'm sorry. You were—you were alive. So was Cinnamon. And I never expected that setting up the fund would leave the Foundation in the lurch, much less you—but there were so many lawsuits. So many. I had to do something to settle them."

"No," I said. "No. That's right. How—how many were there? Victims, that is—"

"Seventeen," Alex said. "That we know of. And that's not counting the ones with his control charms, or that woman who was half skinned alive—"

"Oh, Jesus," I said, sitting down. "Oh, Jesus."

"So I started signing settlements, trying to do good," Alex said, "but found out I'd very nearly signed myself out of a job. The Foundation had to mortgage its buildings to keep paying the employees. So . . . we negotiated with the network to do a special on his challenges—"

"Oh, you son of a bitch," I said. "You son of a bitch! I knew I owed you footage, but here I was thinking you'd do a respectful ten-minute segment on the attack, and you're planning, what, an hour-long spot 'on his challenges.' The only challenge he took last year was *me!*"

"The only person to have beaten him," Alex said. "It would be great TV."

"Christ, Alex!" I said. "What kind of man are you? This is the most gauche, ghoulish—"

"Pull out your thesaurus and throw every name in it at me," Alex said, "but at the end of the day, I'm a stage magician. More importantly, a *television* stage magician. Keeping this show alive is my actual job, as important to me as . . . as your tattoo shop is to you."

I folded my arms and looked away.

"Now, it may seem ghoulish or gauche or whatever, but *this will be great TV*. If I'd told you before you walked in that room, that moment was lost. We need your honesty to make great TV. From that, we can make some money and do a lot of good to help the victims—"

"*I'm* a victim," I said.

"So was I," Alex said. "I almost got killed trying to save you and Cinnamon—because Valentine practically led me to you with a dotted line. Remember, I had your working magic tattoo on me. I was living proof that you'd beat his challenge. He was going to murder me—"

"I remember," I said, staring at him, arms folded. "The old fuck bragged about it."

"Jesus," Alex said. "But . . . working with that psycho made me a lot of money. So, the way I see it, we're both people who stand to profit from a murderer's illicit gains. I've given mine back to those who need it. Frankly, I didn't expect you would—"

"Don't you dare," I said, blood boiling. "Don't you *dare* turn this back on *me*—"

"Given the circumstances," Alex said, raising his hands, "I completely understand, even though I personally don't approve of using Christopher Valentine's money to do anything but set this right. Hell, I'd dissolve the Foundation if I could. Tell me what good that would do."

"It might make me feel better," I said, "but that's a *terrible* reason."

"I agree, on both counts, but . . . *I don't want to use any of his damn blood money,*" Alex said, glaring at me. "And you shouldn't either. We should wash our hands of that fucker and make our way on our own. For you, that's tattooing, but for me, that's television. Now, you may think it ghoulish, but we've got a chance to turn this tragedy into a real success. We'll be able to pay you, *honestly*, without blood money, and keep the Foundation afloat for the legitimate good it does—scholarships and education. We have a chance to make things *right*."

"Fuck that," I said. "Fuck *you*. But . . . but . . . all right. Tell me what I've got to do."

"I would like you to participate in the special," he said—and drew a breath. "And . . . to participate in the show. Five tapings. No further commitment. In exchange, the network will pay you one million dollars, if you're willing to write off the debts of the Valentine Foundation—"

"That's *bullshit*," I barked. "You really want to make it right? Make it *two* million."

Alex's mouth fell open. Cinnamon's did too.

"Fuck," Cinnamon said at last. "That's ballsy, Mom—"

"It's crazy," Alex said, voice slightly high pitched. "There's no way we can—"

"*Quit dicking around, Alex,*" I snapped. "I am *not* stupid. I'm not fooled by misdirection. The network *doesn't care* about your conscience—it's paying a million dollars for me to appear *in the show*, not for winning the Challenge, and the Foundation gets off scot-free—"

"Damn it, Dakota," Alex said, jerking away from me. "Yes, you're right. The *network* agreed to pay you a million dollars, and . . . I hoped to get the Foundation off the hook on what it owes. But if you're that fucking mercenary—fine. We'll make your cut *two* million. Happy?"

I stared at him. I hadn't expected him to say yes. This was insane.

The Valentine affair was a horrific mess. I'd tried to put the pain behind me, but Alex was dredging it up again. I'd been trying to build walls around the avarice spawned by the prize money, and now Alex casually rolled up to my gates with a two million dollar battering ram.

Three words occurred to me: quid pro quo. I didn't need two million dollars; hell, I didn't need *one* million. God only knew when I'd see any of it; Alex was King of the Welsh. What I *really* needed was a second source of info about fireweaving—and Alex was my best shot.

"All right," I said. "I'll do it, for two million, though I'll believe that when I see it. But even though you just put Cinnamon through college, I'll have you know I'm not doing it for the money. I have another price in mind—a price from you, *personally*. Call it my quid pro quo."

"All right," he said, resigned. "Hit me."

—৵

"You teach me fire magic," I said. "*Everything*. Top . . . to bottom."

25. Dungeons and Dancing

When Cinnamon and I left the Valentine Foundation three hours later, I at last felt free. Not because we'd negotiated a better future—that would take some lawyering to finalize—or even because I'd shot all the trailer shots they needed.

No, it was because our *schedule* was finally free.

Our stay in the Bay Area was bookended by unpleasantries—wizards and vampires on Tuesday, and another meet with the Wizarding Guild Friday. But today was Wednesday, and we were free to enjoy ourselves until Cinnamon's award ceremony at Stanford Thursday evening.

Personally, I wanted to go visit the Taido dojo at Stanford—unless I wanted to hop on a plane to Japan, there were so few places I could practice Taido that I wanted to sample all of them—but that wasn't fair to my daughter, who'd never before seen all the sights of San Francisco.

So we took a brief driving tour, mostly to see the twin orange monoliths of the Golden Gate Bridge, then rejoined our vampire friends just as they were rousing themselves. Nyissa was the first up, chatting with Jewel, who had spent the day touring San Francisco incognito.

"Hi," I said, flopping into a chair next to strawberry-blond Jewel and violet-dyed Nyissa, who looked at me, a little shocked, as if they'd just been talking about me. I felt my ears—were they burning? "I just sold my soul for two million dollars. How was your day?"

"Good as can be expected," Jewel said. "You look happy, Cinnamon."

Cinnamon flopped down next to me, grinning, as she'd been doing since I'd shook Alex down and he'd unexpectedly folded. "Mom's gonna . . ." she began, and from the drive over, I guessed she'd say, *Mom's gonna learn fire magic*, which interested Cinnamon *far* more than two million dollars. But Jewel had refused to teach me, and didn't need to know, so I shook my head. Cinnamon caught my glance and said, "Mom's just . . . cool. She took me to the Golden Gate—"

"I was there too," Jewel said, smiling as she pulled out her phone. "Must have just missed you—ah. Molokii's texted; he says he's coming by later. Mind if he joins us for dinner? No. Good. Afterward, I was wondering, 'cool Mom,' if you'd be interested in going—"

"Excuse me," Vickman said, grumpy and haggard. I gathered he'd been up all day and night guarding the vampires on almost no sleep. "The Warlock called. He 'requests' we join him for dinner, privately, with the 'Commissioner.' It sounds innocuous, but also required."

"Well," Jewel said halfheartedly, "have fun—"

"Required of all of us," Vickman said, "*including* you and your friend."

"You mean . . . me?" Jewel said, hand going to her breast. "Oh, crap!"

"Ah, hell," I said. "So much for a relaxing evening."

•

THE COMMISSIONER'S favorite restaurant was a charming little Italian joint in a flatiron building in San Francisco's Italian district, an area called North Beach—though, like Cathedral Hill's missing cathedral, there was no beach in sight. We were ushered up to a private dining room in the building's narrow prow, and found the Commissioner waiting at the far end of a long table, silhouetted by the lights of Columbus Street rising behind him.

Uneasily, we joined the Commissioner, seating ourselves while he stood. The man was dark-haired, solid, and broad enough that if someone fired a missile through the glass, he could have simply stood and shielded us with the bulk of his black pinstriped business suit. There was something off about him, like he was a throwback to an earlier time, and when he spoke, I got a strange tingle of magical resonance . . . both feelings I'd gotten from the Warlock.

"I have asked," the Commissioner said, "the kitchen to spare us the garlic."

Beside me, I felt Saffron twitch. "Thank you, Commissioner," she said.

The vampires sat in polite silence, their guards standing behind them. I'd given up asking them to eat with us. Jewel and Molokii sat on the side of the table to the Commissioner's right; Cinnamon and I sat on the left, and the Warlock took the opposite end of the table.

"So, Ms. Frost," the Commissioner said gruffly, cutting open a roll, then buttering it with long, slow, methodical strokes that implied patience more than indulgence. "I understand we have you to thank for thwarting that little business in Union Square last night."

"Yes," I said, trying a grin. "All part of the service."

The Commissioner looked up at me, blue eyes glinting from behind horn-rimmed glasses. "Of course it is," he said, eyes turning toward Jewel. "And I understand that this is the young lady who was the apparent target of the attack?"

Jewel swallowed, and I nodded on her behalf.

"Apparently," I said. "The precise nature of the attack, its intent and ultimate goal, is yet to be determined. However . . . it certainly *looked* as if she was the target of the attack."

"You understand things are not always as they seem," the Commissioner said. He took a bite of his roll. While he chewed, no one spoke; not even the Warlock. "But things are usually just as they seem. Why might someone take offense to you, young lady? What do you do?"

"I—I'm a firespinner," Jewel said, uncomfortably. "A performance artist specializing in fire magic. Fire magic can be dangerous unless handled properly, and my Order is somewhat secretive. Apparently some fire magicians . . . object to my public performances."

"Understandably so," the Commissioner said, "though I doubt it is for the same public safety reasons that might concern my office. But it does seem a bit much, do you not think? Can you think of no other reason someone might want to hurt you?"

"I'm . . . a Hawai`ian political activist," Jewel said, even more uncomfortably. "I know people who object to that as well, but . . . I've never gotten so much as a death threat in Hawai`i. I can't imagine that my political opponents would travel to attack me here."

"Neither can I," the Commissioner said. "Still . . . I am a bit disturbed to find both your names on two police reports in two days, Jewel Anne Grasslin and Dakota Caroline Frost."

"You aren't the only one," Jewel said, swallowing again. Her delicate hands were not visible; her arms were held straight at her sides, as if she was sitting on her hands.

The Commissioner stared at her. "What is your relationship?"

Jewel and I stared at him blankly, then at each other.

"We . . . met on the plane," I said.

"I gave her a card to my performance in Oakland," Jewel said. "Then, after she saved me that time, I told her about the performance in . . . in Union Square."

"An illicit performance of magic," the Commissioner grumbled. "Well. From the reports, even though the later unpleasantness eclipsed it, it was spectacular. Like a fountain of liquid fire. Too bad I did not see it." His eyes glinted at her. "Do you plan other performances while here?"

"*No,*" Jewel said. "We, uh, canceled our schedule after the second attack."

"Good," the Commissioner said. "Let this blow over, and then we would be glad to have you back in San Francisco. With the appropriate permits, of course. You *can* get permits for fire performance in Union Square, you know. There is no need for you to break the law."

"Yes, sir," Jewel said.

"As for you, Dakota Frost," the Commissioner said, picking up another roll slowly, "are *you* planning any demonstrations of magic?" His eyes scanned my tattoos. "Your clan inks are as vibrant as I have been told, but inking tattoos of *any* kind in California requires a license."

"I know," I said. "Magical tattooing requires an elaborate setup. I don't travel with it. Nor would I trust someone else's setup—I make my own needles, and prefer my clan's own inks. I . . . *am* supposed to give a talk in San Jose on Friday, though, on magical tattoo safety—"

The Commissioner waved his hand dismissively. "No license needed for that," he said, "and safety is something I hope more people would consider when attempting these dangerous manipulations. Back to the matter at hand. I understand you are assisting the police."

"Yes," I said. "In my experience, three incidents of misuse of magic in just two days is an extremely bad sign. I've offered my expertise to the police—"

"Three?" the Commissioner said sharply.

"Oh, hell," I said, and explained the magical mark we'd seen at Liquid before the battle of Union Square. "I assumed the bar staff would have reported that. I assumed wrong."

"Stop assuming," the Commissioner said, leaning back in his chair. "Pass on all the information you have to the police. Cooperate to the fullest, but back off if they tell you to—you understand the complications involved with having a magician on the scene of a crime."

"I do. Fortunately, no one has died—yet," I said. "That makes things easier."

"Yes, yes it does," the Commissioner said, eyes looking up past me. "Let's try to keep it that way. And now, I believe the first course is arriving. Let us put this awful business behind us for the moment, and enjoy the simple pleasure of sharing good food in good company."

And then, surprisingly, we did enjoy a good meal in good company. The Commissioner relaxed once food arrived, and successfully steered the conversation away to safer topics. He and Cinnamon hit it off well, and Jewel and I watched with amusement his twinkle-eyed attempts to follow her explanation of just exactly what "the twisty snake function," was, why its zeroes were so important, and how she had gotten into higher mathematics in the first place.

"Quite the bright flame," Jewel murmured to me.

"Whispering won't help you," I said, trying to ape that wry smile of hers that I loved so much. "She's a werekin. She can hear you anywhere in the restaurant."

Jewel smiled. "It's OK if she hears it," she said. "It's just stating the obvious."

"What about your friend?" I asked, nodding at Molokii. He was ignoring the rest of us completely, deep in conversation with Nyissa via American Sign Language (and sneaking glances at her deep décolletage whenever he could). "Shouldn't you be translating for him?"

"Molokii?" she asked, elbowing him. He looked, and she flicked her hands. *«You OK?»*

Molokii smiled, tilting his head at Nyissa; then he made a curious gesture, thumbing his chin with his right hand, then letting both hands out, wriggling his fingers, blowing as if on a flame—and then gestured at me and Jewel, again with a knowing smile.

My mouth fell open. I couldn't have read that right—either he'd called me a mother of a dragon, or told us to set a bed on fire. But my ASL is rusty, and before I could "speak," Jewel had already had a whole mini-conversation with Molokii and turned back to me with a half smile.

"He says he's all right, and told us to 'go have fun,' " Jewel said, rolling her eyes—and while I don't think that's *quite* what he suggested we do, I'd take it. "Sad as it is, I think he's used to being left out—and I think he's digging having Nyissa to stare at. I mean talk to."

"She is good for that," I said. I was still a little miffed that Jewel and Molokii felt like they could have private conversations right in front of me in sign language, but I didn't press the issue—if they didn't want to share, it wasn't my business. "No doubt about it."

"Soooo. . . ," Jewel said. "Having fun . . . what are your plans for this evening?"

"Stay out of trouble, have a good time, and get a good night's sleep," I said, smiling again. "Why do I have the feeling that you can help with only one of those?"

"You know me too well," Jewel said, with a wicked grin. "Care to go dancing?"

Jewel called up a couple of friends and took us to Bondage a Go Go, a BDSM-themed dance night playing every Wednesday in the SOMA district at a sprawling, multi-level affair called the Cat Club. Bondage a Go Go was *extremely* long running: the Lady Saffron and I had visited ten years ago, back when she was still called Savannah.

Something *else* that was extremely long running was the music. Everything gets periodically recycled in the club scene, and the very same track—*Spank My Booty* by Lords of Acid—was playing when we walked through the door, though then it was "New Beat" and now it was "Old News." Fortunately, the music quickly began to fast forward through the ages.

I noticed other changes—as before, smokers were corralled outside, but now, inside, the ban was actually enforced. Club kids mixed in with the Goths and punks, and even a small contingent of tourists. But the soul of the place was the same—a cavalcade of fetish fashionistas strolling over balconies and catwalks surrounding a cavernous dance floor powered by thumping music.

Like a child in a playground, Saffron laughed and pulled Darkrose onto the dance floor; Nyissa followed, then a lesbian couple Jewel invited joined them and they all began bouncing to the music. Vickman and Schultze hung back, watching; Jewel and I broke off, wandering.

I missed having Jinx here, but I was glad she and Doug had decided to stay in and watch over Cinnamon. My little monster had sulked when I told her they carded at the Cat Club—and that if she produced a fake ID, I'd confiscate it—but had perked up at the idea of math games with my brainiac friends. Unexpectedly, Molokii had decided to hang back and join them.

"You sure Molokii is going to be all right?" I shouted, as we climbed a tight curvy stair toward the second level. I'd felt bad about ditching our friends for a girl's night out, but the four of them seemed happy with the arrangement. "Seems like he'd enjoy all the thumping music—"

Jewel glanced back at me, a bit sad. "Too much confusion," she yelled. "Even when he can feel the beat, everyone else is dancing to rhythms he can't hear—"

"Or yelling to each other in the dark," I said, a notch more quietly as we turned the corner and stepped out into the quieter, warren-like upper level. "Jinx feels the same way. She's not a big dancer, but she used to love people-watching. Now she says it's like—"

"Like pouring salt on a wound," Jewel said, toning her voice down too.

"Yes," I said, not precisely smiling, but gratified as she got it. "Her words exactly."

If this was the same place, it was more crowded than I remembered, but it had the same energy that had drawn Savannah and me so many years ago. I got a charge out of watching the costumes, seeing the gear, spotting the occasional handcuff or collar or leash—though ten years ago, bondage and discipline had been the exciting new thing Savannah and I were discovering, and now it was a nostalgic reminder of . . . if not a happier time, at least a different one.

Repeated slaps—the noise of whipping—could be heard in an unseen room, and the hall was partially blocked by a standing couple—a dazed but happy man in the arms of a dommish woman, who tousled his hair and whispered in his ear in what was almost certainly aftercare.

With barely suppressed grins, Jewel and I stepped around them on either side. That took us on opposite sides of a larger area where a crowd was gathered around a man who was rigging a woman up a rope sling, using knots similar to those in Jewel's bikini. For a brief moment, we could see each other passing on either side of the show, and Jewel's eyes must have caught mine noticing the knots—because when I glanced back down at her, her eyes were gleaming.

We rejoined on the other side of the crowd and walked through a seating area where people were actually dining. *They have a kitchen now?* The Cat Club had expanded since I'd seen it, or maybe I'd been too into dancing with Savannah to notice all that it had to offer.

"So," Jewel said, still trying to suppress that smile, "you're into bondage."

"Whatever gave you that idea?" I said with a smile. "Leather coat, leather chaps—"

"Steel collar," she responded. She winced slightly, chewing over something that seemed like a delicate subject. "If I may ask . . . whose submissive are you? Darkrose's?"

I laughed. "I'm no one's sub," I said. "I was Sav—the Lady Saffron's once, long ago, and I think that gave her the idea to use a collar for the sign of her house. But it's not a sub collar. It's the sign of her protection—a big red neon 'fangs off' to other vampires."

"Ah," Jewel said, half smiling, but falling back into that wince. "And Saffron's a switch, then. So . . . you're not technically a sub, but . . . her human servant, then?"

"Most vampires think that because I'm her 'troubleshooter'," I said, "but, technically, no. I'm not a blood donor, bound by a psychic link or even a part of her 'household.' "

"And Nyissa?" Jewel said. "She sticks to you like glue. Is she *your* sub?"

"What? No!" I said. "That's ridiculous. She's a full-time vampire dominatrix."

"Is she now?" Jewel smirked. "Most interesting. Not her sub either, I take it?"

"We—are—just—friends," I said. "She kidnapped me once, then saved my life."

"Sounds . . . complicated," Jewel said. "I don't mean to be so particular, Dakota, but . . . vampires scare me. I just wanted to be completely sure that—oh, hell, that you were—"

"Completely free, Jewel Grace."

Jewel stared up at me, swallowing. "You know, Dakota," she said, eyes wide, hopeful. "You have a lot of power. You should use it."

I stared at her a long time. Then I smiled. She smiled back. I leaned toward her. Then we kissed, first briefly, then passionately. Her lips were sweet, and I could smell the patchouli on her skin, feel something almost damp in the heavy curls of her hair.

I leaned back, cradling her cheek in my hand. "Well, hello, Jewel Grace."

"Hello, Dakota Frost," she said, head shifting aside so she could kiss my palm.

"You are really sweet," I said, relishing the taste of her lipstick against my lips. Even my Dragon stirred against my skin. *I really like the taste of her lips.* "And I really like you. But I have to take it slow. I've been burned too much, lately."

"Burned, she says, to a fireweaver," Jewel said, with a sudden grin.

"*Badump-tish,*" I responded. "Totally unintentional."

"S'okay," she said. "That one kiss is enough of a start."

A couple at one of the tables was grinning at us, so we finished our circuit of the upstairs, coming out on a balcony almost exactly opposite the stairs we had just climbed. Briefly, I caught a glimpse of Nyissa, prowling on the far balcony, her eye catching mine as she descended. She'd been keeping tabs on us, at a discreet distance. Huh. My bodyguard wanted to make sure we were safe—without interfering. How sweet of her—and I'd thought she'd been jealous.

Jewel and I leaned against the railing overlooking the dance floor and looked down on the world of Goths, punks, bondagiers, and club kids milling about to the music. A staff member was bringing out a ladder, and a shapely young model was bopping next to it, preparing to climb up and do her go-go thing in a previously unused hanging cage that I'd thought was decoration.

"Hey, my friends are here," Jewel shouted over the music, waving to a group on the dance floor—and the small knot of dancers waved back. "You know, we've so been looking forward to coming back here," Jewel cried. "Ready to hit the dance floor?"

"Coming *back*?" I shouted back. "This is a *planned* thing? People know you're here?"

"Yeah," she cried back. "Bondage a Go Go only runs on Wednesdays. The Fireweavers come here *every* time we visit San Francisco, a girl's night out, sometimes with a light-balls performance thrown in, but we had to cancel that after—"

"Oh, God damn it," I said, shoving myself back from the rail. "We're going!"

"What?" Jewel said, as I turned to the stairs. "But, Dakota—"

"When I said cancel everything, I meant cancel *everything,*" I cried, stomping down the stairs, whipping my hand round in a "let's go" motion. "A performance at a club *every* time you visit San Francisco is as big a frickin' bulls-eye as flyers for a performance in Union Square—"

And then, cutting even over the music, the screaming started.

We gathered, forming up, Vickman and I taking point, Jewel and her two lesbian invitees in the center, and the vampires in a triangle around them. Vickman and I pushed through the crowd, past Jewel's newly arrived friends, standing there in shock.

Out by the bar, the screaming and commotion was louder, but it wasn't the terrified, panicked screaming that I expected, accompanied by a strong flow back from the doors. It was a more shocked-relieved-oh-look-at-that screaming . . . and the milling of curious gawkers.

We pushed through the crowd and stepped into the street. Outside, the smokers and the curious were stopped and staring; but as whatever shocking event had died down, people began to disperse, backing away in fear from what they did not understand. And then we could see:

From curb to curb across the street burned a dragon, ringed with symbols written in fire.

26. The Drake Cage

After that, the idea of leaving Jewel to her own devices was over. When the police were done questioning us, we hightailed it back to our fortress on Cathedral Hill. Vickman sorted out a new arrangement with the hotel—the entire block of rooms down a dead-end corridor with a fire escape at the end. Vickman opened up all the interior doors and pulled out chairs and sofas to soft block the L join of the hall, making our wing into an impromptu fort.

Molokii joined us, staying with Jewel and Nyissa, and the rest of us mortals stacked in rooms on either side as the vampires prowled about. As everyone else was settling in, I buttonholed Vickman by the ice machine for a conference.

"Jewel and Molokii have changed their flight to Hawaii to midnight tomorrow," I said. "We keep her with us, and safe, until we put her on the plane. At that point, I hate to say it, she's on her own. We don't have the manpower to start protecting people all over the globe."

"We don't have the manpower to protect the people in this *hall*," Vickman said.

"Yeah," I said. Vickman used to have a dozen men. Most of those were dead now, at the hands of Scara, the enforcer of the Vampire Gentry in Atlanta—another reminder I needed all the allies I could get. "But, damn it, Vick, I'm *trying*. I didn't ask for this. But I still got it."

Jewel padded up, in fuzzy flannel pajamas, fuzzy slippers, and holding . . . well, I supposed the thing in her arms was supposed to be a dragon, but whatever animal the shapeless thing had started its life as was no longer clear. "What?" she asked, reddening.

"I didn't say anything, fireweaver," I said, smirking.

She started to retort, then just looked at me. "I love your smile," she said, and then bit her lip, glancing over my shoulder at Vickman. "Hey, look, it's been a long day and I'm—I'm turning in. I just wanted to say good-night."

I walked Jewel back to her room. "I'm glad you're safe," I said.

"*I'm* glad you're keeping me safe," she replied, clutching the dragon.

"We'll do our best," I said, "but . . . when you get back to Hawaii . . ."

"I'm going to lie low," she said. "Let this blow over, reconsider my approach—"

"OK . . . but don't let the bad guys win," I said. "This country was founded on the strategic withdrawal, but don't let them intimidate you into giving up—"

"That's easy for you to say," Jewel said. "You're guarded by vampires and weretigers and your skin is a living weapon. All I've got are some spinny sticks that become useless at the first tangle, and known and unknown enemies that know just how to tangle them."

"Well, think of it this way," I said gently. "Fireweavers are good at tangling up those around them." Then I leaned down and kissed her forehead. "Good-night, Jewel."

She stared at me, eyes wide. She bit her lip. But before she could nerve herself to kiss me back, she whirled and ran back into the room. "Good-night," she said, closing the door.

"Ah, hell," I said, walking back to Vickman. "Here I was, trying not to let things move too fast, and now *I'm* the one coming on too strong."

"Eh," he said. "She's cute, and you're scary."

I glared at him. He raised an eyebrow. I gave up and retreated to my room, where, despite what I'd told Jewel about a good night's sleep, I ended up staying up the next two hours reading puzzles to Cinnamon out of the codes-and-ciphers book she'd picked up at Berkeley.

Between puzzles, we talked about the code.

The messages were encoded by magic, mathematics rewriting reality, so in theory, the code could be anything. Cinnamon, a talented graffiti artist herself, boasted that she could create the magical equivalent of the Enigma machine, creating a code that was essentially uncrackable.

But in practice, this wasn't the complex, layered graphomantic circuits of graffiti magic, or even the simpler single-layer patterns of tattoo magic; this was *fire* magic—elaborate physical movements, yes, but tracing out a comparatively simple magical shape. Cinnamon even claimed the "seven hundred and twenty basic weaves" were probably just all the ways you could combine six basic elements, what she called "six factorial." As Jewel's tattoo-activating performance at the Crucible showed, the real subtlety in fire magic lay in its caster's *intentions*.

So unless the caster could hold giant tables of letters in their head and think of what they wanted to say at the same time, that ruled out substitution ciphers. More likely, the spell relied on some very simple rule to jumble the letters, so, other than the weird symbols, the message had to be hidden in plain sight, like a cryptoquote—what Cinnamon called a transposition cipher.

Too bad I lost count of how many trillions upon trillions of them she said there were.

At dawn, I woke to find Cinnamon and Jewel already up and chatting in Jinx and Doug's suite. The conversation grew hushed when I entered, and again, I felt my ears to see if they were burning. When Molokii got up, the six of us took a cab up to the Mission district.

There, we met the vampires for breakfast at the Pork Store—to a vampire, "vegetarian" meant "not blood." Our fanged friends spent the night trying to dig up information and had come up empty-handed—whoever the fire ninjas were, they didn't seem to be San Francisco locals.

After the vampires crashed, Cinnamon, Jewel, and I took a day tour of San Francisco with Molokii, Jinx, and Doug. We weren't due at Stanford until the afternoon, so we went to the Palace of Fine Arts and got tickets for the noon show at the Cage.

The Palace of Fine Arts itself is a faux ruin curled around a glittering lagoon—columns and statues of warm brown stone rising through trees and reflected in gently rippling waters. As we strolled through the winding paths, Doug explained that the Palace had been built a century ago for some exhibition, but really, no one in the world cared what San Francisco's most famous attraction *had* been. Everyone only cared what it was *now*—the home of the Drake Cage.

An unearthly squawk echoed throughout the columns, a prehistoric cross between the calls of a bird of prey and a great cat. Following quickly was another in a lower register, then another in a higher; then a dozen more, overlapping each other like a chorus from the *Land of the Lost.* Jinx whirled to Doug, squeezing his hand, her face bursting out in a great sunny smile.

Then we stepped forward in sight of the Drake Cage.

A mammoth faux-ancient rotunda ten stories high stood before us on eight massive columns. Vast scaffolds supported a mesh of invisibly fine netting, obscuring neither the huge Greek statues peering down at us, nor the gleaming eyes of the drakes perched upon them.

They came in all colors: glistening orange, sparkling purple, gleaming cyan. They came in all shapes: tiny, fluttering drakes no larger than butterflies; large, raptor-like drakes the size of eagles; and next to the center cage, a giraffe-tall long-necked drake, patterned scales gleaming green and blue. The giraffe drake fixed a huge jeweled eye straight on us, and my dragon tattoo shifted uncomfortably on my body—I got the disturbing impression it was a stare-off. Then the giraffe drake blinked, stretched that long neck—and once again let out that squawking, trumpeting cry that set off all the other drakes in a cacophonous chorus.

"They don't eat each other?" I asked, bewildered at the variety in the cage.

"Mom," Cinnamon said, as the rest of the drakes joined in the chorus. "We're up."

I blinked. Then I saw a keeper gesturing at the door of the Cage. "Oh! We're up."

"Yes, you are," the khaki-garbed keeper said with a smile. "Enjoy the show."

There are two stands of seats at the Drake Cage. For the less adventurous, there are risers between the columns of the rotunda. For the more adventurous, there is the feature that makes the Drake Cage a worldwide attraction—the dozen center seats in the Inner Cage.

We took our seats in the cramped, mesh-guarded arc at the center, and the khaki-garbed, Kevlar-gloved keeper locked us in. Then he chirped, and the giraffe-necked drake lowered its head, lifted him up and placed him on a kind of crow's nest at the other side of the Cage.

"Ladies and gentlemen," the Keeper said, voice amplified by a throat mic that left his hands free to scratch the neck of the giraffe drake as it dropped him off. "Boys and girls. Monsters and mortals. Welcome to the Drake Cage!"

And with that, the giraffe-necked drake lit up the Cage with a brief spurt of flame, a twisting, napalm-like threader that burned painfully bright.

"It's like liquid fire," I said, shielding my eyes.

"It's not *real* liquid fire," Jewel responded, jamming down her hat—a sparkly number shaped like an octopus whose curled-up tentacles made a scraggly brim. "A drake's *magifouaille* may be better than any human fuel, but it still has nothing on the liquid fire of a real dragon."

Next, the Keeper brought out an amazing sequence of drakes: small drakes and fat drakes, turtle drakes and cat drakes; drakes that flew and drakes that crawled—so many that I wondered how creatures that rare came in such grand variety.

"True dragons have been extinct for thousands of years," the Keeper said, as an Orange-Throated Striking Drake flapped and squawked on his arm like a overgrown cross between an eagle, a gecko, and a fire-burping machine. "Likely hunted to death by early humans."

"*Not* likely," Jewel muttered. "Scientists, thinking they have all the answers—"

"True dragons were one of an entire family of creatures, with a 'family resemblance,' like cats or apes," he said. "Drakes, in contrast, are magical echoes of true dragons mixed with other animals—just like werekin are magical echoes of animals mixed with each other."

I glanced at Cinnamon, but she didn't flinch.

"Like lycanthropes," the Keeper continued, "drakes are mundane creatures with magical infections. Like lycanthropes, there are drakes for every family of creatures in the world, and like lycanthropes, they breed true. But unlike the precursor of lycanthropes, which granted its offspring shapechanging abilities, the precursor drake granted flight—and fire."

The Keeper released the gecko-like Orange-Throated Striking Drake, which flapped up and away in the cage, seemingly glad to get away from the staring eye of the Long-Necked Giraffe Drake, which once again belched a long tongue of fire.

"Thank you," the Keeper said, as the performance concluded and the giraffe drake lowered him to the ground. "Please visit the museum on your way out, and consider a donation which will help the Drake Cage continue its educational mission."

I stood to leave, but froze as standing brought me eye to eye with the giraffe drake as its neck lifted back up. It stared at me curiously, definitely. My tattoo shifted. I swallowed. What prevented the drake from launching a burst of flame into the inner cage?

"Mom," Cinnamon said, tugging at me. "We gots to clear the cage now."

I blinked. Then I saw the Keeper gesturing at the door of the Cage.

"Oh, right," I said, stepping to follow Jewel and promptly bumping my head on the low door of the Cage. Jewel tried to stifle a laugh, and I laughed too, rubbing my head and shagging my deathhawk back to life before I let Cinnamon drag me to the Drakatorium.

The Drakatorium was a large curved building nestled around the Drake

Cage proper. Within, there were more live drakes, drawn from populations that could not coexist in the Cage; dioramas of drakes in their natural habitats; and, finally, a series of exhibits on true dragons.

Dominating this last room was a huge facsimile of a red dragon, its wings as broad as the building was wide and its neck as high as the ceiling was tall. But this was a facsimile, not based on any real fossil—there just wasn't enough left of a "true dragon" skeleton to reconstruct.

We didn't even know whether "dragon" fossils were true dragons or just dragon-touched dinosaurs—the so-called Saurian Drake Hypothesis. Regardless, ancient dragon corpses burned themselves up with magical fire, and it's hard to reconstruct *anything* from charred fragments.

Looking at the statue, my dragon tattoo shifted on my body. *This isn't true.* I didn't like how reactive my tattoo had become, how much it seemed to be feeding intentions back to me as much as receiving them. But I agreed—this knockoff was far too Tolkien for my taste.

I wandered out into the gift shop, and Jewel followed.

"Forget Smaug out there. Look," she said excitedly, pointing to an LCD monitor showing over and over again a short news clip of a glowing, cartoony image of a dragon perched atop the Golden Gate bridge. "I *told* you you summoned a dragon!"

"That's just their logo," I said, pointing at a line of T-shirts, which had a similar but not identical image of a drake atop the Golden Gate. "And it's obviously a special effect—"

"How can you tell?" Jewel challenged, leaning in. "It looks like magic—"

"It just *looks* animated," I said, pointing. The giant image atop the Golden Gate had a distinct drawn outline, like a Disney cartoon. Except . . . "That's not a physical object, it's a piece of art they composited in. It looks like a giant neon version of one of . . . one of my tattoos—"

"Oh!" Jewel said, nonplussed. "So it does."

"That *is* a knockoff of my original Dragon tattoo," I said, shifting uncomfortably. Was my new Dragon jealous of the old one? "Close enough I could sue for copyright infringement. Jeez, come on. This is a *scientific* exhibit. Can't they do better than ripping me off?"

"Oh, don't go all scowly on me," Jewel said, her own irritation fading slightly. She stepped in front of me, taking my hands, pursing her lips into something halfway between a smile and a frown. " 'Penny for your,' as Cinnamon might say?"

"Dragons were the most magnificent creature to have lived in human history," I said, pulling my hands back and adjusting my vestcoat so it rode on my shoulders more comfortably, "and humans killed them so good we can't even reconstruct them properly—"

"Now you're getting how *I* feel," Jewel said, quickly becoming steamed again, jamming down her hat again. "Walking through all this faux-Tolkien, *Reign of Fire* shit, with things that aren't even *half*-dragons stuffed in cages—"

"Would you rather have visited the zoo?" I asked. "Even more animals in cages—"

"Feeling a bit caged myself," Jewel said, glancing around. "Let's get out into the sun."

In the fresh air, I started to feel better, but we couldn't escape cages, not with the Drake Cage looming over us. I made some snarky comment about the huge latticework built around the columns—but, according to Jewel, the latticework had been built *before* it became a cage.

"They had to build it, just to keep what was left of the Palace of Fine Arts standing," Jewel said. "It was falling to pieces. The Palace was built for the Panama-Pacific Exhibition almost a century ago. It was never meant to last as long as it did."

"A metaphor for our modern world," I said, still feeling the nasty aftertaste in my mood from seeing the misleading dragon "reconstructions." "A façade of planned obsolescence decaying under its own weight, desperately shored up by stopgap measures."

Jewel looked at me sharply. "You know, *you* called *me* Granola Girl—"

"Takes one to know one," I said, a faint smile appearing on my face. Then I felt it fade. "Not that I know you, really, Jewel. I mean, I know I like you, and that you spin fire, but I really don't know anything else about you, other than people want you scared, quiet, or dead."

She shrugged. "Born and bred in the surf," she said, "but never took to it."

"What got you into firespinning?" I asked.

"I've always loved fire," Jewel said, looking up into the sky. "Fireworks and bonfires, matches and burnt fingers. When I got older, I started spinning fire batons in luaus, but after I woke up about native culture I . . . turned to poi, then fire magic—and never looked back."

"Cool," I said.

"Hot, *I* like to say," she replied. "Your turn. Who are *you*, Dakota Frost?"

"What?" I said. "Oh! I . . . well, born and bred in the buckle of the Bible belt—"

"But it didn't take," she said.

"Oh, yes it did," I said. "Eighth grade Bible Bowl champion. But when I got into high school, I got into science, and that knocked the edge off—I was raised 'if it isn't all true then none of it's true' and, well, you know."

"I do," she said. "But how did that turn into tattooing?"

"Ah," I said. "Science again. When I got into college, I got into chemistry—and into a great deal of trouble, quite the hell-raiser. On a road trip to Savannah-the-city, much to the consternation of Savannah-my-friend, I was flirting with this sailor, and he—"

"*He?*" she asked.

"He," I responded. "He had a tattoo that moved. And *I didn't know how it worked.*"

That last bit came out more forceful than I intended, and Jewel's brow furrowed a little.

"I had two thirds of a degree in Chemistry with a minor in Physics," I said, "he had a tattoo that moved—and I didn't know *how* it worked. And I *had* to know. I transferred to the Harris School of Magic the next week. Within two semesters, I'd learned everything they could teach me, so I hunted down owners of magical tattoos, then their inkers, found a backwoods skindancer to apprentice to . . ." I spread my tattooed arms. "And the rest is history."

"And that's how Dakota Frost became a skindancer," Jewel said.

"No," I said. "That came later. Once I learned how . . . I just wanted to tattoo."

"But," Jewel said, "isn't skindancing . . . magical tattooing?"

"No," I said. "Magical tattooing is fire poi making. Skindancing is firespinning."

"Ah," she said. "But back to this 'he' business. Were you not out yet?"

"What a forward question," I said. "But as it turns out, I'd already dated girls . . . but I've never stopped dating guys. I'm not straight or gay . . . I'm just Dakota."

Jewel's mouth quirked up. "Oh, that's very clever. I *like* that. I hope it catches on." At my blank look, she clarified, "I'm sorry, I thought you meant, bisexual, like, North *and* South?"

I laughed. "No, I am bisexual, but I meant, I won't be categorized. I'm just Dakota."

"So . . . you're saying you're a force of nature?" Jewel asked.

"No," I said. "I'm saying . . . I like who I like, Jewel Grace."

"*I* think you're a force of nature, Dakota Frost," she said, her eyes flashing hot at me. "Where *was* that sailor's tattoo?"

I smiled wickedly. It had been on his bicep, but it was more fun to let her wonder.

27. Lower Kicking

My breath caught, a fist sailed at my head—and I *backflipped* away from the punch.

Our original plan for the Hilbert Conference, of course, had not involved *any* punching. We'd planned to spend Thursday at Stanford attending talks—though Cinnamon also wanted to hit the Stanford Bookstore's awesome mathematics section—but after the attacks, campus security asked us to wait for an "all clear" before heading over to the auditorium where Cinnamon would repeat her Berkeley talk . . . and receive her Young Investigator Award.

Instead, we hid out in the one place no one could expect us to be, because I'd explicitly declined the invitation—Stanford University's Taido club, where Cinnamon, Jewel, and Molokii got to watch me get my ass kicked . . . before we even *started* to fight.

These guys were hard core. The warm-up *began* with a dozen punches, then moved on to Taido's acrobatics—but where I was used to cartwheels and flips by themselves, sensei Ransu "Paj" Pajari drilled us as if we were in combat, with cartwheel *kicks* and backflip *dodges*.

His fist whistling at my head, I threw myself backward—and two students, holding either side of my belt, gave me enough assist for my body to flip over. I landed awkwardly, wincing—but my physical therapist said Taido's exercises actually strengthened my bum knee.

"I'd pay money to see you backflip away from a punch in a real fight," Paj said shortly thereafter to the ring of students, another student ready by him as he spoke, "but I'm drilling your *reactions*. It needs to be instinct. Don't block with your fists—dodge with your body!"

The student threw a roundhouse kick, and Paj instantly threw himself backward, falling into a defensive tripod, legs folded, one hand supporting him, the other shielding him from the demonstration kick, hovering inches from his face.

"*Foo-koo-tekky*—changing the body axis to avoid contact," Paj said. His eyes narrowed at the student's kick, and he said, "You could let it pass over, but his form's bad. He's left an opening. Never pass on free. So you decide to take the rib."

Paj threw his shield hand down and flicked up his back leg, touching the student's side. "You see," he said, and I *did*—how the defensive movement set him up for the kick, how the kick set him up to retract the leg, shooting it under his body, spinning upright.

"Sensei," one of the green belts asked. "What was that kick? It wasn't *ebi*—"

"*Chai-joe*," I said with a grin. I loved saying the name of that kick; it reminded me of two of my favorite beverages. "More like a roundhouse kick done from the floor."

"It's *shaa-jo*," Paj corrected. "Otherwise our visitor is correct. Frost, show him!"

I blinked. *Me? And my damn mouth.* I let one hand fall to the floor and kicked up my back leg. I held it up there, pointed forty-five degrees at the ceiling, and the green belt grunted; then I pulled it under me and lurched upright. In short, I had none of the grace of Paj.

At least my dragon tattoo wasn't bothering me—it seemed to like my exertions.

"Not bad, Frost," Paj said, perhaps a little too graciously, as I stood there, red-faced, whether from exertion or embarrassment I couldn't say. "We need to work on your form a bit. You're not ready to work it into *foo-koo-tekky*. Again!"

After showing us some of Taido's most advanced kicks, Paj drilled us on its most basic form—*untai no hokei*, a ritualized solo fight where you imagine a sequence of attackers coming at you, whom you dispatch with the *hokei's* signature movement, a wavelike motion.

Regardless of how good you are at *untai*, the best thing to do is to narrow your focus and enter the universe of the *hokei*. To *see* the attackers, leaping between them, shooting your hands at their Adam's apples, landing knockout punches on a third foe, catching him and laying him aside before whirling to deal with the two remaining foes—before returning to the start.

"Good!" Paj said. "Forceful yells, fluid pacing, and believable targets. But you're bobbing. Halfway through the hokei, your stance goes to shit. Focus on your breathing—it should follow the hokei. Conquer your breathing, and your stance will follow. Next!"

I rose and returned to the line of students. Out in the theater seats,

Cinnamon, Jewel, and Molokii watched. Jewel was staring at me, wide-eyed—then giggled as Cinnamon leaned and muttered something in her ear. Only Molokii was unmoved, nodding at me gravely.

"Thanks for joining us," Paj said, shaking my hand after closing the practice with a formal stretchdown and a whole bunch of bowing. "You just pop up everywhere. I think I've seen you in every studio but Fort Lauderdale."

"Thanks," I said, wiping my brow with a towel. "I'm surprised you remember me. I've only been to the headquarters once when you were there."

Paj cocked his head at me. "Full sleeves and a Mohawk," he said, still smiling, but his eyes penetrating. "Six-two, but you carry yourself like six-six. You *want* to stand out."

I smiled tightly. Behind me, I heard Jewel snicker. Finally I said, "Can't argue with that."

Then I hopped down from the stage to land in front of Jewel, Cinnamon, and Molokii.

"Ow," I said, regretting it the moment I landed. "My knees. My thighs. My *ass*—"

"I can help with that," Jewel said. "You know, check for damage—"

"Oh, behave," I said, checking my phone. "Officer Ridling texted me the all-clear, but we're in the conference's afternoon break." I smiled at Cinnamon, then tousled her hair until I disheveled her headscarf. "We'll just have to while away the time in the Stanford Bookstore."

"Yaay!" Cinnamon said, bouncing.

"Haha! Phoo," I said, wiping my face again. "Just give me a minute to wash up—"

"You know, I can help with that too," Jewel said, the smile becoming devilish.

"Behave," I said. "Really. Behave!"

"Don't wanna," Jewel said.

Fifteen minutes later, we emerged into a winding path lined with bicycles that led us back on to the beautiful Stanford campus. We soon lost ourselves in branches and leaves and cottage-like classrooms roofed in Spanish tile. Stanford was a warren, a living Escher print unfolded and flattened out upon itself, M.C.'s delicate etchings of impossible buildings coming to life in a maze of arched arcades and cozy buildings fashioned from warm, rough-hewn gold stone.

It was here, by an empty bird fountain, sitting on a redwood park bench with a plaque that read SMILE, that Savannah and I had shared our first kiss "away." The Bay had been our first trip together, the first time it had finally hit us we could really be together as a couple.

I glanced at Jewel, trying to jam her octopus hat back down over curls which kept trying to pop the hat off. What a delight she'd proved to be. Five months since Calaphase died, three years since I left Savannah-turned-Saffron. Maybe it was time to open a chink in my armor—

My phone rang. "Yes," I said curtly.

"Frost? Carnes," came the reply. "What's the word on Buckhead?"

"Dude!" I said. "We last spoke, what, twenty-four hours ago? Give me a break."

"*Higher*-ups," Carnes said bitterly, "in the Wizarding Guild are leaning on me. If you recall, you asked if I wanted another arrangement. I *do* want another arrangement. I want to help your friend Jewel, and I want your help. But my superiors are demanding a quid pro quo."

"Where is this bookstore again?" Cinnamon asked.

"All right, all right," I said, glancing over at her. "I'll call him."

"Don't you know?" Jewel asked, adjusting her hat.

"But you haven't called him yet," Carnes said. "I mean, as of right now?"

"I thinks it's that way," Cinnamon said. "Down to the left—"

"No," I said. "It's down to the right—"

"What?" Carnes asked.

"Really? *Fuck!* I'm all turned around—"

"Just a minute, baby," I said, stepping slightly away.

"*What?*" Carnes said.

"Sorry, I'm in the middle of two different conversations." I hung back a bit and let Cinnamon, Molokii, and Jewel get ahead. As their conversation about missed turns and Dover books faded, I put the phone to my ear again. When I did, Carnes was laughing.

" 'Catches' you at a bad time?"

"In theory, no," I said, following the three of them closely as they wound around the garden. If I remembered right, this would come out right in front of the church, in the middle of the Quad, and from there it would be easy to get our bearings back. "You were asking?"

"I'm not asking—my boss, the *Professor,* is," Carnes said. "He likes to stay informed, but since, in his words, 'A fae god's visit won't be announced on Wikinews,' he asked me to ask you for an update. Though I don't understand why he won't just ask you when he sees you—"

"When he sees me?" I asked, rounding the corner. Cinnamon, Jewel, and Molokii were ahead of me, my tiger hopscotching over tiles inlaid with numbers—but the main cobblestone surface of the Quad was nowhere in sight—only a long arcade of stone arches. I'd gotten us completely lost. "Our schedule's filled to the brim. I need some advance notice—"

"Wait," Carnes said. "Aren't you at Stanford to see him now?"

"No," I said, picking up the pace. Each time I turned the corner, I got more and more confused—an Escher print, this was. But each time, my three companions were farther away—gaining on them, I wasn't. "Wait, how did you know we're at Stanford? No one knows—"

"I didn't," Carnes said. "*He* did."

"Oh, hell," I said, bolting forward, chasing after my baby as she, Jewel, and Jewel's friend rounded the corner. But when I turned just after them, they were already at the opposite end of an impossibly long arcade of brown stone arches, seemingly farther away now than ever.

And then Cinnamon, Jewel, and Molokii turned the corner . . . and were gone.

I stared. What the hell had just happened?

I whirled around. The archway I had just darted out of had disappeared, replaced by a wide path lined with luxuriant jasmine bushes. I whirled again, and the long arcade I'd seen my friends disappear on was gone, replaced by a classroom building nestled among paths and trees. It was a perfectly normal classroom, two stories of warm brown stone topped with Spanish tile . . . but attached to it, looming over me, making my skin crawl in a way I couldn't quite put a finger on, was a tall, windowless, three-story tower.

I swallowed.

I looked at my cell phone for reassurance—but the call with Carnes had been dropped. *Shit.* Cautiously, I stepped up beneath the archway, and saw a dark green double door. On the right hand door was written, in neat, white letters:

LIGOTTI HALL

Building 26A

Department of Alchemy

Post no flyers or posters

Then the left hand door opened on its own.

—

"Oh, hell," I muttered. "Let me guess. The warm welcome . . . of the 'Professor.' "

28. The Computer Wizard of Ligotti Hall

I stepped through the dark green door—and backward through time, my nose assaulted by competing wafts of memory: the tang of desiccants from Emory University's Department of Chemistry, and the eclectic spices of the Harris School of Magic. Here, at the Stanford Department of Alchemy, those smells mixed, but the feeling was the same.

The wave of nostalgia was not limited to my nose. The colors, fonts, and logos were all different, but otherwise, the room I entered was a perfectly normal front office of an academic department: mail slots and message boards, ratty couches by a well-worn copier, a wide cracked oak counter shielding a pair of administrative assistants.

The younger assistant, a trim Hispanic man, was busy hitting on a Scottish version of Hermione with purple hair and a nose ring. I wondered what the point of their flirting was; as far as I could tell, they were *both* gay. I turned instead to the wiry-haired senior assistant and cleared my throat—and the assistant and student both gave me appraising looks. Were they gay or bi? I realized that I'd slapped a label on them, just like I'd accused Jewel of doing to me.

"Excuse me," I said, reddening. "I'm Dakota Frost. The Professor is expecting me."

"Which one, dear?" the senior assistant asked, pleasantly but distractedly, still scribbling on a Garfield pad. "There *are* thirteen—uh, twelve professors in the Department." When I didn't respond, she looked up sharply. "Oh, dear. You mean *The* Professor. Did he do the thing?"

I grinned. "I'm guessing he did."

The Hispanic assistant slapped his head. "Oh, God, we're gonna get sued. *Again*—"

The older assistant stabbed at a phone. "*Professor!*" she barked, in a voice of authority that made all of us jump. She rose, finger still held on the intercom button, and snapped, "You, as you *well* know, have a visitor, and *shame* on you, *sir.*"

Laughter rippled out of the intercom. "Yes, yes, send her back, Ms. Koch."

Miss Koch released the button. "Follow me, dear," she said, bustling toward the flip-top of the counter. "And I'm so sorry. He's supposed to stop doing the thing—"

"Are *you* the new professor?" the Scottish girl asked, calculatingly.

I glanced back at her—cute, and what a delicious voice. But still . . . "God, I hope not."

As we walked back through the hall on the left, that brief interaction made me start to wonder what I was doing with Jewel. I'm an irrepressible flirt; if a tasty man or woman crosses my path, I'll give them a wink. But I rarely act on it. Why had Jewel been different?

We turned a corner, and the split-brain feel of the Department of Alchemy continued. On our left were normal professorial doors—some dark behind the glass, others lit, and one with a row of students waiting. On the right were classrooms hosting far less normal demonstrations: wafts of smoke, crackling electricity, flickering behind glass that left my tattoos tingling.

We passed a laboratory where students slaved over bubbling beakers that shot puffs of sparkling silver flame, and I wished Jewel was here to see it too. I sighed. What made me latch onto this stranger on a plane, knowing we'd go our separate ways by the end of the week? Maybe that was the appeal in the beginning.

But that's as far as my self-examination got—we were there, at a second bend in the hall, standing before a door with a frosted glass window whose brighter light almost certainly indicated a corner office, and whose dark lettering indicated the turf of:

Professor A. NARAYAN DEVENGER

Department of Alchemy

Chair

Miss Koch knocked, but nothing happened; and while we waited, I examined the flyers on the message board next to his door: a film series, antinuclear protests, and an arrow pointing down at a large box, filled with **FREE(D) BOOKS.** Charming. I liked him already.

"Professor!" Miss Koch snapped. "This is enough. I know you're in there!"

There was a rumble. A large shape loomed behind the glass. "Oh, all right," called a voice, and the rounded shape sank downward. With another, deeper rumble, the shape receded from the glass, and the door slowly opened, all by itself, with no one behind it. "Come in."

Miss Koch groaned. "At it again. He's not tearing you away from anything, is he?"

"Oh, just my daughter, my date, my life," I said, picking up a couple of books from the box. Someone had thrown away a perfectly good copy of Kohen and Egelston's *Biogenic Manadynamics*. "Huh. What do you know, fifth edition. All I have is the fourth—"

Koch snapped her fingers in my face. "Don't let the Professor addle you," she said, checking her watch. "Legend has it people have grown old and died talking to him, so if I don't see you in twenty-five minutes, I'm coming back with a crowbar—"

And then a shimmering light flickered against the glass. I squinted, feeling a slight flood of mana that made my skin tingle—but the sparkle caught Miss Koch full in the eyes. She stopped, tilted her head, then said pleasantly, "—and maybe a cup of nice tea."

"I won't let him 'addle' me," I said, smiling. "And I'll pass on the tea. Or the crowbar."

"Crowbar?" She furrowed her brow, then scowled. "Neither the tea nor the crowbar will be for you," Miss Koch growled through the door, having recovered both her composure *and* her ire. "Both will be for his head, and not in that order!" Then she stalked off.

I pursed my lips, slipping the slim copy of Gamut's *Art of Graphomancy* on top of the fifth edition of K&E. Then I stepped through the door.

I entered a paradise of books and light. The two straight inner walls of the corner office were lined with books; the opposite wall arced outward, with a row of sofas below a curved arc of windows, nearly three-quarters of a circle. At the circle's center, protected by the ramparts of a huge, paper-strewn L-shaped desk, and nearly hidden from view by a parapet of vertical flat panel monitors, sat Professor Narayan Devenger.

Narayan Devenger was a salt-and-pepper Santa in sandals, suspenders, and sport coat. His frayed black T-shirt was emblazoned with a symbol I didn't recognize, an upside-down V in a circle. I couldn't quite place him—his features were Caucasian, his skin swarthy. He was facing his fort of computer screens when I entered, but when I stepped through the threshold, he looked back through half-rimmed glasses at me, mouth breaking into a wide, cheerful, devilish grin.

As Devenger turned around, the wooden floorboards rumbled deeply beneath his Herman Miller chair. Beside me, just behind the door, I saw a stepladder on rollers piled with books on magical tattooing, all by authors I knew: Sumner and Navid, Wilsen and Grayson. Devenger had been checking up on me, right up to the moment I appeared at the door, and then he had turned the simple act of returning to his desk into a little faux-magical show.

Then I remembered how I got here. "My daughter—" I began hotly.

"She's fine," Devenger said, holding up his hands. His face might have been European, his skin Indian, but his voice was pure Midwestern. "No doubt deep in the bookstore by now. I have Carnes's errand boy on loan, shadowing them. You have my word as a wizard—"

"Ha," I said.

"My word as a wizard," he said firmly, "they will come to no harm—"

"Really?" I snapped. "You 'addle' them too?"

"No," Devenger said, so sincerely I started to believe him. "You are described as a skilled magician, highly cantankerous, and a fiercely protective mother. I anticipated your response, and spared your daughter and your squeeze from my little exercise in . . . escheromancy."

He smiled, whether at the magic or the pun I couldn't tell. I stared back—then my mouth quirked up, wanting to smile. Maybe he was putting the whammy on me, but my skin felt no tingle of magic. Perhaps Devenger's happiness was just naturally infectious.

Finally I gave in, smiled, and said, "Still, that was a dirty old trick."

"A whole sequence of them," Professor Devenger said, chuckling.

"Mind if I keep these?" I asked, indicating the books in my hand.

"That's why they're freed," he said, still chuckling. There was a reason this fat, happy, *charismatic* man was a chair of a department. "And I'm sorry for luring you in like that, but I'd heard you'd had trouble being tailed by the DEI and I wanted to talk in private. Besides, this is *Stanford.* The campus is practically built for it. Forgive an old man his little tricks."

"Old man?" I said. Professor Devenger looked at me curiously; I gauged him coolly in return. There was more pepper than salt in his beard, and his tan skin was a smooth canvas, but he was the perfect caricature of a old-school computer wizard—beard, belly, sandals—even down to the upside-down V symbol on his shirt, which I now saw as an AND sign.

No, not a caricature. Devenger wasn't a portrayal of an old-school computer wizard—he was a *snapshot* of one. And while Devenger's name might be on his door, he was definitely *the* Professor—and *the* Professor, *the* Warlock, and *the* Commissioner *all* looked like castaways from *That '70s Show.* And, now that I felt for it, Devenger gave off the same magical vibe.

Three men—three powerful *wizards*—all primarily known by simple, revealing titles, all enduring, "legendary" figures in whatever organization they were a part of, all giving off, when I felt for it, the same whiff of old magic . . . and all curiously frozen in time.

Had they done something to increase their power . . . or extend their lives?

"Enjoying your stay in San Francisco? Having productive meetings?" Devenger asked, glancing at his computer. *Huh*—he'd basically hidden his face, switched to small talk and asked who I'd met with. Maybe he'd guessed I'd guessed the truth. "Seen any interesting sights?

"Actually, three of them: the Professor, the Commissioner, and the Warlock," I said, and Devenger tensed. I said, "You're not the first wizards I've seen who extended their lives—and not the first to fuck with me. I mean, what gives? Does immortality erode the social graces?"

"What an interesting question, Ms. Frost," Devenger said, tilting his head.

"I'd expect that someone with forever to practice a skill would get better at it—"

"You don't expect, you know," I said. "With the Warlock or the Commish, I dismissed it as a quirk. Seeing all three of you in the space of as many days, I started to suspect something. But the moment you ducked your head under your coat and changed the subject—"

"Yes, yes," Devenger said, waving his hands and turning back to me, looking both irritated and embarrassed. "You've made your point and it isn't really that deep a secret anyway. By the way, don't call the Commish the Commish. He *really* hates that."

I blinked. "Fair enough. Now . . . my question stands. What gives? Why the hassle?"

"Nothing 'gives,' " Devenger said, eyes tightening slightly, picking over my tattoos, lingering on my left arm. "Yes, there are spells to extend life, but I'm sure it's merely coincidence that a few old wizards who know them have 'hassled' you—"

"For a wise old wizard," I said, "you need a lot of work on your poker face."

"Asperger's," he said, embarrassed, though he had zero, zip trace of the mannerisms I'd expect from someone on the autism spectrum. "A hundred and twenty years wears off the burrs, but it's still work to control the nuances—or to see them. What did *you* see in *my* face?"

"You checked out my tattoos," I responded.

He sighed. "Which made you target of the Archmage, according to Carnes." He shook his head, his eyes still focused on my arms, now zeroing in on my upper left shoulder. "Entirely understandable. I don't think you even know what you have there, do you?"

"My masterwork, reloaded?" He kept staring at my arm, and I looked at it closely. There, the varied elements of the Dragon were most visible. You could see her claw, a bit of her tail, even a trailing spark of fire—but no special logic. "I mean, it's a magic tattoo—"

"Yes, yes, of course, that's what a skindancer would see. A wizard—an *alchemist*—sees something else." Devenger's eyes glinted behind his glasses. "Evidence . . . of liquid fire."

My eyebrows raised. The Commissioner had used those words. *Jewel* used those words.

Devenger smiled. "For a player," he said, "you need work on your poker face."

"I've heard 'liquid fire' too much recently. I take it it's not just a metaphor."

"No," he said, staring at me, considering. "And while it is a liquid, it's not just fire."

—∾

Then he stood. "Come, Ms. Frost," he said. "Let me show you the fountain of youth."

29. THE FOUNTAIN OF YOUTH

We stood in the precise opposite corner of Ligotti Hall from Devenger's office, on the bottom floor of the windowless tower that was the first thing I'd really noticed when Devenger's escheromancy had worn off. The way my skin was tingling, I doubted that was coincidence.

This room was the same size as Devenger's office, but where Devenger's chair sat at the center of an arc of bright windows, here, a hollow glass tube stood at the center of an arc of dark sound baffles. Above us, two floors had been cut away, leaving a narrow catwalk around the tube, which must have been three stories tall. Barely visible at top was the glowing bulb of a spinning whirligig, ringed with metal sheets—a mana generator.

I knew about mana generators. Georgia Tech had one of the largest in the country, sitting atop the largest magical circle in the country, engraved in a massive single-cut slab of marble that was as wide as the floor of the whole tower in which we now stood.

But the Stanford Department of Alchemy had something different.

The hollow glass tube that dominated the room did not stand in a magic circle. Instead, it rested in a disc of polished marble raised to knee height, engraved with two connected spirals in an asymmetric figure eight. Lazy lines looped out from the base of the larger tube, then tightly wound around a second tube with a rounded top, like a man-sized bell jar. Suspended within this second glass tube was a stack of metal rings, almost tall as a person, and pulsing with power.

Written on the glass, in plain letters, were the words MANA FOUNTAIN.

I stared in fascination at the stack of gleaming rings, which had a vaguely Coke-bottle outline, with a second, rounded bulge near the very top. Near the bottom, at the center of a bulge where the rings grew larger, hovered an amber sphere of glowing liquid. Near the top, in the rounded bulge of the rings that were set provocatively at eye level, hovered . . . nothing.

"Still calibrating?" Devenger asked, his hand falling on the shoulder of a young Korean technician wearing spiky hair, black gloves, and a nose ring—fetching, even though I couldn't tell if he or she was male or female. "Run me one, would you?"

The technician nodded, and Devenger stepped back to the wall, beyond the edge of an auxiliary magic circle painted onto the floor. The outline of my dragon tattoo seemed to raise up on my skin as the bulb above began to glow with power, and I quickly stepped outside the magic circle before the gathering mana brought the damn thing to life. The tingling faded, leaving only a tickling at the back of my mind that drew my eyes to that empty space in the rings.

"I'll wager you've realized why San Francisco's vampires wanted you out here—feeling Atlanta out for territory and power," Devenger said, handing me a dark pair of glasses. Actually, I hadn't realized that, though I'd been unconsciously on guard against it during our meeting with the Vampire Court. "And from Carnes, I learned the fae told you outright—they're hungry for a visit from a small-G god, and wanted to exploit your connection to the Lord of the Hunt."

"Of course," I said, as the machine's whine increased. *I'm so naïve.* In my universe, you don't need an ulterior motive to meet someone when you're facing a mutual catastrophe. I forget everyone else lives in a universe where people won't get up to help you with the lifeboats for fear that they'll lose their seat on the deck chairs of the *Titanic.* "And the werekin?"

"The werekindred? Well, they're always desperate for allies who treat them like people rather than animals—and *you* adopted one," Devenger said, sliding on his glasses. He chuckled. "I think they're your best friends forever. But you must have wondered about the wizards."

"Yes," I said, slipping on my glasses too. "So . . . what *do* the wizards want?"

"Access," Devenger said, as the machine whine hit a fever pitch, "to liquid fire."

The magical capacitor discharged with a bang. Violet lightning shot down the glass collector tube and slammed into the marble. Magic rippled out across it, crackling through the figure-eight in its surface, getting brighter as it wound its way around the second tube. The first discharge hit like a dull blow, but as mana converged on the second tube, I felt an electric tingle as energy concentrated at the base of the giant bell jar, then discharged again.

Even through two layers of magic circles, I flinched from the cattle-prod jolt as mana leapt up into the bell jar, striking the hovering sphere of liquid, knocking a single gleaming droplet up into the shaft. The glittering point of light shot up through the narrow neck of the coke bottle, setting off colored flares of light as it passed each stacked ring, getting brighter and brighter but slower and slower, until it came to a stop at eye level, hovering dead center at the top bulge, blazing like a miniature sparkler shimmering through each color of the rainbow.

I stared at the tiny spark in the fountain, mesmerized. Even through dark lenses, it hurt your eyes—it burned as fierce as a welding arc, as bright as a glint from the sun. But the sparks that came off it were not straight: they curved and twisted, branched and forked like the tracks in a particle chamber—or drawings in one of Jinx's graphomantic designs. The brightness dimmed rapidly, and I took my glasses off in unison with Devenger; then we both stepped forward.

The assistant stepped up with a thick-walled test tube, reaching for a glass panel that allowed access to the inside of the fountain. Then she—he? It?—touched his or her forehead. "Let me get the key," s/he said in an androgynous voice, handing the test tube to Devenger.

"No, I got it," Devenger said, slipping something that looked like a bulky pen out of his pocket. He pointed it at the lock on the fountain, and the tiny glass access panel popped open in a flicker of red, grainy laser light. My tattoos prickled as Devenger shone the device again, pinioning the blazing sparkler of mana in a gritty, shimmering beam, and maneuvering it out of the tube, like using a pair of tongs made of light to grab a glowing coal made of magic.

As it hovered between us, I could now see that the dying spark wasn't a spark at all, but a tiny droplet, glowing with a brightness that still stung the eye. Devenger let it hang there in the air between us, staring at it, then he turned off the device, letting the droplet fall into the tube.

"*Aqua incendia:* liquid fire," Devenger said, raising the tube between us, his kindly Santa face lit amber by the glow—and transformed thereby from something genial to something a little more sinister. "At least, a synthetic variant. Half-life, two weeks."

"Half-life," I said, taking the tube when it was offered. "Like . . . radioactivity?"

"The magical kind," Devenger said. "Magic is life, and life is fire—chemical reactions, whose logic tweaks the rules of the universe. But liquid fire is something more, magic all the way down to the core of its atoms, active with nuclear reactions that produce magical effects. The liquid form of the Philosopher's Stone—the goal of all alchemy."

"A magical version of a radioactive substance," I said, struggling to form my thoughts. "Oh my God. Like the Philosopher's Stone, but real." My brow furrowed as I looked at the tube. "But . . . nuclear reactions are thousands of times more powerful than chemical ones."

Devenger's eyes gleamed. "You're starting to see," he said. "With liquid fire, you can do spells that are impossible by any other means—life extension spells, for example, delivering to every cell powerful magical effects beyond the reach of the best magical generators."

My mouth hung open. I had been a chemist before I was a magician; I could see that, see the power of a compound delivering a targeted magical effect right where it was needed, when the same flux of magic flowing in from the outside would kill a man.

"The fountain of youth in a bottle," I said. "And you can synthesize it—"

"No. From your tattoos, I take it you know about the colors of magic—"

"Colors are an approximation," I said, shimmying my shoulders, making my tattoos spark with the magical "spectrum" of black, white, red, green, and blue. "It's just different fractions of magic, broken down by the 'colors' the human eye can perceive."

"But complex magical effects need complex combinations of magic," Devenger said. "Whether it's a tattoo on your skin, a spell in my mind, or a circuit in a necromancer's dagger, each new color of magic you try to combine makes the mana you need shoot up quickly, like Fermat numbers—all possible combinations of all possible combinations, save one for entropy. Just transforming *one* kind of magic requires a five-to-one gearing of power—"

"And two, seventeen," I said. I *did* know this—it was an obscure trick of the graphomantic arts, something that never normally came up in practice—because combining even three kinds of magic took a gearing of almost two hundred sixty to one, nearly impossible. "And liquid fire?"

"At *least* Fermat number five," Devenger said. "Something like four billion to one."

"Jesus," I said. "You . . . you could do *anything* with that. And you make it, *here*—"

"Nothing over F4. And synthetics are short-lived. The fountain's infinity lens focuses more magic than the Georgia Tech array, but its gearing tops out at thirteen-to-one—there's only so much magic we can concentrate into each atom. Already, the high-fraction manatopes in that sample are gone," Devenger said, pointing at the test tube; the spark was visibly fading. "In a couple of months, that will decay to mundanity. But true liquid fire can burn for *centuries.*"

"That's why they're after Jewel," I said. "She's got liquid fire. *Real* liquid fire."

"Yes," Devenger said. "That performance at the Crucible gave her away. For her finale, she spun poi for *seventeen minutes* without refueling—I've seen the YouTube video. Almost certainly, she doped her fuel with liquid fire. The fire warriors who attacked Union Square did too."

"You saw her performance," I said. "*And* the Battle at Union Square?"

"Yes," Devenger said, tugging at his ear. "That was . . . quite spectacular."

"I'm guessing you're not talking about Jewel's performance," I said, and Devenger nodded. A thousand questions ran through my mind. "Professor, did you see the aftermath? The giant symbol plastered all over Macy's? My daughter thinks it's some kind of code—"

"Almost certainly, but it's not the standard alchemical Zodiac cipher. I'm guessing it's a secret alphabet used by the Order of the Woven Flame—you probably know them better as the Fireweavers. That's just the stage name of performers in a Kanaka Maoli magician's guild—Hawai`ian nativists, historically secretive. Most of their communications are encoded."

"Secret fireweaving codes," I said. "So we just need to find the mapping—"

"It won't be that easy," Devenger said. "There wasn't any obvious pattern in the repeated symbols. Could be polyalphabetic, or perhaps a transposition cipher, scrambling the letters based on the rules of fireweaving magic—but I haven't cracked it yet. Too many possibilities—"

"That's what Cinnamon said." I scowled. "She says it's a code because the magic that lights the tag doesn't connect to the words of the message. I love my baby girl, she's a genius, but I don't believe someone would create a symbol of that size just to send a message."

"Yet people do," Devenger said. "Billboards. And they don't have to be corporate logos—Osama Bin Laden would take out a full page ad in the *New York Times* if they'd let him. A magical sign plastered over the façade of Macy's? Hell of a calling card for a terrorist."

"Fuck me," I said. Of course. An attack on a crowd, followed by a huge symbol slapped over Macy's, *would* look like the act of a magical terrorist. "Let's avoid the t-word. They haven't blown anything up to make a point, though it'd be nice if it was as benign as a calling card—"

"A terrorist calling card, benign? You think it's something *darker?*"

"Jewel thinks," I said tightly, "it's a curse."

Devenger frowned. "Cinnamon's right about the tag—it's hermetic magic. The logic of the sign isn't connected to the logic of the message—but that doesn't mean *the message itself isn't a spell.* It could be vicious magic, bottled up—and ready to spring on whomever decodes it."

I squirmed uncomfortably as my Dragon shifted on my skin.

"So it *could* be a curse," I said. "In her performances, Jewel is burning up a substance that can be used to extend human life, and I can see that explains the attacks on her. But you said that the wizards wanted a piece of me, too. Why? I don't have a supply of liquid fire."

Devenger just looked at me. Finally he smiled.

—∞

"You may not know it, but you do," he said. "It's inked into all of your tattoos."

30. You're All Over the Internets

"The legendary source of liquid fire was the blood of dragons," Devenger said, settling back into his office chair. It creaked a little. "As best as we can determine, while manactive compounds were in their blood, the pure form was an extract from their flame glands."

"Their fire extended our life," I said. "No wonder we hunted them to extinction."

"We thought that once," Devenger said. "Now we know dragons were dying out before humans came along. I once hypothesized they needed some trace element—liquid fire contains elements not common on Earth since the Hadean era—but experiments like the one you just saw refuted that. They could have synthesized the elements of liquid fire in their own bodies, like magical versions of breeder reactors. So why dragons died out . . . is a mystery."

"Dragons . . . *synthesized* . . . liquid fire," I said. "Well, obviously, if it ran in their blood and powered their fire . . . but, somehow, it makes you think, if they could synthesize it—"

"That's the point of all those big, sciency, *precise* words," Devenger said. "You were a chemist before you were a magician, so I'm certain you realize the universe isn't made of secret substances available only at mystical times or places." His voice deepened, sounding like a true wizard. "That which can be made can be unmade—or made another way."

"Devenger," I said. "You can't be serious. Liquid fire is totally unlike tattoo ink, and I don't just mean that it's impractical to ink human skin with stuff that's *on fire*. Most inks have a shelf life of years, but you said that liquid fire has a half life of *months*—"

"*Synthetics* have a half-life of months—like the nasty synthetic elements that come out of nuclear reactors," Devenger said. "But the reactors themselves are powered by uranium. It has a half-life of millions of years. So too with dragon's blood—"

"I don't use dragon's blood as ink," I said. "You have to know that. It's too expensive, even if you buy it in the five-gallon drums to get the wholesale discount—"

"What?" Devenger looked at me sharply. He squinted. "Are you pulling my leg?"

"*Moi?*" I said. "Yes. I've never *heard* of anyone who had a supply of dragon's blood before today. But you clearly suspect I've got another source of the same compounds."

"I love talking to you, Ms. Frost. You don't just keep up, you try to pull ahead."

"I've had to," I said. "And I have good science advisors. I should introduce you to Doug Suleiman at Georgia Tech. He's got an apparatus similar to what you've got here—"

"Suleiman . . . sounds familiar," Devenger said, cocking his head. "Maybe we met at that manadynamics conference in Hawaii—oh, of course. Your graphomancer's new husband. He works at that Tech mana facility, yes? I'd love an introduction to Doctor Suleiman."

"Mister, currently," I said. I didn't like how much Devenger seemed to know about me and my companions. "He's working on the doctor bit."

"Yes, yes," Devenger said. "Supplies of liquid fire are the most carefully guarded secrets in the wizarding world, but it's no secret supplies are running out. Unlike dragonsbreath, human uses of liquid fire are not self-regenerating. The spell used by the Warlock, the Commissioner, and I, for example, binds you to the spirit of an age; periodically, it must be renewed."

"It's not just the fountain of youth in a bottle," I said. "The bottles are running out. And all your efforts to attempt to synthesize it have just taught you it's effectively impossible—unless you had a source that you could study and replicate, and even then, it would *still* run out."

"Making liquid fire the most valuable substance in the world," Devenger said. "Almost certainly the real reason behind the assaults on your friend are a fireweaver's dispute over the use of liquid fire. And the reason for the Archmage's interest, and ours, are your tattoos."

"I am *not* the only magical tattooist," I said, and it was true. "There are easily hundreds of us who ink in the open, maybe half a dozen in the Bay Area alone. I even hope to meet some while I'm here. Why can't you get this information from someone else?"

"There may be hundreds of magical tattooists, but few known for inking tattoos of such extraordinary color," Devenger said—and it was true. "That's the source of interest—or, more precisely, our interest is in your source for the compounds you used to ink your tattoos."

I tensed subtly in my chair. That hadn't precisely been the Archmage's intent, but I had no intention of correcting Devenger—he knew entirely too much about me. I started to worry that I'd come across a stalker. His next actions seemed to confirm it.

Devenger leaned forward in his chair. "I don't mean to seem forward, but . . . can I see one of your tattoos? The butterfly—ah, you gave that one to your daughter, didn't you? Then an asp, or, if you're comfortable, the tail of the Dragon—"

Let me out, let me out, whispered a voice, silky as my own skin . . . and I complied. I released the mana that I'd pent up, bent my head forward, and the head of the Dragon slid smoothly out of the back of my collar and over my head. "Will that do you?"

Devenger looked up and cooed. "Wonderful," he said. "But actually, what I want to show you is on your skin. May I?" he asked, reaching for my hand.

I let him take it, and his grip wasn't soft or grabby like a creepy old uncle; it was firm, gentle, even clinical; like a kindly old doctor. "Many of these pigments," he said, drawing his finger over the surface of my skin without touching it, "are magically active. But the mana lines—the magically conducting circuits—are too effective for how colorful they are."

He glanced at me for permission, then pressed his finger into my skin and drew it along the surface of the asp. Little tingles of mana flickered through the design in his finger's wake, like a dozen little ants made of light.

"It's almost impossible to get that much visible color and that much magical activity in the same ink without using manactive compounds. Even in a mix. The fractions just aren't there. Almost certainly your inks have trace amounts . . . of true liquid fire."

"Every magical tattoo artist in the South does marks this colorful," I said.

"*Every* magical tattoo artist," Devenger asked, "or just the ones from your clan?"

"Well," I began, but most of the really spectacular inkers *were* in my clan. "Well, it's a regional specialty," I said lamely. Devenger raised an eyebrow, but I shook my head. "People make fun of it at tattooing conferences—but no one ever suggested that we use liquid fire!"

"Maybe the tattoo *artists* don't know," Devenger said quietly. "You don't do your own graphomancy; the aforementioned blind witch analyzes your designs. I'll bet you don't make your own pigments, either." His eyes gleamed. "Clan inks? Who's your stonegrinder?"

"*How do you know so much about me?*" I asked.

A crackling growl rippled through the room—from my Dragon, still hovering above me. The tendrils at the tip of its jaw dipped into my view like a glowing moustache . . . and I started to see double, watching through the Dragon's eyes as Devenger leaned back in his chair.

"I'm sorry," he said, "but that's your own damn fault. You're all over the Internets."

I stared at him, then noticed his upraised hands. From his perspective, the Dragon had to be one quick lunge away from biting his head off. There was crackling my skin with magic to intimidate people, and then there was crossing the line into actual threats.

"Excuse me," I said, withdrawing the dragon slowly back into my body. I rubbed my eyes as the double vision faded. "Technically, that was assault. Sorry."

Devenger put his hands slowly on the arms of his chair and let out his breath. "Well," he said, "that certainly wasn't the worst reaction anyone's had to either my little perceptual tricks or my Internet snooping, so shall we say we call ourselves even?"

"Hardly," I said, "and I still want an explanation."

"Magicians survive by being secretive," Devenger said, folding his arms. "To Stanford, I'm just a professor—I don't advertise my role in the Wizarding Guild. It's not hard to figure out, but I never confirm anything in public, so it's hard to push inquiry past speculation. *You,* on the other hand, can't keep your mouth shut, so I can find out anything I want on Wikipedia, including pictures of your tattoos good enough to reverse-engineer their logic—"

"Wait, *Wikipedia?*" I said. "Last time I checked, it didn't have anything on me more than a one-paragraph bio, scheduled for deletion for 'not being notable'—"

Devenger's salt-and-pepper eyebrows lifted. "And I thought you were web savvy. Don't you review your footprint on the web? Don't you set up Google alerts?"

"Maybe . . . I should start," I said.

But Devenger had already turned to the screen, tapped out my name, and ten seconds later found a Wikipedia page on **Dakota Caroline Frost**, complete with that same old out-of-date picture everyone scarfed from the Rogue Unicorn website.

"Damn," I said, leaning over his shoulder. The page kept scrolling down, and down, and down. "That's me all right—all of me. Damn. Last time I looked, there wasn't even a picture."

"Compiled from police records, interviews, TV appearances, the Rogue Unicorn website—*everything* about you is here, down to a list of your tattoos," Devenger said, scrolling down through the page. "Even ones you no longer have, like your original dragon tattoo—"

"Wait," I said. "Scroll back up. There, my daughter's name. Why is that a link?"

"Maybe she has a Wikipedia page too," he said.

Something cold ran up my spine.

"Click on it," I said quietly. He did so, and then a page titled **Cinnamon Frost** appeared, complete with a picture from *yesterday*, from *Berkeley*, of Cinnamon holding her tail amidst that clump of graduate students when I'd been *right there*. My eyes bugged as I read the text:

> **Cinnamon Stray Foundling Frost** is an American weretiger, prodigy, and mathematician, best known for her work on Goldbach's Conjecture and her struggle with Tourette's Syndrome. Frost first attracted the notice of the mathematical community with a Note to *Ars Numerica* in which—

"*Tell* me this damn thing doesn't have her schedule on it," I said.

"What?" Devenger said. "No, how would—"

He scowled, turned back to the screen, and clicked savagely on the page, throwing up link after link in new windows, muttering to himself, reading one page while five others loaded. Unsatisfied, he started hitting search engines until he turned up a blog called *Zetawatch*.

"Oh, hell," he said, tilting a monitor toward me. "Look at this—'Cinnamon Frost at the Battle of Union Square?' "

"Oh, hell, is right," I said, leaning in. "That's us, all right—"

"Look at these older ones," Devenger said. " 'C.S.F. Frost wins Young Investigator Award?' 'C.S.F. Frost to appear at Berkeley'? 'Cinnamon Frost to receive award at *Stanford?* Sounds like your daughter has got an Internet stalker—"

"It's not so sinister," I said, peering at the profile picture. "That blogger is one of the grad students who hosted Cinnamon at Berkeley. That doesn't worry me." Apparently, he'd been at Union Square, recognized Cinnamon, and had taken a picture. I pointed. "*That* does."

The reason the blogger had been at Union Square? To see Jewel's performance. He'd had a front row seat to the whole show, from Jewel's setup to the police aftermath. The final picture of the blog? Jewel, Cinnamon, and me leaving with the police.

"I'm not certain what you mean," Devenger said. "Are you saying someone monitoring these blogs would assume Jewel would be at a Cinnamon event? But why would the people attacking Jewel be looking for math blogs?"

"If they plastered a three story magical glyph atop Macy's, they're egotistical enough to want to know how it was received," I said. "What if they're web savvy? What if they've got a Google Alert? What if they'd already had seen me and Jewel together—"

"And now," Devenger said, pointing at the page, "they have your *name*."

—

"Put it all together," I said, "and Cinnamon's appearances become Jewel's hit list."

31. Putting Out the Illuminati

Our golf cart sped through the walkways of Stanford at pedestrian-scattering speed. Devenger had told me to go ahead, and I'd *started* to run, but fifty paces out, my knee, already abused from the Battle of Union Square and Taido practice, had me limping.

Then Devenger whizzed up in a golf cart, grabbed my arm, and pulled me onboard.

"They should be in Dinkenspiel Auditorium, correct?" Devenger asked.

"The bookstore," I said. "Cinnamon wanted—"

"Damn it," Devenger said, turning the wheel so hard the cart nearly flipped over, sending us careening down a side path. "The auditorium and bookstore are practically on top of each other. If these firespinning hooligans do even the most cursory casing, they'll *find* them—"

Ahead, the path was blocked by a chain, and I started to ready an asp to bite it, but Devenger whipped out his laser pointer, reached around the windscreen and blasted the chain out of the way. Only then did I notice the cart's starter switch was burnt out.

"You're like the Doctor with that thing," I said.

"Laser," Devenger said, adjusting the focus of the device. "Who'd have sonic?"

He blasted another chain out of the way, the cart burst through the low-hanging branches of a magnolia tree, and we emerged into a wide lane leading toward a building with a sloping red tile roof and low gold walls that I recognized as the Stanford Bookstore.

Ahead of us was a familiar scene: screams, chaos, scattering pedestrians, a glowing bubble of flame, and dark-suited figures blasting away at Jewel's diminishing shield. Only this time, Jewel was stuck—because the shield that protected her surrounded a pool and fountain.

And this time my daughter was *in* the bubble with Jewel—and a fire ninja.

Cinnamon's outline rippled like a reflection on water, only standing up above the pool, rather than contained within it. She must have tried to turn invisible—but splashes at her feet gave her away, and the black-garbed fire ninja advanced upon her with a lit poi staff. My heart seized—weretigers were vulnerable to fire, and besides, her foe was more than twice her size. In lycanthropy studies, I'd learned that werekin in human form weren't as strong as vampires. Where a vampire might have the strength of ten men, a werekin might be only as strong as two. But then my heart started again, because that equation apparently didn't apply to lifer weres who couldn't completely change back to human—for Cinnamon was now beating the shit out of the fire ninja.

Fully visible now, Cinnamon was using fists, not claws—she told me once she'd rather die than give someone lycanthropy—but even with her holding back, with each blow, the hulking man was buffeted around like a rag doll. The black-garbed figure was tough—he didn't fall—but he was losing ground, the poi staff falling from his hands, fists swinging wide, flying back as Cinnamon kicked him in the belly. He bounced off the inside of Jewel's bubble of flame and yelled, stumbling forward, pitching inside the rim of the fountain inside the shield.

Outside Jewel's shield, things were going much worse. Figures screamed, stumbling and afire—the fire ninjas weren't being gentle this time. I recognized a prone figure in a leather jacket as Ferguson, lying flat in a spray of cinders next to a cowering security guard behind a bench.

But that was it—no cops, no vampires, no security guards, no other help. With fewer bystanders to disperse, and fewer defenders to resist, the fire ninjas were already turning from the crowd to focus on Jewel's shield.

"Use your Dragon," Devenger urged. "Build on her spell—"

"They've seen that trick," I said, shimmying my arms. "But I have an idea."

"Take the right, then," Devenger said, rising out of his seat, leaning, one hand on the wheel. I rose as well, intuiting what he was going to do. "And cover your head!"

He gunned it, and we leapt out—and rolled. The pavement struck me with a slap I didn't expect, and I felt the bright sting of road rash, heard the scuff as my jacket scraped the ground. *Damn it*, I was going to have to have one commissioned from a leathercrafter, at triple the price. But half of Taido is tumbling, and I followed the first forward roll with a second shoulder roll, coming up at a forty-five degree angle and whipping my arm out at the right-most ninja to fling a tattoo just as the golf cart barreled into the fire ninja in the middle.

Screaming, the ninja was hurled into Jewel's shield, which popped when the cart and ninja slammed into it. Jewel's shield dissipated in prismatic fireworks, but the cart had done its job—focusing the attention of the ninjas on Devenger . . . and me.

My dragon tattoo surged for release. *Let me at them!* But I didn't want to just yet; the fire ninjas might have prepared counters for the spells they'd seen me use. Amazingly, my Dragon *got* that, like an intelligent thing, releasing its power into my vines, making them glow.

The one to the right snarled, whipping a bolt of fire at me. I deflected it with a coil of an extended vine, but as I'd expected, his fire was now more tenacious, more grabby, like they'd tuned their spells to work against me. As I flicked the fire off the vine with difficulty, the fire ninja pointed at me, raising his hand with a swagger, calling me out. *I'll get you.*

Well, fine. *I'd* already gotten *him.*

The fire ninja jerked wildly as the asp I'd flung out at the start made contact with his leg and slid up his pants. He jerked harder, trying to kick it off; I was nowhere near as gentle as I had been the last time I'd sicced one of these on someone. He took a hesitant step toward me, raising his fire sword; then he doubled over and collapsed, as if kicked in the gut.

But it wasn't his gut I'd told the snake to bite down hard on.

I glanced over. Three fire ninjas—the singed one who'd been hit by the truck, the wet, bulky guy who'd been pummeled by Cinnamon, and one I assumed came from the left—were all ganging up on Devenger. They needed the advantage; he was not fast, but he was graceful, using some combination of Tai Chi and Aikido, throwing blows off with style and sending more than one of the ninjas sprawling. No doubt, three-on-one, they would eventually have taken him; but I strode over to them, hauled the big one off Devenger, and belted him smack in the mask.

Ow! I damn near broke a knuckle, and his mask didn't crack like the one Cinnamon hit at Union Square, but I knocked it sideways, making the ninja wave his hands in the air. Frantically, he tried to reseat the mask—and I punched him as hard as I could in the stomach. When his hands went for his midsection, I twisted his mask so I was sure he couldn't see.

I looked up in time to see Devenger's elbow *CRACK* into the jaw of another ninja; then he swirled like a matador and the remaining ninja spun off. I stepped in to assist, then flinched as Devenger's whole front lit up with a bright yellow glow.

Devenger flung himself backward as a gout of flame seared the space in which he'd been standing. He whipped out his laser pen as I extruded my vines, as mana hungry as I could make them, trying to deflect the next ball of flame hurled by the fourth fire ninja. I couldn't stop the blast, but I did tilt it up a little, and Devenger flattened himself to the ground as the roiling ball of flame sailed over him, close enough to singe eyebrows.

Devenger sat up. He flicked his pen. Then he raised it and fired, sending out a red beam of light . . . just as the remaining ninja spun up his fire sword into a complicated pattern that spat forth a torrent of flame.

Devenger's red beam collided with the ninja's fiery blast, scattering it as effectively as if the ninja had been playing the fire over a solid brick wall. Devenger slowly got to his feet, pen raised, bracing himself, keeping his aim, deflecting the stream as I came to guard his back.

I threw up a shield of vines, concentrating on their thorns, then risked a quick glance back at Devenger's device. The laser pointer was scanning a shield spell on the surface of the roiling flame, using the opponent's magic against itself—not just *metamagic*, an extremely advanced technique I'd yet to master, but *programmatic* magic, drawn with laser light. The possibilities staggered my mind. Graphomancy on tap. Devenger would be a formidable opponent.

"Stay with me," he said. "I'm going to push him back."

And Devenger pushed forward, carefully keeping his balance, driving the stream of flame forward as I guarded his blind spot with a coiled spiral made from my remaining vine. The ninja was driven back, but his fellows were recovering. When Devenger reached the pool around the fountain, he stepped inside, joining Jewel and Cinnamon who also stood back to back, their claws and fire poi out. Only then did I notice Molokii slumped against the fantastical shape of the fountain itself, half of his face and much of his hair burnt.

"Dakota! Duck!" Devenger said, diving aside as he suddenly whipped his wand down. I crouched to avoid the flames, but before they hit me, Devenger conjured up a wall of water that hissed as the flames splayed against it. Devenger whirled, stepping into the pool with a splash, drawing the point of the laser through the water, and on its shimmering surface I could see the beginnings of a magic circle. "Everyone together! Everyone together! Around the fountain!"

We all ducked inward, splashing into the basin, and then the wall of water shot upward and merged over our heads, into a clear dome of liquid twenty feet wide, gleaming with shimmering magic more prismatic and beautiful than any soap bubble.

Devenger twisted his device, pointing it straight overhead. Now I could see a tiny bulb glowing, the kin to the mana generator I'd seen in Ligotti Hall. Then I looked past Devenger, out of the bubble, to glare at the fire ninjas.

The fourth ninja was rejoining his three companions, who were now back on their feet. By now, Jewel had re-lit her morning stars, Devenger dropped to a crouch, and I was squeezing my hands hard to build up a charge of mana.

"Cinnamon," I muttered. "Snarl. Show your claws."

Cinnamon glanced up at me, then threw her long, bony fingers out, sharp claws extended, shouting, "Raaaaa!" Then I raised my hands, one over the other, and opened them, releasing the mana into a glowing ball hovering between them.

The ninjas now had fully reformed, a four-man phalanx facing off against us. Jewel whipped her poi around, making them spark against each other, and one ninja elbowed another. Then the ninjas ran off, disappearing into the courtyard of a nearby building.

After a minute, with all four of us staring in all four directions, Devenger let the spell lapse. Water splashed down around us, and I shivered gratefully as the cool water hit my bare arms. After another minute, I waded forward, climbed onto the pool's rim, and hopped out.

—

"Uh, yeah," I said dryly, staring out at the courtyard after them, "you'd better run."

32. A Whiff of Dragon Juice

"Ow." I felt the road rash on my right arm. "At least they didn't leave a message—"

Cinnamon pulled on my arm. I winced and turned around. On the opposite side of the fountain from where I stood was the wide front and long sloping roof of the Stanford University Bookstore. Across its front glass was a cooling mandala of the same type we'd seen at Liquid.

"Crap," I said, watching cracks spread through the glass. "Well, did you get to go in?"

"What?" Cinnamon asked, confused. She folded her arms, hunching a little like she was shivering, and I wondered if the moisture on her cheeks was all from Devenger's shield. "Yes, Mom. They hit us right after we walked out. Jewel threw up a shield, but . . ."

"It's OK, baby," I said, squeezing her. "Thanks for defending my daughter, Jewel."

"They were after me, not her," Jewel said, looking at Molokii's burns.

"You could have run," I said. "Both here, and at Union Square—"

"You give me too much credit," Jewel said, grimacing as she touched Molokii's face. It wasn't as bad as it had first looked, but he still needed immediate medical attention. "He didn't hear. They shouted something before the attack, but he didn't hear it coming—"

"Yes, yes, at the Bookstore," Devenger was saying into his cell phone. He glanced quickly at Molokii. "We have several burn victims, send an ambulance. The perpetrators headed north—four figures in dark clothing wearing masks. Yes, I'll stay on the line."

He pulled out a bright blue Bluetooth earbud and popped it in his ear.

"Do you have any idea who those ninjas were?" I asked.

"Ninjas?" Devenger said. "*Ninjas?* You mean those firespinning hooligans?"

"Well, obviously," I said, "They had the black pajamas and everything—"

"Black pajamas do *not* a ninja make," Devenger said, offended. "*Real* ninjas use stealth. These *gentlemen* didn't. Real ninjas avoid attention. These didn't. Real ninjas use many small blows as prep for a killing strike; these guys . . . let's hope that wasn't what they were doing."

I stared at him. "I may want to ask you more about what you know about ninjas."

"Atlanta has a dojo," Devenger said, seeming to gesture expansively without ever taking his attention off Molokii and the burns on his face.

Frowning, Devenger pulled out his laser pointer, adjusting it carefully. "Let's have a look at you, young man—"

"Molokii is deaf," Jewel said. "And he's not great with the lipreading—"

"Nobody is," Devenger said. "Can you sign for me?"

I started to raise my hands, but Jewel beat me to it. Well, fine. I left them to it; I was pissed at her anyway. Jewel was holding out on me about liquid fire. She'd known what it was, but never let on that she used it—which today might have put my daughter in danger.

While Devenger and Jewel attended to Molokii, Cinnamon and I helped some of the students who'd been burned. The damage was not as bad as it had appeared; the kid who'd been most badly hit had dropped and rolled, and two other victims had been put out by a walrus-mustached visiting parent, who'd run into the Bookstore to get a fire extinguisher.

The worst hit, but least harmed, was Ferguson, Carnes's errand boy. According to walrus-moustache, the fire ninjas hit him the moment he moved to help. The tough little man had been knocked cold by a gout of fire, but his bike leathers protected him. Now, singed but sound, he was helping bandage another victim. He glanced up when my shadow loomed over him.

"When the Guild gave you those tickets, we expected you might throw them back at us," Ferguson said. "And we didn't have this in mind if you did. Scratch that—we thought *something* nasty might happen, but never planned to do anything to you. You gotta know that."

"I know that," I said. "Thanks for helping protect my daughter."

He paused, glaring off into the distance. Now I could see the side of his face was singed, just like Molokii's. True to their debated "ninja" nature, the fire warriors had attacked from the side, taking two of the strongest fighters out first without tackling them headlong.

Cinnamon returned with my smartphone, filled with pictures of the mark on the glass. "Got it comin' and goin'," she said. "Look fast. It's not as bright as the others, a little splotchy. It's almost like they're running out of the stuff that gives it its kick."

I stepped up to the shimmering mandala, which was indeed dimming out, almost gone, unlike the huge mark at Union Square which had lasted three hours. "Lend me your nose, baby girl. Smell that, that weird tang? Is this the same chemical they used at Union Square?"

Cinnamon wrinkled her nose. "Yeah, I smells it. Same thing as Oakland, too," she said, whiskers twitching. "Something funky, like gasoline or olive oil, but it isn't just that. There's something else. Something . . . animal like. Oily, like a lizard . . . but not."

"Damn it," I said. Was she smelling liquid fire? "Extract of dragon glands, maybe?"

Cinnamon hissed. "Like lyke juice," she said, and there was an ominous undertone to those two simple words I'd never heard together before. "If it really is dragon juice, that would be some of the rarest shit on the Earth—and it'd be running out. Because—"

"Because there are no more dragons," I said, shaking my head. She really *was* a genius.

"Everyone all right?" Devenger asked, adjusting his laser as we returned.

Jewel was signing to Molokii, who signed back how glad he was that the "mother of the dragon" had saved his ass. *Interesting.* Then Devenger asked, "Why didn't you use your claws, young lady?"

"What? No way. I'm not gonna give *anyone* lycanthropy," Cinnamon said, hugging her arms to herself again. Only now did I see the blood on her palms where her own fingers had cut her when she'd been hitting the big bruiser. "Not even someone trying to kill me."

The squawk of a siren in "get out of the way" mode sounded. I sighed. "I'm sorry, baby," I said. "I think we're going to miss the award ceremony—"

"No," Cinnamon said, horrified. "But I got so close. Can't we—"

"Not unless the police are extraordinarily quick," I said. Something else struck me. "And I'm sorry for you too, Professor Devenger. I think your cover is blown—"

"Oh, I wouldn't say that," Devenger said, raising his "wand." "Cover your eyes."

Jewel ducked her head and covered Molokii's eyes, and I pulled Cinnamon close and squinted, using techniques Nyissa had taught me to shield my eyes from the influx of mana. Devenger flicked the wand, and its pointer tip began spinning, humming, tracing out an elaborate pattern on the ground, on the walls, on the skin of everyone around us, runes and markings that tore at my defensive perimeter like it was paper. I squeezed my eyes shut, feeling mana sway around me, muttering to myself over and over again, "*it was real, it was real, it was real.*"

"Mom?" Cinnamon said uncertainly. "What . . . what just happened?"

I opened my eyes and looked down at her. She looked dazed. I looked around and saw everyone standing around, a bit dumbfounded; then I looked back at Devenger, at the *wizard*, who was slipping the pen back into his pocket with a wink.

"Here come the men in black," I muttered, sing-song.

"Excellent work, Ms. Frost," he said, his voice seeming to echo inside my skull. "I don't think I've ever seen a more brilliant display of magic. Why, if it weren't for your intervention, I think everyone here might have been killed."

"Uh . . . yeah." I still knew exactly what had happened—except, what had happened, exactly? The memories were fuzzy, like they didn't want to take—and I was an experienced magician. Wasn't there something I was supposed to ask Devenger? It was gone.

I saw policemen walking toward us across the square, and I sighed. "Honey, I'm sorry," I said. "I think we're going to miss the awards ceremony—"

"No," Cinnamon said, horrified. "We got so close. Can't I—"

"Not unless the police are . . . unusually quick," I muttered, forcing myself to reconstruct. The policemen had gotten out of their car, assessing the situation . . . but once Devenger finished putting the whammy on them with his little pointer, they had made a beeline for me. My head hurt. "Remind me not to get on your bad side, Professor Devenger."

"If you were, how would you know?" Devenger asked, leaning back, looking remarkably harmless. "I'm glad I could help you save your daughter and your friends. But please remember—you have access to a source of liquid fire, even if you don't know it, and the Wizarding Guild of San Francisco will help you in *anything* you do if you could procure some of it for us."

The policemen stepped up to me, asking *me* what happened and how I'd saved all these people from the bad guys. I answered their questions, staring at Devenger all the while, who just rocked on his heels, smiling at me like a happy old Santa in a professor suit. With a flick of his wrist, he'd convinced a dozen people that everything he'd done had been done by me.

I was glad he had helped us—because Devenger would be a dangerous enemy.

33. NIGHTTIME VISITOR

Long after everyone evacuated Dinkenspiel Auditorium, long after Security emptied the Stanford Bookstore, the Stanford police finally quit questioning me and cleared us to go . . . long after the canceled conference award ceremony had been scheduled to conclude.

We regrouped with the vampires at Nola, a New Orleans/Mexican fusion restaurant in nearby Palo Alto that Saffron's vampire colleagues claimed was "safe ground," an Edgeworld demilitarized zone where we could hole up until it was time to take Jewel to the airport.

I immediately saw why vampires loved the place—filled with vaguely disturbing folk art, Nola recreated a French Quarter style courtyard, and was surrounded by a warren of little streets and alleys where a dining couple could later sneak off for a little . . . ah . . . "necking."

The waitstaff let us hole up in a private second-floor cubbyhole near the emergency exit. Vickman stood like a statue at the entrance of our area, with a commanding view of the stairs. I sat in a chair just behind him, turned crosswise so my view complemented his. While we did so, Ferguson, bandaged but alert, lurked in the downstairs bar, nursing a beer in a seat that gave him a cross view of the long entryway. Anyone who wanted to hurt my friends would have to go through all three of us, and *then* deal with the vampires—and if they got through all that, they'd face the wrath of our vampire allies for violating their turf.

I took a cautious sip of Jewel's margarita on the rocks—it was surprisingly strong. I gave it back to her and shook my head. "Thanks but no thanks—I want to be able to drive," I said. Jewel smiled and nodded, but kept signing to the hero of the hour, Molokii.

In truth, Molokii was little worse for wear, but half his head had disappeared into a white bandage—so he attracted attention from everyone: our vampires, the server, other diners, even a nod from Vickman. Through Jewel, he kept trying to say he hadn't really done anything, that he'd just been in the wrong place at the wrong time, but the story kept amplifying in the echo chamber until half the table was convinced he'd body-blocked a ball of fire to protect Jewel.

Cinnamon, on the other hand, *had* fought with relish, but, without visible injuries, she felt as if she was being ignored, and now moped with vigor. She'd finished her "hubcap burger" and was now picking at the remains of my vegetarian "jambalaya," glaring at the vegetables.

My phone buzzed, and her ears picked up.

"Is it—"

"Let me see," I said, picking up. I'd been on and off the phone with Devenger and the organizers of the Hilbert Conference all night, as he tried to find a way to reschedule the awards ceremony. I wasn't hopeful, but the text message was worse than I'd feared. "Aw man—"

"No," Cinnamon said. "Oh, no no no. Let me see, let me see—"

"Oh, all right, all right," I said, turning the phone toward her.

The text read: **«Disaster—security has canceled rest of conference.»**

"Oh, no," Cinnamon said, hands going to her mouth. "Oh no oh no oh no, we killed it—"

"What?" Jewel said. "Are you serious? They canceled the whole conference? Why?"

"Security," I said, looking at Vickman, who nodded. I said, "I don't blame them."

I looked back at Cinnamon, and I wanted to kick myself. She was shrinking into her seat. I shouldn't have said I didn't blame them; I shouldn't have let her see the text. I should have stood up and walked off and took the call . . . and she would have heard it anyway.

"I was *so close,*" she said, one hand scooping up her tail. "It isn't fair. *It isn't fair.* I did something, I did something real nice, and someone who didn't know me liked it so much they wanted to give me an award, and we came all the way out here . . . for *nothing.*"

"Not for nothing," I said, patting her knee. "You'll still get the award—"

"It's like . . . it's *not real,*" Cinnamon hissed. "Talkin' to that herd at Berkeley was scary, and I thought they hated me, and I *so so* wanted to run—but they were, like, *real,* real *people,* people that talked to me. Now they'll put the trophy in the mail, and it will feel . . . fake."

I stared at her. I understood precisely what she meant. I had nothing to say.

"You know what *I* think?" Jewel said, leaning in on us, putting her hand atop mine on Cinnamon's knee. "When life deals you a setback, all the cards seem to turn up disaster, and you feel there's no hope, you know what time it is? Time for a *really* decadent dessert."

I laughed despite myself. After a moment, Cinnamon did too.

"However, as much as I'd like to sample those decadent-looking beignets," Jewel said, "I recommend we take a walk to get some coffee, for devious therapeutic reasons of my own—and besides, I *need* to walk this dinner off. I don't want to be any more roly-poly."

"I *like* roly-poly," I said.

"Good to know," she said, smiling.

I smiled and raised my hand for the check.

Schultze took point with the vampires behind him, a spearhead leading us out into the street with our more vulnerable friends behind. As Vickman and I took the rear, I glanced into the bar. Ferguson raised his glass, smiling but wincing, and Vickman gave him a salute.

Our entourage strolled out into downtown Palo Alto, a chic walking neighborhood in the heart of Silicon Valley that oddly reminded me of downtown Stratton, South Carolina—a long, pleasant two-lane, with street parking and trees lit up with strings of white lights, surrounded by a pleasant mix of mom-and-pop restaurants and stores dotted with the occasional Walgreens, Starbucks or Cheesecake Factory. The pedestrians were slightly different—slightly hipper, slightly more diverse, with slightly more homeless lurking about—but, still, it wouldn't have surprised me to turn the corner and find myself on the intersection of Pine and Stratton.

Perhaps all walking neighborhoods were a bit alike, no matter where they were.

As we walked, Vickman and I talked about the "mission." We still had meetings for the Magical Security Council, and Alex had asked me back to the Valentine Foundation to shoot some "pickup shots," but, with Cinnamon's award ceremony canceled, I just felt like getting her out of here. Vickman agreed, but before I broke down, Jewel turned and pointed toward a flashing marquee. "There it is," she said. "The Borders of Palo Alto."

"Coffee . . . in a *bookstore?*" I said. "And a chain bookstore to boot! We're on the other side of the country, in a unique place filled with little gems, and you're going to drag me to a chain bookstore with a chain coffeehouse—"

"Oh, quit your whining, you'll love it," Jewel said. "It's made from an old theater."

The Borders of Palo Alto *was* made from an old-style movie theater, but that didn't tell me what to expect: a long courtyard, open to the sky except for thin netting overhead, between stucco walls and Spanish-style roofs of charming century-old buildings. Round metal tables were filled with coffee drinkers and laptop campers and more of the homeless; the more I encountered them, the more disturbed I was about the Bay Area—not that Atlanta didn't have homeless. At the end of the courtyard, we passed through glass doors and a small café that occupied what must have been the ticket booth, then hooked right into a bright, golden two-level bookstore dominated by media below and books above on what must have been the balcony.

"Wo-o-o-owww," Cinnamon said.

"You see that balcony?" Jewel said, leaning down next to Cinnamon, who was staring about, starry-eyed. Jewel said, "According to my very reliable sources, it has the best math section in the Peninsula, right next to the largest audiobook section on the West Coast."

Cinnamon squealed and bounded off, and I laughed. I grabbed a maple mocha and headed out to the courtyard with Jewel, where we sat with a great view of the climbing Spanish architecture rising above us. I took a sip, smiling at Jewel; she just smiled back at me.

"Thank you," I said. "Mission accomplished—what's wrong?"

Jewel's face had fallen. She frowned, pursing her lips, stirring her steaming hot beverage, then asked, "I hate to ask, but . . . any progress on decoding those messages?"

I took another sip, considering. Part of me still suspected Jewel was holding out, but if she knew what was in the codes, why was she asking me? And if Daniel really was talking to Jewel on the street with fire . . . would she have blithely walked into a trap at Stanford?

"Cinnamon hasn't made any progress," I said. "And no news from Philip neither."

"Funny you mentioned Cinnamon first," Jewel said.

"She is my daughter—what?"

Jewel put her swizzle stick in her mouth and drew it out slowly. "You know, Cinnamon really is amazing," she said, "but do you really think your until-recently practically-illiterate daughter has a better shot at cracking the code than the National Security Agency?"

"Actually," I said, "Philip has *both* the NSA and the DEI trying to crack it. They've got a friendly wager—the DEI thinks they can crack it in a dozen messages, the NSA, ten. Cinnamon thinks we can do it in six if those symbols are, as she thinks, just coded English letters—"

"So Cinnamon's going to beat two sets of spooks to the punch," Jewel said.

"I never said that," I said. "She's just learning cryptography. You can't expect—"

"But *you* do," Jewel said. "For answers, you think of her first, because you're expecting she'll beat them. If she knew cryptography, you'd fully expect she'd have *already* beat the DEI and the NSA to the punch. You really think she's *that* good."

I stared blankly at Jewel. I realized I really did think that.

"I mean, maybe she is," Jewel said, taking a sip and wincing at the coffee's heat. "*Phoo.* It's possible. *I'm* that good, at what *I* do. They fly me across oceans to perform with spinny fire things. But I'm an adult. You can hold me to that standard—"

"They flew her across a continent," I said, "to win a math prize—"

"*You* flew her across a continent," Jewel said. "Even if Cinnamon solves this problem, there'll come a day she can't live up to that . . . that *expectation.* Cut her some slack, OK? Don't hinge your adult plans on the performance of a young child. Let her have a childhood."

"I—yes," I said. "Yes. Absolutely."

"Well," Jewel said, dipping her swizzle stick and licking it. "OK, then."

"So, Jewel Anne Grasslin," I said. "Adult plans. What are you going to do now?"

"Get on a plane," Jewel said determinedly, "go back to Hawai`i—and hole up. And not even on my home island of Maui—I'm going to a different one, smaller, where we've got a little Kanaka Maoli community. Where I learned fireweaving, in fact."

"Where you got your liquid fire, I'll bet," I said.

"Not you too," Jewel said sharply. "Let me guess, you'd love to get some—"

"Jewel, I and my daughter have been caught in the crosshairs for you—*three times*," I said, and Jewel frowned, looking a bit guilty. I said, "If Devenger's right, Daniel's beef with you is over liquid fire, but I don't know if he's right because *you aren't telling me anything*—"

"Dakota!" Jewel said, raising her hands. "I'll tell you what I told Daniel: Yes, I have a supply, and no, I can't give any to you." I opened my mouth to object, but she said, "I know, I know, you'd love some, given the dragon tats that you ink, but—"

"But I'm not asking for any, because I don't use it," I said, and Jewel raised her eyebrow. "Devenger thinks our stonegrinders must have a secret source they add to our pigments, but I'd never heard of the damn stuff before today. Why do people keep so many damn secrets?"

"Power," Jewel said. "Knowledge is power; knowledge of a secret is more powerful. Knowledge of a dangerous secret . . . why, that's the best power of all. Especially if you're self-righteous, convinced you have to keep the secret, convinced the world will burn if you give it up, that motivation will burn within you like a fire. It becomes . . . *empowering*."

I stared at her. She was pretty, and charming . . . but I loved how she thought.

"What's *your* empowering secret, Jewel?" I asked, sipping my mocha, and she shrugged. Jewel *was* holding something back; I needed to lean on her for information, to be smart, to be careful . . . or, hell, I could just put all my cards on the table. "What's hidden in those codes?"

Jewel bit off an angry retort, then sighed. "Dakota, I'm in the crosshairs too—and you're the first outsider who's stood by me. I need you to believe that if I knew, I'd tell you. But other than knowing they're some kind of threat, I don't know what's in the codes—"

"Then let's figure it out together," I said. "Daniel's not going to waste effort on a three story sign saying 'I hate you.' And if he cares about wasting liquid fire, he's sure not going to use it in a giant PSA saying 'please don't use liquid fire in performances, we need it to live forever—' "

"Oh, feh," Jewel said. "Who wants to live forever, *really?* Life is fire. The candle that burns twice as long burns half as bright. Everyone dies. Even the Earth is gonna die. Use it up, burn it out, enjoy it while you've got it. Everything else is wasted potential."

"And that's the conflict, isn't it?" I asked, leaning back, kicking my feet up onto the seat of a chair. "You use more liquid fire in a performance than Daniel probably uses in months. You even dip your defensive poi in it, and this with your supplies running out—"

"Hey," Jewel said. "No one said our supplies are running out—"

"*You* just did, by denying it so quickly," I said, staring up through the mesh over the courtyard into the blackness of the night. "You're using up the liquid fire because you believe in using it, while Daniel wants to use it for . . . a longevity spell, perhaps."

"Maybe, but . . . *yuk*," Jewel said, shuddering. "Daniel's clan does have this wizened old *gnome* they all look up to. They call her 'the Firebrand,' but she's more like a dried-up old *nut*. I know, I know, I'd be happy to look like *anything* at three hundred years—but you wither because you're basically *cursing* yourself for centuries straight. Even if you use the spell *once*, it's like you're stuck in time.

Have you seen what that *does* to people?"

"I have seen that," I said slowly, closing my eyes—the Warlock, the Commissioner, and Devenger, all stuck in the early seventies. Why then? Had they discovered a supply of liquid fire in 1970? Or was there a simpler explanation? The sixties was when the American counterculture got bored with sex, drugs, and rock and roll, and started to turn to magic, so it was just possible that the ageless wizards minted in the late sixties or early seventies were the first generation of them that wanted to go public. I couldn't say. "I've seen it three times this trip, in fact."

"This is why I tell you you can't put magic in a box," Jewel said. "There's nothing in those spells that would tell you they'll stunt your fashion sense, and yet they do. Your whole emotional and spiritual growth gets retarded, not just your aging. Magic is a whole—"

"I know, I know," I said, putting my hands over my face. I tried to get perspective. My mind drifted over Palo Alto, first hovering over Nola's folk-art courtyard, then sailing up over the trees, before coming to rest over the mesh-covered alley to Borders as my friends gathered around us at the table. "You can't reduce magic to its parts without missing the big—"

"*Dakota,*" Jewel hissed, her hand closing on my wrist. "You gotta see this."

My eyes opened in shock—but the third-party image of myself and my friends in the courtyard didn't go away—if anything it got *stronger*, fighting in sudden double vision with the image coming from my own eyes up through the mesh of the courtyard—where my own Dragon, my *original* masterwork, perched atop the rooftop of Borders in full glowing Technicolor life.

The double vision abruptly ended as the Dragon flinched and snapped its head, as if stung by the feedback from my own visual cortex. It *roared*, a full-voiced throaty trumpet worthy of the Tyrannosaurus of *Jurassic Park*, and chairs and tables around us suddenly rattled and overturned as patrons heard it, saw it, then screamed and stumbled away.

"That's . . ." Saffron said. "Dakota, that's—"

"That's *my* Dragon," I said. "My first masterpiece."

I rose to my feet, staring up at it, staring up at *my own tattoo* brought to life, thirty feet high, glowing like neon but solid as a fist, its thick Imperial talons cracking and crumpling the ridge of the roof that was its perch, broken tile sliding down the roof and into the netting.

Mesmerized, I stared at the glittering coils, the sparkling blue eyes—and realized I'd seen the tattoo like this before, when I killed Christopher Valentine with magic. He'd shut down my other tattoos with pitch and tied me to an altar, so I'd been forced to detach the Dragon to fight him off; but instead of returning to me once it saved my life, it had *consumed* him, growing opaque, glowing with power, rearing with pride—then bursting through the roof.

I nodded at the Dragon in respect, and the Dragon glanced down at me in the briefest acknowledgement—then the vast magical beast trumpeted, launched itself, and again flew away, disappearing into the night sky with three huge beats of its powerful wings.

A huge chunk of masonry cracked loose and tumbled down into the mesh. One by one, the strands snapped, and we all leapt back as a piece of stone, stucco and Spanish tile the size of a mailbox smashed the table in front of us and then shattered on the floor.

"What . . . the *fuck?*" Cinnamon said, staring up at the sky.

"Holy shit," Vickman said, staring at the dented table.

"Holy shit," Jewel repeated, staring up at the sky, though I got the feeling she meant it in entirely different way than Vickman had. "*And* . . . what the fuck?"

What had just happened?

That had been *my* Dragon. I thought of that tattoo. Of all the time I spent tattooing it; of the tattooing talk I was supposed to give in Burlingame. Of the colors of the tattoo; of the colors of Castro Street which we were supposed to visit on Saturday. Of the magic fire the Dragon could breathe; of all the fire magic we'd seen over this crazy week. Of the horrific circumstances under which I'd detached it, saving myself from Valentine's knife . . . and of all of this week's chaos, and the unknown horrors it might promise. That chaos had robbed Cinnamon of her award, had forced Jewel to flee, and had woken my new tattoo to a weird kind of life—but *my* mission, the mission to secure the funds for Cinnamon's future, had been accomplished.

I thought of all of that . . . for all of five seconds.

Then I revisited my command decision.

"Screw the Bay," I said. "Let's get the hell out of Dodge."

34. The Player of Games

In under two and a half hours, we were on a plane, flying out of the San Francisco Bay Area. We were back in Atlanta by morning—and then things slowed down *considerably*. There were no more assaults by crazy fire ninjas, no more mysterious messages writ in fire on the streets, no nighttime visits of improbably detached tattoos grown impossibly stronger.

But we were not out of the woods. Not by a long shot.

We still had to face the music.

"So, Dakota Frost," the lich rasped, "your mission to San Francisco was a failure."

Like a vulture, the lich loomed forward, dead white skin of his skull gripped by dark rivulets of black hair, white pinpricks gleaming in the black sockets of his eyes. His lips parted in a piranha smile, his cold bony fingers reached out . . . and he drew his queen across the chessboard in one decisive motion. Then the sparks in his eyes shifted up to me.

"You failed, as I said you would, but even more spectacularly—home three days early, with your tail between your legs, with nothing to show for your expensive boondoggle," the vampire said. "Your move, Dakota Frost."

I swallowed. The "lich" was Sir Leopold, the leader of the Vampire Gentry of Atlanta. Saffron might be the most physically powerful vampire in the city; her master, Lord Delancaster, held the highest public rank. But Sir Leopold, the dark vulture with white skin standing in an Victorian suit like a failed reanimation of Professor Moriarty, held the keys to the kingdom.

I blinked at the chessboard, trying to think. I hadn't expected to be playing this game. When we'd arrived at the lich's mansion to give our report, the sun had barely set, but the bony old creature was already waiting for us; I hadn't known he was that resistant to the sun. Even now, the warm glow of twilight still leaked in through the open windows of the study, forcing Nyissa, my ostensible "bodyguard" to remain bundled up in her dark traveling cloak, huddled in a chair as far from the light as possible while *I* had to stand before the lich.

Cinnamon shifted in her chair. I scowled—I didn't like having her here, but I had hoped to drop her off with her schoolmate Joya, who had not yet arrived at the lich's house. Then I realized Cinnamon was nervous because the lich was waiting for me to speak.

"First off, it wasn't your mission," I said, "it was a trip for Cinnamon—"

"And yet you failed to bring home even a plastic statuette," the lich said.

"The 'mission' wasn't a complete failure," I said defensively, eyes flickering between Cinnamon and the chessboard. Nothing to show for it? No, I came back with a contract for two million dollars—but I wouldn't tell the lich that; above and beyond it being none of his fucking business, I didn't want these ancient, powerful vampires to have too clear an idea of how much treasure was stored at my castle. "We had to leave early, but we learned a lot."

"Really," the lich hissed, gesturing at the chessboard. "Show me."

Oh, hell. I glared at the chessboard. It was early in our game, but the position was already confusing, and I was a knight down with no real plan. The symbolism wasn't lost on me. The lich wasn't playing with me—he was playing me, and wanted me to know it.

"We learned some games aren't worth playing out," I said, tipping over my king—and the lich hissed. "We were under fire, almost without reason. We made friends, we got aid from allies—but when you're down before you start, sometimes the best move is to regroup."

"I did not mean you to demonstrate it so literally," the lich said, laughing softly. "But I did warn you. That San Francisco is a warzone. That you sought allies where others have tried and failed. That you lacked the knowledge you needed to make the trip a success—"

"Well," I said, "like I said, we learned a lot—"

"What did you learn?" the lich hissed. "That there is far more to magic than you know? That your child was too young for the schools you indulged her fancies on? That the people who owe you are no likelier to give you your due to your face than over the phone?"

I narrowed my eyes. "What are you saying?"

"This . . . trip," the lich rasped, "was not the business of the Council. It was not even a vacation. It was a thin excuse to gather your loved ones under the wing of new allies, with a new source of funds. Surely you see that was futile now. You cannot escape our grasp—"

"If you mean to say you had us tailed while we were out there, we could have used the help of those agents when we were under attack," I said evenly. "If you mean to say you were actually behind those attacks . . . you will find you cannot escape my wrath."

The lich chuckled softly. "You and I are too dangerous for cheap threats or stunts. I simply meant that you will not find allies in San Francisco useful enough to keep you out of the situations you . . . and yours . . . have created."

Cinnamon drew herself up even more tightly in the chair.

"You know, this creepy insinuation thing, it's not working for me," I said. "If you're referring to the graffiti attacks, those could have happened just as easily in San Francisco as they did here. Remember, the Screetscribe hated all vampires, not just Atlantans."

Something flickered behind the lich's eyes, ever so slightly, so I rolled on.

"If you're referring to cleaning up that mess . . . the Streetscribe's black-book is circulating widely now. We have to not just clean it up here, we need to stop it from starting there." I said. "Yes, we had to bail without meeting all the people I wanted, without even Cinnamon's award. That doesn't mean we didn't find allies. They might even be useful to you."

The lich considered that for a while. Then, slowly, he smiled.

"I think they shall be useful . . . to me," the lich said. Then his bony hand reached out and righted my king. "Which turns to my next lesson—some games you cannot easily stop playing, Dakota Frost. It is still your move—even if you know, in the end, you are going to lose."

That hung in the air like a lead balloon.

"Ooo, boogedy," I said, taking his queen with my knight.

The lich blinked. "You fool," he said, moving his knight. "I have you forked—"

I moved my king—because I had to, I was in check—but I'd get that knight before he forced mate. "If I'm going down, I'm going to have some fun."

The lich hissed and knocked the pieces from the board.

"Oh, you concede?" I said. "How wonderful for me—"

"No, for you are a fool, and are not seeing what I am trying to teach you here," the lich said with a hiss. "Even for one such as you, who delights in the rules of the game . . . you have much to learn before you can win. Girl! Reset the board!"

I blinked in shock; he was speaking to Cinnamon. She glanced away from him a moment, then seemed to jerk and hopped out of her chair, gathering the fallen pieces from the floor.

"Don't, Cinnamon," I said sharply. "I won't have you doing his dirty—"

But when I glanced up, the lich had drawn a long bony finger to his lips. Nyissa had stood as well, slowly letting her dark hood back to show pale skin, violet hair—and glittering jeweled lace choker covering her healing scars. She too put her finger to her lips.

I suddenly realized that twilight had passed and true night had fallen. I swallowed. Nyissa shifted, rolling her poker between her fingers imperiously . . . but with a hint of fear. There was a quiet creaking in the old bones of the house in which we stood; then a sliding panel opened.

The Lady Scara stepped from the shadows to see Cinnamon placing the chess pieces back in place on the board between me and Sir Leopold. Scara was a black, matronly vampire, whose eyes literally glowed red with the closest thing I'd ever seen to pure bottled hate.

"We are done with you here, girl; you are not needed in the Council tonight," the lich said harshly, cuffing Cinnamon behind the ear—for show, I hoped. "Lord Iadimus is here. Receive him, then go entertain his daughter while your mother details for us her failure."

"Yes, Sir Leopold," Cinnamon said, quickly turning away and bolting out. My blood boiled, but I kept my mouth shut. The lich, it seemed, was actually on my side against his protégé, Scara, and was willing to put on a little show to protect Cinnamon.

Scara watched Cinnamon go, then turned her red gaze back upon us. I could feel the flush of "heat" from her gaze, a mana field flooding out of her irises, as a prickling along my tattoos. I didn't need to feel the religious symbols on my knuckles burn to know she meant me harm.

"You cannot shield the stray from me forever," she said, and I could not tell whether she was speaking to me or the lich—but I could tell that Cinnamon remained on Scara's little black book of enemies. The vampire said, "One day there will be an accounting."

"Maybe," I said, moving my king's pawn forward two squares, "but not today—"

Now Scara knocked the pieces from the board. "Enough games," she hissed.

"You forget yourself," the lich said softly to her, eyes still on me.

"I see through both of you," she said.

Cinnamon opened the door to the study, and beyond her, I saw a tall, blond man kiss the forehead of a tall, blond girl; Lord Iadimus, and his dhampyr daughter, Joya. Lord Iadimus stepped forward, and Joya stepped back, quickly darting off with Cinnamon.

"The Lady Saffron is detained," Iadimus said coldly, eyes quickly flicking over me, the lich, Scara—and the scattered chess pieces. "But since she was a witness in San Francisco, we wished to interrogate her separately in any event. We have a quorum. Shall we proceed?"

"Of course," the Scara said, brushing past Nyissa—then her dress caught on the end of Nyissa's poker. Nyissa's eyes bulged—Scara was the vampire who gave her those scars. Scara slowly looked aside, to fabric hooked on metal. "Do you need the lesson again, my dear?"

"Do *you?*" Iadimus asked, stepping forward quickly, releasing her dress. Iadimus had saved Nyissa from Scara—saved me too, though I guessed that was incidental to protecting a fellow vampire under truce from unprovoked violence. He said, "Behave yourself."

"As you wish," Scara said, sweeping forward. "Another time."

Iadimus shook his head, almost imperceptibly, then followed. The lich was impassive . . . but did he look pained? Then that ancient monster followed his protégé—and the second vampire that he needed to keep his protégé under leash—into the chamber.

Damn it! This was precisely what I'd feared when Saffron became a vampire—not that I'd get sucked *on* by a vampire, but that I'd get sucked *into* her vampire world. Now I was about to enter the lion's den with a vampire who was my former *enemy* as my only protection.

Nyissa and I stared at each other helplessly . . . and then joined the Gentry in court.

35. To Summon a Dragon

The Gentry interrogated me for hours, a long session over a conference table where I explained we were still in communication with the fae and werekin we had not had the chance to meet with before I hit the eject button. And, disturbing as they had been, the attacks had actually made our mission easier; defending Jewel gave us instant credibility.

I was just explaining what I'd learned about liquid fire—oh, and the many requests we'd had to broker a meeting with Lord Buckhead—when Scara hissed softly and raised her hand. Nyissa shifted, ever so slightly, but she remained completely silent while Scara spoke.

"And what of the dragon?" Scara said.

"And what of it?" I said evenly. "I had to defend Jewel—"

"Do not dissemble," Scara snapped. "I do not mean that little display in Union Square. We have seen your tattoo magic. I meant the summoning."

"The . . . summoning?" I said, perplexed.

"Of the spirit of a dragon," Iadimus said, so seriously that I realized it was not just poetic language. "Ghostly visions, first sighted when you arrived in San Francisco, and continuing until you departed. Even excluding the Union Square sighting, there were five visitations—"

"All of that was me," I said dismissively. "I used my dragon tattoo, first in Oakland, then in the Square, later at Stanford, and . . . and . . ."

And then I paused. I'd only used my Dragon three, maybe four times.

"You used it in the Square twice, at the same time?" Scara asked, and my eyes widened. I *had* gotten double vision—and several people had referred to the *dragons* at Union Square. Scara continued, "And used it atop a theater at Palo Alto? *And* atop the Golden Gate Bridge?"

"Atop the Golden Gate? That was *real?*" I asked. "I saw the video at the Drake Cage, but though it was a promotion, ripping off one of my designs—"

"We are not talking about your tattoo magic," Scara barked.

"Yes, we are," I said. "I still don't quite know how, but the sighting at Borders in Palo Alto *was* one of my tattoos, or more technically a *projectia.* I have no idea how it survived, but Cinnamon snapped a picture and it was very definitely generated by my original masterwork, the one I detached and used against Christopher Valentine. Based on my reaction to that brief glimpse of video, the one atop the Golden Gate was almost certainly the same one."

Scara glared at me, then at Nyissa. "You saw it, Nyissa—was it hers?"

"I—" Nyissa said, her hand going to her throat as her voice came out as an unexpectedly ragged croak. Then she drew a breath and said, "I never had the pleasure of seeing her original masterwork upon her skin, but the apparition certainly had the . . . confident lines of her style."

Scara and Iadimus looked at each other. "Still, that could fit," Scara said.

"What are you talking about?" I asked.

"We are given to understand," Iadimus said, "*you* summoned that dragon spirit. If true, you would be the first person to do so . . . in at least a century. Perhaps more—"

"But I never—"

"Perhaps unwittingly, it seems, by launching a tattoo which it could inhabit."

My mouth dropped. I'd never considered the possibility that something could possess a *tattoo*, but there was nothing to stop it from happening. Complete tattoos were normally inked with Euler angles that made that difficult, but released from the body and disintegrating—

"You admit it is a possibility," Scara said.

"Most definitely," I said. "Skindancers ink magic tattoos inside magic circles to prevent stray spirits from inhabiting the magic. Normally a *projectia* is reattached, or is small enough that it disintegrates quickly; but this was a masterwork, filled with two dancers' magic."

"More like a probability," Scara said.

"Perhaps," Iadimus said. "Do you have a source of liquid fire?"

"What? Not you too," I said. "No, I don't have a source, but—"

"I take it you know the substance's value. Do not be concerned. Vampires have no need of it; we have our own source of eternal life," the lich said. "Iadimus asks because, according to legend, a dragon spirit can only be summoned by a spell using liquid fire as a component."

"Only *true* liquid fire has the concentrated magic needed to summon a dragon," Scara said, and I squirmed in my chair as my Dragon squirmed on my back. The vampire said, "Or so the legends go. I do not know if I believe those stories—ah. But I see you do."

Damn it! "I—I have heard that *theory*," I said. "That true liquid fire is a . . . 'concentrated' form of magic, capable of accomplishing what many, many wizards working together could not. As for the summoning . . . I don't know. It sounds convincing, not knowing more—"

"So," Iadimus said. "Was your tattoo inked with liquid fire? Even in trace amounts—"

"No. I don't have access to any, nor do I even recall *hearing* about it before this trip." Then I scowled—I *had* learned a thing or two on this trip. "*But* . . . I have heard a wizard allege that there must be some compatible compound in the pigments I use."

"I used to be a wizard, and I concur," Nyissa said. "The House Beyond Sleep feared the skindancers of Blood Rock and their unusually potent magic. Before the Lady Frost brokered a truce, I worried they were using vampire blood . . . but liquid fire is a better explanation."

"I have never heard my master or any of the stonegrinders refer to liquid fire," I said—realizing, as I said it, that that meant nothing. "Of course, while legend may *claim* that liquid fire may be required for a spell, according to modern science . . . a substitute could do."

"If that's true," Nyissa mused, "when you empowered your dragon masterwork in Union Square, using the magic of Jewel's shield, which we know used liquid fire, and in quantity . . . perhaps you *accidentally* summoned the spirit of a dragon."

All the other vampires hissed, and Scara rose from the table.

"Leopold was right," she said. "You have exposed us all to unnecessary risk."

"How?" I asked. "I'm not contradicting you. I need you to explain this to me."

"Liquid fire extends human life. Dragons are supposedly the only source of liquid fire," Iadimus said patiently. "And their spirits can only be summoned by magic that uses liquid fire, or something very much like it. Something that can be potentially used for the same purpose."

I leaned back in my chair. *Now* I could see where this was going.

"So some cult of ancient wizards," I said, "is going to try to steal my supplies—"

"No, you fool," Scara said. "Who cares about your supplies?"

"What Scara means," Iadimus said, "is that you are their target."

"Do what?" I said. "But . . . if they want liquid fire, what do they need *me* for?"

"I have seen this before, over the centuries," the lich said softly. "The supplies of liquid fire rise and ebb. When they rise, arrogant youths drink deep in the hope of endless life; when they ebb, desperate old men fight to the death over the extra day granted by that last drop."

"But the supply should have long since run out," I said. "Dragons are extinct—"

"But their eggs keep," the lich said with a cackle. "Oh, they keep. And there are legends—"

"When the spirit of a dragon is sighted, an egg is about to hatch," Scara said.

"And the summoner of the dragon's spirit is the one who will crack it," Iadimus said.

I let my chair fall back to level. I hadn't seen where this was going at all.

I stared at the vampires. These were the Gentry, deadly and manipulative, creepy old monsters who'd killed one of my friends and who'd tried to kill me. And yet they continued to surprise me, this time with knowledge of legends and . . . concern for my welfare?

"By summoning the spirit," Scara said—and then her voice softened. "That is, *if* you summoned the spirit, you *may* have started a war for liquid fire." Then her old venom surged back. "And if that *stunt* in Union Square convinced desperate wizards you are the herald . . ."

"They'll move Heaven and Earth," Nyissa said, swallowing, "to get to you."

"Surely," I said, "surely you don't really believe—"

"What we believe is irrelevant," the lich said. "Somewhere out there,

Dakota Frost, an ancient wizard is dying. Only dragon's blood will save him, or so he thinks; liquid fire from a dragon's egg, revealed only by the summoning of the spirit of a dragon.

"And you are the first person to have summoned a dragon in over a hundred years."

36. Off the Deep End

Dreamily, I strode through a tunnel of shimmering blue-green light. Myriad fluttering shapes broke the sunbeams into ever-changing shapes beneath my feet. The day was almost perfect . . . then a dark shadow loomed above me, blotting out the sun.

I looked up. The vast shape sliding effortlessly overhead had a body longer than a car, fins wider than I was tall, mouth big enough to swallow a child—though Taroko, the Georgia Aquarium's newest whale shark, was a filter feeder that never ate anything larger than a pea.

The huge shark turned lazily, first showing its white belly, then the distinctive gray and white panther pattern on its sides. As Taroko slid overhead, Cinnamon squealed and hopped; on each bounce, her head rose almost to the glass top of the Ocean Explorer tunnel.

"Ta-RO-ko Ta-RO-ko," she cried, "the-SPLENdid-and-MAGnificent!"

I sighed, and smiled. At last, things were back to normal.

After the Gentry's ominous warning, things were tense at the MSC—but no thieves snuck in to steal my nonexistent supply of liquid fire, no thugs leaned on me to divulge the location of my mythical dragon's egg, and there were no more sightings of my possibly-possessed tattoo.

Even the Dragon on my back had gone disappointingly quiet.

And so, without data, I was left with what I had—inking new asp and vine tattoos to get back to full strength, researching liquid fire to find out what I could, trying to crack the code with Cinnamon, and injuring myself trying to learn fireweaving as remotely instructed by Alex.

After we had signed the contracts, Alex had honored his part of the bargain—sort of. He had started to teach me regular fire*spinning*, not magical fire*weaving*, insisting that I learn to spin poi before setting them on fire, and that I get comfortable spinning fire before I tried magic.

It was hard to argue with that.

I tried learning the theory, but, as Jewel had hinted, fireweaving was not simple, and trying to learn enough of it to reverse-engineer what the fire ninjas were doing—or what she was doing—was taking far longer than I expected, especially since the basics didn't use magic.

So it felt good to finally get a glimpse of normal life—a field trip with my daughter.

No; it was more than just that. I'd taken her across the country to win a prize, only to have hers snatched away while I got mine. Now I was determined to make it up to her, to spend as much time with her as I could. It wasn't just a field trip; it was an unspoken apology.

We left the glass tunnel and its rainbow schools of fish to find an enormous plate glass window as big as the front of my house—another view of the same six million gallon tank. The tank's newest star guests, Taroko and his companion, Yushan, slid past every few minutes, and I watched them closely. The Taiwanese whale sharks had adjusted well to their first month in the tank, sliding effortlessly through the waters. Their distinctive pattern would make an interesting full-body tattoo; I wondered if I could weave swimming magic into it. I'd have to talk to Jinx.

"That's most of the exhibits. Ready to go?" I asked, after Cinnamon and I eventually returned to the mammoth atrium of the Georgia Aquarium. All around us were engineered micro-worlds: rivers, lakes, the deep sea. "Get everything you needed for your report?"

"What? No! Let's . . . um," Cinnamon said, whirling, eyeing the river exhibits we had already gone through an hour earlier. Then she caught the second question. "What? Oh."

"I take it the 'oh' is also a 'no,'" I said, pulling out my buzzing smartphone. "Come on, Cinnamon. What did you need to see to finish your report?"

"Oh, God, not that old thing," Cinnamon said, ignoring my question and peering down at the phone. "That's *so* last month. Why don't you gets an iPhone—"

"You means you want me to get *you* an iPhone," I said, checking the call—it was Ranger. She was an artist friend who shared my newfound interest in firespinning. "And maybe I will, but as for me, this thing isn't even seven months old. Besides, are iPhones even out yet?"

"Mom! Didn't you see the lines? *Eeeveryone's* gots them at school," she said—and I suddenly realized yet another downside to sending Cinnamon to an expensive private school—her friends all had parents who were rich, rich, rich. She said, "You gonna get that?"

"No," I said, thumbing the call to voicemail. "I don't want to be rude cell phone lady—and I don't want to distract you from doing your homework. All right, young lady, once more with feeling—this time, fewer pretty pretties, more taking notesies."

While Cinnamon was getting notes and taking pictures for her field report on the Indo-Pacific reef, Ranger texted me: **«Want to see some live dragons spin fire?»**

My jaw dropped. Numbly, I thumbed an affirmative and pocketed my phone. I couldn't read that and not think of Jewel. She'd called when she landed, but promptly disappeared—no calls, no email, not even a text message, nor did she respond when I'd texted her. After a few weeks, I'd started to think that Daniel had gotten her—I'd heard from *Carnes* more recently—when on the sixth of August I'd received a postcard from her:

Hey Skindancer, miss me? Hope you worried, but you needn't. I'm safe, sound, and as far from the public eye as can possibly be. No wires on this isle! This may be a few days getting to you—Molokii will send it when he next goes to Maui. I trust you, but who knows who reads the mail? Thanks for saving me. And thanks for showing me your Dragons—both attached and unattached. Wish I'd gotten to know you better—I had fun with you.

Thoughts of hot kisses from a might-have-been—your Fireweaver.

A "might have been." She was right. It was hard to imagine a more difficult long-distance relationship, between the attention hound and the underground princess, one grabbing the spotlight, the other trying to lay low on the other side of the planet.

True to form, the airport Maui postcard had no return address and was postmarked the first of August, more than a week after the date on Jewel's handwritten note sent near the end of July. It had taken Molokii longer to mail the card than it had taken the card to reach me.

That worried me at first—Molokii was quiet, by necessity, but he didn't seem like a slacker. Maybe the "isle" was on the other end of a ferry? No, Molokii drove cars. Well, even then, they could still be on the other end of a ferry. I hoped nothing sinister was hidden behind the delay. Maybe I was getting paranoid, but with my job as leader of the Magical Security Council, it was easy to see why. Every week, it seemed, I learned of a new threat.

Everything worried me now, but I didn't see what else I could do, other than keep a lid on Atlanta and keep talking to Carnes and Kitana. We all wanted to find the attackers, but I wasn't going to patrol the streets of San Francisco, much less fly to Hawaii to fight fire ninjas.

It didn't take long for Cinnamon to finish her third circuit of the aquarium, this time on point. Once outside in the bright bright blinky light, I immediately pulled out my phone and called Ranger. "Hey, girl, what you got for me?" I said.

"Oh, did I get your attention?" Ranger asked impishly. She sounded like she was smiling; that was a relief, as last I'd seen her she was recovering from a graffiti attack—just out of a burn ward, walking with a cane, and days from being homeless. "Thought you'd never call back—"

"Bull, you knew I would," I said. "That text was tailor-made to turn my head."

"Was it now," Ranger said. We'd been emailing about firespinning ever since I got back from San Francisco—but we hadn't actually spoken. "Well, now that I've got your attention, hello, Ranger, how are you, are you out on the streets or not—"

"You know how to pick up a phone," I said. "But, since you asked, how are you—"

"Off the cane," she said, "And off the streets. In fact, the lawsuit has been settled to everyone's mutual satisfaction, so the Candlesticks Apartments are back in business just in time for the Rise festival, which I am promoting. Like live music, fire, and hot guys hanging from wires?"

I raised an eyebrow. "At least the latter two are intriguing."

"Oh, but the first is too," Ranger said. "Ever seen the Loch Ness Dragons?"

"No, but I think I'd like to," I said, smiling at Cinnamon, who nodded vigorously. "My daughter would too. What kind of scene is Rise? Still like the old days—"

"Yep. Twenty-one and up," she said, and Cinnamon let out a sharp exhale and spun off. "Not quite BYOB, but it won't be a full bar. We're still trying to work the kinks out with the landlord. But, hell or high water, the Dragons go on at nine tonight—"

"*Tonight?* Hell. Well, let me work out the kinks with my daughter," I said, winking and tousling Cinnamon's hair and headscarf. "If Mom can get permission to do something cool, she'll be there tonight at nine. See ya—"

"I've been to wilder parties than you," Cinnamon said as I hung up the phone, "had more boys than you, did more drugs than you, been more drunk than you—"

"On that last one, I highly doubt it, my little werekin friend," I said, "not with all those Niivan organelles cleaning the alcohol out of your bloodstream before it hits your brain—"

"How do you knows that?" she said.

"From your textbook on Extraordinary Biology," I said, not breaking stride. I looked back, and my bouncing tigger was stopped dead, staring at me with a dropped jaw. "What? You can't expect me to help you with your homework without trying to learn it myself."

"Do you gots to do everything I do?" Cinnamon said. Her voice was oddly resentful.

"No," I said. "Just the fun stuff. Don't worry. I don't think I'm going to be doing any number theory or code breaking. I think that's all you, baby."

"I'm not a baby," she said hotly, "and I should too be able go to your stupid party—"

"You'll *always* be my baby," I said, gathering her in my arms and kissing her forehead, "even when you win the Nobel Prize. But don't be too eager—you may have had it wild and rough at the werehouse, but the Rise Festival could throw even you for a loop."

PUFFS OF FIRE blossomed in sequence up the sides of a thirty-foot arch of welded metal, meeting at its apex in a burst of flame that illuminated an endless sea of half-naked humanity beyond. As the flames faded, the arch lit up with the neon letters RISE ATLANTA.

There were jugglers and firespinners and men on stilts. A dead-white bald man in goggles carved a burning wooden sculpture with a blowtorch, and a dreadlocked black woman with fuzzy boots did elaborate tricks with Tarot cards that seemed to glow. A thoroughly Native American man dressed as a chief wove his way through dancers of all nationalities performing an Indian-from-India traditional. There were welded sculptures and neon flowers, hemp garments and handwoven silks, Tesla coils and kinetic mobiles. Stages with live bands were surrounded with stands of indie records. And, at the heart of the festival, at the center of a crowd of appreciative women, were two slender young men in a breathtaking tug-of-war, pulling at each other via long cords embedded in fishhooks embedded in the taut skin of their bare, muscular chests.

I smiled. Burning Man, writ small.

I paid my fee and waded into the muddy crowd. Far too many people were crammed into the irregular no-man's land behind the featureless black-and-white converted warehouses that were the Candlestick "Apartments." A dancer pirouetted by, whirling sparklers—a bit late for Fourth of July, but I'd allow it. There were three distinct stages, with a folk band and an alternative band and a space band, all partway through sets—but nothing even remotely resembling Loch Ness Dragons, and it was already eight-fifty-five.

Then I got a text, from the ever "reliable" Ranger. **«Where *are* you?»**

I sighed, flinched as lightning crackled overhead, and replied**, «Next to the Tesla coil. Where are my dragons?»**

«On the docks. Come in through the Tower.»

I looked back saw a tall, beige four-story tower—the eponymous Candlestick itself, originally a guard tower and now supposedly where the landlord lived. Beneath the Candlestick was a wide, white blocky structure—into which crowds were already streaming.

Ranger texted me instructions that led me in through the warren of apartments behind the "stage"—literally, a bunch of amps and a big disc set up on the loading docks—and one of Ranger's friends led me down into a tiny roped-off area next to the sound booth.

Ranger was a beefy woman, kind of a cross between Bettie Page and a crossing guard, wearing a beret and twirling a cane which was by now almost certainly for show. She gave me a quick hug and pointed me to the stage while wrestling the mike from the sound crew.

"All right, it's nine-oh-five and we promised we'd start on time," she squealed, a mess of static and feedback. "Give it up for the Loch Ness Dragons!"

The stage went black. Spotlights flared. Drums rolled, crisp and military. And then a rough scream rippled out through the crowd—as *bagpipes* began to play.

Two female drummers in dark mascara and military uniforms marched smartly onto either side of the stage; behind each of them were big, burly bare-chested bagpipe players in kilts. They marched out, the bagpipers really wailing on their instruments, the drummers less so; and the moment I noticed that, I saw, behind the weaving spotlights, a wan, goateed drummer at the back of the stage, filling out the rest of the drumbeat.

Two dancers in dragon masks bounced onto the stage, and I realized the pale drummer was part of the real band and the "drummers" were just two more of the dancers when the stage *exploded,* a huge spray of flame roaring out behind the bagpipers, silhouetting a kilted female guitarist standing back to back with a Goth-punk female violinist.

"Good evening, Atlanta!" screamed the guitarist, leaping forward, kilt flaring, landing with her big black chunky boots planted on the disc, seemingly staring straight at me as she began wailing away on her long bass guitar. "We are the Loch Ness Dragons!"

The guitarist flicked back her rainbow bangs, leaned into a driving bassline, and began prowling forward in place as the spinning disc began turning beneath her feet. The bagpipers joined her on the spinning disc, marching in place beside her as she started to really wail.

I glanced at Ranger, who smiled back at me. This worked. The song was a cover, but I hadn't quite placed it yet—the Loch Ness Dragons were *tight* and had totally made the song their own. There was a flare of light, and Ranger cocked her head at the stage, smiling.

I glanced back forward—and then my eyes went wide in shock.

Behind the singer and the bagpipes was a spray of flame, a shimmering fan, sparking through all the colors of the rainbow with a distinctive, artistic, almost Chinese flair to its repeated arabesque pattern—and then I felt my dragon tattoo stir against my skin.

This wasn't just fire spinning—it was fire *magic.*

I stood on my tiptoe, but I already knew what I would see. Behind the wailing lead singer was a lithe, curvy dancer dressed only in a dragon mask and silks and leather bits. Her face was hidden, but she wore long leather bracers, and spun a staff tipped with points of flame.

—&

It was Jewel, spinning like she was on fire.

37. Jewel on Fire

"Surprise, surprise," Jewel said, mouth quirking up in a devilish smile.

"Fancy meeting you here," I said, feeling a smile and a frown struggle on my face.

We were "backstage" at Rise, in a big "living room" someone had carved out of the loading docks' receiving area with a Persian rug and a few sofas. The Loch Ness Dragons were still stuck pressing flesh and pushing CDs outside, but when I asked Ranger about the spinners, she grinned, led me backstage, and introduced me to Jewel with, "Your groupie is here."

I plopped down on the couch opposite Jewel and Molokii as they cleaned up.

"So, Jewel," I said. "When were you going to tell me you were in town?"

"I, uh," Jewel began, reddening as she slipped on her flannel shirt. "But isn't this a nice surprise? And, for the record, I *didn't* know I was going to be in town until Ranger strong-armed the Dragons into adding this performance, and when I found out she knew you, of course I—"

"You slipped me a backstage pass," I said, smiling halfheartedly. "Yes, that was a nice gesture, and this is a wonderful surprise—but also random, and last minute. What if I couldn't have made it? Would you really have come to town without even calling me?"

"Dakota, don't be like that. I really didn't know I'd be here," Jewel said. She bit her lip. "But, if you hadn't made it, I might have taken it as a sign. I got attacked like, a half dozen times when I was with you—once just because I tagged along with your daughter. You're dangerous, Dakota. Call me superstitious, but I wanted to give us a little breather while I'm laying low."

I grimaced. Jewel had drawn precisely the wrong lesson from the Bay Area—she'd been the target of those attacks, and I was just a bystander. But I could see it—she claimed she'd never been attacked before meeting me, and I too saw the wisdom of getting the hell out of Dodge.

And she'd said *us*. How promising. But still . . . "This is laying low?"

"Not calling anyone directly," she said. "Communicating by word of mouth—"

"An invitation to a performance," I said, "of *public fire magic*—"

"Unannounced, wearing a mask," Jewel said. "I just want to spin. I don't need to be top billed or center stage or any of that. I'm happy to be someone else's window dressing, hanging out in the background, creating beauty with fire, completely anonymous—"

"Spinning the most distinctive fire magic in the world," I said. "That's how I recognized you, Jewel. Not from that beautiful curvy body, or those sexy leather bracers you wore at your last two performances—but from your style of spinning. I recognized your magic—*first*."

Jewel's face drained of color. "Oh, *shit*."

"Aren't these guys *great*," cried an unfamiliar voice I oddly still recognized—and then the lead singer of the Loch Ness Dragons vaulted over the sofa, big black chunky boots banging onto the coffee table. Molokii slid off the sofa onto the floor, and the singer spun, kilt flaring, plopping herself down into the seat he had just vacated, squeezing his hips with her boots and wrapping her arms about his bare, muscular chest. "And I don't just mean in bed."

My mouth dropped open, and then I saw Jewel roll her eyes and lean forward. "She plays with the other team," Jewel said in a stage whisper. "*Most* embarrassing."

I blinked. This was coming a bit too fast; then I realized I was technically in the Loch Ness Dragons' greenroom and should say something nice, like about their band or something.

"You guys rock," I said. "But Infernal called. They want their song back."

"Infernal *loves* us. Every time we play *Sorti de L'enfer, Rechargé* they sell dozens of copies of the original album," the singer said. She had a way of tilting her head forward and staring under those hanging rainbow bangs at you. It was very distracting. "We used to open for them. We got the spinny disc thing from them after it shorted all their amps on one tour."

"Sean," Jewel said, "Dakota Frost."

"Dakota—oh! Your unrequited," Sean said, giving Molokii a hug.

"Not so much unrequited," I said, "as uninvited—"

"Really?" Sean said. "She talks about you all the time, and didn't invite you?"

"I did too invite her, just . . . not directly," Jewel said, her curvy face flushing with color, and I smirked at her. She said, "The timing was . . . inconvenient. We didn't know we were coming in town, and we were sort of lying low—speaking of which, Dakota just—"

"Well, I'm glad you could make it," Sean said. "How'd you ding your . . . ?"

Curious, I followed her eyes and touched my forehead. "Oh!" I said, feeling the little lesion. "I was . . . uh . . . well, I was practicing firespinning and—"

"Were you now," Jewel said, raising an eyebrow. "I feel less bad about pining. But I still don't understand. That's a hell of a welt you got. What were you spinning with?"

"Well, I don't have the, the poi that you guys have," I said defensively, "so I got some string and some blocks of wood—"

"Blocks of wood!" Jewel said, hands going to her face. "Whatever possessed you—"

"The house is being worked on," I said defensively. "Some scraps were lying around, with holes in them so I could tie in some twine—"

"*Lōlō!* I thought you were smart!" Jewel said. "Dry beans in stockings. I'll show you."

"Alex told me to try that, but it sounded confusing," I said, smiling tightly. "I'd say I look forward to you showing me, but since I'm not sure I'm ever going to see you again—"

"Ouch," Sean said, winking at me. "Anyway, Dakota doesn't look like she wears stockings. Or does she, Jewel?"

"What?" Jewel said, reddening. "I—I dunno—"

"You could ask her, you know," Sean said, leaning back, putting her feet up on the table on either side of Molokii, who put his hands on her boots. He looked like a kid in a candy store under her relentless attention. She said, "Good things come to those who ask."

"I think the phrase is normally 'to those who wait,' " I said, "but speaking of asking, I *love* those boots." They were even bigger and chunkier than they looked on stage, polished like she was an army officer, with big old buckles and snaps, coming all the way up her calf just beneath the high white socks tied off just below her knees. "Where did you get them?"

"Cohen's," she said, rocking her boots back and forth. "They're vegan, you know."

"Really?" I said, staring at them—more for the chance to look at her legs than the boots, to be honest. Even though the boots and socks covered her skin, they accentuated the flesh you could see beneath the kilt. I heard a slight noise, and glanced over at Jewel, who was staring at me . . . no *glaring* at me, jealous. I smiled back at Jewel, and said to Sean, "Something about your outfit makes me wonder whether you're wearing the kilt Scottish proper."

Sean stared at me brightly beneath her multicolored bangs. "Since you didn't answer my question about how you wear stockings, I think you'll have to ask one of the Dragonriders about how I wear my kilt," she said, tousling Molokii's hair. He smiled and touched her hand.

"Dragonriders?" I said. "I thought you were the Loch Ness Dragons."

"We are," she said, once again reaching down to wrap her arms around Molokii's bare shoulders. "The Riders are what we call our *groupies.*"

"Oh," I said, feeling my face redden. "I think I just bit off more than I can chew."

"She does have limits," Jewel said, making a note with her invisible pad and pen.

"You knew that," I said. "I seem to recall receiving a critique about them—"

"About your rules," Jewel said, leaning forward, "But that was before I knew you."

"So, are we good now?" Sean asked, looking between us. "By which I mean you two."

"Yeah," I said, smiling at Jewel. "I wasn't mad, I was just a little hurt—"

"Don't be. This stop was unplanned, a favor to Ranger," Sean said, "and Jewel really was trying to lay low. No billing, no publicity, we even added the masks, a nice touch—"

"And *still* spinning the most distinctive fire magic in the world," I said.

"So?" Sean said. "That's why we always try to get the Fireweavers. They're the best part of our performance, better than any light show."

"So you've done this for them before?" I asked, and Jewel seemed to sink lower in her chair. "*Aye yae yae*, have you learned nothing of what I have taught you? Look, I want you to cancel the rest of your schedule with the Dragons—"

"And who are you to tell her to do that?" Sean said. "I thought you were split—"

"Dakota's . . . head of magical security for the Southeast," Jewel said, and, before I could correct that little exaggeration, she launched into a vivid account of the attacks that had happened in San Francisco. It was worse than even I'd known—Jewel had neglected to tell me about Daniel's death threats, or that some of his ninjas had torched the fireweaver's safe house in Sunol. "To the *ground.* Fortunately, no one was killed, but . . . Dakota wasn't there to stop it."

"Holy . . . fuck," Sean said. "You should do what she says."

"Don't puff me up so much," I said, shifting as my Dragon squirmed against my body. "I'm not an expert at this or infallible. I'm not trying to ruin your tour here. And going on tour is a good idea—it's far from your normal haunts, it keeps you moving, isn't predictable—"

"Tonight," Sean said. "Isn't predictable *tonight.* The rest of the tour—it's on *everything*, our T-shirts, website, MySpace—"

"Including galleries of photos, I bet—including Jewel," I said. "Damn it—"

"I'm sorry," Jewel said. She was halfway between pouting and crying. "I . . . look, San Francisco may be his nominal home, but Hawai`i is Daniel's birthplace and stomping ground. I didn't feel *safe* there. I thought if I got far away—"

"It's not your fault," I said; though that wasn't *quite* true, it wasn't quite false either. "You're new at this, and frankly, no one should have to put up with this shit—"

"Hey Dakota," Ranger said, clomping in to the room. Her face broke out in a grin when she saw me sitting opposite Jewel. "I do good, hooking you up with your honey?"

"You did great," I said. "Like I said, a tailor-made text."

"I told you," Ranger said, smiling at Jewel, "*told you* I could get her here."

"Hey Ranger," Sean called, leaning forward, kissing Molokii's ear. "We do good, hooking you up with some crowds?"

"You guys were *awesome*," Ranger said, plopping herself down on the couch next to me and hooking her cane over her shoulder. "Ow. Even last minute, you *packed* my *house* and Staniel says you sold *out* of your own CDs. I owe you guys the hugest favor—"

"Which I'm calling in," Sean said. "Can you take on a pair of Riders for a few days?"

38. The Unexpected Dragon of DeKalb County

Things progressed quickly after that. It didn't start as dating—Jewel and I hung out late that night, discussing a plan for her safety, Jewel and Molokii swung by the Rogue Unicorn the next day to follow up, and Cinnamon and I cooked dinner for both of them that evening.

Ranger, good to her word, found friends that could take Jewel and Molokii, and we didn't see either of them the next day. But they planned to stay in town the week while they figured out their next move, and I planned to see as much of Jewel as I could before she disappeared again.

They met us for lunch, then for dinner, then again, and again. Jewel was a delight—feisty and challenging one minute, sweet and apprehensive the next. I couldn't tell whether she was more scared of the situation, or me . . . but this time, she didn't run and hide.

Well . . . not physically.

A few nights later, Jewel, Cinnamon, and I hosted Doug, Jinx, and our mutual friend Jack Palmotti for dinner. I was experimenting—vegan pepper "steak" made from portabellas for Jinx and me . . . and fried kidney slices with shitake mushrooms and shallots for Cinnamon.

Doug raised a curved blood-red slice of kidney dubiously, then shuddered as Cinnamon wolfed another one down with her big toothy grin. Jinx bumped him with her shoulder, not turning her head, and Doug turned the slice on his fork. He said, "It looks . . . different—"

"Nothing ventured," Jack said, spearing one for himself. He had a shaggy Einstein haircut and moustache, brown rather than gray, and had served as Cinnamon's foster parent briefly during the adoption. "Mmm. Not bad, Dakota. You should try my kidney pudding."

"Fuh—*yeah*," Cinnamon said, another one already on her fork, her fangs gleaming. It was amazing how much control she'd regained since her poisoning, but the full moon was not long behind us—and this close, she really put the *ravenous* in *werekin*. "I *loved* that—"

"Gimme the recipe," I said, after I swallowed my pepper 'shrooms. I had tried a tiny bite of the kidney, and it *was* good, but as a general rule, I tried to limit my intake of meat. "I guarantee, it will not go to waste in this household if an animal died to produce it—"

Doug froze with his fork still in his mouth, and Jewel and Cinnamon giggled.

"Rich," he said at last. "Which reminds me, Cin, I *did* find that Gaines book cheap—"

"Dover books are your friends, let me tell ya," Cinnamon said. "How is it?"

"Rich," Doug said, chewing a little. "But I don't think it's going to help us—"

"Which book is this?" I asked.

"*Cryptanalysis*," Doug said, and Jewel grimaced. Doug put down his fork. "Normally, I'm skeptical of older references, but this seems solid. The problem is, we don't have enough code to *de*code. Five messages, sixty characters each—all we *really* know is the alphabet."

"Assuming there aren't low-frequency letters that haven't shown up," I said. "Like Z."

"Good ciphers don't do that, Mom," Cinnamon said. "They reworks it to mix it up."

"Yeah," Doug said, looking at Jewel. "Have you seen more messages in Hawaii?"

Jewel was staring off, uncomfortable. Then she realized Doug was talking to her.

"Me?" she asked. "What—no. No, I haven't seen any more of those stupid curses."

"They're not curses," Doug said gently. "Well, what about the symbols? Are they—"

"Secrets of my Order," Jewel said flatly. "I'm sorry, I can't share fireweaving secrets—"

"Well," Jack said with a grin, "if we're going down the rabbit hole, I'll take my leave—"

"Sorry, Mr. Palmotti," I said. "I know you don't like Edgeworld business—"

"No, that's OK, Miss Frost," Jack said, standing, dumping his napkin on his *very* cleaned plate. "My babysitter's expecting me home, and I have a *long* drive early tomorrow morning."

"I'll help clear," Jewel said, picking up her own plate. "I'm serious—I'm not supposed to talk about the Order." She paused, plate in hand. "Look, I appreciate all you guys are doing to track down the people that hassled me . . . but it was half a country away. Can we let it rest?"

Jewel stared around the table, taking in our silent reactions. After a moment, she nodded, then took some of the cleared plates and stepped to the kitchen. Cinnamon hopped up to help, then saw the remaining kidney slice and speared it with a claw. She bit into it, filled her hands with plates, and skipped after Jewel and Jack, humming and purring to herself.

"If you leave kidney drips on my hardwoods, you're wiping them up, young lady," I said mock sternly, and Cinnamon smirked back at me. We'd both spent time wiping down the hardwoods together when we moved in. I looked at Jinx. "I love that kid."

Jinx leaned forward, conspiratorial. "Jewel really won't tell you about her magic?"

I frowned, leaning forward as well, lowering my voice. "Not a word of it," I said. "She says there are seven hundred and twenty ways to perform the basic weaves, and until I've learned all of them, she can't even *think* of telling me the details of the actual magic."

"Oh, Dakota," Jinx said. "And this with people trying to *kill her.*"

"We should figure this out," Doug said. He frowned. "Look, Dakota, Cinnamon's great, she's a *genius*, but she's also like a howitzer. If you roll her in place and point her at the right problem, she can blast it away, but she doesn't know enough math to do it all herself yet—"

"I know, I know," I said, scowling. "When I've been helping her with her homework, we try to take half an hour or so to look at the problem, but . . . look, I've been helping her as best I can, Doug, but honestly, I'm no cryptographer. I'm just a chemistry dropout—"

"Oh, Dakota. A dropout with three years of chemistry under her belt?" Jinx said, slipping something out of her satchel. "With all the math frontloaded, followed by a year sucking down all Emory had on graphomancy? You can't fool me, Miss Frost. You've got the math."

She slid a small blue book to me—a copy of *Cryptanalysis* by Gaines.

"They had a second copy," Doug said. "And I could use a third eye on the problem."

"Maybe your friend won't help you help her," Jinx said. "But you can help anyway."

I stared at the little blue book, staring at the grid of letters on its cover. Then I took it.

"Thanks, guys," I said. "As much for the vote of confidence as anything. No promises."

We all said our goodnights, and Jewel, Cinnamon and I cleaned up. Very quickly, we were developing a little domestic routine: pots and dishes, leftovers and garbage, counters and floors. It made things easier on the nights my bodyguard Nyissa wasn't over to help out.

Afterward, we retired to the front porch . . . to enjoy the Atlanta summer.

On a typical night before Jewel's arrival, I'd have practiced Taido or spinning in the front yard, while Cinnamon watched from behind the elaborate iron bars that made a "safety cage" out of half of the porch, struggling through her homework while I struggled through karate moves or dinged myself in the head with wood blocks. Then, on good nights, Cinnamon and I would curl up on the sofa together and work on her homework, or try to crack the code.

Now Jewel and I practiced together, her with glowy plastic LED balls, me with beans in stockings ($1.68 bulk at Whole Foods, $4.49 on sale at Target), spinning in the front yard while Cinnamon watched from her safety cage, cussing through an English assignment.

Jewel kept refusing to divulge the secrets of fire magic . . . but she *had* agreed to teach me the basics of fire *spinning*. Or perhaps "agree" was not the right word—after hearing more horror stories about me and my blocks of wood, she practically demanded it.

"Woow—*fahh*—wow," Cinnamon said, lifting her head from her homework, staring at Jewel, who was whirling through move after complex move as I just kept hitting myself. Cinnamon sat up straight. "They stops in the *air*. How are you *doing* that?"

"Just practice," Jewel said, whirling the LED balls around her in an elaborate flower, then seeming to make the poi stop, one above her head, the other at her feet. When she pulled them out of the pause, she brought them fluidly into a counter-rotating weave, her hands darting in and out of the intricate pattern the poi made in the air. It looked effortless, unless you were trying to do it yourself, in which case it looked impossible. "No magic, no liquid fire. Just practice."

My faux poi smacked me in the head again. I was having trouble "keeping my planes," just holding the poi in a single plane in front, at the side, or behind. If they were going in the same direction, I could do it, but as soon as I tried to get them out of sync—on purpose, that is, yes, it's a technique—my body wanted to start dancing, left and right, sway this way and that, my planes disintegrated, and, sure enough, I smacked myself on the head yet *again*.

"Thank God, no more blocks of wood for you," Jewel said, giving me a crooked smile as she made making her glowing balls seem to freeze in the air again, then whipped them back into motion. "But don't worry about hitting yourself. It's OK. Even *I* hit myself—"

"Oh, I'd pay money to see that," I said, shifting as my Dragon stirred on my back.

And then Jewel promptly klonked herself on the head.

I laughed, but that faded quickly as Jewel's poi just tumbled down around her. Her eyes rarely followed her poi, but now she wasn't even paying attention to them, just staring upward, upward at the top of my house . . . and yet somehow, straight into my eyes.

I whirled. Atop my house, thirty feet high, glowed the *projectia* of my Dragon.

"Get inside," I said. Jewel didn't move, so I reached out, grabbed her arm and pushed her toward the house. *Oh, God.* I'd done that without turning my head, seeing through the eyes of the Dragon as it looked down on us. We were linked. "Go to the safe room, both of you!"

Jewel bolted for the porch. Cinnamon reached out through the bars of the safety cage, lifted the were-safe latch, opened the gate, and pulled Jewel inside. Then they ran down the narrow stairs into the safe room Cinnamon used when she changed.

The Dragon sat atop the house, much as it had at Borders; only this time, it picked its perch with care, shifting its weight without cracking my roof. It stared down at me with glowing, sage eyes resting deep in its half-lion, half-lizard head; staring not just at me, but also at my new Dragon tattoo, which had frozen on my body, like a cat avoiding a larger challenger.

I stood transfixed, uncertain as to what to do.

"*The egg is hatching,*" the Dragon said. "*Beware.*"

With one flap of its wings, it lifted off the roof, then shimmered and evaporated.

I stood there, stunned for a moment. Then I cursed out loud.

"Oh, great!" I shouted. "Cryptic fucking phantom! Say what you mean! *'BeewAAAare!'* " I said, wiggling my fingers. "Beware who, or what, for what reason? I inked you as an icon of wisdom, not a symbol of confusion! At least give me the fucking Ides of March!"

Like a gopher, Cinnamon poked her head over the rail of the porch. "What was that?"

"My Dragon, honey," I said. "My old tattoo, just like we saw in Palo Alto."

Now Jewel poked her head up. Clearly, they hadn't run down the stairs at all. "Is it gone?"

"Yeah," I said. "Sorry to scare you—I don't think it was a threat, but yeah, it's gone."

"Why were you shouting?" Jewel said. "Did . . . did it have something to say to you?"

"Couldn't you hear it? No?" I asked—then glared at her. I shifted, scratching over my shoulder as my new tattoo abruptly began moving on my back. "Damn it! Settle down, you itchy ink! But I'll bet you know *exactly* what it had to say, don't you, Fireweaver?"

Jewel bit her lip. "Hatchsign?"

I nodded grimly. "If that's what you fireweavers call it," I said. "I had to learn that from the vampires, Jewel. From the vampires! They made me look like an idiot."

"I'm sorry," Jewel said.

"And another thing," I said. "The timing—I'm *not* fooled. You claimed you were trying to summon a dragon, and then *my* Dragon appears—where you and I have been together! Here, Palo Alto, even the Golden Gate Bridge when we were both there! Tell me that's coincidence—"

"I'm sorry," Jewel said. "I swore an oath! I can't tell you!"

"*Fine,*" I said, pulling out my cell phone and thumbing through the contacts. This one I didn't have on speed dial . . . but maybe that would have to change. "No wonder you're afraid of me adding rules to magic. Yours are a straitjacket."

"Who are you calling?" Jewel asked.

"Someone I should have called the moment we saw that tattoo at Borders," I said. How the hell had my tattoo resurrected itself? It shouldn't have lasted an hour, much less nine, no, *ten* months now! Surprisingly, the phone picked up on the third ring. "Hello, Zinaga, it's Dakota."

"Is that your old master?" Jewel asked.

"What? No!" I said; Zinaga, my former fellow apprentice, laughed on the line.

Then a gruff male voice came onto the phone. "What the hell do you want, Frost?"

—☙

"Hello, Arcturus," I said grimly. "Time to throw myself at your feet again."

39. The Tin-Pot Kingdom

Dozens of miles to the east of Atlanta, and maybe half that south of Stone Mountain, deep in a warren of sharp hills and deep valleys where few roads go and fewer phones get more than one bar, lies Blood Rock, Georgia—a tiny hamlet of rednecks and recluses living in the shadow of a stadium-sized boulder that runs red with Georgia clay each time it rains.

If you haven't lived in the South—I mean, really *lived* in the *South*—you might think I'm picking on the residents by calling them rednecks. I'm not. They'll tell you that themselves—or, as the owner of the Grist Mill Café once said, "You work for a living, in the sun on a car, or out in a field, you get a red neck too, you pasty city girl!"

But when I say recluse—well, this time, I mean it.

Blood Rock is *not* Atlanta—it's the backwoods. They call Atlanta the City in the Forest because green trees seem to explode out of every square inch of ground we haven't covered with concrete—but out near Stone Mountain, the trees grow taller, leaner.

Here, Sherman never marched; here, progress never bulldozed old growth to the ground. Off the main highways, the trees loom over the roads, long trunks rising sinuously like slender sentinels, and the rare houses stare at you through oddly paired windows, like eyes.

The last time I'd been here, I'd driven the windy roads to the top of Blood Rock proper, seeking an audience at the Stone Rose Sanctuary, the stronghold of Nyissa's vampire clan, the House Beyond Sleep. But that was the new Blood Rock; today, I headed deep into Old Town.

Down two miles of menacing dirt roads, farther down a quarter mile of perilously bumpy driveway, and behind trees leaning ominously like crossed spears, hid the home of Arcturus, my former tattooing mentor. When my Prius rattled to a stop at the end of the drive, the house proper was still obscured by magnolias and pines. Only the front porch was visible, making Arcturus's spacious split level seem smaller than it really was. Unimposing, but not quite innocuous; he deliberately let the grounds and façade run down, to give it that flavor of menace that implied it was possibly guarded by a redneck or recluse with a shotgun.

Arcturus, of course, was far more dangerous than either.

On the porch he sat, squat as a fireplug, skin like weathered wood, hair like Einstein—Arturo Carlos Rodriguez de la Turin, AKA Master Skindancer Arcturus. Where my tats are an exercise in skill and restraint, his are bold, rough designs with the raw power of folk art. That isn't just a difference in skill; I'm an artist, and ink to create beauty; Arcturus is an engineer, and inks to create power. The broad, thick lines of his tats can carry a lot of mana, and his designs have the magical logic to back up their brashness. As egotistical as I am about my art, I have no illusions—Arcturus has the harder nose, the willingness to ink something that doesn't look pretty if it gets the job done—so he gets more done.

As I got out of the car, Arcturus stood, scowling; beside him, Zinaga, his apprentice, leaned back off the wall and prepared to face me. Her hands kept clenching and unclenching, and as she did so, little sparkles shimmered up through the elaborate white lines inked upon her dark olive skin. Zinaga was an expert in light magic, every bit my equal in her area of expertise—and because of her choice to specialize, a complete zero in Arcturus's eyes. She hated the very air I breathed. I tried my best not to return it; she didn't deserve the treatment she got.

"Arcturus," I said, nodding to him. "Zinaga."

"It pisses me off it takes a fucking catastrophe to get you back here," Arcturus said.

I frowned. Surprisingly, that hurt. "I'm sorry," I said. "I have no excuse."

"Typical, Frost," Zinaga said, folding her arms, gleaming white lines rippling across her arms in a beautiful moiré pattern. She was skilled, artistic, athletic, and had great skin—all the makings of a good skindancer. "The studio hain't got a revolving door."

"I know," I said. "But the Magical Security Council isn't just a game, either."

"So skindancing is a game?" she asked, spreading her arms. "Frost, this is an *art*—"

"Ease down," Arcturus snapped. "Look at her ink. Clearly she cares about her art—"

"And she doesn't?" I said. "Come off it. Give her some credit. She stayed, I went—"

Zinaga hissed, turned, and walked inside.

"Frost, show sense," Arcturus said. "Being nice to her is worse than being a dick."

"No, it isn't," I said. "Because I mean it, and if I keep it up, one day she'll get it."

Arcturus rubbed his face. "All right, I suppose I needed to hear that. I needed to go into this with no illusions that you're actually here to learn something—"

"Hey," I said. "Don't be an ass. I know I've treated you like dirt, I know I should muddle through on my own, but I thought you might be interested that my masterwork has survived over half a year detached from my body. So . . . you wanna help me figure out how, or not?"

Arcturus stopped rubbing his face, drew his hands down, and finally smiled. "All right, Frost," he said. "Come on in."

I gave the whole story, everything I thought was possibly relevant: the five sightings of my masterwork in San Jose and the one in Atlanta, Jewel's superstitions and the vampires' theories, the strange link I seemed to have with the tattoo, the oddly suspicious timing of the sightings when Jewel and I were together—even the unexpected movement I was getting off my new dragon tattoo—and the weird vibes that I got whenever it became active.

"It's," I said, struggling for words, "almost like it's . . . *talking* to me—"

"Dakota, I don't want to disturb you, or insult you," Arcturus said carefully, rubbing his hands together, "but there is a distinct possibility you're talking to *yourself.* You yourself said that the tattoo gets energized when you're enraged, or aroused—"

"Hey," I said, my cheeks reddening. "I never said—"

"I can read between the lines," Arcturus said. "But you also said that the tattoo quieted when you wanted it to. That sounds less like a separate personality rather than an extension of your own. That new tattoo of yours is . . . a complex design—"

"It's fucking insane, is what it is," Zinaga said, shaking her head at me in something between admiration and disgust. "I can't believe you inked something that complex—I mean, I know you got the chops to ink it, Frost, I just think you were reckless to ink that nest—"

"I had the design extensively vetted," I said evenly. "Not just by Jinx, but by the Marquis—and that's after I double-checked all the Euler sums myself—"

"See what I was saying," Zinaga said to Arcturus. "That's more than ego—"

"Let it go." Arcturus shook his head. "The point is, this new design may have unforeseen features. All tattoos absorb your mystical intent; they wouldn't work otherwise. But this one is so complex . . . you might be getting intent echoes. Reflections of your own thoughts—"

"Damn it," I said. "I . . . I can see that's possible."

"The alternatives are all worse," Arcturus said. "It's your own design, so I think we can rule out a control charm, and it's hermetic, so we can rule out external intents. That leaves the idea that your tattoo picked up a stray spirit. You inked it encircled?"

I gave Arcturus my best withering look.

"Fine, fine," Arcturus said. "Are you certain that—what's wrong?"

"I . . . *did* activate it once, before it was fully complete," I admitted.

"Jesus!" Arcturus said. "You activated an incomplete tattoo—"

"Not intentionally," I said. "I was being attacked by vampires right after having my vines forcibly stripped from my body. I tried to activate *them*, I ended up activating it . . . and it was still in four components. The feedback damn near tore me to pieces—"

"But even then, it wouldn't have picked up a stray intent," Arcturus said. "You're a careful inker, Frost. Each of the components was piecewise hermetic, right? So—"

"Think that leaves the notion you're talkin' to yourself," Zinaga snarked.

"*Fine,* I'm talking to myself. A magical circuit *could* create weird perceptual effects. But we're avoiding the big mystery—*how* is my original masterwork still active *ten months* after it detached from my body? It actually looked stronger. In fact, it looked *solid*—"

"I'll give you another mystery," Arcturus said, avoiding Zinaga's glance. "A student walks out on her master, then waltzes back in almost *nine months later* expecting him to solve her problems for her. You always want to cut down the easy road to get the quick answers—"

"Damn it, Arcturus," I said, glancing at Zinaga, who now refused to look at me or Arcturus. "You think you got an explanation, spill it. I don't have time to play games here. People's lives have been threatened, may still be at stake—"

"You don't know that there's any connection between the threats on this Jewel character and the appearance of your original masterwork," Arcturus said. "It could just be coinci—"

"I don't believe in coincidence!" I snapped. "Not when dealing with magic or mystery or threats or anything else smelling of danger. Someone is out there. *Bad people* are out there. But they're not going tell you their targets, their plans, or their methods—they're going to keep all that hidden. But they're always *after* something, and *that* they can't hide. When you glimpse the enemy sniffing around, you don't sweep it under the rug. You go on high fucking alert!"

Arcturus frowned. "You'll never see it coming," he said. "Trust me—"

"You never—" I began, and stopped. Arcturus had lost his family to a kidnapping. He never spoke of it. When he said "you'll never see it coming," he meant *he* hadn't seen it coming. Somehow, I doubted that—but I wasn't going to use that against him.

"You and I," I said, "are going to have to differ on this, because the few times I've had to deal with 'someone' out there who meant me harm, weird shit started happening *long* before the bad guys ever reared their ugly heads—"

Arcturus's mouth slowly opened, his eyes staring into the distance.

"And weird shit is definitely happening now. Magical signs that keep glowing without a power source are one of them. Tattoos that survive long after they should have dissipated are another. They're similar enough that it makes me mighty damn suspicious—what?"

Arcturus's eyes had snapped back to me when I'd drawn the connection between the dragon signs and the appearance of my original Dragon—a connection I hadn't made until I'd spoken it, right then. But he quickly shook his head and tried to brush the connection off.

"Fire magic and tattoo magic are powered in completely different ways," Arcturus said. "Linear discharges versus planar connectors. There can't be a connection—"

Zinaga hissed. "Damn it, Arcturus—"

"Settle yourself down," Arcturus said. "This is between her and me—"

"*I-am-not-stupid,*" I said. "I know there's a connection you don't want to tell me—"

"You don't know a damn thing," Arcturus said. "You think you know so much, but you still quit before you learned to tell shit from sand. If you're so smart, why do you need that blind witch or that mangy half-wolf to do your designs—"

"I have independent graphomancers *review* my designs because *that's the law,*" I said. "And I know the flow of mana is essentially the same, no matter how it is collected. I took five semesters of magic before I came out here, Arcturus. I'm not an idiot, and I'm not blind—"

"What you're not," Arcturus said, "is part of this studio. You left. Twice."

"So?" I said. "I had to leave sometime, Arcturus. The chick must leave the nest—"

"Don't lecture me with fortune cookies, Frost," Arcturus said. "You're not the master."

"What does that matter? I'm dealing with a real problem here," I said, staring at Zinaga. She was even more independent-minded than I was; no wonder Arcturus was treating her like dirt. "Is the only way someone can have a relationship with you is worshipping at your feet?"

"No, I'm asking for a basic level of respect," Arcturus said, voice rising. "You can't learn anything unless you show your teachers a basic level of respect—"

"In *grade school*," I said. "Maybe even high school. But by *our* age, you're supposed to be sharing knowledge amongst adults. You're supposed to learn that attitude in college because professors can be wrong, and in life you will be penalized if you take their word for gospel!"

Arcturus leaned back. "You and I will have to differ," he said icily. "I was educated in an older school, and I demand to receive the same level of respect I gave my teachers."

I stared at him. "If you had me drive an hour and a half out here to demand I grovel," I said, "I'm leaving and not coming back."

Arcturus stared back at me. "If you think you can do without me, fine. Go, then."

I glared now. "Whatever has been discovered, can be rediscovered," I said, standing. "I have scientists all over the country lined up to help me figure this out."

Arcturus laughed.

"Real scientists, not closet wizards trying to lead everyone astray so they can keep magic for themselves," I said, standing. "So they can set up tin-pot kingdoms in backwater nowhere—"

"Dakota, siddown," Zinaga said.

"I told you, settle down," Arcturus barked. "This is between master and student—"

"Ain't *I* a master now?" Zinaga said coolly, and I raised an eyebrow.

Arcturus scowled. "Well," he said, "well, technically yes, but she's my student—"

"I thought she just fired you," Zinaga said.

"*She* fired *me?*" Arcturus said.

"A teacher is hired by the student," Zinaga said. "Don'tcha know that?"

"A *master*," Arcturus said, practically underlining the word with a growl, "takes an apprentice. Don't you know that?"

"Yeah, I sure do . . . because *I am a master*," Zinaga said. "And didn't you say it was high time I took on an apprentice?"

Arcturus's face turned red as a beet. "Don't!" he barked. "Don't you dare—"

My eyes widened. "Now, now wait a minute," I said. "I'm not agreeing to—"

"Both of you, get over yourselves," Zinaga said, leaning back against the wall, shaking her head. "Every time you get together, you squabble like little kids. It's embarrassing."

Arcturus pointed at her. "Zinaga, this is my studio—"

"Oh, shut it, Arcturus," Zinaga said. "I ain't the fucking help. This may be your *house*, but it's *our* studio. You remember that talk about partners . . . *partner?* Well, I won't have my partner acting like a dick to our star . . . to one of the studio's former students!"

Arcturus's face became even more mottled, and he clenched his fists on the table—but he didn't respond. As for me, I couldn't get over what I'd just heard: Zinaga had walked straight up to the edge of calling me the studio's *star student*—

"Wipe that smirk, Dakota," Zinaga snapped. "You are such a total ass."

I frowned to hide my smile. "Yes, yes I am. Sometimes it's hard to shut off."

"So," Zinaga said, folding her arms over her chest, so that her tattoos gleamed. "We're going to help you, Dakota, because it's pretty damn interesting that a tattoo inked in this studio is still live nearly a year later, and the 'studio' oughta know how, right, Arcturus?"

"Yes, we need to know," Arcturus said, "but she left, Zinaga. We can't just—"

"Why not?" I asked. "If the studio is you and Zinaga, why can't you just—"

"The 'studio' *ain't* just 'Arcturus and Zinaga,' " Zinaga said. "It's a whole lot more."

"Damn it, girl," Arcturus said. "Partners or no, this . . . this is a sacred trust—"

"*Arcturus,*" Zinaga said. "Think about what this girl can do. It's *time.*"

Arcturus scowled, looking at her, then at me. "All right," he said. "All right. You're right." Then he glanced up at the calendar on the wall. "Damn it. We can't do the formal ceremony for a few more days yet, but if you're saying it, it *is* time."

I drummed my fingers on my arms. "All right, I'll bite. Time for what?"

—

"Time, skindancer," Arcturus said, "to stop being an apprentice, and become an initiate."

40. Fire on Jewel

"Who kicked your puppy?" Annesthesia asked.

I stared off into the distance. It was Thursday morning back at the Rogue Unicorn, the tattoo studio where I held court, and I was in a *foul* mood. After all that buildup, Arcturus had told me to come back to Blood Rock on the next new moon for my "initiation."

I was *incensed*, but they ignored my pleas for urgency, broke out a six pack, and told me to chill, so there was nothing for little old designated-driver me to do but grit my teeth, say farewell to the drunks, and drive back to Candler Park to stew for seventy-two hours.

I *hate* waiting. It wasn't even eleven yet, so I didn't have any customers to pick on; only Annesthesia, our coquettish receptionist, who could give better than she got. Finally, I lowered my copy of the *Journal of the American Academy of Dermatology* and smiled at her.

"Arcturus," I said.

"That would be . . . the only person other than me who can take you down a peg?"

"Right the first time."

Annesthesia smiled. "On that note," she said. "You have a visitor. I'm letting her stew."

"We're not even open yet," I said, "and even so, it's not like you to let customers stew. Normally you springload them on me when I'm stepping out of the bathroom."

"I didn't say *customer,*" she said, "and you're less of a wasbian than you let on."

Now I smiled. "Jewel," I said.

"Right first time," she said, smiling. "I'll show her right back."

"No, let me see what she's doing," I said, and we both scurried down to the tattooing room—still dark, so we were almost invisible to our sole visitor in the waiting room: Jewel. She stood there, in harem pants and a leather top, staring at the Artists' Wall, both hands behind her, holding a shapeless fringed purse over her shapely rump, her heavy copper ringlets shifting as she looked first at my picture and bio, then at the gallery of tattoos I had inked.

"Maybe I was wrong," Annesthesia said. "You *do* have a customer."

I felt my dragon tattoo shifting against my body, its tail slowly running over my belly, like I was rubbing my hand over my stomach. It wanted to slip lower, and my cheeks reddened. I now could see the wisdom in Arcturus's idea that the Dragon was just mirroring my intent.

I stepped out, and Jewel turned with a slight yelp.

"Oh! Hey, Skindancer," she said, putting her bracer-wrapped hand to her breast. She made even embarrassed reactions look graceful. "You startled me."

"Hey, Fireweaver," I said, smiling and giving her a hug. It felt so good to have her around again, especially with our "first meeting" barriers down and without fire coming down around our heads every other minute. "Did bad old Annesthesia make you wait?"

"I told her I didn't mind," she said. "I had planned to bum around this little alt-culture mecca you've got here, a surprise find in the Deep South—"

"Atlanta is *not* the Deep South." My mouth quirked up; I was still mad at Arcturus, so I said, "You wanna see that, I'll show you the town where I learned to tattoo."

"I'll pass on the dueling banjos, thanks," Jewel said, flicking her hand, making me scowl. "Oh, you're cute when you pout. Anyway, I strolled over when I thought it was time, but I was a few minutes early. Forgot my watch."

"I can fix that for you," I said. "Tattoo a working watch right on your wrist."

Her jaw dropped. "You can't seriously do that," she said. "Oh my God. You *can*."

"One of my more popular tattoos," I said. "Call Alex Nicholson back in the Bay. He can vouch for it—he got my first one, and it's been running for . . . what, eleven months now? The newer designs are better, though, calibrated to a solar day—"

"Wow," she said. "That's . . . that's impressive, not what I wanted but—"

"So you were planning on getting a tattoo," I said, smiling slowly.

Her face reddened. "Uh, I—not exactly planning. Thinking about it."

I waved my hand about the shop. "Well, while you're thinking, why don't I give you a little tour, show you what we've got, tell you all the questions you ought to be asking of your magical tattooist and studio, and what answers you need to get, else you should run—"

"So what should I be asking?" Jewel said, smiling.

"For a tattoo studio? Clean, and licensed, for starters," I said, pointing at the Rogue Unicorn's business license on the wall, and beneath the licenses the tattooists themselves needed to ink magic in Georgia. "And for a magical tattooist? Knows a magic circle and how to use it."

"I'd think," Jewel said, "that knowing the magic would be more important—"

"*Using* a magic tattoo," I said, "is a lot like casting a spell. It needs mana, a well-formed intention, and some word or gesture as a trigger. *Inking* a magic tattoo, on the other hand, is just specialized tattooing. What you really want is for your inker to have a good graphomancer."

"And you have a good graphomancer?" Jewel asked, mouth quirking in a wry smile. "Let me guess, the best?"

I smirked back. I didn't just catch the dig; I caught that she'd gone from asking about tattooists in general to me in particular. "Absolutely," I said. "Jinx."

"The blind Goth girl?" Jewel said. "I knew she was a graphomancer, but *your* graphomancer? Vetting *artwork? Really?*"

"She's only partially blind," I said, and sat down on our overstuffed couch, stretching my long arms out over its back. Jewel now had a choice—she could keep standing, she could sit in the chair . . . or she could sit next to me. "And she has the best software in the business."

"Well . . . the best do use the best," Jewel said, surveying the gallery again; then, giving me a quick glance over her shoulder and a glimpse of a wry smile, she clutched her frilly bag and sat down next to me. My arm fell on her shoulder. "Oh, she thinks she's soooo smooooth."

"Sometimes," I said, giving her a brief squeeze.

Then she surprised me by leaning against me, head resting on my shoulder. I got a tingle when her warm curves pressed against me, and then another when her slightly damp copper ringlets spread out over the exposed skin of my arm.

"You are *so* arrogant," Jewel said happily. "What tattoo should I get?"

I looked at the flash on the wall, started reflecting on the designs in my book. But what a tattooist has done in the past should never be the starting point of a design; the *client* is the starting point. So I thought of Jewel, what she liked . . . and what I could do.

"An octopus," I said suddenly, and Jewel drew a breath. I ran my hand over her bag—the fringes of the floppy purse were really tentacles reaching out from an octopus design. "A firespinning octopus, whose limbs move when you move, juggling balls of flame."

"Oh, Dakota," Jewel said, hand going to her breast. "That would be *perfect.* Where?"

"I, ah," I began, unexpectedly embarrassed. "I'd . . . I'd need to see, uh—"

"Would you need to see me naked?" Jewel asked, grinning at me.

I swallowed. "Only if you were certain you wanted it someplace you could hide."

"Never," she said, standing and twirling. "Or did you just need to see me turn around?"

"Yes, I—" I stammered . . . then stared at her, caught the sparkle in her eyes, the open invitation. I remembered her words about my power. "Take your top off," I said, my voice now sure, more commanding. "Leave the bra, since you don't want to hide the tattoo."

Jewel swallowed, then unbuttoned her jacket, revealing that oh-so-interesting hemp rope bikini—and those flame designs on her back, not tattoos but something else, an inked scarification process I hadn't seen. Inwardly I shuddered—cutting is *not* my thing.

"Like what you see?" Jewel said, finishing another pirouette.

I did. Jewel's curves, as always, were awesome—rippled shoulders, strengthened by spinning; the soft roundness of her breasts, curving under the hemp; the graceful belly and hips beneath them. Delicious—but my options for the tattoo were limited. "Drop the pants."

Jewel flushed, glancing around the waiting room at the door, at the reception desk, eyes widening like a frightened little doe. I stared at her, at that hemp bikini—it was shibari, rope bondage, as much a sign of BDSM as was my collar. Whose submissive was *she?*

"Do it," I said, voice growing slightly more commanding. Inside, I felt awkward. I might be forward, but I'm not actively butch, and I've never taken a dominant role in a relationship. Not once. But I wasn't asking her to do anything I hadn't asked of other clients. "I need to see."

Jewel nodded her head, dropped her eyes—and pulled the drawstring on her harem pants, and they fluttered to the floor. She stood there, half covering herself, half not, embarrassed. I stood up and walked around her, looking at the designs on her legs. They disturbed me.

"I really wasn't kidding about my need to see," I said quietly, kneeling beside her. The flame design was elegant, but the ridges of flesh were almost certainly made by a cutting procedure and not a brand. "I had hoped to use the outside of a thigh, but . . . may I?"

"Oh, please," Jewel said, eyes half closed, drawing a breath.

But as much as I wanted to touch her, that wasn't what I was after. I held my hand carefully over the skin of her thighs, tracing the design, flexing my skin to generate mana and feeling the shimmering response from some pigment buried beneath the design.

"Tickles," Jewel said, opening her eyes. "Oh, my God. You're not even touching me."

"These are magically active," I said, standing, waving my hands over her thighs, her back, part of her forearms. I stared at the patterns, at first distracted by the curves of the canvas, then increasingly intrigued by their logic, the feel of their pigments. "Ah. Fire retardant?"

"Damn, you are good," Jewel breathed, watching my hands move. "That's exactly it."

"Clever. But they're fixed in place by the scars. They would interact badly with magical tattoos, which need to move. I'm afraid for the design I have in mind we're limited to your upper chest, over your collarbones here . . . or I hate to recommend it, a tramp stamp."

"Oh, she wants to stamp me," Jewel said, smirking once again, finally coming out of her submissive haze. She glanced at the door to the walkway. "As delicious as this is, I'm worried about the dinging of that bell and shocked *o-mi-gods*. May I at least put my pants back on?"

I reached down and grabbed her harem pants, spreading them open. Jewel blinked at me, eyes doe-wide again; then she stepped into the pants delicately, first one foot, then the other. I stood, drawing the pants up her legs, then tying the drawstring about her waist.

"We do have a height difference," she said; beneath that mass of copper hair, I could tell she was staring dead center on my chest level as I finished the knot. She looked up, those heavy ringlets falling back, the slightest whiff of patchouli drifting up. "So . . . what do you think?"

I reached in to my pocket and pulled out a sharpie. "I'm thinking . . . here—"

"As much as I want you to do that," she said, seizing my hand with both of hers before the ink could touch her flesh, "it would knock my feet out from under me. On paper first?"

"All right," I said, clasping my other hand over hers. Her hands were trembling, but her eyes held nothing but admiration. "On paper first, especially given your existing marks. I want to get the design vetted by Jinx anyway; she's the engineer to my architect. Come into my office?"

The Rogue Unicorn shares the second story of the Make-A-Wish building with the Herbalist's Attic, a magic supply shop. The stairs up are behind the building, so the "back" of the studio is streetside. That's where I hold the primo spot—the corner office of the Rogue.

I bumped my computer on, tossed my lanky body into my comfy-chic Herman Miller chair in the crook of my L-shaped glass desk, and spun around, smiling up at Jewel, framed from behind by broad windows overlooking Little Five Points, Atlanta's alternative culture mecca.

I was proud of my little throne room overlooking the Vortex restaurant and its cartoon skull; the view looked a heck of a lot better since, in a moment of fiscal foolishness after winning the Valentine Challenge, I sprang for some workmen to re-open the bricked-up side window.

But for once, Jewel had no eye for me, nor even for the colorful sights of L5P beyond. Her back was turned, but I could see, reflected in the glass cabinet atop my butcher's block, her mouth hanging open as she stared into the tall display case.

At first, I thought my pretty little dragon junkie was staring at my gift from

Lord Kitana—the dragon's tooth dagger, on prominent display high in the case. I was about to give her the spiel when I realized her eyes were aimed lower, at a long glass tube . . . holding a white, spiral horn.

"Oh . . . my . . . God," Jewel said. "Is that . . ."

"Oh, I'm just a big softie," I said, standing up with a grin. I unlocked the cabinet, slipped on blue nitrile gloves (reusable, if you autoclave 'em) and reached for the latch with the side of my thumb. Jewel's hand rose automatically, toward my precious magical supplies.

"Hey," I said, and she withdrew her hand. "No touching. Many of those are clan inks; I'm not supposed to even let the other tattooists use them. And *that* is the real deal. Not just naturally shed, but vestal gathered—and I know you too well to think you're a virgin."

"Oh, really?" Jewel said, pressing a hand to her breast. "I've never been with a guy."

I stared at her for a moment, stunned speechless.

"You did *not* just say that," I said. "For the record, lesbian sex is not sloppy seconds. It *counts*, both in practice, and for the purposes of magical virginity—"

"Of course lesbian sex 'counts.' I didn't mean—" Jewel began, then shook her head. "But if there's no, uh, penetration, *real* penetration, then I don't understand why it, uh, 'counts' as sex for the purposes of *magical* virginity—"

"Oh, what kind of lesbian magician are you?" I asked, opening the cabinet, carefully withdrawing the engraved glass tube with its long horn, holding it up at her eye level. "But, for the record . . . you lose *magical* virginity through interpenetrating auras."

Her eyes went even wider as she inspected the long, gleaming, spiral horn. This one was recently shed, just weeks old, and looked unreal—a shimmering spiral, translucent and gossamer, glittering silver threads woven through it picking up so much light it looked like it was glowing.

Of course, with horn this new, maybe it was.

I pulled out the needle case the horn had been resting on—a narrow mahogany box that held the remnants of my last horn and the needles I'd made from it. I set the case on my glass desk, and gently put the horn cylinder on it. Then I closed the shades and killed the lights.

The horn gleamed in the dark, an icicle of light, sparkling as echoes of sunlight rippled through the slow threads woven through the horn. It was so beautiful, even I gasped, but Jewel was no longer looking—her head had been turned by the magical pigments in my case.

In the magic light of the horn, the glass case glowed to life, shimmering colors shifting from vial to vial as slow echoes of magically filtered sunlight resonated with first one kind of pigment, then another, a dozen principal colors and thirty mix-in pigments: prismatic gold, newts-eye green, firecap red, butterfly blue, dandelion yellow, coals-eye black. In the slow kaleidoscope of the unicorn horn, the case became a Technicolor display of fireflies.

I stood behind Jewel, one hand on her shoulder. Eventually, Jewel turned her head.

"Magic tattooing is a little more . . . complicated than fire magic, isn't it?"

I shrugged. Between banging my head, stumbling through forms of power, and watching all Jewel could do, magic fire seemed complicated enough. But

Jewel swallowed, turned away—then saw the horn, and clapped her beautiful, delicate hands to her face with a squeal of glee.

"Oh my God!" she said. "Oh my God! It's glowing! It's really glowing!"

"That it is," I said, leaning over her as she leaned over it. It sat in rings of etched glass that protected it from stray mana and, well, "spirits," if you believe in such things. After seeing that dragon, I was less of a skeptic. "I'll make the needles for your tattoo from it."

"Does . . . does every tattoo use a brand new needle? For health or something?"

"Every time," I said. "For health reasons, of course, but for the art too, and most of all for the magic. You don't want some scratcher muddling your hide with a worn-out needle filled with stray mana traces it picked up from half a dozen other pigments."

Jewel leaned closer to the horn, still not touching it. "You don't like scratchers, do you?"

"I love my work," I said, standing, oddly irritated. I sat down on the edge of the butcher's block, the cabinet to my back. "No, that's not it. I care about the people getting tattoos. They're permanent marks. Every time you pick up the needle, you have to give it your A game."

Jewel turned around. She stared up at me, an unreadable expression on her face. Then she turned around, carefully picked up the edges of the mahogany box without touching the horn atop it, and turned around, proffering it to me. I took it and locked it back in the cabinet.

When the cabinet clicked, her arms wrapped around me. She squeezed me, just for an instant, then spun me round, laced one hand in my deathhawk, and pulled me down to her.

Her wet lips touched mine, I smelled patchouli, and my mind dissolved into bliss.

41. All Yours

"You," Jewel said, kissing my knee, "are the most flexible person I've ever met."

We lay in my bed, afraid to move. I didn't want it to be over. I lay behind her, curled about her, right leg hooked over her, knee drawn up to her chin, toes downward between her thighs, pointed, like a blade. I caressed her cheek with my right hand, then set my hand on the bed and lifted. I slid my left hand down from above her, down her back, under her curvy rump and beneath, seizing my own big toe, drawing it against her. She gasped. Her thighs clenched.

"Ohhh," she breathed. "How do you do that? Your hands are *everywhere.*"

"Long arms," I said, slipping my right arm down around her breasts, my hands once again cradling her cheek. Everywhere I touched her . . . "You are *so* soft."

"And you are *so* strong," she said, touching my biceps. Her fingers played over them, warm, sliding against my skin and sweat. "Are you a tattoo artist . . . or a weightlifter?"

"Both," I said. "But most of my muscle is from being a martial artist."

Jewel shivered a little, then curled up even more. "I'm not into fighting."

"You don't have to be," I lied. Then I realized we were intimate now. I couldn't start a relationship based on lies. I had to tell her what I really thought, regardless of consequences. "I don't really believe that—everybody should know how to defend themselves."

"Or become a pacifist," she said.

"Or become comfortable getting your ass kicked," I said.

"Is that what you were doing?"

"I said kicked, not licked."

She laughed, and I released her, rolling on my back. Jewel had been *so wonderful.* She wasn't "experimenting," or just "curious," or inhibited—she knew what she was doing. Tribadism wasn't a dirty word to Jewel, and she held no expectations that interfered with our enjoyment.

She was a sub, but didn't demand that I act as a domme. She was extremely experienced, but didn't press me any further than I wanted to go. Even her odd hemp undergarments revealed her relaxed nature. They *were* shibari, Japanese rope bondage, but when I asked about them, asked about something she was so obviously into that she never went without it, she just shrugged and said, "Sure, that's my thing, but I'm in no rush, Dakota."

She was *so* refreshing. When Savannah and I had dated, we were just learning. Michael too. I barely remembered the parade of clumsy, groping men and shy, halting women in the drunken stupor I fell into as I dropped out. Then Calaphase—ouch. I drew a sharp breath.

"You're glowing," Jewel said, hand brushing gently down my thigh. "Literally."

I looked at her. She was sitting up, all soft curves in the shimmering light. I stared at her fondly, looking at the strange almost-tattoos she had. Then I realized there was nothing to illuminate her in my dark, spare bedroom, and I sat up and looked in the dresser mirror.

I was the light in the darkness. My tattoos were shimmering with magical power. Of course; skindancing was based on body movement . . . and sex was the best dancing of all. My skin glimmered with magical afterglow, just a hint, just enough to see my outline without detracting from the glow of the magical circuits rippling over my body.

My Dragon slid over my body, slow, sinuous, luxuriating in the afterglow of power. Now I could see what Arcturus had said about it reflecting my intent—when I wanted to fight, it reared for battle; when I wanted to be intimate, it caressed me like a second lover.

I drew a breath, and a pulse of power rippled across the body of the Dragon. Mana sparkled through the jewels, glittering flares escaping into the air like stardust. Roses bloomed, releasing wafts of mana; butterflies flapped, making the mana drifting off me coil in the air.

In the mirror, in the light of my magic, we were *not* a traditional couple, even by lesbian standards. I'm long, muscular . . . lanky; she's curvy, generous . . . fat, some would say. My tattoos, even her scarification, are beautiful—to us; that taste puts us in a definite minority.

Jewel shifted, looking at me. "Why are you crying?"

"It's nothing," I said, wiping the tears. In that magic moment, seeing us both together, I had put *him* from my mind. I did *not* want to go back there. But Jewel put her hand on her curvy hip, scowling, and I gave it up. "Just thinking of . . . of my last time with my last boyfriend."

"Oh, *thanks,*" Jewel said, turning away. I could tell she was really hurt.

"It's not like that," I said, drawing a breath. Jewel looked at me, concerned. "Calaphase wasn't just the last person I'd been with. He was the first person I'd been with in a while." I said, staring off. "He was killed in front of me maybe an hour after we hooked up for the first time."

"And I, somehow, reminded you of him?" she said, horrified. "Oh, God. Quick, call Nyissa! We need to get some bodyguards up in here, pronto—"

"What? No, I—" I began, then stopped. She was smiling, and I snorted. "You—"

"You laughed," she said simply. "I thought you needed it."

I took her hand. "You reminded me of him because being with you was such a wonderful experience," I said. "I pray to God that there are few other similarities."

"No penis, for one thing," she said smugly.

"Nor fangs," I said. "Though you do bite."

Jewel swallowed. "Fangs? I didn't think you went in for that . . . that sort of stuff."

I stared at her. A year ago, I would have said the same thing. But being with Calaphase had opened my eyes to vampires—they were just people. And her "that sort of stuff" line reminded me too much of Saffron's attitude about tattooing before she pulled the stick out of her ass.

"I've been where you're coming from," I said. I don't know what was wrong with that, but it was like I'd slapped her. "No, it's OK. It took becoming friends with a vampire for me to see I was treating them like 'the other.' And once we were friends, things sort of . . . evolved."

I looked away. Back there again, in that sad space. *Son of a bitch.*

"Hey, let's always be honest with each other," she said. "Even if it hurts."

I smiled, sure she didn't realize the door she'd opened. "Fine for you to say, Miss Won't Teach Me About Fire Magic—"

"Keeping secrets is not dishonest," she said. "There's plenty I'm sure Cinnamon has told you in confidence you'd never dream of telling me, and that doesn't make you dishonest. Can't you accept I've made promises that matter as much to me as Cinnamon's trust matters to you?"

Slowly, I nodded. "But—"

"But this is magic, and you're the head of the brand-spanking-new—"

"She said spanking."

"Ha. The brand-new Magical Security Council, a self-appointed post, if I understand the story right," Jewel said. "Is there nothing you've learned that you wouldn't feel safe sharing? Nothing that you learned in confidence that you don't feel allowed to share?"

I nodded again. I did have many, many secrets.

Jewel nodded in response, then nodded a second time.

"Let's promise—always be honest with each other. We may not—yet—be in a position to share all each other's secrets. We may never be. I may never learn the intricacies of the MSC, and you may never become a fire initiate. But we can be honest in what we do share."

"Honest," I said, extending my hand for an in-air brotherly clasp.

Jewel stared at it a moment. "Honest," she said, taking my upraised hand, "and on that note, you are the *butchest* butch I've *ever* dated."

"Ha," I said, squeezing her hand back. "Honestly, I'm not—I think you bring that out in me. It's been a long time since I've been in this role in a relationship." Then I felt it all rushing back. I pulled my hand away, and my face became a mask. "Sorry. It's—"

"It's OK," Jewel said, pulling closer to me. Her hand fell, very gently, on my knee. "It's OK. You can let it out. You don't have to be the big bad butch biker twenty-four seven, three hundred and sixty five. You don't have to be that at *all*. It's OK to be hurt. You loved him."

"I did," I said, staring down at my hands.

"And he's *gone*," she said firmly. "He's gone."

"He's gone, and I miss him," I said. Now tears started to flow—not a flood, just a few . . . but each drop was pent-up pain. "Not just him. I've got so many regrets. I miss the roads not taken: Calaphase, and Philip, and Savannah. All the things I could have had with them—"

Jewel drew a sharp breath, then drew her hand gently up the curve of my thigh, up over my hip, touching my stomach. "Don't you have something else now?"

We kissed, glow and glitter and sweet patchouli. My eyes closed, and I lost myself in her soft, wet kisses, her cradling hands, the warm curves of her body against mine.

"You don't have to share," I said, opening my eyes again at last. "I'm all yours."

42. A Spring in Her Step

"You have a spring in your step," Arcturus said.

"She's datin' again," Zinaga said.

I raised an eyebrow. "That I am, God help me."

True, I was happy to have finally connected with Jewel—but even under the joy of a new relationship, I'd felt a clock ticking these past seventy-two hours leading up to the new moon, getting increasingly antsy for the chance to finally get some answers about my old Dragon.

When the eleventh came, I wound my way back through the red clay and kudzu maze of Blood Rock, and again found Arcturus and Zinaga on his porch like a Deep South version of the minotaur and his wife. But this time, Arcturus was subdued, and Zinaga was beaming.

"What's his name?" she said with a challenging smile.

"*Her* name," I said, "is Jewel. The firespinner we talked about."

Zinaga's smile cracked, just a bit, but she recovered. "I'm *so* happy for you," she said, but Arcturus harrumphed at her. Then she softened a little bit. "All right, you made your point, Arcturus. If *Frost* can learn to behave, I'll try not to shove my foot in my mouth."

I was already climbing the steps, but Zinaga stood and raised her hand, stopping me. The position left her still a half head above me, looking down, trying to look haughty, with Arcturus standing behind her, watching grimly, arms folded.

"Why are you here, Frost?" she said.

"Because you asked me?" I said, and Arcturus rolled his eyes. Oh, wait—that was the same question he'd asked me, so many years ago. "To learn how to ink magic."

Zinaga stared down at me in triumph. "So you wanna join our studio?"

I rankled . . . but then thought about what Jewel had said, more than once, about me being arrogant. I was here for their help, and, hell, I needed to learn a new level of humility if I was going to run the Magical Council successfully. Practice made perfect.

"Yes," I said at last. "Yes, I do."

Zinaga's mouth quirked up. "You willin' to be *my* apprentice?"

"With all due respect to my former master," I said with a nod to Arcturus, "yes."

Zinaga let her mouth fall open, a slight ahhh, like a little orgasm. I looked at her and then Arcturus in alarm, and he shrugged. Then Zinaga shook her head.

"Well, as much as I might like that, you're outta luck," she said, raising her hand before I could say anything. "As far as *I'm* concerned, you're *way* past apprentice. You're skilled, your book learnin's powerful stuff, and you've put what you learned here to good use—"

"Thanks, I—" I said . . . and then shut up when she glared.

"But you're not ready to be a part of the studio, because you never finish anything," Zinaga said. "I'll sponsor you as an initiate, Dakota, but I *insist* if you do, that you gotta make a college try at learnin' everything Arcturus and I wanna teach you, within reason."

Arcturus shifted on his feet. I looked at him, tilting my head oh-so-slightly at her. Arcturus smiled tightly, then nodded. I think both of us were more proud of Zinaga at that moment than we'd ever been. I'd be her learner if it helped her grow into a teacher.

"All right," I said, smiling.

"What?" she said, dumbfounded. "Just . . . 'all right?' No quid pro quo, no demands—"

"Check her," Arcturus said. "I think she might be a pod person."

"I mean, damn," Zinaga said, "what did that girl do to you, Dakota?"

I laughed. "Quite a lot, as it turns out. Can I come up on the porch now?"

"Sure thing," Zinaga said. "Well, I don't care how all gooey you've gone now, it won't last. We'll have answers for you, but—did you skip food, like I told you?"

"I did not eat," I said, rising on the porch. I saw why Zinaga had stopped me—I had a head and a half on the both of them. I enjoy being tall, but people don't enjoy being intimidated, especially when trying to establish authority. "I took you seriously."

Arcturus and Zinaga looked at each other, then shook their heads.

"Pod person," he repeated.

"Rocked world," she shot back.

"I'm standing *right here*," *I* said.

Arcturus and Zinaga welcomed me inside. Before we got started, Arcturus reminded us of the date and asked for a moment of silence. After a brief double take, I nodded. It had been six years, but apparently memories of 9/11 were stronger in rural Georgia than in urban Atlanta, and we all raised glasses of Zinaga's awful-but-it-grows-on-you limonshine in remembrance. After a grimace and a difficult swallow, Arcturus shook his head, clapped his hands, and took us out to the sandpit to practice.

At first, Arcturus and Zinaga ran me through a set of skindancing moves—but it wasn't much of a test. I *had* been practicing what Arcturus taught me, and I could perform all the basics on cue. Soon we were practicing together—no, *dancing* together—close, collegial, so natural I regretted not practicing together from the beginning. But the reason we hadn't was my own impatience to get on with tattooing without building a proper foundation for skindancing.

After almost two hours, Arcturus grunted, and we went inside.

Then came the grilling.

We sat in the studio for what felt like hours, drinking a strange, spiced tea while Arcturus and Zinaga asked pointed questions—ostensibly, about my masterwork, the Dragon, but soon I realized the tattoo was just an excuse to probe my knowledge of skindancing, top to bottom.

At first, I was almost insulted when Arcturus and Zinaga began asking about my tattooing setup—how I drew my magic circles, how I prepared my needles, how I kept my inks pristine—but I was able to convince them that yes, I *did* know how to prevent magical infections.

Then they asked about the logic of magic. At first I thought I had them—I thought I *lived* graphomancy nowadays—but that bravado cracked as they drilled deeper. I didn't remember half of what Arcturus had taught me, and I stumbled, more than once.

Fortunately, what I *did* remember . . . I knew better than them.

"The scales aren't what makes my new dragon tattoo powerful, it's their *pattern,*" I said. "Whether you call it the mystical complexity of the beating heart, or high Fermat number mana emanations, it's the Euler matrix of the scales that routes the possibilities of magic—"

"Fine, you know the mechanics. Let's come back to *your* question." Arcturus's said, eyes boring into me. "Your old dragon tattoo, still flying around. We've established it's a *projectia.* But how is that possible? Magic doesn't just happen. What are its sources of power?"

"Ah, hell, let's see . . . first and foremost, the beating heart," I said, feeling like I was back, not at the studio, but at Emory University, in my Physics of Magic class. "Source of the life force, generated by the action of muscles and transmitted by the pumping of blood—"

"Reducing it to mechanics again," he said.

"Yes, but not just mechanics, I know that you can't reduce magic to components, but the components we *do* know help me remember," I said. "Mana also comes from moving muscles, generating it in the fire of contraction. It comes from stretching skin, releasing pent-up mana."

"Good," Arcturus said. "Now—"

"There's also the mind, the firing of neurons," I said. "And almost all tissues generate mana, even bone and teeth, in lesser and lesser amounts. Then there's the life force of the Earth itself, conducted through ley lines; and the mana in 'spirits,' loose graphomantic designs."

"So why isn't the Dragon just a spirit?"

"It was glowing, and it damaged a roof. So-called 'spirits' are usually spell remnants—graphomantic kinks left in the fabric of mana when a spell collapses. Like a knot on a loop of string, they can't come undone by themselves, but they get so weak they're normally invisible, untouchable. Unless some yahoo inks a tattoo outside a magic circle, or forgets to close a tattoo circuit, only ley lines or psychic disturbances can charge them enough to radiate."

Arcturus began to speak, but Zinaga raised her hand.

"Nice recital," Zinaga said. "Any other possibilities for its power source?"

I racked my brain. "Well, there's liquid fire," I said. Zinaga smirked, while Arcturus just looked uncomfortable. "Liquid mana, the magical version of radioactivity. Derived from dragon's blood, it can now be made in the lab, in tiny amounts—"

"But neither one's a real practical source," Zinaga said quietly.

I stared at her. "Oh, hell. And you've got one. That's a secret worth keeping."

Arcturus nodded. "Maybe us backwoods hicks aren't as dumb as we let on."

"Maybe not," I said.

"And maybe all the pieces are out there," Zinaga said, glaring at Arcturus. "You see how close she got, me just asking a few questions? You saw the videos I showed you. She's approaching your power level. You couldn't ask for a better defender."

"You had me at 'she's ready,' " Arcturus said, standing. He let out a half laugh. "It's part of the ritual, but the whole idea of quizzing *you* is ridiculous. Except for those things we haven't told you yet, we'd be better off asking *you* what to ask an initiate. Zinaga's right. It is time."

Zinaga and I looked at each other.

"All right, apprentice," Zinaga said. "Time for the next step. Don't screw this up."

Then we rose together, and followed Arcturus out of the house into the woods.

Behind Arcturus's split-level is the hexagonal sandpit we used just for skindancing practice. Beyond that is a vegetable patch, oh-so-familiar from harvest time as an apprentice. Beyond that are the grapevines Arcturus let go fallow after he developed a bee allergy.

And beyond that . . . is the deep green forest. Kudzu and underbrush so thick the woods beyond are dark as velvet. My eyes widened—the kudzu was kept from engulfing this place, how? Fighting kudzu could be a daily struggle—Arcturus's garden must be magically warded.

Zinaga drew the kudzu aside with her hand, and the vines I had never before noticed seemed to shimmer, their branches rearranging between the movements of my eyes, like magic tattoos do. A spiritual ward—you didn't want to go past this point unless you'd already been.

Arcturus stepped into the verdant tunnel. Reluctantly, I ducked and followed, stepping out of Arcturus's oasis of relative modernity into an ancient path, one carved by the footfalls of men and animals, a deeper part of the South than even the most committed Southerners ever see.

Shifting rays of light cut through the tunnel like angled shafts of gold. Highlights danced off wide glossy leaves and moss-covered trunks. Worn stream stones dotted the path like fallen diamonds. Columns of gnats sparkled at the edge of the light, like ghosts made of static.

Arcturus passed an ornate wooden bowl, varnished and nailed into a tree. Similar work hung in the Curio Shop in town; here, it marked a barely visible fork off the path. We passed more forks—this was a backwoods alley, connecting Blood Rock's most reclusive artisans.

The path switchbacked down a steep, shadowed hill. Fallen trees bridged rippling streams, with only a rope handhold as a sign of habitation. The trees loomed oppressively now, the pine needles and dense kudzu letting in only the barest slivers of sunlight. Frequently, I had to duck my head, as Arcturus and Zinaga strode under branches which would have klonked me.

But the path was more than just overgrown. All of Georgia's trees were represented: spruce pine and red maple, black walnut and water oak. The kudzu faded, replaced by gray beards of Spanish moss and vivid fringes of resurrection fern, though you rarely saw either in Blood Rock. Fruit trees and edible fungi wedged in between medicinal shrubs. I hadn't had the knowledge or experience to see it before, but I could see it now—this forest was *cultivated.*

Then we emerged into a place that I knew—the Stonegrinder's Grove.

43. THE STONEGRINDER'S GROVE

The Stonegrinder's Grove was sparkling and fey, shafts of light mixed with flowers and butterflies. A ring of giant live oaks guarded a cluster of rounded stone huts. A low fire sparkled within a ring of stones, but its smoke dissipated into the leaves of the trees. The air was rich, scented like a spice rack's or a butcher's, reminding me of turned earth . . . or turned stomachs.

The last time I'd visited the Grove, for my induction, I'd been led here blindfolded—and that after an hour in the back of Arcturus's old Ford Econoline. But this was within walking distance—he must have driven to Stone Mountain Village and back just to throw me off.

And last time, the Grove had been practically deserted. Now? A small tribe of rough men and fit women worked the village in furs and exposed midriffs, tight jeans and tattooed chests. An Asian girl in male Native American leathers and paint spoke with a shirtless Native American man in black designer slacks, jeans jacket over one shoulder. Both saw me and went silent. A young girl who reminded me of Cinnamon hopped up onto an oak limb.

All of them were barefoot, buff, covered in bangles. Dreadlocks and hair beads were common; red necks and beer bellies were not. The grove was as far from the dueling banjos of *Deliverance* as I could imagine. I felt like I'd stumbled into a commune in California.

But there was more to it, things I hadn't been able to see the first time I was here, an antsy college dropout so eager to start tattooing that I'd barely looked around while Arcturus pressed my thumb to the Sanctuary Stone that marked me as a magician of Blood Rock.

Now the Sanctuary Stone once again hung in the throne room of its maker, Nyissa. I had spent years in the Edgeworld—five in Little Five Points tattooing the magical, four in the orbit of vampires, and a solid year dealing with the fae—and living with a werekin.

But something more than glitter sparkled on the too-pale skin of a girl; something less than human lurked in the too-wide eyes of a boy. The whole community felt touched by the fae. These were *real* Edgeworlders, living on the knife edge where the two worlds met.

A hot, bald, intense young man sitting beneath the girl's oak limb saw us and rose. Like the Native American man, he wore dark jeans beneath a bare chest rippling with muscle and angular, tribal tattoos—Zinaga's work, with some of Arcturus's smaller pieces thrown in.

"Master Inker," he said, staring at Arcturus. "This the new candidate for initiation?"

"I am," I said.

His head didn't turn, just stayed fixed on Arcturus. "I wasn't speaking to you."

Arcturus chuckled. "Oh, I hadn't yet seen the humor in *this* collision," he said, shaking his head. "Dakota, this is Gabriel Finch, head of the Stonegrinder's Guild. Gabriel, this is Dakota Frost. She's in charge of preventing the abuse of magic in the southeast."

"Self-appointed," Zinaga said, "meet self-appointed."

Finch shot her a glare. "I wasn't talking to you either—"

"That's *Master* Zinaga to you, Finch," she said.

Finch now glared at Arcturus. "You elevated her without asking us?"

"I told you," Arcturus said, "*I* decide when my students are ready to leave the nest."

I cleared my throat. "I'm honored that Arcturus and Zinaga have chosen me to take this next step . . . but I don't understand why the Stonegrinder Guild would care who was initiated or elevated in the Skindancers' Guild. What exactly am I getting initiated into?"

"Initiates are the children of a symbiosis between skindancers and stonegrinders," called a strong female voice, and I turned to see a dreadlocked woman standing at the entrance of the largest hut. She parted a bead curtain and stepped out. "A symbiosis to guard our secrets."

The Grinder was a pale, fit woman with blazing blue eyes and red dreadlocks woven through with a thousand extensions and beads. A headdress of feathers and bones sprayed back over her dreads; a staff with antlers hung loose in the fingers of one outstretched arm.

The woman's bare midriff rippled with muscles even I envied; her bracers and bangles and beads and bows would have been the envy of anyone at Burning Man. But the flared bell bottoms on her low-rider pants tickled a reminding, and my eyes drew over her closely.

She wasn't a modern primitive. She was an aging hippie—scratch that, a NON-aging hippie. She had already been weathered when I saw her at my initiation—but she hadn't aged another second in nearly ten years. She was hiding it under layers of modern adornment, but there was something distinctly . . . *seventies* about this strangely ageless woman. She had the same look, and, if I felt for it, even the same magical resonance as the Warlock, the Commissioner, and Devenger—a powerful wizard, stuck in cultural time, reeking of ancient magic.

Which meant she had a source of liquid fire.

But rural Georgia wasn't the West Coast. Drakes hadn't been seen here for millennia, hadn't been common here since the Ice Age, so there was no native source of the faux liquid fire Jewel called *magifouaille*. And dragons themselves, or Saurian Drakes, or whatever they really were, never ranged north of Mexico—so I had a hard time believing there was some secret crèche of dragon eggs or deposit of dragon amber the Grinder was mining for liquid fire.

Which meant there was more to this little backwoods village than met the eye.

"I am the Master Grinder," she said.

"I remember," I said. "You pricked my thumb."

She raised a painted eyebrow. "You're not the same child I remember."

I laughed. "I wasn't a child," I said, "but I did have a lot to learn."

"And still do," the Grinder said. There was something oddly . . . *addled* about her eyes, like she wasn't looking directly at you, not ever. "Skindancing can be *practiced* by anyone. But *creating* a skindancer requires both ink, and inking—a grinder, and an inker. Each are difficult skills, easily abused. We guard ourselves by showing our secrets only to chosen initiates—"

"And by entrusting our deepest secrets to different branches of the Guild," Arcturus said. "I am not a really a 'master skindancer,' I'm a Master Inker of the Skindancing Guild. The Grinder is a Master Grinder of the Guild. The Grinders and the Inkers train their own—"

"But we vet all Initiates to the Guild *together,*" Finch said pointedly—and I realized that he might have an actual point. He looked at Arcturus, then me. "Two branches, but *one* tree. We must *all* accept you, Frost, before any of us can share with you our deeper secrets."

"We will test your knowledge," the Grinder said, and Arcturus snorted. She arched an eyebrow, then extended her hand to the firepit and the stone seats around it. "We will challenge your wisdom. We will question your loyalty. If you pass, you will become one of us."

I smiled tightly at her. "Well," I said. "I'm game."

Once again, I found myself in a circle, sipping spiced tea while being grilled about magic. This time the questions were lathered with a bit more woo-hooery (I hate that phrase, but there's no other polite way to describe that New Age nonsense) but it was nothing I couldn't handle.

And nothing Arcturus and Zinaga hadn't just prepared me for. They just leaned back, quiet, sharing smiles with the Grinder, who grew similarly reticent, sitting to the side with her chin propped up on her fist, head and headdress tilted askance while Finch kept grilling me.

At first, he grilled me about my tattooing setup: how I prepared my needles, how I stored my inks, how I drew my magic circles—asking subtle questions designed to see if I knew how to prevent magical infections. Next, he tried to crack my knowledge of graphomancy. Good luck.

Finally, he switched to pigment grinding—something I'd learned even less of from Arcturus than skindancing. But I'd spent three years in chemistry before dropping out, and now Arcturus leaned forward, hands steepled together, as interested in my answers as Finch.

These questions were hard. Finch drilled me mercilessly on the five colors of magic, their relationship to human perception, and how that could be realized in chemical structures. I had to use *everything* I'd learned, even the newest alchemy knowledge I'd picked up from Devenger and his books, and I wasn't sure I would get the answers right. But, again and again . . . I did.

"Fractions of magic are more interesting than spectra of light," I said. "Less like a line, more like a fractal tree, with complex, interwoven possibilities. The higher up the tree, the farther out you can fall, like a Pachinko machine. That's why we use Fermat numbers—"

But Finch was only half listening to the answer to his own question about why firecap ink could create such amazing magical colors. Instead, almost the moment I began talking, his eyes started flicking over my shoulder, in the direction of the sun, setting behind the trees.

I relaxed. We kept talking, shifting from my knowledge to the lore of the Skindancer Guild, and Finch kept trying to trip me up, standard job interview stuff with a little mysticism thrown in, but I wasn't fazed, or fooled. I just sat cross-legged, at the ready for the real test.

When the last rays of the sun faded, Finch stood up.

—❧

"Enough talk," he said. "Show us how you dance."

44. Skindancers, Duel

Oh, had I been *waiting* for this.

I stood in one fluid move, uncoiling my crossed legs in a corkscrewing motion which made the tails of my newest vestcoat whip around me as I whirled to standing. I raised my right hand in the traditional skindancer bow, then began the Dance of Five and Two.

Skindancing isn't like traditional dance, or even ballet—the moves aren't designed to look pretty, but to build power, stretching the skin over exercising muscles to generate mana. Worse, if one move builds mana, its mirror takes it away, so even the basic footwork is complicated.

The Five and Two draws out a pentagram, a quick, light-footed sketch in one direction, then repeating it again, switching right for left, always building power. It can look awkward, but I've practiced until it's perfect, feet flickering through the J-steps.

I didn't wait to be given direction. When Arcturus had said they were better off having me quiz initiates, I realized that knowing the shape of my art was just as important as the details. I had to show them my scope. So when the Five and Two was done, I really cut loose.

I whirled into a pirouette, curling my arms in the proper *port de bras* to capture magical power as I flicked my legs up in complicated sequences of *battements*. The turnouts and pointed steps weren't really ballet, but I'd been practicing ballet to help with skindancing.

Because if *I'm* going to do something, I want it to look *good.*

I whirled, then abruptly stopped, discharging all the mana I'd generated into a gleaming bubble of power the size of a bowling ball. The sphere of power gleamed from red to green to blue to gold and back again, showing I'd mastered channeling different kinds of power.

I was just preparing to re-absorb the power and show off the magic of my marks when Finch began clapping. "Not bad," he said, raising his right hand in the traditional skindancer salute. "Now let's see how you use it."

And he blew a kiss to me, sparkles glittering off his hand and wafting toward me in the air like a trail of pixie dust—and then a tattoo bee shot through the sparkles like an ink bullet, puncturing my bubble of power into a spray of Technicolor fireworks.

I flinched as mana sparked around me, but I was prepared. Finch didn't like me, and I'd had no illusions a fairy grandmother blessing was winging to me on that kiss. I twirled my hand as I turned out my feet, uncoiling my vine as I grounded myself to drain off power.

Savage tribal marks leapt out of Finch's skin, a thicket of dark razors, swirling around him as he swept his hands in a circle, his feet nimbly hopping through a complex dance called the Seven Three Five. Razor bees streamed off his tattoos and swarmed me, biting, stinging.

By now I had two vines out, whipping them around, batting the bees away. But Finch's magic was strong, and I was forced to bring my asp tattoos to life, sending the coiling snakes down the vines to bite at the scalpel hummingbirds he'd added to the mix.

A mistake—Finch stamped his foot, and his tattoos surged out in a spray of abstract shapes. The angles overwhelmed me, and I felt a surge of mana drawn out of me, chilling my core and making my heart race—and then my asps twisted free and fell away.

My eyes bugged as my asps flopped on the ground. Finch had used metamagic, applying his magic to mine, forcing my tattoos to become *projectia.* No, I realized, as an asp thumped against the root of a tree, not just *projectia*—they drew so much mana they had become *solid.*

Finch drew in power for another attack, and I angled myself backward, legs stretched out in a move drawn more from Taido than from ballet. I threw my hands forward, pretending to fire another burst of energy or launch a tattoo—and Finch's abstract angles surged over me.

My pulse raced. My body shivered. Mana surged through me—not just from my heart, but up through the ground. I'd become *real* good at drawing mana from other sources, and now I used Finch's metamagic against itself, drawing mana from the ley lines beneath our feet.

Let me loose, whispered a voice, *let me loose*—and I saw no reason to deny her.

"*Spirit of fire,*" I said, "*come to life.*"

Smoothly, my dragon's wings slid out of the slits cut in my coat. Gracefully, its tail slid out of my pants leg. Powerfully, its arms hulked out of my sleeves, mirroring my movements. Fueled by Finch's metamagic, the dragon became more solid than it ever had.

"That's your masterwork," Finch said, his angular armor wavering.

A low crackling rumble erupted from the dragon's throat. "Sure you want to bring this one to life?" I asked, trying to keep the tremor from my voice as mana poured through me like a conduit. My boots were smoking. "Sure you can handle this *projectia* flying around—"

"Damn it!" Finch swept his hands aside, the angled shapes dissipating. My own dragon partially evaporated as the metamagic subsided. So it *was* still tattoo magic, requiring a beating heart; I stole a glance at the asps, and watched them fade. He said, "You weren't supposed—"

"You had a chance to tell me the rules before picking a fight," I said.

"That's not the point! You're supposed to react," Finch said, stomping forward like he was spoiling for a real fight. "*Of course* an inker can pull out a masterwork and beat someone without one. You're supposed to match magic for magic, not pull out PhD level charms—"

"Whoa—match magic for magic, with you using *metamagic*, which I haven't even had the opportunity to learn, because it's clearly a secret?" I said, glaring down at him. "What is this, capoeira, where you get baptized to the mat? Is that it? Did I have to lose to get initiated—"

"Oh, you'll lose," Finch said—and punched at me.

I fell back into an improvised Taido middle stance. I had a head on him, but no way am I going to underestimate a guy in a fight—guys have twice the upper body strength of girls, and Finch could do me serious damage if I wasn't careful. Still, I repelled a flurry of blows.

"We're done," I said, after he subsided. "This isn't a fistfight—"

But I'd made another mistake, this time turning to leave in the hope that backing down would help defuse the brewing street fight. I felt, rather than heard, the swish of the punch aimed behind my ear. I didn't think—I just shifted down and to my right, caught his hand and tugged. Finch's momentum carried him over my left leg, flipping him so he landed on his ass.

"You all right?" I asked, hand on his shoulder, less to comfort him than to keep him from popping back up. "Anything wounded other than maybe pride?"

He surged under my hand, then blinked and raised his hand to mine. "Yes," he said, face a struggling mix of anger and admiration. "You pass. Yes, the fight was supposed to be a lesson in humility—but you not only can fight, you know when to *stop* a fight. *Of course,* you pass."

"I'll drink to that," Arcturus said, raising a drink which had appeared in his hand.

We once again sat around the fire, drinking yet another strange brew Finch assured me was an important part of my initiation later that evening. I was still rattled from our almost-fight, but Finch was treating me like his new best friend, and was telling me about Grinder traditions.

The little werekin girl kept trying to eavesdrop, and her presumptive parents, the Asian woman and the Native American man, kept shooing her away. I lost her for a while, and then I spied her, again up on a thick live oak branch, watching us. I swear her ears were tufted.

"Is that young girl a werekin?" I asked, and she ducked back behind the tree branch. Entertaining, but you couldn't be a mother and not realize that kid was a person—and not part of the show. "A werelynx? We should get her together with my daughter, set up a play date—"

"Khouri has no interest in a 'play date,' " said the Asian woman, archly, sitting up straight and haughty even though the girl was peeking up over the edge of the branch, her interest piqued. "Especially not with a tame werekin who's never seen forest."

"Cinnamon's a street cat, and Atlanta's the City in the Forest," I said. "I'll wager she had a harder upbringing than Khouri—no role models, no parents, no education. Though she's a real quick study; I'll wager she could tutor Khouri if she needs help with her math homework—"

"Khouri doesn't have homework," said the Asian woman, tossing down her mortar and pestle. "You can dance, you can even fight, but you have not learned what's important. You've not learned our traditions. We have our own ways here, and we'll train her in them—"

"If you want to indoctrinate your children, there's always Sunday School and Bible Study," I said. "Or Wiccan Hour, or meditation, or home prayers, or whatever. Trust me, your children will have no trouble choosing their path. After all, you did."

"And now that we've chosen, we want to pass it on," she said, folding her arms. She had leather bracers like Jewel's, but where Jewel's were mostly proof against fire, this woman's intricate beaded gauntlets were laced with magical symbols. "What's so wrong with that?"

"You chose this life," I said. "She didn't. You're choosing for her. Even down to who she plays with." The woman's face faltered, and I raised an eyebrow. "Khouri *does* have someone to play with, doesn't she? No? Would *you* really want to have grown up all alone?"

"No," the woman said, licking her lips.

"Well, if you want to find a playmate for Khouri, I've got a werekin who's a bundle of springs," I said. "Cinnamon's a little older, a bit surly sometimes, but she's a real good sport and a total softie on the inside. I'd be happy to bring her by. And she is a whiz at math and science."

"Is she?" the Grinder said, looking at me calculatingly. "Are *you?*"

"Well, I could say yes, and you could just take my word for it," I said, looking back at her, equally calculatingly; she'd just asked something I'd love to know about *her*. Then I quoted Feynman, "But if you really want to know, 'the sole test of any idea is experiment'—"

"Thank the Goddess," the Grinder said. "At last, someone to tell the whole story to."

"I thought I handled it quite well," Arcturus said, "when you first told it to me."

"*You,*" the Grinder said, and Arcturus fell silent. "All that knowledge you're so quick to discard chasing each new mystery. Mysticism helps you train your body to dance, but it will not help you grind a perfect mixture. We need both learning *and* wonder." Arcturus looked down; then the Grinder turned her strange eyes on me. "Come," she said, rising. "You are ready."

The Stonegrinder's hut was a stone and moss version of a hobbit hole—underground, but cozy and comfortable, not crude and cold. Another fire flickered at its heart, warming it; its smoke curled up in a strangely corralled column, slinking out a hole in the roof.

All around the room were piles of worn textbooks: chemistry, geology, mathematics, all *very* old. I flipped through one, examining its yellowed pages—it had the bad typography and dense math of something turn of the *last* century. Perhaps the Grinder's job involved preserving the stored knowledge of her predecessors . . . or perhaps she was not just old, but *very* old.

On a terraced column that reminded me of a stone cat condo rested the stonegrinder's tools—stone pots and modern droppers, handmade brushes and Pyrex glass. Dozens, no, hundreds of little bottles were piled everywhere. On the highest platform rested a lacquered skull.

"Oh, hey," I said. "Who's Yorick?" I stared at it with a slight smile, then noticed a stick behind the skull. Slowly, I realized it was a thighbone. It was yellowed with age—real human bone. At last I said quietly, "And how did you get him?"

"Through nothing untoward," the Grinder said, stepping up opposite me with that slightly addled stare. She took the skull and flipped it over, tossing into it herbs and powders. Then she reached for the thighbone. "It was given freely to my master by *his* master upon his death."

The skull and thighbone were her mortar and pestle. *Yuk.* I turned away as the noise of grinding filled the cabin, unsure why that left me so unsettled. It was touching, in a way, and probably magic of great potency. Arcturus, Zinaga, and I all sat around the Grinder's hearth.

"Never met him," Arcturus said, "but his student initiated me. Good man."

"Charming," I said. "What is this initiation going to involve?"

"We are going to give you the Skindancer Gift," Zinaga said.

"But first," Arcturus said, "we're going to let you in on the Skindancer Secret."

—

"Before the first life," the Grinder said, "before the first death, there was the first *fire*."

45. Born in Flame

In the gloom of her cabin, the Grinder flicked the contents of the skull toward the fire. Glittering powder sparkled out, the fire flared . . . and then the air above it grew dark, though still sparkling, like a night sky full of stars. Slowly, I realized the pinpricks *were* stars.

"A view of space?" I asked. Then the view expanded, moving in upon a star that grew into a sun, *the* Sun, with outsized planets curling around it in elaborate crystal tracks. My brow furrowed. "Scale's off. So . . . a magical planetarium, showing me what you want me to see?"

"You think," Arcturus began, "that *only* scientists know *anything*—"

"Be silent," the Grinder said. "Yes, Dakota, the Eye of Truth only shows what you would call a reconstruction. But is a 'scientific' reconstruction is better because you've seen it on TV? They're just special effects, cobbled together by thieves and liars and fools."

My skin prickled. A whispered voice said this was . . . *true but inaccurate—broad brush.* But still, something raised the hackles of the Dragon on my skin, and soon I nailed it—the Grinder had called people who worked in television fools, and *I* was now in that category. And Alex—

"I'll give you thieves and liars. But I'm working to change the fools on TV part."

"My point is, the Eye of Truth is not half-truths tarted up with a little flash," the Grinder said, tossing another pinch of powder at the fire, apparently not seeing the irony as the magic made her own image flare. "Like false color images of planets from NASA, magical lore seen with the Eye of Truth is a *view* of truth *as we know it.* As we learn more, the view expands."

"This lore isn't that different from science after all," I said. "Tell me the story."

"You were probably taught the Sun formed first and all the planets grew around it," the Grinder said, waving her hand. The planets whirled backward, blurring into a glowing, knotted red cloud. "The opposite is true. The Earth and its sister were ancient, *ancient* bodies—"

"The Earth . . . and its *sister,*" I said. I *knew* this, and not just from the cryptic murmured assent of the magical dragon on my back. I knew it from a more prosaic source—a cover story in *New Scientist*. "You mean the planet that stalked the Earth . . . *Theia*."

"Yes," the Grinder said. "Greeks told muddled tales of the titans Theia and Hyperion, the parents of Helios, the Sun. They were not far off. The proto-Earth and the body scientists call Theia are the nucleus around which the solar system formed. The Sun is an Earth-child."

The image ran backward further, stars spinning, the cloud expanding, evaporating, leaving two tiny planets sailing alone through the dark. The Grinder released her hand, and the stars moved forward again, the icy twin worlds dancing around each other in the night.

I felt my forehead furrow. "How did that work—"

"Theia and Hyperion traveled long in the dark. Perhaps they were orphaned in the death of another star; perhaps they date back to the origin of the universe. No one knows—because of the First Cataclysm. When they fell into the Cloud, its dust stripped them to their bones."

Abruptly, a glowing gold column swam up at Theia and Hyperion. They impacted in a flare of light and a growing shock wave, the ice boiling off their surface, streaming away like planet-sized comets as they slowly came to rest . . . and the gas began to collapse on them.

"Theia and Hyperion were the nucleus of the solar system," the Grinder said. "In that sense, we owe them everything: the light, the water, the very core of our world. But we do not know our parents. Whatever they were like before the First Cataclysm is all but lost to us."

"But not completely lost, or how would we know what we know?" I said, with a little smirk—then my eyes widened. "My God. Not all lost. There are traces. What kind of traces? Was there a civilization on Theia? Were there . . . artifacts?"

The Grinder grimaced and cocked her head, not precisely a no.

"Unclear," she said, nodding at her column of smoke and its magic images. The cloud was reknotting again, its central core thickening, thick sweeps forming in inner and outer orbits. "But what is more important is that, before their child killed them, it gave them new life."

The Sun lit up in the center of the cloud. It boiled away the gas at its core, leaving arcs of pebbles that coalesced into Mercury, into Venus, and, farther out, into Mars. But in the orbit of the Earth . . . Theia and Hyperion danced around each other, covered with oceans of fire.

"I . . . know this," I said hesitantly. "From geology . . . this is the *Hadean* era?"

"When stones fell like rain," the Grinder said softly. "The ground flowed like water, glowed like sunset. But Theia and Hyperion had already cleared their orbits. Their skies calmed. Rock cooled, froze, floated like pack ice. And under that dim new Sun, life began again."

In the cracked rock of a broken continent, under the looming red moon Theia, the caldera of a volcano swelled in a heaving mass. The veined red surface bulged outward like an egg—then burst, birthing a burning creature with teeth of stone, scales of steel and wings of fire.

"Oh my God," I said, shifting in my seat. "Dragons are . . . *Hadean* life."

"Life, born in fire, powered by *magic*," the Grinder said. "Perhaps jump-started by the remnants of what came before; perhaps not. We do not know. We *do* know Dray'yan life ruled for an eon. Longer than the dinosaurs, the flame-beasts basked under the young Sun."

"On their twin worlds," I said, "doomed by the very star they created."

"Why doomed?" Zinaga asked. "*I've* heard the story, but how did you just *know?*"

"College physics," the Grinder said, tilting her head. "Explain it to them."

"Things need speed to stay in orbit," I said. "Theia and Hyperion were doomed as soon as they hit the cloud. It stole their velocity, made them fall toward each other. Even if they didn't impact right away, the Sun would eventually jostle them into each other."

"It's the three body problem," the Grinder said. "It isn't stable."

I glanced at her. The Grinder *also* had training in science before she joined the Guild.

"Life as we know it began beneath the feet of the fire beasts," the Grinder said. "As the worlds cooled, Vai'ia and Ni'iva began to flourish in the embers of Dray'ya—"

"Vai'ia? Ni'iva?" I shook my head. "I keep hearing those words, but I don't understand them. I don't care whether you think of them as midichloreans or the living Force or whatever, I always just thought that stuff was woo-hooery. Now you're telling me all of this is real."

"Vai'ia is the spirit of *life,*" Arcturus said. "Of the first life that formed on Earth—"

"A layer of bacteria, born in the cooling crust of proto-Earth," Zinaga said, and Arcturus scowled. "Living in the coals of Dray'yan life, but not consuming that life—thriving in the embers, living off magic. The first—what's the word you used, Grinder, auto—"

"Autotrophs," I said. The Grinder was twisting her staff, showing me a layer of sparkling moss beneath the feet of dragons, like a bed of pearls. "Life that feeds itself given a source of energy. And Ni'ivan . . . let me guess. The first heterotrophs, the first life eating other life."

"The first death," Zinaga said. Among the jeweled moss, mushrooms began growing—strange, glowing and fantastic, some as large as mountains. "At first, magical fungi which ate the decay of other life forms and turned it into more life. Later, it became more aggressive."

"On both worlds, I take it," I said. In the magic window into the Grinder's supposed past, rocks hurled into space by impact on one world landed on the other . . . then flowered into green moss and silver threads. "So that's not why you have a third word. Vai'ian and Ni'ivan are fancy words for autotrophs and heterotrophs, defined by their source of energy. Vai'ian draws energy from the environment, Ni'ivan from other life, so logically, Dray'yan life would be . . . life that provides its own source of energy?" Then all the pieces clicked. "Life built on liquid fire."

"Precisely," the Grinder said, smiling in triumph. "Life that is its *own* source. Life that is more than just fuel for magic, but feeds on it, consuming only the tiniest fraction of real matter in the cycle. A nearly infinite, practically endless source of magical power."

"There's no way forms of life based on that would ever fall to predators or disease," I said. "You said the First Cataclysm. I've already guessed there was a Second, when Theia finally impacted Hyperion. Did that kill off the dragons?"

"No," the Grinder said, twisting her staff. Theia impacted Hyperion, shattering both worlds. A ring of silvery material formed, then coalesced into the young moon, but on the newly formed Earth, new dragons were born in calderas. "It was the cooling that killed them."

As the new Moon cooled, it glowed with a shimmering silvery light. But the new Earth just cooled and cracked as the red seas of lava faded. Impacts ceased, volcanoes became rare, and the great flame beasts began dying, falling and crumbling to dust, one by one.

"Even the fire that seems to burn forever may one day go out," the Grinder said. "As the surface grew cool, Dray'yan life retreated underground. Vai'ia and Ni'iva followed, digging into the mantle, a thick layer of life woven through with silver threads of death."

"I know the next part of the story. As magic died, non-magical life flourished on the surface . . . and Vai'ia and Ni'iva *infected* it," I said, steepling my hands. Beneath the dark crust, green and silver threads warred, then reached up, twisting life. "Making werekin and vamps."

"And drakes are the same kind of thing," Zinaga said. "Magically infected creatures—"

"So this *is* the Saurian Drake hypothesis," I said, and the Grinder grinned. "Dragons in the fossil record are just infected dinosaurs, mutated by dragon organelles. There *are* no real dragons—none, at least, in recorded history. Or even in the fossil record—"

"Oh, they're in history *and* the fossil record," the Grinder said. I stared at her. I'd been a chemist, Arcturus an anthropologist; I was becoming convinced *she'd* been a paleontologist. "And I'm willing to bet, as sharp as you are, you've already guessed where."

"No," I said. "You're talking about things the size of mountains stomping over the Earth before the days we've even got fossilized *pond scum*. If creatures that powerful, that vast, had survived for any length of time, we'd notice. There'd be traces—"

"Mass extinctions," the Grinder said.

"Oh, Jesus Christ," I said, crossing myself.

"What killed the dinosaurs?" the Grinder said. "Not mammals nibbling their eggs, I'll tell you that. Did they teach you giant impacts? Volcanic eruptions? Let me tell you how the most successful mortal creatures in history died, Dakota—there was a *hatching*."

"No," I said . . . but from the thing on my back, I felt, *this is truth.*

"The last one in recorded history was . . . Krakatau, perhaps?" the Grinder said. "Pompeii, almost certainly. Mount Saint Helens . . . may have been a failed one."

"Erupting volcanoes are dragons hatching?" I said.

"Not *every* volcano," she said. "But *any* volcano. A hotspot might be mating sign. A magma pool could nurture an egg. And even if there was none of that . . . a hatching would definitely cause a volcanic eruption. Even if it failed—"

"Please stop this," Arcturus said sharply, and the Grinder fell silent.

"You're getting into the rationalist weeds. Magical power is derived from the spirit, not organelles or eruptions. The Skindancer Secret is that there are three sources, not two: Vai'ia, Ni'iva, and Dray'ya. If you rationalize things too much, you miss the energy, the meaning, the wholeness—"

"I *think* I understand you . . . but do you really think anything she's said is wrong?" I said. "Either from a perspective of skindancer lore, or from our scientific interpretations? Because I gotta tell you, I found her little magical Powerpoint pretty damn convincing—"

"No, she's not wrong," Arcturus said, frowning. "Dakota . . . I'm sorry."

"For . . . what?" I said, surprised he said it with such . . . heart.

"For always giving you such a hard time," Arcturus said. "When we first met, I was a younger man. Well, it wasn't that long ago, but I was a new master; you were one of my first students. And your intellect is . . . well, intimidating. I've been defending my ego."

"*My* intellect?" I laughed. "You *do* understand I'm the dim bulb of my circle—"

"You mean the blind witch and the vamp queen, don't you?" Arcturus said.

"You think they're *so* smart just because they're scholars," Zinaga said.

"Well, yes," I said. "I'm not going for a PhD in vampirology, or graphomancy—"

"*You* were studying chemistry," Arcturus said. "To become a college professor."

"I dropped out," I said.

"You switched majors. A budding *college professor* came to study with *me*—and then quit because you thought I had no more to teach you. Great way to make me feel like a master, but we must move past that. What makes you discount yourself, compared to your friends?"

"I went to work," I said. "I work for a living, and they gave that up to study—"

"Did they?" Arcturus said. "I hear the witch's a practicing graphomancer, and the vamp's some kind of politician, and neither of them have graduated yet. Truth is, all three of you worked while you learned. Now tell me, Miss 'Dim Bulb' . . . which one of you got your Ph.D. first?"

I stared at him. I wanted to laugh, but didn't. "I do *not* have a Ph.D.—"

"You attained mastery of a subject matter. You created a masterwork that made a unique contribution to the field—two of them, one of which rests on your skin and the other which is still flying around. And today, you defended their principles before a council of guildsmen."

"You said I'm just an initiate," I said. "I'm not a master yet—"

"A master is a position in a studio," Zinaga said. "It's not a measure of learning, but status and responsibility. Like a professor, you have to be accepted into a studio and in turn accept students to be a master. An initiate just means an accepted member of the Guild—"

"The same way a 'doctorate' means membership in an academic guild," Arcturus said. "And don't tell me I don't know what that means, Dakota. I *do* know. I have a doctorate, in anthropology. That's the game. You have to have a doctorate to give a doctorate, and . . ."

Arcturus sighed, then smiled, both proud and sad.

"You're one of us, Dakota Frost," he said. "You *are* a Skindancer."

A chime sounded. The Grinder checked her wrist—which bore a normal-looking digital watch hidden beneath all the bangles and feathers—then stood. Arcturus and Zinaga did so as well, and after a brief baffled glance, so did I, facing the Grinder.

"Welcome to the Guild, Skindancer," she said. "Time for your graduation ceremony."

46. Droplets of Liquid Fire

"At midnight," the Grinder said, stretching forth her hand toward a faery circle, "on the night of a new moon, when the Ni'ivan light of the Sun is hidden, and the Vai'ian light of the Moon is dark, then, and only then, can Dray'ya, Earth's first life, truly blossom."

The four of us stood at the edge of the faery circle, staring at the fantastic eruption of mushrooms around it. They were narrow and rounded and puffballs and oysters, red and blue and white and gold. They glowed like neon, lit from within—but they were not the true prize.

At the center of the ring, in a blackened patch of soot, grew a cluster of firecaps.

My head was spinning from the simple implications of the Grinder's words. The Moon was *Vai'ian*, the spirit of life, its silvery form the biosphere of a whole world knocked into space by a giant impact. Werewolves drew their power and their curse from that surge of life force.

The Earth was *Ni'ivan*, a world of death, a deep web of fungal decay beneath mossy remnants of life, flowering into a new biosphere after that titanic impact. Vampires didn't catch fire because sunlight was their enemy; it was because the sun was too much of a good thing.

And beneath them both, down where the Earth was still so hot that rock flowed like plastic, a third form of life flourished, *Dray'yan*, the last remnants of dragons, their magical cells infecting normal Earth life, producing drakes. But the infestation wasn't limited to *animal* life.

"A Dray'yan fungus," I said, watching the firecaps grow before my eyes. From tiny nubs, they quickly grew into miniature gnome's caps, white tipped with red, rapidly swelling and variegating before my eyes into red cones rimmed with flames. "A *dragon* fungus."

"A dragon fungus," the Grinder said. "This is our secret. Where others see only a battle between two forces, we see the harmony of all three: Vai'ian, Ni'ivan . . . *and* Dray'yan. Magical power comes from these three spiritual sources. These three sparks of life—"

"These three kinds of organelles," I said, stepping closer to the ring, shifting a branch. It crackled under my hand, and I was surprised to see the bark was burned. "The organelles only represent rules of magic. The compounds they're made of will retain a touch of that magic—"

"And a touch of that spirit," the Grinder said.

Around the ring, moss gleamed, glowing green and verdant right up to its edge. Within the ring was no life but the firecaps, guarded by an inner circle of singed white mushrooms as big as cantaloupes. Even the trees around it were twisted, their bark darkened with soot.

"So what's the initiation?" I asked, staring at it warily.

"We are going to eat firecaps," Zinaga said.

My eyes widened. "You can't eat firecap ink," I said. "Even if it's nontoxic in the skin the stabilizers aren't meant to be *ingested*—"

"Not firecap ink," Arcturus said. "Raw fire caps."

"Fire caps," I said, "are a poisonous fungi. In their raw form, they're a neurotoxin—"

"Still thinks she knows everything," Arcturus chuckled. "Firecap ink is one of our most important pigments—but why? It's because fire caps are also the source of our power. Consuming them cements our mystical connection to the Dray'yan life force—"

"Let me speak her language, Arcturus," Zinaga said. "Fire caps are magical fungi, filled with Dray'yan organelles, drawing their power from them the same way that weres and vamps draw power from Vai'ian and Ni'ivan organelles in their bodies. But like vamps and weres—"

"They can infect you, filling your cells with alien magic," I said. "Fire caps are filled with dragon organelles, and you're suggesting that we eat them so they can infect us?"

"Yes," the Grinder said . . . as the fire caps caught fire.

A bonfire leapt up in the middle of the faery circle, its magic rippling against my skin before I felt the heat. The mushrooms around the fire caps glowed to life in a thousand colors as the air was rent by a tearing, crackling cry that sounded disturbingly like a drake.

I stepped toward the singing fire. The fire caps burned without being consumed. Their pointed caps, now fully red, were darkening to black, tattoo-style flames etched into their sides. Tiny sparks fell from the base of the caps, then rode the flames up into the night.

"This is how they spread their spores, though they rarely take root in any place a human sets foot," the Grinder said, leaning her staff over the flame, catching the sparks in a dark velvet sheet that made them look like tiny stars. "I will share the spores with my apprentices."

"Shades of the burning bush," I said, staring at the caps resisting the flame.

"They *will* burn, eventually, but only for a minute," the Grinder said. "Then, we will quench them. Fire caps must be consumed or harvested before they caramelize."

"Browning—*the Maillard reactions*—makes them edible," I said, my chemistry flooding back to me. "But it breaks open the Dray'yan organelles, spills liquid fire out into the cells, reheats them from within—and caramelization makes them poisonous again."

"Yes," she said.

"They grow only in faery circles, magically insulated from the modern world," I said, talking through the knowledge. I had to be sure my facts were right, teasing out the implications. "Already rare, they bloom only once a month, or less, at midnight—and must be harvested within the minute. By someone with knowledge—or you'll get killed."

"Yes," she said.

"The magical world would tear this grove apart for this knowledge," I said.

The Grinder laughed. "Perhaps," she said. "But those truly in the know would not. We respect each other's privacy, we Keepers of the Secret Flame—"

"Last person who called himself that tried to skin me alive."

"Frost, relax. It just means 'guardian of liquid fire,' " Arcturus said. "Many groups of people call themselves that. *All* Skindancers are Keepers of the Secret Flame."

"And we keep each other's secrets," the Grinder said.

The fire abruptly went out.

The Grinder moved quickly to the edge of the circle, turning over a small hourglass. Khouri, who I had not seen hiding there, scampered forward with a bowl, holding it out as the Grinder carefully selected and picked red-hot fire caps with her bare fingers.

"This is how firecap ink is harvested," she said to Khouri, wincing, tossing a cap into the basket, one eye always on that hourglass, so quickly running out. "Just after the flame, just after midnight. See this one, child? White streaks. No good."

"I see that," Khouri said. "And this one? Too burnt?"

"Yes, child," the Grinder said. "Toss it there. I will show you how to mulch them."

Quickly, they filled the bowl, then the Grinder pronounced them finished. Khouri gasped and scampered off, then ran back with a pitcher, just as the hourglass was running out. The moment the last grain fell, the Grinder poured the water in, releasing a cloud of steam.

Zinaga, Arcturus, and I crowded around the Grinder and Khouri, smelling the sweet steam rising from that bowl. As the fumes evaporated, we saw at the bottom of the bowl perhaps two dozen black mushrooms, their tips glowing with red flames.

Then Khouri grabbed one, popped it into her mouth and scampered off with a giggle. The Grinder hissed, shaking her head, but still smiling. Then she turned to us. "Pick four. One for Arcturus, one for Zinaga—and two for you, Dakota. You have some catching up to do."

Eagerly we reached into the bowl, seizing the hot, wet, steaming mushrooms. We laughed as our fingers touched, Arcturus and me slapping each other's hands away and Zinaga trying to referee. But we all came away with gleaming fire caps, warm to the touch.

I cupped two of them in my hand. "And what about you, Grinder?"

"I've had my share," the Grinder said wearily, and she looked far older. "For now."

"This is *already* in me," I said, raising one mushroom in my fingers, watching the light of mana steam off the glowing red flame pattern on its tip.

"In firecap ink. Droplets of liquid fire are in my tattoos, breaking down, flooding my bloodstream, collecting in my fat—"

"And you can feel it," Arcturus said, and I did: the power flowed from the mushroom, tingled through my body—and made my dragon shiver. He said, "That's the secret of your tattoo flying around, Dakota—*dragon ink*. It keeps our tattoos alive long after they leave living skin—"

"Firecap ink . . . is essence of dragon," I said. "Devenger was right about my source of liquid fire. And here I thought . . ." and I grimaced as I said it, as ridiculous as it sounded to me now, "I thought my tattoos were powered by the magic of my beating heart."

"They are . . . *on* your skin," Zinaga said. "Off your skin, they'd disintegrate without a seed of high mystical complexity. This is the secret weapon of our clan—pigment choice. That's why our designs are so long-lived. Dragon ink is best of all, a constant trickle of mana—"

"My tattoos," I said, "are powered by *mystical nuclear reactions*."

"Yes," the Grinder said. "It is so. Are you afraid?"

"Afraid," I said, "and delighted. Inkable liquid fire . . . and you let me have it."

Arcturus smiled thinly. "We put more trust in you than you give us credit."

"All those questions about my tattooing setup," I said. "From both you and Finch. I thought you wanted to know whether I knew how to prevent magical infections, but you were *really* asking questions designed to show whether I was *sharing my inks*—"

"Which you do not," Arcturus said. "What's the phrase? Trust but verify?"

"Without knowledge, firecap ink *is* just ink," the Grinder said. "With knowledge . . . it is essence of dragon, a secret of our power. A secret to longer life. But only one secret. First, we entrust you with this; once you have taken this step, you will be ready to take another."

"You should have done this a long time ago," Arcturus said. "She's right. You do have catching up to do—and this is a matter of a sacred trust. When you eat this, you will be an initiate. On pain of death, you may speak to no one of what you have seen—"

I held up my hand. "Hell to the no," I said. "I understand the need to keep some things secret. But this system is too fragile. We're not going to leave secrets like this to us four Lords of the Sith, waiting for some *decappite* out of the *Da Vinci Code* to erase this knowledge forever."

"We can't trust anyone else with this knowledge," Arcturus said.

"More than you know," I said. "In the olden days, maybe ink without knowledge was just ink, but nowadays, we understand the physics of pigment. Devenger got a good guess about what was in my tattoos *just by looking at them*. Give him a bottle of ink and a gas chromatograph—"

"Goddess," the Grinder said. "You must not tell him of this—"

"I won't betray your trust, but you must help me build something you will trust. This is important. This is precisely what I've been fighting. Thank God this had nothing to do with the fires, or the keeping of this secret could have left everyone in the city of Atlanta dead."

Arcturus frowned. He'd helped me crack that problem; even he saw that.

"She is the next generation," Zinaga said. "Heck, I might even do the same thing."

"What are you talking about, Dakota?" Arcturus asked. "Some kind of secret library—"

"Decide later," the Grinder said. "Eat now. It is time."

We looked at each other; then we raised the firecaps to our lips and ate.

To call it an explosion behind my eyes makes it sound trite. Warmth passed my lips, heat flooded my mouth, then fire ignited my spirit. The taste was of mushrooms and cinnamon toast and just-singed marshmallows, the best smores *ever* dissolving into my mouth and soul.

I filled with fire. Then I opened my eyes to a new world. Streamers of mana—of *magic*—were everywhere, ever-present and ineffable, climbing from the circle to the trees, from the rocks to the skies, each woven with their own song, each written in their own language.

And us skindancers? We *burned* with magic. Our skins glowed, not just from the tattoos, but from the magic they left behind. I knew I had been getting more powerful, and now I knew why. Every time I released a tattoo, a little was left behind, leaving me a stronger foundation. Each time I re-inked, I introduced more dragon ink to my cells.

The fire seemed to reach my core. I drew in a breath, seeming to feel the inner surface of my lungs for the very first time. Heat climbed up my spine, my brain filled with light—and magic began pouring out of my eyes in an unstoppable signal of my power.

Arcturus, Zinaga and I stared at each other, eyes glowing with inner fire.

47. STRIKE TO THE HEART

I stared at the police cars around the Rogue Unicorn, dumbfounded. At first, I thought someone had robbed the Herbalist's Attic; then I passed the Star Bar and saw the glowing magic circle crackling next to the Rogue's brushed aluminum unicorn sign, and my heart pounded.

The fire ninjas had attacked my tattoo shop.

I'd stayed up all night in the Stonegrinder's Grove celebrating my initiation—learning secrets, practicing initiate's rites, setting up a play date for Cinnamon and Khouri. Exhausted, I'd crashed at Arcturus's for a couple of hours before driving back to Atlanta and the Rogue.

Of course, I'd left my cell off the whole time—because cell phones could be tracked. Earlier this year, higher-ups in the DEI forced Philip to roust Cinnamon's werehouse because I hadn't been paranoid enough to cover my tracks. Given what I just learned, the last thing I wanted to do was leave a trail deep into the mystical heart of Blood Rock.

That left me incommunicado, and so when a policemen stopped traffic, I hurriedly beeped my phone on. I'd received over a *dozen* messages and texts—all since 6:17 a.m., and when I looked up, an ambulance was lumbering out of the Rogue's driveway. *Shit.*

The policeman waved the cars in front of me on. I dropped my phone and slid the Prius forward, flicking on my right turn signal. The policeman shook his head—then got a closer look and waved me in quickly. I'm a little past having to pull the "dad on the force" card now.

The Prius bumped down the steep drive, I pulled my car in to the far end of the lot, and stepped out, surveying the crowd of policemen, looking for the officer in charge. My usual cronies—my "uncle" Andre Rand, my officer friends Horscht and Gibbs—were absent.

But I had allies on site. Ordinary Atlanta police detectives dress sharp, but these men and women dressed sharper, like stylish extras in a noir movie: dark suits, dark gloves, and dark fedoras—the Black Hats, Atlanta's Magical Crimes Investigation Squad.

That meant my friend McGough was here, but he was nowhere in sight. I recognized some of the Hats, but only vaguely, by sight; they remained nameless to me, like . . . well, like extras in a movie. But soon, another dark-suited—but hatless—detective saw me.

"Ma'am, are you one of the tattooists at this studio?" he asked crisply, eyes running over my bare, inked arms. I nodded, shaking his hand with my best bone-crushing big butch biker grip, but the big man didn't bat an eyebrow. "Sergeant James Parsons, APD Commercial Robbery."

"Dakota Frost," I said, "Chair of the Magical Security Council."

"Oh, this is *your* shop," he said, now raising the eyebrow. He cocked his head at the huge spinning magical symbol on the side of the building. "Figures. Officers following up a burglary report found that magic mark. The Black Hats are on site, but they've not given the all clear—"

"I'm more worried about who was the ambulance," I said, shifting uncomfortably.

"The witness slash victim who called it in," Parsons said, flipping out a small notebook and checking it, though I had the feeling this detailed man in his crisp suit had that name stored away precisely between those graying temples. "Your shop neighbor, Miss Weston—"

"Maude?" Maude Weston ran the Herbalist's Attic. "Oh no. Is she all right?"

"Miss Weston is fine, ma'am," Parsons said reassuringly. "There was a small scuffle, but she's fine. She reports that she came in early this morning and I think she may have surprised the perpetrators by changing her schedule. We did try to contact you, ma'am—"

"Please, Sergeant, it's Dakota, or Miss Frost," I said, laughing. I found myself liking this calm, straightforward, detail-oriented man. "Sorry, I had to turn my cell off. I was visiting my old master, Arcturus, and he hates them."

"Your old master, eh?" cracked another voice. "That's a man I'd like to meet."

"Hey there, you old toad," I said, turning around with a smile.

"Hey back at ya, you tattooed witch," McGough responded. He was a short, tough little man with a trimmed goatee and slightly wilder hair, wrapped in a long duster two sizes too big for his frame and two shades too dark for Atlanta's heat. "How the hell are ya?"

I glanced up at the police tape, the officers pouring in and out of the Rogue Unicorn . . . and the crackling magical symbol twenty feet high, rotating on the south side of the building, clearly visible even in plain daylight. "I don't know, you tell me."

"Ah, stupid question," McGough said. "Well, what I can tell you is—"

But then McGough ripped off his sunglasses and stared at me strangely.

"Have you been bitten by a vampire?" he asked.

"Not lately," I laughed—or tried to laugh, though it was a bit forced. McGough damn well knew I'd been bitten by a vampire earlier that year—Calaphase, my lover, an hour or so before his death. At my tight expression, McGough cursed and shook his head.

"Another foot in my mouth, sorry. Well, have you become a werekin, or . . ." McGough trailed off, staring at my eyes closely. I didn't say anything, and after a moment, his mouth fell open. "Ah . . . Dakota Frost, Skindancer. You're an initiate in the order now, aren't you?"

"Jesus," I said. "Did you get that just from my eyes?"

"From their aura," he said, his own eyes tightening. "And you just confirmed it."

Cold facts clicked together in my brain—McGough now had enough information to track down Arcturus. He somehow knew I'd been initiated. Thanks to my big fat mouth, he knew I'd just been to Arcturus's home. And even though I had turned my phone off *while* I was there, I hadn't been smart enough to shut off my cell phone *during the drive to his house*. Hell, they could probably have tracked my movements with the GPS in my Prius.

Knowing where I'd just been was enough to pinpoint where my initiation happened.

Of course, Philip Davidson of the DEI knew where Arcturus was, by similar means—but *unofficially*, when he was helping me elude the police earlier this year. Now, the DEI hierarchy didn't know everything Philip knew—but he kept warning me to be more careful.

Thinking about what I had learned, and had let leak, made me nervous. Philip had earned my trust, and, so too had McGough—but McGough was a covert wizard from a competing order, with conflicting loyalties, who'd just guessed I had been initiated into a rival order's secrets.

Maybe Arcturus and the Grinder weren't wrong to be paranoid.

"Perhaps I did, perhaps I didn't," I said. "Can we discuss that later? Privately?"

McGough's voice lowered. "Sure," he said curtly, then turned back to look at the Rogue.

"Was there property taken, Detective?" Parsons said curtly.

"Yes, sir," McGough said. I realized that Parsons outranked him. McGough was huge in my world, the Head of the Magical Investigation Squad, but he was just a Detective. Commercial Robbery handled more crimes—and a Sergeant was a bigger fish. "I need more time, though."

"What's the holdup?" Parsons said. "Are there or aren't there rogue marks inside?"

"It's a magic tattooing shop, sir," McGough said, and Parsons drew in a breath. "I've got the willies, but I don't know what's normal for their shop. With your permission, I'd like to do a walkthrough with Frost to verify what's been taken. She's quite the sensitive herself."

Parsons thought about that for all of two seconds. Then he nodded.

"Miss Frost, I've heard good things about your participation in other investigations, especially after that graffiti scare," he said, withdrawing a pair of latex gloves from an inner pocket and handing them to me. "Please make me willing to pass those good stories on."

I slipped them on. "You're not coming?"

"No. I'm not a magical investigator, and I wouldn't know how not to screw a magical crime scene up," he said, gesturing to the Rogue.

I laughed again. "Well, I'm not really sure what I can do."

"You can sense whether or not something's magicked," McGough said sharply, "and know enough not to touch it. The Sergeant would be going in blind and uninformed."

Parsons took no offense, just nodded. "You all . . . do what you do, and I'll control the scene until you give the all-clear. Don't worry, I'm patient. I'm not paid by the hour."

I looked at the gloves. "I'm going to assemble my own evidence kit," I said.

"I'd prefer you call us first, but if that isn't practical," McGough said, raising the yellow tape so we could step under it, "you want gloves, booties, and baggies for evidence. Get yourself a Moleskine or voice recorder, and a point-and-shoot, though I know some good DSLRs—"

Inside the yellow tape, we followed a second taped line that wove through the lot and up the stairs. Officers with cameras and rulers photographed a trail of half-formed footprints left in ink, and I grimaced at the thought of the magic lost. Criminologists with baggies and tweezers extracted dark fibers from a twisted nail on the wooded stairs. Dark-suited men from McGough's unit roved the upper landing with digital dowsing rods that recorded video, angle, and distance.

A Black Hat waved his hand over the doorframe of Maude's shop, nodding significantly as we approached. McGough waved a wand plugged into a voltmeter over it, making the device yowl. I held my hand over it too, immediately feeling the mana—and its magical affinity.

"Fire magic," I said quietly. A ripple shuddered through my tattoos, a resonance echoing off the Dragon, some of the vines—anything, in fact, using firecap ink. I grimaced, shrugging my shoulders to settle the Dragon. "Using some quite expensive fuel, I'd guess."

McGough's eyes bugged, as did the Hat's. I grimaced. I had a long way to go if I was going to learn to keep secrets. But McGough and the Hat seemed to understand. We all looked at each other, silently, then the officer nodded . . . and McGough and I went in to the Rogue.

As I rose up the steps, my first thought was that someone must be playing with a black light. Then I realized I could see more than I had before—traces of magic, woven in the stairs, curling out of the Herbalist's Attic, climbing out of my own shop in faint tribal waves.

I wasn't just feeling magic anymore. I was seeing it.

But once inside, the Rogue Unicorn wasn't as damaged as I expected. The front office wasn't trashed; the tattooing room was barely touched. At first, I was elated; then my heart fell as I saw more Black Hats farther in, following the taped line.

I knelt, waving my hand over the ink-stained footsteps; feeling a tingle, I cursed, rose, and went deeper into the Rogue, following the ink-stained footprints back along the taped line, following it to, at least in my mind, the heart of the studio—*my* office.

Inside, I stared at my shattered magical supply cabinet. On it, I could see tiny flecks of magic pigment, formerly invisible to my eyes. From it, wafts of magical effects oozed out like a slow-moving rainbow. Brightest of all was one central spot that burned like fire.

The place where I'd kept my firecap ink.

I had always known my inks were valuable; but until today I really had no idea.

48. THE MSC ON THE CASE

The fire ninjas now had a new source of liquid fire.

I needed help. I had to tell McGough. I looked at the door of my office, wondering if I should close it. No, I didn't know if they were done dusting for prints. Finally, I motioned McGough into the office and over to the front window, as far forward as we could get.

"Guys, give us a minute," McGough ordered, and a couple of technicians got up and walked out, tapping other Black Hats and officers on the way out. In moments, we were alone. Of course, my office could be bugged, but I had to get this party started. McGough said. "OK, spill it."

"I have reason to believe a magical component of enormous value was taken—"

"They left your unicorn horn," McGough said. "Tossed it looking through the case. Ended up under the desk. I had the boys bag it, but it may have been, ah, violated." He studied my face, then pointed at the cabinet. "So I take it you mean what was on this stand."

"No," I said, feeling a pang. "That was just a dragon's tooth dagger."

"Jesus," McGough said. "That has to be worth a quarter million dollars—"

"Three hundred and fifty thousand," I said. "Ignore it. They took it as a diversion. Seriously. That dagger sat for seventeen years in a shop window in San Francisco. Anyone could have taken it at any time. I think the shopkeeper was hoping it would walk for the insurance loss."

"And you're shrugging that off," McGough said grimly. "What did they get?"

"A supply of liquid fire," I said, mouth suddenly dry. "I didn't even know I had it."

"Jesus," McGough said, eyes wide. He looked at the cabinet, then me. "Jesus. You had that shit lying around . . . in *tattoo ink?* No wonder your colors are so awesome—and you just found out. Of course. New initiate. I'm surprised they let you have the ink before—"

"Damn it, stop being so smart," I said. Frankly, I'd been surprised that they had, until I realized that it was a test of a candidate's loyalty—and that the rules of the Skindancing Guild predated the tools of modern chemistry. "I'm *counting on you* to keep this secret—"

"Oh, yeah," McGough said, rubbing his chin. "The Wizarding Guild won't want that knowledge going around anymore than you do. And we need your pet spook in on this—"

"Do we really want to bring Davidson in?" I asked. "He's good at keeping secrets only so long as his bosses don't decide otherwise—"

"Give him more credit," McGough said, still rubbing his goatee. "Davidson didn't trigger that werehouse raid—*you* did, when you called in that attack on Tully. And it was the right thing to do. Don't beat yourself up about it—or blame him. Sometimes, crap just goes down."

"Tell me about it," I said, staring at my broken cabinet.

"Who knows how freaking valuable that ink was?" McGough asked.

"Nobody that *I* know who doesn't already have their own supply," I said. "But . . . I'm told that supplies of the real deal, of liquid fire, may be running out."

"I've heard the same rumors," McGough said. "Shit. And you've had everybody and their brother in here, haven't you? All right. All right. This is how we handle this. Put a Magical Security Council hold on this investigation—"

"I can do that?" I said.

"Same thing you did with the magic graffiti," McGough said. "The investigation goes forward normally, but the MSC and the Black Hats get first crack. No public announcements, control of all evidence, complete lists of everyone that's been on site—"

"I got it, I got it," I said. "You get that started inside, I'll talk to your boss."

I picked my way out of my office, carefully avoiding the broken glass, and wormed my way out of the Rogue and past the Herbalist's Attic. Parsons was staring at the giant spinning symbol glowing on the side of the building, and I motioned to him.

"I'm putting an MSC hold on this investigation," I said quietly. "Police procedure keeps going forward as normal, but the Black Hats get first crack—and no announcements, complete control of who sees the evidence, we need lists of everyone on site—"

Parsons nodded, without batting an eye. "All right," he said, motioning to an officer. "Though I've never worked under a MSC hold before. I don't know how that works—"

"Me neither," I said, and he glanced at me. "Same procedure we used for the magic graffiti, but we need to make it formal now. Something that's not going to tie your hands, but . . . some heavy shit may have gone down here and we can't let that out, not just yet."

"You, me, and the Detective can powwow once we've got the scene under control," Parsons said. His eyes glinted with excitement, like he'd seen something valuable, something I didn't yet understand. "Thanks for taking me into your confidence, ma'am. I won't let you down."

He walked off. I took a deep breath. When I started the Magical Security Council, it was almost a joke, a pure bravado play designed to keep my daughter out of trouble and defuse a brewing human-vampire-werekin civil war. But now . . .

I really *was* the head of the Magical Security Council.

I called Tully and clued him in. Cinnamon's childhood squeeze was becoming a reliable right-hand man—perhaps because his service to the Council kept Scara off his back. We picked out a team, and Tully hung up to alert Philip in the DEI while I gathered more info on site.

After the call disconnected, I stared up at the spinning magical mark crackling against the side of the building. *I* had to crack this thing. Me, and the people under me. The war for liquid fire had reached Atlanta, and by God, they were going to regret ever bringing it here.

With my new eyes, I could see more structure than before—circuits of power, ratchets of rotation, projectors of light—and that revealed more clearly why Cinnamon thought it a code. The spinning letters were cut off from the rest of the magic, intent almost encapsulated.

Already, I could see there were no new symbols in the design. If I was right, there was a shot that some obscure letter like Z hadn't shown up yet, but if Cinnamon was right, if all the letters were evenly distributed, the chances were better than nine in ten we had them all.

Twenty-six symbols, twenty-six letters in the English alphabet—one-to-one. It felt right. Five messages, now six, sixty characters each—totaling three hundred. It felt hopeful. Sixty characters, in eight billion combinations . . . with six more trillions following that.

It felt hopeless.

I scowled. Someone *could* read this, and I *would* crack it. I pulled out my phone to take a picture—then sensed something. I turned and saw Jewel, standing a few feet away from me, outside the yellow tape, staring up at the symbol, holding her octopus bag in both hands.

"Jewel," I said warmly, glad that at least one thing in my life was going right. But when she heard my voice, she swallowed. She'd been looking at the symbol intently, like she was *reading* it—but now she looked at me with fear. "Jewel, what's wrong?"

"What's wrong?" she said. "You were attacked because of *me*—"

"You don't know that," I said, trying sound reassuring, but she shook her head slightly, a look of pity on her face that usually meant someone thought I was completely out of my depth. "You *do* know that? Jewel, if you have *any idea* what this means—"

"I—" she began, then looked away. Then she stared back at it. "I won't lie to you. The *symbology* is an ancient fireweaver's curse. Jinx may think it's hoodoo or whatever, and maybe it is, but Daniel isn't content to just beat us. He wants us to suffer."

"And you know this because—"

Jewel struggled with something. "Well . . . because of the symbols." She gestured at a trio of signs at the center of the circle. "Ancient symbols put together to form a simple meanings, like subject, verb, object. These symbols mean *guardian*, *transport* . . . and *prison*."

I glared at the symbols—three of them, at the center of the message. Each message had these, and I'd just assumed they were part of the design. *Damn it!* Three more symbols that made . . . what? Nothing? A key to the code? Or another gazillion combinations on top of the mess?

"Daniel is trying to do something with these messages," I said. "To communicate, to cast a larger spell, hell, maybe it is a curse. I don't care to speculate; I have to *know*. They attacked my place of business. It could have been my home, or, if you go back to Hawaii, *your* home—"

"I—" Jewel said, and then her eyes went wide. "I hadn't thought of that."

"I'm not minimizing the public assaults on you, but this attack, and the one on your friends' home in Sunol, are worse. It's one thing to attack a target of opportunity when they're out and vulnerable. A planned attack on someone's stronghold is something else entirely."

"Jesus," Jewel said, hands tightening on her purse. She looked at me, struggling with something, then sagged. "Dakota . . . you're right, more than you know. I do know what the message means, and this is something else entirely. I . . . I really need your help."

"I *am* trying to help you," I snapped, "but I need information. You have to tell me *everything you know* about this fireweaver code—"

"The code isn't important," Jewel said. "The *message* is. I couldn't translate the code if I wanted to, and even if I could, it's a secret for initiates—but we're past that. More than moldy old secrets are at stake. Dakota, I've got to . . . I've got to come clean. Can I trust you?"

"Of course," I said, looking at the spinning symbol. "So . . . the message is important. What does it mean? The *guard-transport-prison* part, that is? Does that mean this curse is designed to . . . what? To get you arrested—"

"No," Jewel said reluctantly—and something about the tone of her voice chilled me. "It uses the language of a curse, but it isn't really a curse. It's just to get my attention." She raised her phone. "And I don't need to translate it . . . if Daniel's done it for me."

I stared at the phone in horror, seeing a text from UNKNOWN NUMBER: **«we have what you lost-come back to maui»**

My blood ran cold. "Jewel," I said. "Is this what I think it is?"

—ᘓ

"It's a ransom note," she said quietly. "They've taken Molokii."

49. PHILIP TO THE RESCUE

The *Georgetown* was a Moffat-class airship—eight hundred feet long, held aloft by seven million cubic feet of helium, with five Shadowhawk stealth copters in its belly. Itself sheathed in stealth fabric, the *Georgetown* sliced through the air quietly . . . taking us all to Hawaii.

"I didn't know we had these," Jewel said, staring out the forward observation window.

"Just declassified," I said, standing behind her. "Apparently, black agencies have been using them for years to get strike forces where they're needed. The Department of Extraordinary Investigation uses the *Georgetown* because the whole craft's mystically shielded."

"Jesus," Jewel said, pressing her hand to her throat. "Way to feed a girl's conspiracy theories, Skindancer! Tell her the U.S. Government not only has black helicopters, but can drop a whole stealth army on magic users any time it wants—"

"Well, not an army, Fireweaver," I said. "Maybe a platoon."

"Dakota," Special Agent Philip Davidson chided. "Giving away all our secrets?"

I turned around. Philip leaned against the jamb of the door to the observation lounge, devilish goatee framing an easy grin. He'd stripped off the jacket of one of his thousand-dollar suits, but he still looked handsome in a subtly patterned white shirt and narrow tie.

"The *Georgetown* is all over CNN and the History Channel," I said. Remembering, I grinned. "Speaking of which, I finally did get the full story on how you got mugged."

"Oh, God," Philip said, standing up straight, hand behind his head. "I deny it—"

"A—*hem*," Jewel said pointedly, elbowing me.

"Ah," I said, putting my hand on her shoulder. She was actually jealous. I liked that. But things had moved so fast—"Sorry I didn't get to introduce you earlier. Special Agent Philip Davidson, please meet Jewel Grace, our special informant—and my current girlfriend."

Philip and Jewel looked at each other, forced smiles on their faces.

"Well," Philip said, "pleased to meet you, Miss Grace."

"Likewise," Jewel said frostily, shaking his hand.

"Did Dakota explain how this works?" Philip said. "We're going to a safe house in Maui which will serve as our base of operations. We'll use a cell rerouter and land lines that will make it appear that we're in Honolulu, but we'll be able to strike quickly—"

"So I don't see why you needed us," Jewel said stiffly. "While I can defend myself, I don't approve of violence, Special Agent Philip Davidson. I deliberately focus on defensive spells. I'd be useless in a firefight."

"I certainly hope it doesn't come to that," Philip said, "but if we end up dealing with some nasty fire magic . . . I'm given to understand that there's no one better than you."

Jewel pursed her lips. "So, what's your role in this circus?" she asked me.

"Your bodyguard," I said, laughing.

"And I'm yours," Nyissa croaked, stepping from the shadows, pale face and violet hair seeming to glow inside her hood. Her eyes fell over Philip, drinking him in, and he looked both uncomfortable and intrigued. "But I agree with Philip. Let's not let this turn into a fight."

"Our first priority is rescuing Molokii," Philip said. "I'm not allowed to use the word *ransoming*, and the United States government does not negotiate with terrorists. But . . . we will facilitate an, ah, orderly transfer, if you decide to meet their demands—"

"I'm not sure I can do that," Jewel said. "They want me to abdicate."

"Do . . . what?" I said.

"Of course," Philip said, putting his hand to his forehead. "Necker Island—"

"How do you know—" Jewel said, then stopped herself. "Damn it. The lawsuit—"

"I'm sorry," Philip said, "but I have to know everything about the kidnap victim and the potential ransomer to understand how to fight the kidnapper. Dakota, Necker Island is a heritage site that Jewel's Kanaka Maoli group sued the government to get back. Successfully."

"And now that you've got a chunk of land to call your own . . . Daniel wants to lay claim to it. That's the point of all the attacks, the messages," I said. My eyes tightened at her. "All those messages we couldn't decipher . . . were challenges to your authority."

"I am a Fireweaver Princess," Jewel said. "One of a small number of individuals with a magical bloodline who can command our Order and lead certain key rituals. Daniel's a low-ranking prince, challenging my"—her face screwed up in distaste—" 'throne.' "

"Jewel, you told me you were going to come clean," I said. "Molokii's life is on the line here. We need to know everything you know. You claim you can't decipher these messages, but you've got a hell of a lot of context we don't and you need to cough it up now."

"You always were too smart for your own good," she said, eyes fixed on me. "Yes, I know the point of those messages, and more you haven't seen. He's demanded that I yield, that I keep quiet, that I defend myself, that I defend my actions—and that I give up my crown."

"That's pretty damn specific. I thought the one on the Rogue was a ransom demand," I said. I'd wrestled with it for the whole trip, trying every trick in Cinnamon's books to find a handle, and now Jewel just coughs it up? "The one you *claimed* you couldn't decipher—"

"Of course I couldn't decipher it," Jewel said. "It's ancient ritual challenge magic, and I'm no historian. But I don't need to decipher it . . . Daniel has been sending me texts." She pulled out her phone. "The last one was just before we took off."

I looked at Philip. "Could we track him with that?"

"No," Philip said, with a quick shake of his head. "A disposable phone, untraceable—"

"How do you know?" Jewel said. "I haven't even shown it to you yet—"

"He probably read it before you did," I said, and Jewel hissed and turned away.

"The call was made from the airport in Los Angeles," Philip said. "I doubt they moved Molokii on a commercial aircraft, but some of their people may have. That leaves us about twelve thousand suspects, but we've narrowed it down to about two hundred likely—"

"I hate this!" Jewel said, turning and stomping to the forward window. "A secret strike-fortress in the sky, full of black helicopters, led by a man who sifts through the people like they're grains of wheat! Why did you show me this, Dakota?"

"Why are you still keeping secrets?" I asked. "I'm trying to save your best friend."

"And there's a living calculus to that," Philip said, hands in his pockets. He didn't look hurt by Jewel's accusation—he just looked resigned, standing there in his expensive clothes. "I don't recommend negotiating with terrorists . . . but is your title worth Molokii's life?"

Jewel's head lowered . . . then she looked back at me, fearfully.

"I can't," she said, voice so quiet we could barely hear her over the drone of the engines. "Daniel doesn't care about titles, just what he can do with one. He wants to lead a very specific magical ritual, which will have a very terrible result. *We've seen hatchsign*, Dakota, and now the Order of the Woven Flame is split between those, like me, who want nature to take its course, and those who . . . well, want it to happen so badly . . ."

"That they're willing to kill," I said, "to get a supply of liquid fire."

Jewel looked at me in shock. I don't think she expected me to be that up front, but I'd never have gotten Philip to spring for this expedition if he hadn't had an inkling of what was at stake—and neither Philip nor I had realized how key Jewel was to the whole affair.

"Oh, Jesus," Philip said. "We've got a magical war over a dragon hatching."

"Precisely what Devenger was afraid of," I said. "This is such bad news—"

"You have no idea. Wizards nearing the ends of unnaturally extended lives don't care about consequences," Nyissa said, her voice ominous beneath her hood. "Trust me, I was one. I became a vampire because my side lost the *last* war for a supply of liquid fire—"

"When was this?" Philip said. "I haven't heard about a recent magical war—"

"You've heard of it," Nyissa said. "Before your time, but you've heard of it."

"Almost everyone on Earth has heard of it," Jewel said. "And everyone on the Indian or Pacific Oceans heard it when it happened. The wizards and the fireweavers battled over the last hatching, and it got . . . far . . . before someone a lot like Daniel finally got their way—"

"And failed," Nyissa said. My Dragon shifted on my back, whispering dark things to me about wizards and their crimes . . . which Nyissa quickly confirmed when she said, "The spell went horribly wrong. It killed the hatchling . . . and thirty thousand people—"

"In an explosion felt round the world," I guessed, and Nyissa and Jewel glanced at each other. That confirmed it, so I continued, "One that darkened the skies for an entire year. The war was fought in 1883—and ended when the entire island of Krakatoa was blown out of the water."

Philip scowled, then turned back to the captain's deck.

—☙

"Wonderful news, *magicians,*" he said. "We land on Maui in forty-five minutes."

50. The Exposers Exposed

"OK," Jewel said. "Philip may have a point—magic is dangerous."

The *Georgetown's* route had been dictated by the intersection of winds and tourism. The airship had slipped over a lush forest on east edge of Maui just out of sight of the town of Hana, then climbed the cloudy and increasingly cracked slopes of Haleakala volcano.

As we'd passed, I'd found myself transfixed, staring in fascination at the upper ridge of the crater—the tip of one of the largest mountains in the world, as measured from the seafloor—but from the *Georgetown,* we could not see the crater floor, as our route carefully avoided too close an approach to the observatory complex called Science City.

After much careful maneuvering, the enormous ship settled, completely undetected, in a secluded ridge valley that everyone assured me was "near the Kona highway." There, on a half-hidden airstrip at the edge of forest and desert, the *Georgetown* had set down for eleven minutes, disgorging me, Jewel, Philip, and two of his agents into waiting black SUVs that spirited us away toward the DEI's Maui compound. The waiting agents shoved us into the cars so fast that I bumped my head, and before my door was closed, the airship was lifting off.

Our driver had looked at me strangely, but I ignored him. I couldn't stop thinking about the *Georgetown.* Where did they hide the thing? The captain claimed that Maui's winds limited where it could land, so where was it going? A hangar near the cliffs . . . or over the water?

"Well," Jewel said frostily, turning away from me in the back seat, staring out at a fading ocean sunset muted by the black glass of the SUV, "I guess me admitting my long-cherished beliefs were wrong wasn't as much of a surprise as I thought it would be."

"Which beliefs?" I asked, unwilling to risk a guess.

"I never really put two and two together before," she said. "I knew that magic could be incredibly dangerous, but I'm used to hearing that from people like Daniel, who have their own agenda. And I knew non-magicians feared us, but I thought it was just prejudice."

I grimaced. It wasn't just prejudice—Nyissa made that clear. The enmity between wizards and vampires? They had been harvesting each other's mystical blood, at least since Krakatoa. The fear normal people had of wizards? Whispered stories of Krakatoa, and disasters like it.

"I used to believe the same thing," I said. "I *hated* all the secrecy in the magical world. I *chafed* at all the restrictions. Now . . . after all I've learned? I don't know anymore." I shook my head. "It's all fun and games until someone blows up a mountain and blots out the sun."

"It's not that funny, is it?" she asked dryly.

"Not one bit," I replied. I stared off into the distance. "I . . . saw a monster earlier this year," I said. "Huge. Fists bigger than elephants. Veins like fire hoses. Head the size of a hill. Scary thing was, it wasn't even the real monster. It was just a long-distance *projectia*—"

"Jesus," Jewel said.

"It was an evil thing a sad and wounded wizard let in to avenge the death of his family," I said. "I'm not one of those man-was-not-meant-to-know types, but they have a point. Liquid fire creates the same kind of fear. People will break the sky trying to live forever."

"Are you suggesting we give it up to you?" Jewel asked, with an edge to her voice.

"Not at all," I said. "I've got my own source—"

"Jesus, Dakota," Jewel said, dropping her voice to a whisper. "Do you want the spooks to know that? It's bad enough you told them why the hatching is important—"

"Philip's proved himself, and if we are at war, we need all the help I can get," I said, though I lowered my voice too—not that I thought it would help; now that the war was on, all of this would come out. "Still, if this is a war over liquid fire . . . I think I could probably replicate it chemically. Other practitioners are learning to synthesize it in other ways. One of those approaches, ultimately, will succeed. Once there's enough to go around—"

"You think scarcity is the problem?" Jewel said.

"Basically," I said. "I'm not saying it's the only problem. There's something effed up with all the practitioners I've seen who've used liquid fire as a longevity treatment, but I have no doubt we'll be able to make tattoo ink and firespinning fuel—"

"You're missing the point," Jewel snapped.

I didn't say anything; I just looked at her and waited for her to let it out.

"Look . . . I *love* spinning magic fire," Jewel said. "Don't get me wrong. I'm not about to give up my supply, but . . . I see that preserving life is more important than spinning fire a little longer. And I don't begrudge anyone who's used liquid fire to lengthen their life.

"But those . . . those aged *things* aren't the problem," she said. "*Dragons* are the problem. Everyone knows what happened the last time one hatched, and you know why wizards fought over it. But liquid fire isn't just a byproduct of a hatching. It's the catalyst for one."

My eyes bugged. "Liquid fire can *cause* a hatching?"

"Hatchsign is only the half of it," she said. "It's the sign of a newborn dragon's spirit on the move. But this world long ago cooled past the point that would support a true dragon's life cycle. There's just not enough fire, or magic. Eons can go by before conditions are right—"

"Unless some *magician,*" I said, now feeling the flavor of the word the way Philip used it, "decides to trick the poor bastard into hatching. How does that even work? If the egg is ready to hatch, then it seems like it would hatch, or not—"

"I don't think hatching begins with a conventional egg," Jewel said. "I mean, there's an egg. That's where liquid fire is harvested from. Even if the dragon hatches successfully, the yolk tailings themselves are a form of liquid fire. But I think the spirit of the dragon *makes* the egg."

We were pulling up a narrow, bumpy drive to a sprawling compound of linked cottages surrounded by a white stone fence. Fields of dark green shaded into the distance in the dying light, flaring with gold flowers like a frozen field of fireflies. Narrow plots of carnations hugged the road as we pulled into a circular turnaround in front of the compound. I stared up from the cluster of huts to the looming slopes beyond. Far above us, the tip of the dark triangle glowed with fire where the top of mount Haleakala was still touched by the last rays of the sun.

"Cinnamon read up on volcanoes for class," I said. "She told me lava forms like rain. Droplets of molten rock, deep within the earth, turning liquid under heat, trickling upward under great pressure, collecting in huge lakes beneath the surface, waiting to explode. Maybe that's where dragon's eggs grow. Waiting for humans to fight over them."

We got out. A Chinese-American man stepped out of the shadows and spoke to Philip. His eyes seemed to glint in the darkness, like he was a closet werekin, or touched by the fae. Then a new thought occurred to me . . . was he, perhaps, touched by liquid fire?

The man turned toward us. "I am Mr. Iloa," he said. "I—"

And then his neck practically popped as he turned to stare at me.

"What?" I asked. I wondered if he could see the new fire in my eyes.

"I," Mr. Iloa said, regaining his calm, "am the owner of this compound. My family have been longtime friends of the Department . . . and the Department has been a longtime friend to us. We provide this space for those the Department needs to shelter. Please respect it."

"Thank you, Mr. Iloa. We will," I said—then pulled out my phone, which was off. "But I was told this is a DEI safe house. Does this mean it is safe, or not safe, to place a call? I don't want to give away our location, but I have a twitchy weretiger daughter back home—"

"I understand," Iloa said, a smile creeping onto his face. "I have a daughter too, though not so twitchy—but her children might give your child a run for your money. Please be discreet, but otherwise consider yourselves welcome guests in our home."

Nyissa stepped forward, no longer hidden deep within her cloak, but walking openly now, hood thrown back, violet hair flashing over that porcelain skin. "Thank you," she croaked. "I believe Special Agent Davidson called ahead. May we discuss the arrangements?"

"Please," Iloa nodded, gesturing to the rest of us. "Enjoy my hospitality."

Philip led us into the spacious foyer of the house. All the cottages were airy, open—and had not-so-obvious features, like a maze of bushes, well-spaced brick pillars, steel doors and grates, and even retractable steel shutters, that in minutes could turn this place into a fortress.

Or a prison.

"Are you Cinnamon's mother," Jewel said, as I texted furiously, "or her BFF?"

"A bit of both," I said with a smile. "Oh, to have been friends with her in school."

"Let me sync up with field command," Phillip said. "Then let's plan our next move."

Philip disappeared into an inner secure room. Jewel and I set down our bags, Nyissa's chauffeur set down hers. I stood, but Jewel sat on the edge of a chair, brooding. A federal agent built entirely of muscle stepped up to take our bags—then stopped, staring at me openly.

"What?" I said. I no longer thought it was the magic in my eyes. "*What?*"

"It's . . ." the man began, eyeing me strangely. "You really don't know?"

"Dakota," Philip said grimly, motioning to me, "could you join me in the security room?"

"What's happened?" Jewel said, and Philip was silent. "What's wrong?"

"This," Philip said, again beckoning to me, "is a delicate situation—"

"Damn it, don't cut me out!" Jewel said. "This is Molokii's life—"

"No, it isn't," the other agent said. "This mess . . . is all about Miss Frost."

We gathered in front of a giant flat panel, where a third agent typing away did a quick double take looking at me, then, without a word, began digging in his browser history. "The first site's already taken down, but I'm sure someone snagged it—ah, here we go. Steel yourself."

He hit the link—and a promo played for Alex Nicholson's TV show, *The Exposers.*

"You've seen him performing illusions—coast to coast," Alex announced—as a short, swarthy, white-haired wizard appeared: Christopher Valentine, the man who nearly took my life, performing card tricks, escaping a straitjacket, and appearing with his *projectia*, a magic double.

"And you've seen her performing magic—on the news," Alex intoned—as a tall, tattooed, Mohawked punk grrl appeared: *me,* inking Alex's wristwatch in my studio, uncoiling my vines at Cinnamon's talk at Berkeley—and releasing my Dragon in Union Square.

A succession of quick shots of Valentine made that murderous bastard look like a saint. They showed him yukking it up on *The Late Shift with Jack Carterson*, accepting a key to the city from a mayor, and cheerfully interrogating a woman with a crystal ball.

Me? They caught me at my most biker, riding my Vespa at an angle that made it look like a Harley. Shots Daniel Ekundayo had done at my dojo were spliced together to make me look like Jackie Chan. Clips of me kicking a punching bag so hard my tattoos glowed.

They made me look like a savage.

"Dakota Frost is the only magician ever to beat Christopher Valentine at his Chal-

lenge," Alex said, again over clips of the inking, showing my detailed setup, showing my needle on Alex's skin—and that faker Valentine watching from a gurney. *"And then she killed him."*

My face flushed. My vision went red. I heard a whine and distant voices.

"Don't you want to know why?"

And then Christopher Valentine was leaning into the camera, candid, and smiling; deep down I knew it was a lie, but for a moment, just for a moment, it wasn't Mirabilus holding a knife, but the Christopher Valentine I'd admired as a child—the wizard and debunker.

"Because we'll get to the truth. Even if it kills us," Valentine said, winking.

And then *I* appeared, angry, flushed and aggressive, barking, *"I said, no cameras!"*

Then my vine whipped out, and the screen went black, and the title card faded in:

THE EXPOSERS EXPOSED:
VALENTINE VS. FROST

"Oh my God," I said, putting my hand over my mouth. Then I left the room.

Philip, Jewel, Nyissa, and the agents swarmed out after me, as I whipped out my cell phone and began punching numbers into it rapidly. I actually had Alex on speed dial, but I wanted. To punch. Each number. Straight through. The dial. To his face.

Mr. Iloa stepped in from outside, looking at me dial curiously.

"This *is* a safe house, Miss Frost," he said. "Don't make *too* many—"

"She just saw the trailer," Philip said, as I raised my eyes and stared at Iloa.

Mr. Iloa's eyebrows went up. He scooted past me, extending his arms.

"Everyone, if you could please join me in the kitchen—"

"**ALEX!**" I roared into my phone.

"What? Who is this?" Alex said, blurry. "Do you know what time—Jesus. Dakota."

"You were supposed to run everything by me first," I said. "That was the contract. You run the videos by me, and I approve them. Approval not to be unreasonably withheld, but tell me, what's so unreasonable about not wanting to be portrayed as a murderer?"

"Dakota, I—" Alex blurted.

"You walked to the edge of slander!" I yelled. "Trashed *my* reputation for *your* show—"

"I did *not,*" Alex said. "Lloyd-Presse leaked it. Even *I* hadn't approved it yet—"

"You were the announcer," I growled, cracking my neck as my Dragon snarled, *let me loose, let me at him!* And I felt like doing it. "You *knew* what the video would be like—"

"No, I didn't," he said, despairing, and I knew I had him. "The same reading could—"

"*Alex!*" I yelled. "You lying son of a—"

"Dakota. Dakota! What, what do you want?" Alex said. "I'll do anything—"

He babbled, but I wasn't listening. My rage was subsiding. I'd spun around in my anger, seen Jewel looking in from the kitchen—then remembered where we were, and why we were here. What was my reputation worth, compared to Molokii's life?

Come to think of it, what were a few secrets worth, compared to Molokii's life? I had the Princess of Fire right here in the kitchen, yet getting information out of her still seemed like pulling teeth. Not that I didn't understand her caution about the elixir of immortality—

But I had a second initiate, right here on the line. One who was a thoroughly modern magician, who spoke my language, who—if our conversation about the Dragon *projectia* at Union Square was any indication—was at least as up to date as *I* was.

"Enough," I said, a cold plan forming. I turned away from Jewel, walked away from her, walked straight out of the house, and, for good measure, lowered my voice so only Alex would hear me cut her out and put him in her place. "Damage's done. You have to make good."

The line was silent while I stared up at brilliant stars against velvet Maui night.

"All right, Dakota," he said, resigned. "How much do you want?"

"It's not about money," I said.

"Don't get stupid," Alex said. "It's not all about money, but that's what I can get you—"

"That's where you're wrong," I said. "One of my friends has been kidnapped."

"Jesus," Alex said.

"I can't play around anymore, Alex. It's not about me, it's not about the money, it's not about my trashed reputation or the T-Rex-sized lawsuit I could slap on you. One of my friends has been kidnapped, and I need all the tools I can to find him, and I need them yesterday—"

"God," Alex said. "Of course, Dakota, but what do you want from *me*—"

"Fulfill your promise. Send me *everything you have* on fireweaving, *right the fuck now!*"

51. SUMMON THE DRAGON

"When I learned you were from Hawaii," I said, "I imagined us coming here."

After my confrontation with Alex, I'd stormed off, and Jewel had settled our bags in our cabin. She'd drawn me away from the others, fixed me tea, massaged my shoulders. No longer burning up inside, I leaned on the railing of the porch of our cabin, staring over the hillside.

Jewel stared out next to me. The safe house had once been a carnation farm, and wild ones grew under our porch. Our cabin was well defended behind a high fence and a twisted knot of volcanic rock that the DEI now used as a guard tower, but the view was still amazing.

The sky was black as crushed velvet, sparkling with stars as bright as glitter. But the broad slopes of Maui before us were not dark; the moon smiled thinly down on us, its disk still lit with earthshine, its waxing crescent bathing the mountains and ocean in dim green light.

Cinnamon had railed that the moon was new enough for her to come, that she could have helped, both with the codes and with any "running," as she put it—but even though she drooped her ears in her best *poor-me* face, there was no way I was bringing my child into a war zone.

That was sad; before our trip to the Bay, she had never been on a vacation, and after I met Jewel, Cinnamon told me she wanted to come see Maui. I had too—a dream of touring the sun and sand and, before I met Jewel, of finding a cute girl in a grass skirt.

But the Maui I got was *not* what I had envisioned.

First, it was cold on the mountain, and getting colder. But it was more than just night chill—we stood at the collision of climates. Upslope, Haleakala was verdant, practically rainforest; downslope, where the rains petered out, it looked like the surface of Mars. The wind carried no voices. Here, there were no tourists, no beaches, no cute girls in grass skirts.

This was as far from the Hawaii of my imagination as you could get.

"The water would have been blue and sparkling," I said.

"That's the Caribbean," Jewel said, leaning on the railing next to me.

"I'd never been here," I said heavily. "In my fantasy, the water would be great, and we'd play in the surf. With a beachball and bikinis. Bouncing in the water and the waves. Then we'd roll on the beach as the sun set, getting sand in all the inconvenient places."

"I wanted that too," Jewel said—and then she hissed. "No, I didn't."

I stared at her. This new "let other people talk" thing was working for me.

"Of course I wanted you to come here," Jewel said quickly. "But it could never happen. You had a daughter, in school—and where would you find a math program for her? I mean . . ." She smiled. ". . . that creature is absurd, Dakota. Of course you have to put Cinnamon first."

"She is that," I laughed. "And, yes, I do."

"But I never wanted you to come *here*. I never wanted you to become a *tourist*." She spoke the last word with venom that surprised me—and the venom in the next surprised me even more. "*Maui*. You have no idea what it's like to have a name known all over the world—"

"I'm starting to learn," I said.

"I'm sorry," she said, lowering her head, staring at the flowers. "Growing up here, you learn to hate the tourists. I'm as tired of people coming here to gawk at Maui as you are tired of people making fun of Southerners for your accents."

"Fair enough," I said. "Still, the tourist industry funds the island, doesn't it?"

"No," she said, "tourism only funds *itself*. Or take Science City. They say it creates local jobs, but really it's just a resort for eggheads—*atop our sacred moun-*

tain. Maui has everything from sugarcane to supercomputers—everything except a way to live that lets us be left alone."

I leaned on the railing, lowered my head too.

"I'm not trying to fight with you, Fireweaver," I said. "What do you want?"

"I want," Jewel said, drawing her breath in ragged, "to get my best friend back. To stop Daniel from seizing control of the egg. And, when I'm pissy, for the damn thing to actually hatch and to burn all the interlopers off the island, starting with that damn observatory on Haleakala."

"A real live dragon," I said, shifting, "might not stop with just interlopers."

"I know that," Jewel said, scowling, staring through her hands at the flowers. "And who am I to decide who's native and deserves the island? I hate playing 'other' games. So I'll settle for saving Molokii—and the island."

"The whole thing?" I pressed. "Everyone on it?"

"Yes," Jewel said. "I'm sorry. I didn't mean to make you think that I really wanted to kill all the interlopers on the island. You just mentioned tourism and it hit one of my hot buttons. So, yes, Little Miss Subtext, I'd give up my 'throne' if it meant saving everyone on the island."

"Hey," I said. "Fireweaver. It won't come to that. Hopefully, Daniel's group will contact you again soon. You *pretend* to give up your throne in exchange for Molokii, and then we rely on the DEI's enormous spy-gathering power to track him back to his destination."

"All right," she said. "It's not my preferred plan A . . . but I'll do what I have to."

"That's . . . great," I said, feeling a wave of relief. Jewel was really starting to open up. If she'd cooperate with us, if she'd let us help her . . . we might actually be able to, you know, help her. I leaned back from the railing, energized. "Really great. We may win this yet."

I leapt the railing, cursing myself when I landed. The damn knee was still bugging me, but I wasn't going to let that stop me. I felt the ground—soft grass, good enough for my purposes—then slipped off my vest coat and chaps and folded them over the railing.

"You're . . . practicing?" Jewel asked, stunned. "Like, karate?"

"Every day," I said, stretching my elbows forward, popping my shoulders, one, then the other. "Martial arts rely on unnatural movements. Especially if we're about to go into battle, I need to stretch out, to test myself out, make sure that I'm not rusty—where are you going?"

"To get my spinny sticks," she said. "You practice karate more than I spin, but karate's a hobby for you and spinning is my life." She paused, then raised her hand in the air. "Shame on me. I mean, shame on me! I could be going into battle too! I need to practice—"

I laughed. "Fair enough, Fireweaver. Put some music on, and let's dance."

"I . . . didn't bring a stereo," she said. "Just my practice sticks—"

"Oh, for the love of Pete," I said, ferreting in my chaps and pulling out my new iPhone and its pocket clamshell charger dock. I unfolded it, plugged it in, and found my practice mix. "What kind of dancing magician are you?"

"We don't dance," Jewel said, disappearing inside. "We keep our feet on the ground."

That was one thing we would have to differ on, because keeping your feet planted was one thing a dancer should *never* do. The drums of Sleepthief's *Dawnseeker* thumped out of my practice mix, and I closed my eyes, starting with the rhythmic warm-up of capoeira.

Few skindancers were also martial artists, so I was designing my own eclectic martial art, using Taido's acrobatics as a base. Capoeria was new to my mix—Brazilian, dance-inspired, practiced to music, starting with a swaying, back-and-forth movement called *ginga*.

My left foot darted back as I brought up my left hand as a guard, then I nimbly mirrored the movement in time to the music. Instruments started to wail around the drums as my body soaked in the rhythm, my feet becoming lighter with each mirrored sequence of steps.

Then the song exploded into a soaring soundscape, and I shifted into Taido's dance of the eight steps, *unsoku happo*, which traced the basic footwork in an elaborate choreographed pattern that built speed and strength while teaching reflexes of offense and defense.

I was fast at *unsoku happo* until I started thinking of it as a dance—and then I got faster. Springier than *ginga*, but still friendly to throwing in capoeria's fluid *esquiva* dodges, *unsoku happo* keeps my feet moving because my feet have to move. I can't stay planted.

The rhythm sank into my bones, and I moved beyond martial arts into skindancing, launching into the Dance of Five and Two. I'd pulled guards and stances from capoeira and Taido into it, but this was a dance, *this* had the right sums, *this* generated mana.

Before the world kicked my ass last year, I'd been satisfied with tattooing, ignoring the "dance" in "skindancer." But no more; I had rediscovered not just the other half of my art, but my own love of dance, and I was as determined to perfect the art of my dance as I had my inking.

The chill mountain air stung my skin as I danced, and I felt winded; all this traveling and talking had left me rusty. But as I moved, I acclimated, warming up, feeling my muscles stretch out, then slowly, surely, feeling my magic surge outward from my heart to my skin.

My power poured into my tattoos, and my vines unfurled around me as I moved. When I first tried this, years ago, with Arcturus, I got so tangled I fell on my face. Now I spun freely, my vines swirling around me fluid as thought, shedding leaves in a circle like a storm of autumn.

Jewel stepped to the top of the stairs, morningstars alight with liquid fire.

She descended the stairs toward my whirlstorm of magic. Her delicate feet touched the grass. Passing vines caressed her, tingling me to my core. She drew a breath, swirled slowly, entering the vortex, hands raising and falling, letting glowing leaves whirl around her.

Now I could see the delicate threads of my own magic. Not just the visible fire, but the invisible structure—the surging arcs, the crossing lines, the subtle pulses as one kind of mana changed into another. I could see my own intents come to life, writ large upon the air.

I no longer feared what would happen if my living magic touched her skin.

Jewel whipped her morningstars behind her, low to the ground, then brought them together in front of her, their cords crossing, the two flaming balls spinning around each other like a fiery buzz saw. Mana flooded off them, empowering me, and I spread my wings.

The Dragon unfurled around me, head rising, wings unfolding, tail uncurling, lifting me off the ground even as it brushed Jewel's feet. Her skin rippled against my projected tattoos and I gasped. The Dragon's wings snapped, hurling me into the air on the strength of her magic.

As my maelstrom of vines and leaves lifted into the air, Jewel let her morningstars fly apart, creating another dome of magic, lifting me higher. The vines and leaves drew power from her, but it was the Dragon that they powered. Her wings flapped, drawing me higher.

Before, when I rose over Union Square on stray mana crackling off Jewel's shield, I'd been disconnected and overwhelmed. Now I was connected and *aware.* No longer cut off by her shield, I could *feel* her through the magic—feel her love, and feel her love of the Earth.

Maui fell away beneath me as I rose on a pillar of magic and flame. The cracked slopes that slipped away around me were more complex than they were on the ground; forests spotted the slopes like patches of moss on a hillside. My own magic lit up the landscape.

Then I saw it—my *original* Dragon.

My breath caught as it shimmered into existence along the horizon. I don't know if it truly faded in, or just approached from the distance, but it appeared, growing closer and larger at the same time, leeching off my stray magic the same way I was being powered by Jewel.

By now, my maelstrom of vines and leaves had swirled out around me into a hurricane of autumn colors: sinuous vines, flowing leaves, glittering gems embedded in flowers, fluttering butterflies flying with sparks, a giant swirling vortex of mana fueled by love and fire.

My original Dragon wove itself through them all, a giant sine wave of blue scales and green gems snaking itself through my magic-generated forest. No longer a pale imitation of a Chinese dragon with tribal influences, it was a living behemoth of magical power, embodied and real.

I gasped, my body falling slack, my new Dragon's will keeping me aloft while my old Dragon slowly inscribed a full circle around me. My leaves dissipated, my new Dragon's wings furled, and as I slowly began to sink, my old Dragon sang to me:

—

"*The egg is ready,*" the Dragon said. "*Be prepared.*"

52. COMPROMISED

"You've compromised my safe house," Mr. Iloa said, quietly, though the force with which he delivered his words made them seem like a yell. "Endangered this mission, the life of your friend, the lives of everyone who lives here—and ruined this place for future use."

Iloa had summoned us all to the main house, where he had proceeded to rant at Jewel and me about the irresponsibility of "our little magical stunt" and to berate Philip for his "lack of judgment" in bringing us here. He looked calm, but was winding up to an explosion.

As for me? My cheeks were burning. I'd screwed up, royally.

"I'm sorry," I said, for the third time. "I never intended to—"

"You agreed to respect my hospitality," Iloa continued. "You yourself said you would protect our privacy. Yet you have violated both." Mr. Iloa glared at me—and then he turned to Philip. "I'm withdrawing my invitation. This is no longer a safe house."

Philip looked like he'd been slapped. Of course. His bosses would blame *him* for *my* gaffe. Me, I seethed. Raking *me* over the coals was one thing. Taking it out on Philip, disrupting the mission, possibly endangering Molokii's life? That was something else entirely.

I had been ready to take my medicine, but now I had to show leadership.

"I want you out of here," Iloa said. "Out of here by morning—"

"No," I said, shifting as my Dragon slid against my back.

"Excuse me?" Iloa said, turning to look at me.

"No, we're not leaving," I said, quietly, just like Iloa had. "We stay, and we finish the mission. This is not just a kidnapping. We're dealing with a magical crisis which may kill everyone on this island. Remember Krakatoa, the explosion felt round the world?"

"I don't need a history lesson," Iloa snapped—then his eyes widened, fractionally. I *had* gotten through to him. "Yes, I—" he began, then recovered his anger. "That doesn't matter! You lit up a mile-high magical sign over *my house!*"

I looked him straight in the eye, calm, apologetic—but firm.

"Yes, yes I did," I said. "Unintentionally, but I did. I'm sorry, and it's very *unfortunate* that my practice had unexpected magical fallout—but that 'fallout' confirmed we're following a good lead and that there's real danger. We need to stay, and finish the mission—"

"I'm not a part of your mission, and you are not in charge of me, Miss Frost. This is *my home*, and you have no authority," Iloa said. "You didn't suddenly become queen of Hawai`i just because some idiot put you in charge of magic in *Hicksville*—"

My nostrils flared. Nobody talks to me about Atlanta that way.

"Read my file, did you?" I asked, cracking my neck. "Then you missed the backstory. Do you know how I got appointed Chair of the Magical Security Council, Mr. Iloa? Someone tried to destroy my city, and no one would step up to defend it—*so I appointed myself.*"

Everyone was quiet.

"Philip's right. I did let too much of my magic out while I was practicing—but that could only give *you* away, not *call down hatchsign*," I said. "The same hatchsign we've seen over Palo Alto and over my literal home. Now it's over your home. If you won't deal with it, I will."

"But . . . but still," Iloa spluttered, "You have no real authority—"

"*One hundred fifty thousand* people live on Maui. That's all the authority I need." I said, trying to wrestle my anger back under control. "I'm sorry, Mr. Iloa, but I'm commandeering this installation under the authority of the Magical Security Council."

"This is not an installation," he said. "It—is—my—home—"

"And I'm trying to *save it* from being buried in a pyroclastic flow. You should be tossing me the keys and heading for the airport, rather than arguing and risking being burned alive," I said, turning my back on him. "Philip, control your man. I don't want this to come up again."

Then I strode out of the room, down the porch and into the night. *Damn it, damn it, damn it!* I had wanted to show leadership, and I ended up picking another fight. Bravado or no, the MSC had no authority here; we'd be lucky if Iloa didn't kick us all out on the spot.

My dragon squirmed actively on my back now, seething with my own rage. I was no longer sure I bought Arcturus's story that it just mirrored my intent, but neither did I completely buy the idea that I'd somehow picked up the spirit of a dragon, not with my old tattoo flying around dispensing cryptic wisdom about the timing of the hatching. This situation was mysterious, and dangerous, and possibly disastrous. Why couldn't Iloa see that?

I clenched my teeth, boots crunching on the path. I shouldn't have let the Dragon sweep me up into the sky. Irresponsible! I'd gotten carried away by the literal *magic* of my girlfriend and had endangered the mission—and rather than owning up, I'd doubled down.

Before I was halfway to my cabin, footsteps sounded behind me. One set was clearly trying to be quiet, stealthy; the other wasn't exactly *trying* to be quiet, but was stealthier. I felt a tingle of mana as Jewel came up on my right, and then Philip joined on my left.

"So this is the famous Dakota Frost bravado in action," Jewel said.

"I did screw up and I will apologize to him in the morning," I said, pulling out my phone. "But we've just seen hatchsign, and we should be focusing on how to interpret it, not quibbling over how fast you got us here or the unexpected strength of my defensive spells—"

"Dakota, Iloa knows that," Philip said. "He tries to play the wise sage, but he's really quite touchy and hotheaded about the little kingdom he's built here. You're not the first to run afoul of him—but I think your crack about being burned alive rattled him. He's still pissed, but he sees the danger. He's going to come around—and let us do our work."

He rattled some papers in his hands. I glanced at them, then the three of us scurried over to one of the lampposts that lit the path. The sheets were seismic maps, hot off a printer, which recorded new activity in volcanoes around Hawaii.

"We were suspicious of Hawaii before, but we're almost certain now," Philip said.

"Is it on Necker Island?" I asked. "The one Daniel wants to take—"

"No," Jewel said. "For the record, it's called Mokumanamana—"

"And it's extinct," Philip said. "The dragon will hatch from an active volcano—but there's a problem. We've got at *least* three sets of suspicious seismic activity from volcanoes located in the Hawaii region—"

"Three dragons," I said. "Jesus—"

"Don't get excited," Jewel said. "It could be *any* volcano, but not *every* volcano."

"If we buy the idea there's only one spirit," Philip said. I stared at him, wondering if he was going to suggest that if one dragon *projectia* could pick up a spirit, perhaps another one could too—but what he suggested was actually far worse. "The thing you saw flying around might be a dragon spirit looking for a volcano . . . because all the suitable ones are taken."

"Please tell me you're joking," I said. "That would mean—"

"A mass volcanic eruption," Philip said. "That's a worst case scenario. Assuming one spirit, that still leaves us three possible sites in Hawaii alone—Kilauea. Lothi seamount, two or three others. The seismographs even picked up a rumble in Pu'u o Maui—"

"In Haleakala crater?" Jewel finished, head twisting toward the slope. "It's *extinct—*"

"Dormant," Philip said. "Maybe not so dormant anymore."

"Crap," Jewel said. "Oh, *crap!* Should we, like, move or something—"

"It's the *least* probable candidate," Philip said, "and for any normal-sized explosion, I think we'd have time to get to safety. From something the size of Krakatoa—well, Jewel, I can't precisely tell you where would be safe. It was heard thousands of miles away."

I thought about what the Grinder had said about hatching causing extinctions, but I didn't know how much of that was poetic license, how much was as a result of an explosive hatching, and how much was a result of a mountain-sized fire-breathing creature roaming the earth.

My tattoo shifted, and I got a disturbing sense of . . . protest. Like a denial that my Dragon would ever do such a terrible thing. I frowned. I wasn't clear whether this was a real voice, or me talking to myself. I wondered how I could ask a question without giving up too many secrets.

"The way Nyissa told the story," I said carefully, "made it sound like the Krakatoa explosion was so bad because of the war—because the hatching was disrupted and went wrong. Do you think a normal hatching could cause that kind of damage?"

"I don't know," Philip said, "but the scientists that *I've* talked to think that as the Earth ages, it becomes harder for dragons to hatch normally. That worst case scenario I mentioned? The Cambrian extinction may have been caused by a clutch of dragon eggs detonating."

"Jesus," Jewel said.

"May He help us," I said. The Grinder was right.

My cell phone vibrated with a text, and I pulled it out, afraid of what new horror would be dumped upon us. But when I stared at my phone, I wanted to whoop. But Jewel was standing right there, so I controlled my expression, simply nodding and putting it away.

"So . . . we've learned we're in the right place. Philip, even that's no excuse for my behavior. When I set out to practice tonight, I really didn't anticipate that I'd end up half a mile in the sky. I'm sorry."

"It was worth it to see Iloa's face," Philip said. "Still . . . he could cause problems."

"I have an idea," Jewel said. "Let me apologize, because this is my fault."

She twisted her delicate hands around each other, glancing at me, embarrassed. "I added my magic to Dakota's practice. I wanted to see what would happen. I'm sorry."

"I have a better idea," Philip said. "We'll *both* apologize for her. Together, we can smooth any ruffled feathers—and Dakota cements her fearsome reputation."

"Hey," I said.

"Someone has to back up all that bravado," Philip said. "It sure can't just be you."

"Gee, thanks," I said. "No, seriously, thanks—and again, I'm sorry."

"No worries," Philip said, putting his hand on Jewel's shoulder. "Besides, that gives the two of us a chance to catch up."

"Do you have dirt, Special Agent Davidson?" Jewel asked.

My friends walked back the path to clean up my mess. I watched them go, then turned on my heel and purposely strode toward the cabin, hoping I could quickly find my laptop, get on line and check my email. That last message ping on my phone had set a fire under me.

If I'd read the title right, Alex had just sent me every fireweaving manual in existence.

53. Ye Gyde of Secryts

After I received Alex's email—and spent the next two hours downloading an enormous rip of the *Gyde of Secryts to ye Weaving of Fyre*—I took a moment to savor the irony. I had to download the latest version of Adobe Reader to open a three-hundred-year-old document.

I'd texted Cinnamon for help, but it had to be past two a.m. in Atlanta, so I wasn't surprised that I didn't get an answer. Either she'd turned in early, or, more likely, was late coming back from her midnight run—weretiger sleep patterns are weird. Regardless, I was on my own.

In the kitchen of our cabin, I'd spread out everything I had on the case: my notes on the hatchsign, Philip's seismic maps, the DEI's dossiers on Daniel and his likely fire ninjas, and the photos of the symbols that the ninjas had left everywhere from Maui to Moreland Avenue.

The promise of immortality was screwing everything up. Everyone around me had their own agenda, their own secrets, all about what liquid fire could do, how they could get it—and how they could keep it. I was convinced that the answer was cracking that code.

I had to know what Daniel was trying to tell Jewel.

I didn't know precisely what I would find. Details of Daniel's demands? Or, given Jewel was still being a little cagey, the secrets he demanded she keep?

It was too much to hope for a location, but I hoped to find a magical signature I could track, some clue—anything.

But I'd been hoping others could solve the riddle for me—relying on Cinnamon to crack it, cajoling Philip to pass it to the NSA, even leaning on Jewel to tell me outright. But what if Arcturus was right? What if I wasn't a dim bulb tattooist who needed to rely on others?

What if I had the smarts to crack the code?

Now, I had no illusions—I wasn't an NSA-trained codebreaker, and I couldn't multiply million-digit numbers in my head. But even Cinnamon, budding genius, was consumed by punishing self-doubt when her defective early education left holes in her knowledge.

Fortunately, ignorance is correctable.

Cinnamon and I had already gone over the code, both individually and in consultation with Philip's experts, so I focused on the new piece—Alex's fireweaving manuals. These were the secrets Jewel was trying to hide. The ones Daniel threatened to maim her for performing.

Here had to lie the answers.

I stared into the text, trying to read the arcane script with its ancient spelling: *ye who vse yese rvnes, ivdge karfulli, ye magiks of fire* . . . Then it hit me—the spelling of the fireweaver's text wasn't just archaic. It used *y* for *th everywhere*—as if even the spelling was a code.

I skimmed the text—*u* everywhere was *v*, *j* was *i*, *qu* was *kw*, *z* was *x* . . . and there were two different variants for all the common vowels, used seemingly at random. So common letters were split up, and rare ones combined—breaking the frequencies. Perfect for a code.

That was what had stymied the NSA, the DEI, even Cinnamon—the alphabet of symbols. Without knowing what they corresponded to, you needed an enormous amount of text to guess the letter frequencies—but the fireweavers tuned their spelling to destroy that information.

But *what were the symbols?* I searched the document for the word *code* and got dozens of references, none relevant. *Cipher* yielded nothing, not in any spelling, not *cypher* or *cyfer* or *sifer*. Symbol—nothing; *simbol*—hundreds of matches, effectively useless to me. *Alphabet?* No.

Then, on a guess, I tried *alfabet*—and found the phrase *ye alfabet of rvnes.*

It was a table, mapping runes to the peculiar spelling of the fireweaver text.

"Bingo," I said, pulling out a piece of tracing paper and laying it over the latest message. *Every* symbol in the ring was found in that table in the document Alex sent me. Soon, I had a ring of letters written down—sixty letters, in fact, in five concentric arcs. And all still gibberish.

I stared into the ring, willing it to resolve like a set of Cryptoquotes. Nothing.

What had Philip said? A good field code had to be simple enough to be encoded quickly, something an agent could easily remember, but still baffling to the enemy. And for a practitioner using magic to send a message, what would be simpler than the rules of graphomancy?

I stared into the smallest disc, at the runes etched on its surface, at the symbols and lines that connected them. Beyond the obvious lines, there was a logic, like one of Cinnamon's cat's cradles, a spiral woven through the lines that hit every letter in a specific order.

I traced the pattern, but the runes were gibberish. Of course. Encoding the letters along the lines of the magic would be as obvious as writing them out in straightforward order. Damn it! How would Cinnamon do this? She'd be able to crack this code between two of her tics!

Or maybe not. I realized the whole idea was hopeless because the disc was symmetric—for each path through the maze, there were many others like it, formed by rotating the pattern. Twenty-four of them, in fact, one for each possible starting point—each letter in the outer ring.

No, there were only six letters in the center ring. You could only turn the pattern six ways. I tilted my head, like Cinnamon would. Six ways break it into groups of ten—not along the lines of the magic itself, *but along the paths that a fireweaver would use to create it.*

Six ways. Once, Jewel had said there were seven hundred and twenty different ways to do the basic spinner's weave . . . but Cinnamon had called that "six factorial." Could it be as simple as writing out the message along the tracks that *had to be* left by a fireweaver's poi?

I paged back through the manual. Before the rituals, before the spells, before the expert moves—back to the basics, the firespinning equivalents of the skindancer's dance of the Five and Two. Sure enough—*the simplest spins had magical numbers.* The weaves were complex enough that an outsider wasn't likely to figure out how the letters were laid down, but . . .

To an initiate, the code would practically write itself.

I pulled out my practice poi and swung them experimentally, imagining the arc. The message would be written inside from outside, five letters out, five letters curling back. I picked an arc and got PSWIL and OSTFR—nonsense. Wait, OST FR . . . and my name was FROST . . .

What was that Cinnamon had said about quirks of the code making things line up?

My heart began thumping in my throat. I tried spinning again and quickly found another arc through it: NDEAI OKTLO—*Daniel took?* Another: NGTOE OMAUI—*gone to Maui?* In moments, I had it. In arcs through the pattern that just looked like nonsense . . .

```
NDEAI OKLTO STFRO ASSCP NGTOE UIOMA
IBGRN STFRO ISSHE ROAUF BLCLA ANKPL
```

. . . there was a hidden order, unlocked by the simplest of keys:

```
DANIE LTOOK FROST SCAPS GONET OMAUI
BRING FROST SHEIS OURFA LLBAC KPLAN
```

Daniel took Frost's caps, gone to Maui. Bring Frost, she is our fallback plan.

"Oh shit, this is bad," I whispered. But not because of what the message said, nor the ominous personal implications of that fallback plan. No, it was because of the key that unlocked the pattern, a key I'd found purely by accident of my name lining up with one of the patterns.

OSTFR. Five letters, taken from FROST . . . letters 4 and 5, then 1, 2, and

3. ASSCP. Five letters taken from S'CAPS . . . letters 3 and 1, then 5, 2, and 4. The whole message was jumbled by repeated application of the pattern 45123, then 31524, over and over, in and out:

`31524 45123 45123 31524 31524 45123`

Again, there was a hidden order, taken from two simple sets of five letters. Cinnamon had shown me this trick—take a word and write down the order of its letters in the alphabet in order to get a scramble code. Something simple . . . something easy for the recipient to remember:

`JEWEL GRACE GRACE JEWEL JEWEL GRACE`

My skin felt clammy. My gut clenched. Because I hadn't just stumbled on it by accident. I'd seen the OSTFR, realized it was a scramble . . . and looked for the first five letter word that came to mind. JEWEL didn't unlock my name . . . but it unlocked the very next sequence.

And then the two words of her name unlocked the whole rest of the message.

"The message was meant for her," I whispered. It wasn't *from* Daniel; it was *about* Daniel, from Jewel's group—meaning, it wasn't a ransom message *about* Molokii, but probably instructions *from* Molokii himself. "And like it asked . . . she brought me to Maui."

I heard a sizzling—and looked over to see Jewel at the door, lit morningstars in hand.

"You always were too smart for your own good," she said—and struck.

54. ADVANTAGE, JEWEL

I barely had time to raise my hand and murmur *shield* before the blast struck. The ball of flame didn't burn like a fire, but hit like a linebacker, knocking me sideways out of my seat, and I winced as heat magically rippled from my projected tattoos to my living skin.

I hit the floor and rolled, kicking with one leg, trying to use Taido to get distance and right myself. But Jewel ran forward with me, striking again and again with her morningstars, battering me like they were real versions and not their magical namesakes.

"Go down," she muttered. "Damn it, Dakota, quit fighting me, go down—"

"Never—had a problem—with that before," I said, weaving as blows rained down around me. My shields worked against magic, against blows, against bullets—but not fire, which stung like a bitch. "Maybe you should—

have stuck to—your old style of foreplay—"

"Damn it!" Jewel said, swinging her fiery balls and chains backward and forward, crossing them at speed before me, creating a flash of magic which impacted my chest and knocked me, winded, against the far wall. "I'm not trying to hurt you—"

"But I'm trying to hurt you!" Nyissa roared, leaping upon her.

Jewel screamed as Nyissa impacted her shield, then stumbled back. I gasped, trying to regain my breath, as Nyissa struck her again and again with her hands like claws, sparks flaring as vampire-hard blows caused her shield to bow and bulge and its flames to flicker, then gutter.

But just when I thought Jewel's shield would collapse, Nyissa jerked her hand back, shaking it out—and a burn was visible on that pale skin. In that moment, Jewel regained her footing, switched up her weave—and her barrier of flame strengthened, redoubled.

"You want to hurt me?" Jewel said, mock-wounded. "Good luck with that."

Nyissa snarled, full fangs, then leapt, whirling around Jewel, trying to penetrate her fiery shield, trying to gain advantage. At first, it looked like the advantage was to Jewel; even with vampire speed, Nyissa couldn't outrun the whirling balls of flame.

"Can't take the heat?" Jewel smirked, hands whipping around her. As fast as she was, I could now see that she could make the patterns of flames in her magic move even faster. "And I've barely started cooking—"

"Hell with this," Nyissa snarled, withdrawing a wand from her cloak. "*Extinguere!*"

I caught a glimpse of Jewel's wide eyes, blotted out by the brilliance of a cold beam of ice blasting from Nyissa's wand like a concentrated snow machine. Jewel's firesticks guttered, but did not go out, and she performed a concentrated figure eight, shedding snow away.

Gasping and dumbfounded, I struggled to stand as a scene from Harry Potter played out before my eyes. I'd known Nyissa was a wizard before she became a vampire, but unconsciously, I'd assumed that since she wasn't a powerful vampire, she hadn't been a powerful wizard.

But she'd built a ward big enough to shield all of Blood Rock.

As Jewel adapted, so did Nyissa, turning the beam of ice first into a stream of chunky snowballs, then into a icy jet of water, then to surging waves of mana that caused the spin of her poi to wobble. Jewel yelped in pain as one of her poi singed her arm, and Nyissa smiled.

"What's that you said?" Nyissa snarled, slowly arcing around Jewel, adjusting the focus of her strange shimmering beam of frost to cause the maximum disruption to Jewel's shield. "You haven't started cooking? Looks like a dish best served cold to me—"

"What's that *you* said?" Jewel growled, slowly stepping back, planting her feet more carefully, hand movements growing more and more complex as she tried to prevent Nyissa from blotting out her fire or tangling up her chains. "The hell with this?"

And she split her morningstars apart, creating a simple shield before her with one spinning stick, and whipping the other straight behind her, shielding with her body a disc of flame she created in the air, a disc that sang with an eerie, resonant wail.

Nyissa blasted the shield with another torrent of ice, but it just bowed back, evaporating the white specks and blowing them away in a churn of steam and fog. Nyissa flicked her wand in a complicated motion, then watched as a tangle of magic rippled off the shield.

Nyissa raised her wand, staring at Jewel, considering; then she hissed, full fangs.

"A magic circle," she said. "The simplest shield. Perfect defense. No offense."

Nyissa motioned to me, and, gasping, I levered off the wall, joining her. Jewel just stared back at us from inside the bubble, smirking, the shield gleaming before her while the spinning ring sang behind her, shimmering and hypnotic.

"She's really good at this," I said, "but her fuel can't last forever—"

"Dakota, fetch my poker from my luggage," Nyissa said. "Now—"

"That's right, go on," Jewel said, twirling the ring behind her. "Fetch, Dakota."

"What's the ring for?" Nyissa said, leaning in with her wand. "You will tell me—"

"You'll find out soon enough," Jewel said—and the front door exploded.

I turned, expecting fire ninjas—and saw Molokii and the Fireweavers instead.

Nyissa whirled, wand whipping out, but it was too late. Molokii's blast hurled her body into the kitchen. The backwash of the impact knocked me off my feet again, leaving me dazed. In moments, two Fireweavers had seized my arms, and a third raised a stinking white cloth.

"Jewel," I said, struggling, trying to gather my forces, "you don't have to do this—"

—⁂

"I'm sorry, Dakota," Jewel said, waving to the guard with chloroform. "Put her out."

55. High Priestess of Pele

Something foul and pungent was shoved under my nostrils, jolting me to awareness. My body bucked instinctively, struggling against something before I was even fully conscious. I was all too familiar with this scene. I'd been knocked out, I'd been captured—and I'd been bound.

"Welcome back, Skindancer," Jewel said. "I'm sorry it came to this."

I jerked fully awake. My arms were bound behind me, some kind of rope harness, and I was covered with some sticky, icky goo. I was kneeling on a towel, and a pair of fireweavers stepped forward to take my arms, not roughly, but almost kindly, helping me to my feet.

"The plan was *so simple,*" Jewel said, her voice echoing in my ears as the world spun around me. "Fake Molokii's kidnapping, get my butch biker babe to ride to the rescue, then convince her she just *had* to perform her part of the spell to win his freedom."

"What?" I asked, dizzy and blinking. Torches and flame swam around me, illuminating the sweaty bodies of the fireweavers, bone and metal decorations, and a gleaming cauldron, but the real star was the scenery—a stark landscape of red and black rock, piled volcanic cinder, rising above us in a conical peak. Now we really were on the surface of Mars. "What—"

"We'd even bought dark robes and masks from Maxi's for all the celebrants," Jewel said, waving her arms, "but then *you* had to speed dial Philip before I could even say, 'let's not tell the police.' I mean, seriously? Who calls in an *airship* in response to a ransom demand?"

"What," I repeated, twisted in the arms of my guards, half struggling against them, half leaning on them. I looked left and right, disorientingly seeing the same spiky-haired fireweaver boy twice—my guards were twins. I looked down at the web of beige ropes crisscrossing the sticky black goo smeared over my body, and finally marshaled myself. "What the hell—"

"It's liquid latex," Jewel said, as I squirmed uncomfortably beneath the ropes. Actually, I have to admit the *ropes* weren't uncomfortable—the coating of goop was. "Piled on thick, on top of all your tattoos. Sorry, Skindancer, but it was necessary to shut you down—and thanks for giving me the idea in your shop as you pulled on the gloves."

I struggled, but the hemp quite artfully kept my arms pinned behind my back without putting too much pressure at any one point—*karada*, Jewel's favorite fetish, the Japanese art of bondage that carefully used ropes to limit the motion of the joints.

The latex, on the other hand, clung to my body, stinging like it was magically active. Mercifully, they'd left me in shorts and a T-shirt, but they'd smeared the goop everywhere—including places where no one, not even Jewel, had the right to touch me without asking.

"You—*you* put this shit on me—"

Jewel nodded. "Of course. Underneath the latex is a layer of henna, inscribed in a way to short-circuit your designs. Only I know your tattoos well enough to do that. And besides"—she smirked—"I didn't want anyone else groping that beautiful body."

"You bitch!" I felt violated, even though we'd been intimate. "How *could* you?"

"Never underestimate a man's ability to underestimate a woman," Jewel said, with that wry smile I'd loved—until now. Before, I'd read it as inviting and delightful; now, I realized, it was just a scornful and vicious *smirk*. "Apparently that holds true for butch lesbians as well."

I looked away. I'd love to say that I was angry with her, but survival instinct had already pushed me past that. There were half a dozen fireweavers around me, and we stood within concentric rings of torches. The crescent moon glinted off the hood of a Range Rover.

But it was the totem-guarded cauldron that worried me the most. It was squat, six-sided, with complex runes covering its silver panels. Beaded threads stretching from its six corners connected it to six feathered totem poles set with crystals and elaborate magical glyphs.

The spell wasn't fully active yet, but the liquid fire in my eyes revealed faint traces. Lines of magic arced between totems, a gleaming bubble pulsed around the cauldron, and a cylinder of power rose from a casting point set before it—all sparkling with magic symbols.

This wasn't Wicca or skindancing or even graffiti magic, all of which depended on a magical practitioner or a magical substrate to make it work. This was *technical* magic, a complex configuration of graphomantic lines designed to channel enormous power.

This was magic as a necromancer would have wrought it, trying to squeeze every last bit out of the surge of a death—but the fireweavers had power. They had a source of liquid fire, so either they were running out, or this spell required simply *staggering* amounts of mana.

My eyes traced the beaded threads hanging from the totems around the cauldron, out into the rings of torches. Soon, I saw the torches weren't concentric rings—they were one spiral, the threads winding out from the cauldron, braiding together, in widening circles.

My eyes followed the spiral as it straightened out, snaking lazily up the reddish-grey, sloping conical hill. At first it was hard to see, given the distance and the nearer flames around us . . . but soon I was certain that the torches spiraled back around the crown of the summit.

I'd seen this in Devenger's lab—an *infinity lens*, a figure eight made of two spirals, one bigger than the other, focusing magic from a source onto a target. Magic as Archimedes would have wrought—*give me a lever and a place to stand, and I can move the world* sort of shit.

"What are you doing, Jewel?" I said.

"You'll see soon enough," she said, smirk fading ever so slightly. "You know, at one point, I'd hoped to tell you directly, to let you in on the secret and bring you in, but you always were so damn sure of yourself. Not *once* did you ever show sympathy for our cause—"

"Damn it, make it easy on yourself," I said, studying the totems. The largest held a silver disc, stamped with a crescent moon split by a dagger, over a burning house wrapped in a braided chain. "The *dragon* doesn't need all this crap. Jewel, *talk*. You *know* me. I *will* figure it out."

Jewel stared off into the distance. Then she sighed.

"Behind us is Pu'u o Maui," Jewel said. "Largest cinder cone in Haleakala, one of the sacred places of the Order. And inside it, a dragon is hatching—the spirit of our people, made manifest. But you know all that, dragon herald. You can feel it. I can see it in your face—"

"You're seeing what you *want* to see," I said, scowling; but I did feel . . . *something*, some connection, some echo in my core, strangely interrupted, that made my skin crawl and my tattoos itch. Still . . . "But if it is the 'spirit of your people made manifest' why all this mumbo jumbo? You seem to be pretty well stocked with liquid fire," I said. "Enough for performances—"

"No. That's what we call faux fire," Jewel said. "Even that's too precious to use in its pure form. For performances, we use filtered white gas mixed with the tiniest drop of faux fire. Faux fire itself is regenerated, continuously, in braziers that burn gold—"

"Shh, Jewel," Zi warned. "She doesn't need to know our secrets."

"Thanks, Zi, I wouldn't have picked out that detail," I said, smirking at him. "Burning gold in liquid fire to make more fire—a reverse philosopher's stone. Neat—but it can't possibly sustain itself forever. That's why you wanted my firecap ink. That's why you need *me*. You don't have anything to trigger this spell with—"

"You don't know anything," Zi snapped.

"I know *you can't escape the second law of thermodynamics:* a closed system always runs down," I said. "No matter what tricks you use to stretch your supply, if you have no living source, no *input*, the magic *will* run out. And while you traveled the world trying to provoke a hatching, *Daniel* looked ahead at what you needed and gathered it all up to spike your plan."

"You always were too smart for *anyone's* good," Jewel said. "Yes, you're right. Over time, faux fire becomes useless for the ancient spells, worthless for the deeper magicks. I never quite understood what the keepers of the secret flame were yapping about."

"Gold isn't magical," I said. "Burning gold in magic fire may yield magical byproducts, but they'll be less magical than the source. It's like fission—the radiation from decaying atoms may create radioactive byproducts, but always with less potential energy than the source.

"But a dragon's heart is a living philosopher's stone, transforming energy into enormous magical complexity, like fusing atoms with magic. From there, the magic will run downhill, becoming simpler and simpler. It's entropy—the loss of order is . . . *inevitable.*

"It's Nuclear Magic 101," I said. "I hope you're taking notes. There will be a test—"

Zi slugged me in the stomach, hard enough to stagger me. Thunder rippled from the caldera, the ground shook, and I stumbled as my dragon twisted against the henna. My guards grabbed for my arms as I fell, making me cry out as my arm twisted under the sudden strain.

"Enough," Jewel said—but the other fireweavers looked approving. Behind her, Molokii signed something to another fireweaver, Yolanda, who walked off to a crèche of equipment near the Range Rover. Jewel said, "She's tied up tight. You do not need to hit her."

"Have you gone soft?" Zi glared at her, then me. He shook his head. "Don't tell me you've fallen for this woman, not after all that scheming! I don't care if she is the herald, we can't just spill our secrets to her! Daniel's right, you're endangering the Order, princess—"

"I said, *enough,*" Jewel said, striking the ground with her foot—and, incredibly, the ground echoed it, shuddering under our feet. The fireweavers murmured, looking between Zi and Jewel. "And here, it's not princess, it's *priestess.* Unless you think Pele will come for you?"

Zi drew a breath. "No, of course not," he said. "Only you can summon Pele."

"Pele?" I said. There was "spirit of their people made manifest," and then there was the plainly ridiculous. "Surely you don't think the dragon is *literally* the reincarnation of *Pele*—"

"Maybe," Jewel said defiantly. "No one understands a dragon's life cycle. There's a spirit, and an egg, and the one precedes the other, before both are joined in the birth of the dragon. Who knows where that spirit comes from?"

"Not Hawaiian myth," I said, squirming in my bonds, staring at the cauldron. This spell needed liquid fire—and if Daniel took my inks, the next best place to get it was my blood. "Dragons date back to the Hadean, when stones fell like rain into oceans of molten rock."

"How poetic," Jewel said. "But that just shows how little you understand. Whether she's really Pele doesn't matter. Even whether we *believe* she's Pele doesn't matter. All that matters is the role that the symbol plays in our ritual—"

"This isn't just technical magic," I said, my suspicion confirmed. "It's *ceremonial* magic. A ritual designed to harvest the collective intents of a congregation. But you still need enormous magical power to catalyze it—a ley line crossing, a bloodline *mashiach*—or a blood sacrifice."

The words hung there in the air, ugly and true.

"No one's going to get sacrificed, Dakota." The ground shook, and then Jewel scowled as Yolanda returned from the crèche with an *athame*, a blessed dagger that was used as a magical weapon in ceremonial magic. "Yolanda, I was serious earlier. I *forbid* human sacrifice—"

"I heard you, princess," Yolanda said, quickly glancing at me, then back at Jewel, "and killing your girlfriend is not Plan A. But we're running out of time. If the anointing fails, we *have* to have a fallback plan ready *before* Pele hatches!"

Again, a silence stretched, broken only by the guttering of torches in the wind.

"Yolanda," Jewel said—and now *she* quickly glanced at me, then back at Yolanda. I scowled. Jewel had known that sacrificing me was a possibility all along. I wondered if she was merely acting when she said, "We have to be better than Daniel. Tell me you're not serious."

"I am. I don't want that dragon to fly free to ravage Hawai`i—or to die, blowing the top of the mountain off. That would leave none of us alive, much less no liquid fire. But, I hope we don't have to . . . uh, you know." She glanced at me. "The ceremonial anointing will—"

"You don't want it to fly free or die?" I asked. "What are you trying to do?"

"The hatchsign has been flying too long," Jewel said. "If we could have called it down earlier, perhaps—no matter. At this point, with the physical egg this mature, Pele doesn't really need our help to hatch. At this point, we have two choices: thwart the hatching—"

"You're going to *abort* her," I said, with growing horror. "A dragon, still-born—"

"No, *Daniel* wanted to thwart the hatching," Jewel said angrily. "To take a rare, beautiful, and independent creature and harvest it for its blood. That *is* what humans have done throughout the ages. But there's a better option, a more humane option—to seize control of it."

"To seize control . . . of the hatching?" I said. "You mean of the *hatchling?*"

—∞

"We can't let Pele fly free," Jewel said. "But she *will* live . . . under our command."

56. TO ENSLAVE A GOD

"You want to . . . command the hatchling?" I stared again at the torches, the totems, and at last saw it—this was a *control charm*, writ large. More properly, a *geas*, a spell to steal a living thing's will. The Dragon on my back convulsed. "You're planning to *enslave Pele?*"

"Dakota—" Jewel began.

"You're going to take a rare, beautiful, and independent creature and make it a slave," I said, bile growing. "You have the hubris to capture a small-g god, and the cruelty to doom something meant to fly to a life in captivity. You're going to *enslave* a *dragon*—"

"Enslave her or kill her," Jewel said flatly. "Those are our choices. No matter how much empathy you or I feel toward Pele, she'll become a monster the size of a mountain. She could destroy a city with a flick of her wing. She must be tamed, or destroyed—"

"She's not an animal. She's *communicating*," I said. "Communicating with *me*—"

"Yes, and I'm sorry, dragon herald," Jewel said, "but that's why the spell will work. We haven't tried it, but we're confident we'll tame her—as confident as we can be given this is a three-hundred-year-old spell from our spotty old records—"

"You don't need old records, you need the *latest knowledge*," I said. "For example, if you think baptizing me in that cauldron will let you collect the spiritual essence of the liquid fire in my tattoos by some kind of magical osmosis, you're out of luck—"

"She's . . . she's just trying to throw us off," Zi said.

"Skin acts as an *essence filter*," I said. "Higher fractions of mana don't penetrate. That's why tattoos need graphomantic designs rather than directly projecting a caster's intent. If you want the essence of magic in my blood . . . you're going to need to bleed me out."

"We add sandalwood oil and hyssop in the act of anointing," Yolanda said. "And the cauldron is steeped with a mix of jasmine and cinquefoil for projection. A *minor* cut to start the bleed, amplify that through the infinity lens, and—what? What's wrong with that, Frost?"

"That's . . . that's really good," I said, staring at the lens and totems. "But an infinity lens tops out at a thirteen-to-one gearing. The most you can concentrate in that cauldron is a twelfth of the power within my skin. For what it looks like you need . . . it would still kill me."

"We won't have to," Yolanda said, looking at the blade uncertainly in her hands. "The circuit started to activate as soon as we brought you into it, even with you covered with that goop. I think the spirit of the dragon has bonded with you—"

My eyes went wide. Maybe they'd realized about my new dragon tattoo what I'd long suspected. But Yolanda immediately showed she was off target—and hopefully, her misunderstanding was something I could use to my advantage.

"The spirit of the dragon was summoned to you every time you cast your dragon tattoo. Sometimes even when you don't cast it," Yolanda said. "If you stand at the casting point, the infinity lens will amplify the emanations of your tattoo—"

"Maybe," I said. "But I'm not casting a fucking *enslavement spell*."

"You won't have to," Yolanda said flatly. "When the spirit of the dragon tries to pass the upper focus of the infinity lens, it will become trapped, charging up the Dragon's Noose. Jewel will take your place in the circuit, and when Pele hatches, the Noose will bind its will to hers—"

A voice whispered against my skin, oddly distant, oddly muffled, but clear enough in source and intention that I was now certain that it wasn't me talking to myself, nor was it coming from the Dragon *off* my back. Something alien spoke to me . . . through my new tattoo.

Don't let them make a slave of me!

I scowled. All right then . . . *I'll do my best.*

"I can't believe I'm hearing this, Jewel," I said. "No matter how much you pulled the wool over my eyes, I watched you deal with the people around you. I know how much you care. I can't believe you'd enslave a dragon just so you can spin fire—"

"You don't know me at all," Jewel said. "To hell with the liquid fire. Sure, we'll take it from her maw once we've tamed her. But we have to tame her, because if she hatches freely, she'll destroy our world. If we can seize control of her, though, she'll destroy what *we* want."

My mouth fell open.

"Do what?" I said. "You want to use a Hadean Dragon . . . as a *weapon?*"

"Why not?" Jewel asked, extending her hand, encompassing both the cauldron and the caldera. "The Americans cracked the atom to make a weapon, even tested it practically on our doorstep. Why can't the Hawai`ians crack the dragon's egg to do the same thing?"

"Why do you need a weapon?" I said. "The atom bombs are on your side—"

"On *America's* side," Jewel said, eyes flashing. "Our conquerors."

I set my mouth. Almost from the beginning, Jewel had described herself as a Hawaiian native, as an activist, as politically active—and I'd read enough on it to understand the issues that mattered to her, or so I thought. But I never realized how far she wanted to take it.

"You're not a Hawaiian nativist," I said. "You're a Hawaiian *separatist!*"

"Not originally," Jewel said. "But the more people that come here, the further we natives get squeezed out. But it's not just the rich and the powerful that are squeezing us out—it's your whole country, taking our land for granted as if it was its very own.

"We tried to work with the system, Dakota, we tried. Tried to create reservations for Hawai`ian sacred land. Flawed as they are, they at least would have preserved some buffer for the old ways. But the thanks we got for working within the system—was *that!*"

And she pointed over my shoulder. Puzzled, I followed her gaze. Far out, atop a distant ridge, were the twinkling lights of a construction site, reflecting off a half-finished dome. I'd seen the lights earlier from the safe house—good, we hadn't gone far.

Something tickled the back of my neck. My eye caught a shimmer of movement, passing behind the dome. Without even seeing it clearly, I knew it was something I'd expected all along, and quickly, I looked away, staring at Jewel, hoping none of the others had seen it yet.

Then I looked back, as something tickled the back of my mind. Suddenly, I realized what the dome was. I'd seen it flying in. Jewel had mentioned it. I'd read about it in *Scientific American.* But I still couldn't quite put two and two together.

"You're upset . . . about a telescope?" I said.

"It's on sacred ground," Jewel said. "They call it Science City, and it's on sacred ground. They're burrowing hundreds of feet into our sacred rock to put up a . . . a temple to the sun, desecrating our lands, which they've already shit on for decades—"

"You're upset," I repeated, "about the *Advanced Technology Solar Telescope.*"

"Frost knows what it is," Yolanda said, staring at me.

"Of *course* I know what it is!" I roared. "My girlfriend is a Hawaiian political activist and I looked up what that meant because you're *supposed* to understand what your partner is into! What flabbergasts me is that you think it is worth going to *war* over a *telescope!*"

"That's just a target of opportunity," Jewel said. "Pele is hatching. As much as we love her, as much as we practically worship her, we cannot let that happen. The devastation would be awesome. We must kill her . . . or tame her. And if we've tamed her—"

"You'll make her go to war," I said, "from which the devastation would be awesome—"

"We aren't out to hurt anyone," Jewel said. "We just want to cleanse our land—"

"Oh, great," I said. "Whatever happened to a spell turning back upon its owner?"

"Karmic redress!" she said. "They destroyed our *heiau*, so we'll destroy *their* temple—"

"And no one will die in that incendiary outrage?" I asked.

"We are trying," she said, "to *defend Hawai`i*—"

"What, from a telescope?" I said. "Get real—"

"You think you know *everything,*" Jewel said. "This place is sacred to us—"

"To the people who lived and died here centuries ago," I said. "Not you—"

One of the fireweavers punched me in the gut. I doubled over, wheezing for effect. I'd needed to lurch forward anyway, and had tightened my abs and started mouthing off, figuring my flapper would win me some blow or cuff or shove that would give me a little cover.

"Enough—remember *kānāwai māmalahoe,*" Jewel said, outstretched finger warning both me and her fellow weavers. "This land is ours. It's sacred. And it's being desecrated. And it isn't the first time that our land has been ruined by American scientists.

"You heard Philip—they marched us off Mokumanamana, our sacred island, at gunpoint! It took three years in *Federal* court to get our land back. *Three years!* And when we finally did, we found that so-called *scientists* from Fish and Wildlife had razed the sacred *heiau* we'd spent a decade rebuilding because they thought it was *vandalism* by *trespassers!*

"The Americans, they've always been the same. They came here and took our land like they owned it. They tortured our people and turned them into trained monkeys in their tourist traps. They even pretended to convert our god Pele to their own joke religion by dropping rocks upon her. I quit Christianity after I learned what the missionaries did, and—"

She broke off, clenching her fists, savoring some feeling of rage.

"The spell will work. Pele will hatch, and the Noose of Will will tighten around her throat as she rises from the flames. Liquid fire from her egg will nourish our firespinning, and living fire from her maw will cleanse our sacred lands. Together, we will retake Maui, Pele, and her people. Under her, at last, the people of Hawai`i will again be free—"

"You know, Jewel," I said, mouth quirking into a smile, "I believe you're monologuing."

Jewel fell silent, sighed, shook her head. "Only you, Dakota, could make light of this—"

"But wait, there's more," I said, grinning. "If you're the villain, then I'm the hero, and it's in my contract to say, 'but wait, you've forgotten something.' "

Jewel turned to me, head cocked, hands on her hips. "All right, I'll bite. What have I forgotten, Dakota Frost?"

—&

"You've forgotten, Jewel Grace," I said, pulling my hands free, "that I'm the most flexible person you've ever met."

57. Rumble on Pu'u o Maui

I rammed my elbows into the chins of the twin guards on either side with solid *CRACKs*. I wasn't quite free of the *karada* when I started—my arms were still pulled back behind me—but I had managed to work a few thorns of my vines through the liquid latex, and by the time I completed my motion, the whole array of ropes fell away from me like hemp confetti.

Then I went to the closed universe of the Taido form *untai no hokei.*

My hands shot out to either side, bladed fingertips nailing the twins in their throats before they recovered. As the guard in front of me whirled to act, I kicked up once, twice, first one connecting with his nuts, the second one with his chin as he hunched over. He toppled back.

On instinct, I spun like a top, a move called *sentai*—shielding my face with one hand, then firing off the opposite punch into the breastbone of a chunky guard behind me. I winced as volcanic cinder ground into my knee—but something crunched in his chest, and he fell.

I whirled back with another *sentai*, just as the front guard was recovering, lifting my arm just enough so that my wild punch hit his chin. His teeth clicked shut, a bit of blood splattered, and his head flopped back. As he sagged forward, I caught him with both hands.

My eyes went wide—I'd thrust my hands into the air a hundred times in this part of *untai*, but never actually caught anything but air. The form worked. Holy shit. The *form* had *worked*. Of course, I'd made a complete salsa of it, using its movements in the "wrong" order—the *natural* order for the situation I'd been in—that I was *still* in. Letting my breath out very slowly, I twisted to the side, letting the guard fall to the bloody gravel on my left, my body relaxing into an attack posture as I faced the twin who had held my left arm.

He was staggering up, hand at his throat, recovering. Then his eyes flicked behind me—and I threw both hands to the ground and shot one leg back up in an *ebigeri* "shrimp" kick. My foot slammed into the twin running up behind me, pain spiked my hands as they ground into the gravel—and I felt ribs break beneath my heel with an ugly *CRACK*.

I popped back up to find the other twin in front of me, his fist flying at my face. Without thought, I backflipped away from the punch, just like Paj had drilled us. My feet connected with his chin, I caught myself, turning the failed backflip into an awkward cartwheel—and whacked the recovering twin in the head, who flopped back to earth in a rattle of volcanic cinder.

I landed and whirled to face the remaining twin. He froze, blood streaming from his nose, his hands held up in a sloppy boxing posture. I crouched in the stance my instructors called *chudan*, my legs splayed low and wide, my bleeding hands held forward like blades.

He ran.

"What the hell!" Jewel cried, standing by the cauldron. Molokii was moving toward me, fists raised, but Jewel jumped forward, hit him on the shoulder, and gestured frantically. He jerked and ran off toward a cache of gear. "Are we not fireweavers? Stop her!"

I turned to follow him, but a blast of fire slammed into my back, winding me and nearly knocking me off my feet. I whirled to face this new attack, falling into a low stance called *jodan*, legs coiled like a spring, front fist forward, back hand shot back up behind me.

Zi and Yolanda faced me, poi whirling around them in shimmering arcs, creating magic bubbles of flames around them. On the left, Yolanda brought her poi together, creating a momentary impression of a flower; then the flower jetted forth a stream of flame.

Heat flashed against my face and I flinched back—but the magic-infused latex was as much a barrier to her magic as it was mine. The fire roiled off me, eerily repelled by the coating on my body, dissipating into colorful streamers of magic, like a kaleidoscope to my new eyes.

"Whoops," I said, as they hesitated. "Hadn't thought that through, had you?"

Then I moved in on them.

Bubbles of magic surged around me, like pulsing jellyfish made of flames, as Zi and Yolanda danced around me, trying to gain the advantage. Unfettered by spinning, I darted back and forth between them, aiming lancing kicks, forcing them back, moving them apart.

Then a third fireweaver attacked me from behind, a hoopspinner. Her waist ground in an undulation that would have done Jewel proud, and six fire sticks jutted out of her gyrating hula, creating expanding rings of flame that rippled out over me in buffeting waves.

But the latex barrier that still contained my magic also repelled theirs. The flames washed over me harmlessly, held back inches by an eerie repulsion. Now, here and there, I was getting stings and burns as movement wore the latex off, but I was protected enough to move in.

I jammed my body between two of her firesticks, stopping the spin, shoving my shoulder against her magic barrier. Darkening waves of mana churned before me as the shield weakened. The fireweaver tried to move back, but I lanced in and punched her jaw.

She bounced back off the inside of her field and fell into a triple punch—then just fell. I caught the hoop, let her collapse out of it, then turned back toward Zi and Yolanda, who were weaving back and forth, carefully getting into position, prepping a new attack.

Why hadn't they attacked me from behind while hula-girl had me distracted? Then I realized that while fireweaver magic was powerful, it wouldn't be easy to get two giant jellyfish of fire to fight together. The magic would interfere with each other—aha! *That's it!*

I tensed, squinted, analyzing their magic—then saw my opening.

"Catch!" I said, tossing the hoop high so it landed atop Yolanda's bubble of magic, rattling back and forth, the flames sparking off the field. The firespinner tried to maintain her shield, but the hoop sank into the magic, the poi intersected, and the field blew apart.

I cartwheeled in as Zi fell back, slipping one ankle into a hole in his shield. A fiery ball on a chain whipped around my ankle and jerked the poi handle out of his hands. I kicked the poi off desperately, looking up to see Zi stare at me in shock as his shield disintegrated.

His remaining poi hit him in the head, discharging all its mana at once, and Zi went down. I should have felt relief, but unexpectedly, I was gasping for breath. I firmed my stance and looked around, fearing another attack. Most of the fireweavers were down or running, but Jewel still stood guard over the cauldron, now with lit poi in her hands.

And one fireweaver had stayed, placing himself between her and me.

Molokii faced off with me, monkey's fist poi spinning. Briefly, he transferred them to one hand, not even missing a beat in the complex pattern he was spinning; made a quick gesture, then took the poi back in two hands. To an outsider, it looked like he was calling me out.

To someone who spoke sign language, it read, *time for the main event.*

58. TAKE THE RIB

In that brief moment, I took stock. Underneath the layer of goop on my skin, my new Dragon squirmed, singeing me with trapped power. Outside the circle of power, my original Dragon curved, trailing lazily across the sky like a distant comet, unnoticed except by me.

Before me within the circle, Molokii weaved within a *double* bubble of magic, whirling the biggest pair of knotted "monkey's fist" poi I'd ever seen, the blocky knotted wicks blazing with a full load of faux fire, burning white and, to my new eyes, just s*treaming* magic.

My eyes tightened. Molokii's shimmering barrier wasn't bubbles. His shield was two nested baskets woven from flames, swirling around each other constantly, like one of Cinnamon's mathematical diagrams brought to life in colored streamers of fire.

I shifted my shoulders, feeling the latex peeling away from my body in places. The fire and fight and volcanic cinder had left me a mess of bruises and burns and scrapes and blood, and my Dragon was moving, but not enough skin was exposed to let me reactivate my magic.

Or maybe it was the henna. When I tried krumping—flexing my stomach rhythmically to build up magic within my body, that trick that had served me so well—I instead felt electric shocks rippling over my body, followed by a hot cable burning across my belly.

Molokii smiled viciously, then began flicking his poi left, then right, fluidly, building up some new attack without ever losing his cross-weaving shield. But the patterns I could now see in his shield gave me an idea, and before he could deliver his blow, I ran.

Molokii laughed, a rough bark, but the laugh died when I retrieved the hoop and poi of the firespinners, guttering now but still afire. I threw the hoop down, then began whirling the two monkey-fist poi around me, focusing on the simplest spin possible—two parallel planes.

Molokii snorted, resuming his complicated weave, eyes on me as I moved to a weave of my own, wrists crossing over each other, poi arcing around me in a three-beat pattern—then I added another twist, making it a five-beat weave, the simplest possible beat that could sustain a magical pattern—the fireweaver's equivalent of the Dance of Five and Two. It was complex, far too complex for me to keep up for more than a minute before clocking myself in the head, but at the same time it was simple, far too simple to do any projective magic. Yet it had the right math to serve as the basis for a crude shield—as long as the right intent was behind it.

"*Spirit of flame,*" I murmured, "*shield my path.*"

A weak, guttering sphere shimmered into existence around me, a soap bubble compared to Molokii's huge web of flame. Molokii nodded, then idly flicked a wrist left, then right, one poi seeming to stop midair, the other looping around it, creating a focused blast of fire.

My shield wavered, nearly popped, at this slightest bit of Molokii's magic. He flipped his poi in and out, creating a whirlwind around him, the shimmering basket weave never losing its grip as the spinning vortex blasted volcanic cinder on me from all directions.

Then I threw my poi away—straight at the join of his baskets of fire.

The guttering balls of fire bounced off the weaving shield, getting drawn up into the sky by the churning of the weave, their chains flicking up and getting tangled not in Molokii's poi, but in the patterns they made. Molokii cursed, refocused, tried to reinforce his shield.

Then I shoved the hoop into the thicket of magic.

The hoop was sucked in and churned up in an eyeblink, its ring twisted into a pretzel, its firesticks spinning around crazily, their arcing creating just the right twist of mana to disrupt Molokii's shield. By itself, that wouldn't have been enough to destroy the pattern, but after throwing two whole fireweaver's sets of gear as impromptu monkey wrenches into Molokii's magic gear-works . . . the whole outer shell of the basket blew apart.

And then I ran in with a flying side kick.

This wasn't Taido, the martial art that I practiced now; this was *taekwondo*, the martial art I'd started with. Old reflexes kicked in when I ran forward, triggering a flash of memory of my college karate instructor, hearing his words, guiding my body into a devastating side kick.

I bounced off Molokii's still-solid inner shield and fell to the volcanic cinder.

Molokii stumbled back a step, but recovered, reinforcing his shield. He laughed as he saw me fall to the rough volcanic cinder, thinking I'd failed. But a Taido student is as comfortable on the ground as they are in the air, and I lanced back with a back-leg shrimp kick, buffeting him.

I'd known I wouldn't be able to break his inner shield with one kick—but now I was too close for him to build up another wicker fire barrier or volcanic blast, and I planned to stay there, using the latex they'd coated my body with to protect me until I found an opening.

At first, Molokii struggled to get his bearings as I danced around him using Taido's distinctive lancing, acrobatic footwork, *unsoku*. He had plenty of tricks in his playbook, but so did I—his waves of fire, I dodged under, and his whips of flame, I cartwheeled over.

But Molokii had the strength and speed to gather himself. He flicked one poi behind his head in a lazy figure eight, maintaining an umbrella-like shield while he drew the other poi's chain in, whirling fast around his fist, building up an ersatz boxing glove made of flame.

Then he began pummeling me with his blazing fist of fire.

Molokii was strong, and with his magic behind it, the blows threatened to knock me off my feet. My protective latex coating was disintegrating, my tat-toos were still shut down, and the burning pain began to wear at my will, making me stumble. Molokii grinned—and punched.

The flaming fist screamed at me, and faster than thought, I threw myself to the ground. No; I didn't *throw* myself; I did *foo-koo-tekky*, Taido's gymnastic defense, dodging with my body, rather than blocking with my fists. I arced to the side, body coiling like a spring, catching myself on two hands and one foot, the other leg cocked back as I faced Molokii's side, recalling Paj's words, echoes of advice Molokii never heard: *His form is sloppy. Never pass on free.*

I was beneath the edge of his shield. I saw the opening—and took his rib.

My leg popped out in a perfect *shaa-jo* side kick, slamming into his torso. I felt the bone snap, heard the crack, saw a silent cry pass his lips. But I was already moving, retracting the foot, shooting it under me and whip-coiling back upright just as he was canting over.

He staggered back, trying to recover his spinning rhythm, wincing as the movement required him to bend his side; and, in the open space between his flailing poi, I surged in, slamming both hands into his chest and hooking my forward foot behind his heel.

Molokii flew back, head cracking against a rock, his poi falling to the earth.

I stood upright and drew in a ragged breath; I was even more winded than before. Was it the altitude? Then I stepped up to Molokii's splayed form and kicked gravelly sand over his poi. The surging blue flames of Molokii's faux liquid fire fought against the volcanic cinder, sputtering, but in moments, the squarish burning wicks hissed and went out.

Then I turned to Jewel.

Jewel stood there before the cauldron, guarding it—a post from which she hadn't moved almost since the start of the fight. Her morningstars were aflame, whirling around her, creating a shield at once far lighter and far more subtle than any of her companions. There was no way I was going to breach that—I'd seen what she could do at Union Square.

But after what I'd done to her friends, why was she here, and not running? There was no profit in it—her spell was done. Or did she need to do something to complete it? Or . . . someone? Surely she didn't need *me* to complete it! Yolanda said the circuit activated as soon as they'd brought me into it. Jewel couldn't imagine she could force me into the casting point on her own, and even if she did, she couldn't imagine I would participate—

But then Jewel expanded her shield, slowly, a ring rippling out from around the first one, expanding around the cauldron. I tensed, preparing for an attack, but the ring slowed, stopped, intensified into a wall of flame, a *dome* of flame—protecting both Jewel and the cauldron.

The fire reverberated against the curves of the infinity lens. My new dragon tattoo squirmed on my body as the lower focus of the infinity lens glowed brighter in my liquid-fire-enhanced eyes, echoing the flames of Jewel's shield, becoming a true shield of its own.

From overhead, the lens must've looked like the eye of Horus—a circular inner shield making the pupil, with an oval lens around it, trailing off into a curved tail that snaked up the slope. I was trapped between the iris and the corner of the eye, in a patch of volcanic cinder.

Maybe she just meant to pin me until her friends regained her wits. But Jewel glanced aside, to my old Dragon curving through the sky, then set her feet a little more firmly, like she was bracing herself. What had she said? Pele didn't need their help to hatch?

Maybe she didn't need my help to cast another spell; maybe she just needed to keep me in the lens until the hatching began. Because the first spell had *already* started, and she wasn't trying to corral me. She was just protecting the cauldron—had been, from the start of the fight.

Maybe, just maybe, all she had to do was keep me from overturning that cauldron.

"Don't make this difficult, Dakota," she said. My mouth opened. I couldn't believe she was doing this. I stepped up to her, but she intensified her inner bubble, raising her hand. "Stay back," she said. "I mean it, Dakota! This will all be over soon. Till then, stay back—"

"I loved you," I said, staring at her. "I won't hurt you."

"Well, good," she said, a bit rattled. "The spell's activating, I don't know how—"

"I do," I said, very quietly.

"—but the lens is *charging.* We planned to catch it on hatching, but before that, it must embody." She cocked her head at the Dragon in the sky. "Daniel wins after all. The spirit of the dragon will tangle itself up in the control charm as it tries to reach the egg—"

"Killing her," I said. "I won't let you do that."

"You can't stop it," she said.

"It won't work, you know," I said, stepping closer. "This is not what you think—"

"That's bull. You told me how you lied your way out of that mess with Cinnamon—"

"The girl who cried wolf, eh?" I said. My new Dragon squirmed on my skin, now almost burning me with surges of magic, making me almost forget the stings and pains from my recent fight. "Then we're at an impasse, because no matter what you think, *the spell won't work.*"

"Let's wait," Jewel said, "and see."

The poi whirled around her in a vicious arc. The burning wicks passed near my face, the sound like oncoming traffic, the heat like flooding waves. Light flared sinister against her face, and I stared into that smile, that vicious smile, wondering how I had come again to this point.

Jewel was just like Savannah. I'd fallen for her, I'd thought I loved her. And maybe she'd loved me. But in the end, Savannah had been more interested in her little project than what it had done to my heart. And Jewel? Like Savannah, on steroids. How had I loved her? Yet I still did.

"Jewel," I said, my eyes flickering upward. For all her crazy villain talk, she'd still defended me against the fireweavers—at first against physical violence, and then later when Yolanda threatened to sacrifice me. Maybe . . . "I thought we really had something."

"We," she began, and our eyes met. Her smile cracked a little. "We really did."

I stared at her in sadness and pain. "Then how did we go so wrong? I loved you, Jewel. I'm not going to hurt you. I'm not even going to fight you. But I'm going to the top of that mountain, and I'm going to stop this spell—and *you will have to kill me to stop me.*"

And I stepped right up to the flaming wall of her magic, feeling its heat, hearing its rush. Somehow, I had to break down her determination, break down her defensive spell. I don't really know what I intended to do—step into the flames? Disrupt its magic? Use harsh language?

At that moment, all I knew is that I wanted her to see my face—and see how I hurt.

Jewel met my gaze defiantly. Then her façade cracked, admitting a twinge of sadness. My own lip trembled as Jewel's poi sizzled past my head. Jewel's smile faded into pain. Then her poi slowed. Then they stalled. Then she let them drop into the cinder.

"Oh, God," Jewel said, falling to her knees beside her poi. "Oh, Dakota, I'm so sorry."

I closed my eyes. It was all over but the shouting. I reached out, tousled her hair briefly; she smiled up at me, then dropped her eyes once she saw what was in my face. I kicked volcanic cinder atop her poi, and she cried out, realizing it was too late to back out now.

"Oh, God," she said. "What have I done?"

"The right thing, for a change," I said. "Now help me save Pele."

59. The Ouroboros and the Cauldron

"*Save* her?" Jewel said. Her eyes jerked aside to her extinguished poi. "I—I won't fight you, Dakota," she said, shifting her weight, maybe thinking she could nab the poi of one of her fallen fireweavers. "But you can't save her. You're—you're going to have to kill her—"

"I am not going to kill her," I said, reaching down and seizing Jewel by the shoulders. She tried to shrug me off, then began hitting me, uselessly. "Stop it! If you go for those poi, I swear, Jewel, I will kick your ass."

"What did you say," Jewel said, striking me again, "about not fighting me—"

"What did you say," I said, trying to hold her still, "about me lying—"

Jewel smacked at me, uselessly, then landed a good one on my chin.

"Not bad," I said, leaning back, feeling my jaw. "Twist your fist a bit more—"

"Damn it!" Jewel said, fists shaking in rage. "Don't taunt me—"

"Don't tempt me," I said, seizing both of her wrists and holding them firmly. I glared into those eyes, those eyes that I'd loved, and she stared back at me defiantly. "I've got a dragon about to die in the hatching. *How do I save her?*"

"You can't," she said. "You mustn't! If it hatches free, it'll cause an *extinction*—"

"*It* will cause?" I said. "You mean *she* will go on a rampage? Why, Jewel?

She's not an animal. She's a sentient creature! Where can she go? What can she eat? She's a creature of lava and fire, Jewel! There's no place on Earth fit for humans that is a proper environment for her!"

"You don't know that," Jewel said, glancing over her shoulder. "You can't risk it—"

But I wasn't listening to her anymore. I stared after what she'd stared after—the cauldron. She was still thinking that the spell could work, without me in the circuit, without liquid fire. I thought it through carefully, then redirected my attention to her.

"Turn around," I said sharply. She stared at me blankly, and I poked her. "Now!"

Jewel turned around, and I knelt and searched her. She laughed, halfheartedly, then shut up as I made her put her hands on her head. I felt her familiar body under my hands, cursing the context. I spun her around, then searched around me, kicking the fallen morningstars away.

"Find what you were looking for?" she asked, hands still on her head.

"Yes," I said, patting her down once more. "This was just a precaution, but even when I searched you, you still looked at the cauldron. You claimed you had no liquid fire, that you needed me to make the spell work—yet you still expect something to happen. What?"

"Go fuck yourself," she said bitterly.

"Jewel! You expect something to happen. The same thing *Daniel* expected to happen. If the egg explodes, there's no way you could harvest liquid fire out of that—it would be burned up, buried underground, lost forever." I shook her. "How is this supposed to work?"

"Might makes right was bad for me," she said. "But apparently good for you—"

"Jewel! I am not the one trying to enslave a dragon! What will happen?"

She tensed, hands still on her head. "If you're so smart—"

I spun her around and put my face into hers.

"You're right, Jewel. Pele *is* ready to be born," I said. "But I didn't guess that because I watched my old tattoo flying around. *I can feel that from her.* I have been living with her in my head, on *my back* for the last eight months—"

"Buh," Jewel said, eyes widening. She glanced aside at my flying dragon tattoo, curving less lazily, picking up speed as it approached the crater. "Not *that* tattoo—but the one *on you?* I guessed, the first time I saw it manifest, suspected it even on the plane—but *how?*"

I grimaced, partly from the memory of the accident, and partly from the knowledge I now had of Jewel's skill at deception. Her reactions looked so convincing—but even as surprise had spread across her face, the words she'd spoken meant she'd really known it all along.

"I activated it before it was complete," I said. "Four segments, connected to my body, using myself as the core element—an open magical circuit. Damn near tore me to pieces when Pele's spirit embodied it, and dumb old me thought it was a magical back reaction—"

"No wonder the Noose activated—it *is* true." Jewel's mouth opened, her eyes fixed on my skin. Her hand lifted off her head, as if she was going to reach out to touch, but I put my hand back atop hers and pressed it down. "Damn it,

Dakota, it's a dragon's spirit. Let me touch—"

"*No,*" I said. "I lived with her on my back—in my head—for almost nine months. That makes her my spiritual child—and *you* were going to enslave her. I'd die to protect Cinnamon, and I'd most definitely die to protect Pele. So do not fuck with me. *What is going to happen?*"

She glared at me hotly.

"All right," I said. "You want me to Sherlock this. All right. *Fine.* I'll do it."

I straightened up. I stared over her shoulder at the cauldron. Then I cocked my fist and pointed it at her face. She flinched, hands jerking out of my grasp to protect her face, but I gathered them with my free hand and put them back atop her head, pinning them there.

"Everyone's the same," I said, staring at the cauldron, holding her hands beneath mine. "I wanted beauty, and love, and sex, and I fell for you. You want the same thing, so you indulged it, but that was never your real goal. You just want . . . I don't know. To spin fire."

She tensed under my hand, and I realized I'd gotten it. "That's it, isn't it? It's not just that everyone's the same—*we're* the same. Forget world domination. You're just like me—you just want to practice your art. You want to spin fire—and you need fuel like I need ink."

Jewel clenched her jaw.

"We *are* just the same," I said. "You never cared about a telescope on a mountaintop or being a priestess of a cult or even about the promise of immortality. You just wanted a source of liquid fire . . . but you didn't want to hurt a living creature just to practice an art."

"It's just an art," Jewel said. "Dragons are rare and beautiful creatures—and the target of my obsessions, and the mystical totems of my order, and, maybe, just maybe, the embodiments of the gods of my people. I'd *never* kill a dragon to spin fire, not if I could avoid it—"

"But seizing a dragon is a dangerous proposition," I said, cocking my head. "People have tried enslaving drakes, but no one's succeeded with a *real* dragon in recorded history, or we'd know from the devastation left not just in the historical but the geological record."

"Right," Jewel said quietly. "But I wouldn't risk destroying the world just to spin."

"So this . . . this is new," I said. "Some dangerous permutation of the old magics that no one's ever been crazy enough to try. Even you . . . you might be willing to *try* the spell, but you had to have a fallback plan. You even *said* you had a fallback plan. Daniel's plan."

I stared at the six torches, then at the lines beneath them. A six pointed star. The Star of David? No. An alchemist's symbol? One of the triangle bore symbols of fire. The other of water. Symbols of earth and air were woven into two rings. That was the symbol for . . .

"The Philosopher's Stone," I said, and Jewel sagged under my hand. "The symbols of this setup are those of the Philosopher's Stone. I read Harry Potter, I know that's not just for transmutation, but that it's the legendary key to immortality. But liquid fire is the *real* key—"

"Like you said," Jewel said quietly, "this is a very old spell."

I shut up.

"Liquid fire is the key to immortality," she said. "Not that I care. Everyone dies. But harvesting it from a real dragon isn't practical—and not just because the dragon might object. It's because the flames themselves may consume the fire before it's harvested.

"There are two parts to the Dragon's Net," Jewel said. "The ouroboros, and the cauldron. The ouroboros—the snake eating its tail, originally, the dragon eating its tail. The ring of torches atop the mountain will trap the spirit of the dragon, catch it in a loop.

"I thought we could use that to take control of the dragon. The so-called Dragon's Noose. It works on drakes, after all. But if you don't let it hatch—if you prevent it from incarnating, force the spirit to circle endlessly in the Net, it builds up mana until the egg *explodes*."

"If the detonation was great enough, it would evacuate the air," I said. "Kill any flames before they started. Hopefully, leaving enough liquid fire to be harvested from the crater—but there's no way you could count on that. No way to be sure it wouldn't burn off or boil off—"

"Or simply drain away," Jewel said. "Either way, it creates a huge blast of mana—a blast that kills the dragon, but feeds back along the threads of the infinity lens. Mana that transmutes the matter in the cauldron, leaving the Elixir of Cintamani, a form of liquid fire."

"Whether she lives or dies, you get your liquid fire," I said bitterly. "You can't lose."

"I already think I have," she said, staring at my fist. "You're going to try to free her, aren't you? You'll fail, and wreck the spell—or succeed, and wreck the world. Either way, the liquid fire will be *wasted*. You're a bigger fool than I thought you were, Dakota—"

"Than you *thought* I was?" I stared down at her sadly. "The loser here, clearly, is me."

She hissed. "I didn't mean that—"

"Yes you did, and yes I did. I've already lost you," I said. "Now I'm about to lose the dragon too. Ordinarily, I'd be on your side here, protecting the world, but I feel more kinship than that. I'm more than just the herald, aren't I. I've got the spirit of this thing living on my skin—"

"Maybe," Jewel said hesitantly. "You're resonant with it, sure, but no one can tell. Hatchings don't happen often enough for us to know for sure. You have a second copy of the dragon spirit flying around you. For all we know, that's it. I don't really know—"

"You don't really know, yet dragged me out here as your fallback plan. You really want to play that game?" I asked, raising an eyebrow. She just glared up at me, jutting her lip. "Jewel, do you know what you call me when you think I'm not looking?"

She looked at me, baffled, and I pinched the back of one hand, flipped the hand over and waggled two fingers over it, and then held both hands parallel. Her eyes went wide as I said, "Skin-dance-agent. Skindancer."

"You can read sign language," she said, eyes wide. "How—"

"Of *course* I know ASL! *My mother was deaf!*" I said, and Jewel flinched. "I should have seen it. You never asked about me, my family, my history—never even gave me a chance to sign to Molokii, just insulated him away from me in your private little bubble where you thought you could talk about me without overhearing. You assumed I was a mark from the beginning!"

Jewel's eyes were still wide. "What . . . what did you overhear?"

"Nothing much," I said. "You were too good for that. But you know what Molokii called me, always, since he never realized I could understand him?" I raised my right hand, thumb to my chin, then let both hands out, wriggling like flame as I mimed blowing. "*Mother of the dragon.*"

Jewel's eyes widened further. She shook her head.

"No," she said. "He meant . . . he meant your tattoo—"

I shook my head, cupping an eye and touching my hand, then running my fingers over my arms before making the flame motion again—*art-body-dragon.* "That's *dragon tattoo*," I said, then twirled my hands in the sign for *wear.* "And this would be *dragon wearer*—"

"Damn it!" Jewel said, shying away from me.

"But the real key is, you're upset," I said, reaching out again, planting her hands back on her head. "You knew it from the beginning, but hid it. It's important knowledge. Knowing I'm the bearer means something. I can do something with that knowledge to stop this."

I stared up at the hillside, at the ring of torches at the limit of my vision.

"And I know *exactly* what to do. Sorry, Jewel," I said—and punched her in the face.

"Ow!" she said, head bouncing back, holding her nose. "What was that for?"

"I'm sorry," I said, holding up my hand. "I was trying to knock you out—"

"Well, thath didn't do it," she said, raising her other hand. "Shit, nothe bleeding—"

"Sorry!" I said, making a fist. "I don't have a lot of practice knocking people out—"

"Wellth, don'th do it agianth," she said, raising her hand to fend me off. "Jerthk—"

"I am sorry," I said, seizing her shoulder, spinning her about and rolling her into my arms in a headlock. She reached for my hands, but I was already applying a sleeper hold—and *that* was something I could do reliably. "I am so sorry, but I can't trust you not to try to stop me."

Jewel's hands gripped at my fist, then sagged. She was faking, of course, but I just shifted my grip. In seconds, her whole body went slack in my hands, and I lowered her to the ground. Grimacing, I pinched her nipple, hard, and when she didn't cry out, I knew she was out.

"Sleep tight, Jewel," I said. "It will all be over in a minute."

—&

Then I stepped over her, through the line of torches . . . and climbed toward the crater.

60. THE SACRIFICE

Rough volcanic cinder crumbled away beneath the shoes I'd stolen from Yolanda. At the base of the slope, the friable rock had sifted down to a rough red gravel that, during the fight, had scraped my soles and palms raw and left my knees bleeding. Now, at least, I could walk.

But as I climbed the rumbling slopes of Pu'u o Maui, following the line of torches of the infinity lens toward the smoking summit, I no longer faced volcanic gravel. Stones the size of my fist tumbled past—sharp, ruddy Swiss-cheese fragments, rattling down into the dark.

The more I climbed, the more winded I became—it was *definitely* the altitude. I'd felt a touch of it back at Iloa's, but this was higher, and colder, and now that I'd peeled off as much of the latex as I quickly could, the thin air was chilling my skin as well as starving my lungs.

But I couldn't stop. I was driven on by the desire to stop Jewel and to save Pele. To save this thing on my back—at least, if I was right about what was on my back, and Arcturus wasn't right that it was feeding my intentions back onto themselves until I'd driven myself insane.

I stumbled. "Fuck," I said, wincing as a rock ground into my already wounded hand. I raised my head to see a spray of what looked like eagle feathers around one of the torch totems. Palm leaves were woven into it, and herbs I didn't know wound round it twice, like a caduceus.

I got to my feet, glaring at the beaded threads and ribbons that connected the torches of the infinity lens like an endless velvet rope. I tested the threads. I was tempted to cut them, but I knew too much mana was flowing. The magic could leap through the air to close the circuit.

Halfway up, the spiral of torches now far below me looked small and non-threatening, as innocent-looking as an aerial shot of a luau. The torches above me looked like a ring of lights around an event. Even if some park ranger saw this driving by, or someone spotted this from the air, by the time anyone realized what this string of torches was, it would be far too late.

My skin was burning now, my body twitching every time my Dragon tattoo tried to come to life. It was still bound by the tattered latex, but tearing at it, still inhibited by the henna, but short circuiting it, its tattooed claws seeming to cut me as it struggled. It was stronger than I.

Arcturus was wrong—I *had* caught something in the four elements of my Dragon, some quintessence of the Dragon's spirit, growing ever since that fateful day when I faced down the vamps and activated the pieces of my tattoo before it was completely assembled.

Something tickled the back of my neck. From some unseen source, I felt renewed strength. I climbed on, letting rock fall away behind me, making better time as the slope evened out. As I neared the summit, I saw out of the corner of my eye an old familiar friend.

My original Dragon flew through the air beside me, grown vaporous and huge, stretching its mana thin in favor of size. Vast and sinuous, it played up its Chinese roots now more than its Western heritage, snaking around the top of the crater in an ever-growing circle.

My new Dragon half-tore her way out of the latex on my back as I crested the ridge, writhing and screaming. I could feel her claws raking me, feel burns where mana she tried to release was short-circuited by the henna. Then I spasmed in pain, nearly losing my footing.

On my belly, a peeling patch of latex started to smoke, and I doubled over, beating it out, scraping more of the dried sticky goo off me, keeping my fingers raking despite the pain until the line of henna paste was scraped off in my fingernails. The henna had left a stain on my skin, but it didn't conduct as well as real tattoo pigment, and the magical circuit was broken.

I must hatch. Let me free! I must hatch. Let me fly!

My new Dragon struggled to tear her wings loose, struggling to get free, struggling to get to the egg—struggling to trap herself. The line of torches was adorned with feathers and leaves and sigils of gold, so inviting to the spirit—but on the ground beneath it was something sinister.

It was hard to see the whole design, but I could guess the black sooted lines of runes stretching out over the summit were a pentagram. The infinity lens's final ring of torches arced just inside its inner pentagon, with more runic circles inside and outside it.

My new Dragon flapped her wings, desperate to free herself, and I saw how the hatching would have worked if the fireweavers hadn't interfered. Sooner or later, the spirit trapped in my Dragon would have grown strong enough to fly free, coming here to land in the egg.

But this structure was an attractive nuisance, a magical trap, luring the dragon's spirit out before it was ready, trapping it before it could hatch. I considered destroying the torches, but the pattern was too huge. I could work for hours and not make a dent, and I had just minutes.

I staggered forward, wondering if I could make it to my destination before the Dragon tore herself free, but the closer I got, the more frantic she became, desperate to free herself, desperate to merge with the projected emanations of the egg.

I had to get her *inside* that circle, directly atop the egg. If I let her free before then, she'd be swept up into the infinity lens, become twisted into an ouroboros, and build up mana until the egg blew apart and tore her spirit to pieces.

But the circle had absorbed the egg's emanations and amplified them, causing a superstimulus response like the human response to sugar or a cat's response to catnip—if I crossed the line, the Dragon would try to free herself. She would have to.

Trying to save her would make her kill herself.

Then my old Dragon snaked down out of the sky, cutting me off. I glimpsed a glowing eye as it rippled past, then it picked up more speed as it slid toward the line of torches. Was I wrong? Was this the real spirit of the Dragon? No—but the infinity lens still caught it.

The old Dragon screamed as the magic whipped it round, faster and faster, forcing the tattoo *projectia* to bite its own tail. The smell of burning skin burnt my nose, but the lens was not powering up—because this was not the real spirit of the dragon.

Where a real dragon's spirit was a generator, turning matter into magic, building power up almost forever, my original dragon tattoo had a finite amount of liquid fire from the original ink . . . and the infinity lens was draining that dry, tearing the tattoo to pieces.

But as the lens flickered and the tattoo twisted, my new Dragon relaxed on my back. The old Dragon was close enough—it could fill the real spirit's role in the circuit, freeing the spirit from its pull, if only for a moment. My old tattoo was sacrificing itself for my new one.

I imagined my old Dragon saying "go" but it didn't—it just screamed. I felt the wings of the new Dragon merge with my back, felt her settle, then I ran. My knee pounded, my stomach burned, my whole body was on fire, but before I knew it, I was through the barrier.

Magic assaulted me, a thousand blinding pinpricks, like I'd run through the hot, sparking column of smoke of a burning campfire. I fell forward on my face and hands with a rough cry, yelping further as rough cinder tore up the insides of my arms.

I struggled to stand as I slid down into the pit, coughing as actual hot smoke filled my lungs. That's right—Pu'u o Maui was one of the volcanic vents that had reawakened with the stirrings of the dragon's spirit, and hot gas and ash steamed out of the caldera below.

Coughing, slipping, bleeding, I slid down toward the rising smoke and fire on a small avalanche of red crackling gravel. Unable to stop myself, I flopped onto the cascading rock, crying out as sharp edges stabbed at my belly, throwing my arms wide despite the scrapes and pain. Slowly, I slid to a halt, bloody and in agony, just yards from the hot center of the crater, mercilessly pummeled by rocks the size of oranges still tumbling down around me.

I raised my face and winced. Heat was rising in shimmering waves, hot miasma rising off a red glowing circle in the crater's floor. In terror, I scrambled back, thinking it was lava—but the circle had a slight bulge, and as it brightened from red to gold, I realized what it was.

It was the top of the dragon's egg.

Red cinder rocks tumbled away from the dome as it slowly rose. The glowing bulge was so gently sloped that the whole egg must have been *unimaginably* huge, but still, the dome rose, near pure gold now, veined with dark red, shoving the surface of the crater away.

Mana streamed off the egg in a slow-motion aurora. With my new eyes, I could pick out individual streamers of power, roiling with the most intense colors of magic I'd ever seen. The Dragon on my back surged and swelled to life, seeming to bulge outward, like a backpack.

Heat stung my face. I struggled to get to my feet as the new dragon tattoo tore free from my back, half manifested, half pinned by henna and latex. Magic limbs and coiling tails flopped around me, and I kicked and stumbled, frantic. I had to stay in the caldera to let the spirit of the dragon incarnate, but I had to get away from that red-hot egg, or I'd be burned alive—

A massive glowing claw slammed down on my arm.

I crouched there, arm pinned in agony against the hot rock, as my new Dragon unpeeled herself from my back by magic. What had been writ upon two square meters of skin now reared ten meters into the air on a flood of mana, trumpeting her new life in a ghostly cry.

—ↄ

Then the Dragon leaned her head forward and was sucked into the egg without a sound.

61. A Fearful Sound

I huddled there for a moment, drawing in my arms, watching mana shimmer into the egg, seeing my own tattoo merge with the red-cracked gold surface until it all but disappeared. Was it gone forever, or would my tattoo always exist as a mark on Pele's spirit?

Then I thought of Krakatoa. Of all the people who had died because wizards interfered with a dragon hatching—and the egg had exploded. Who knew what all this muddle of magic—firecap ink, a dragon tattoo, the Dragon's Noose—had done to the dragon's spirit?

I put my burnt, shaking hands together and prayed. Prayed the egg would not explode, prayed the dragon would hatch safely, prayed if the dragon did hatch, it wouldn't turn on the human race. Prayed that no one would die, and that everything would be all right.

The ground shook. The egg shuddered. Light began pouring out of its golden, domed surface, dark only at those strange red cracks which seemed to suck in the light. Then the rounded surface of the egg heaved upward, discharging a spray of cinder around me.

A sound like a crack of thunder—or a cracking egg—ripped the air.

I stood, turned, and ran. Ran up the slope. Scrambled up the gravel. Grappled with the rock as I fell and crawled and scrambled and ran again, coconut-sized cinders tumbling around me, parts of the hillside sliding so fast it seemed like I was running in place.

The egg shuddered again, throwing a wave of rock up the slope toward me. Somehow, I kept my feet under me and the sliding rock under my feet and kept running, finding sure footing at last, pounding to the top of the slope in an agony of pain and burns and blood.

Before me, the ouroboros of my old Dragon whirled in a maelstrom of tattoo magic, spinning so fast the torches no longer burned with chemical flames, but were rainbow sparklers of purely magical fire. The shield shimmered before me, a wall of magic waters.

It had burned me, but I'd gone through it before. I didn't stop now.

The magical maelstrom caught me and spun me about, spinning me round and round, but my momentum kept me going, tumbling me out of the circle, throwing me sprawling onto my back as the chasm behind me erupted in a blast of magical flame.

On some level, at the back of my mind, I expected to see the head of Pele rise from the crater, to see a fiery creature rise from the pit like a wyrmic phoenix. But what flew up from the crater made more sense: fragments of egg, glowing white hot, on a shell of burning yolk.

The yolk splashed against the inside of the magic barrier, infusing the infinity lens with a titanic amount of living mana. The egg fragments flew on, sailing out across the valley, lighting the whole of Haleakala crater end to end with golden fragments of the sun.

A blast of mana swept over me as the infinity lens charged with magic, overloaded, and then discharged itself onto the waiting cauldron far below with a crack of thunder. Smacked down to the earth again, I lay there, gasping, as liquid fire fell down around me like rain.

Wherever droplets landed, puffs of magic burst forth, and more than magic. Roses and jewels and butterflies blazed into existence and disappeared into whiffs of flame. There was too much mana for anything to take hold, but I could see how dragons had sparked life on the Earth.

Droplets splashed around me, hot as sparks, but did not burn me. They touched my skin, warm as coals, but did not burn me. They fell into my lips, fiery as chili peppers, but did not burn me. The hot liquid fell down my throat like liquid honey, quenching a thirst I never knew I had.

I lay my head back against the rock, content.

"I always did have an affinity for fire," I murmured.

I don't know how long I lay there, dazed, as life was created and destroyed around me in a rain of magic flame. At last, the fall of liquid fire ceased, and still I lay there, smiling, breathing in a delicious smell half between wet grass in the rain and the ozone tang of lightning.

But then I heard another slow intake of breath, and raised my head.

My original Dragon perched on the edge of the crater, fully materialized, solid as the rock that it sat on. It was something entirely new—not a *projectia*, not a drake, not even a real Hadean Dragon. This was a dragon of human legend, brought to life by an immense blast of mana.

It drew in a breath, and I tensed, wondering whether it planned to roast me—or merge.

"*Soon Pele will fly,*" my Dragon said. "*And you must flee.*"

My eyes bugged. I got to my feet. And if I'd thought I'd run before, I flew now. I skipped down the hill, running, tumbling, slipping, falling. More than once, I fell on my face. More than once, I bloodied myself in pain. Not once did I stop. I just scrambled on.

I'd read the stories of Krakatoa. I knew what was coming.

The fireweavers were recovering as I barreled down the hill toward them. Even from a distance, I could see the cauldron glowing with a blaze of golden light—apparently, the spell had worked. I didn't know whether to cheer or curse; I just ran down into the circle.

The spell had worked, but the fireweavers were still a mess. Someone was helping Molokii to his feet, Zi was helping Yolanda, and the twins were sitting with Jewel, who was holding her nose and head gingerly, a bit dizzily. She saw me and jerked back in shock.

"Dakota!" she said, confused and appalled. "My God. What happened up there?"

"Get in the cars," I shouted. "Get in the cars and drive! Now now *now!*"

"Frost," Zi snarled. "You'll pay for . . . for . . . what's happened?"

"Pele's not dead. She's hatched, and *rising,*" I said, running past them, scooping up Jewel and running toward the knot of cars. Fireweavers began falling in around me and we ran down to their trucks, a Range Rover and Jeep Cherokee. "Get in the cars and drive! Now now now!"

"Damn it, help us!" Yolanda said, struggling with the cauldron.

I looked back, thought about it for half a second. It would serve them all right, to lose their lives because they were so concerned with that liquid fire. But that fire was life, centuries and centuries more life for people like the Grinder or the Warlock. It was worth the risk.

I dropped Jewel by the Range Rover. "Open the trunk!" I shouted, not waiting for her response, running full tilt back toward the cauldron. I seized one handle, Zi seized the other, and we lifted, and screamed, hot metal burning our hands as we ran, but we kept running, the hot liquid splashing us until we sloshed the cauldron into the back of the Rover, already packed with passengers shocked and astounded at what we'd shoved in the trunk. "Jewel! *Drive!*"

I slammed the gate, and the Range Rover started off, splashing the glowing fluid around the inside of the car. Briefly, I wondered whether it would seep down and set the car on fire, but I had no time for that. I ran over to the Jeep Cherokee and practically leapt in the open door.

It squealed off. Zi was driving, Molokii was half-unconscious in the passenger seat, and two more fireweavers were crammed in next to me. Everyone was tense, breathless, and scared as the hillside shook beneath us . . . then seemed to slide out beneath us as the earth moved.

Zi barely kept the car upright, following the glowing taillights of the Range Rover and the unearthly light streaming from its back window. Then light from behind us reflected off that window, and I turned to look back behind me.

Pu'u o Maui was rapidly becoming not a cinder cone, but a glowing crater, explosion after explosion hurling concentric rings of rock away as golden liquid bubbled and boiled out. Cracks appeared in the earth around it, spreading over the floor of Haleakala caldera.

"How big is that egg," I yelled. "How big is it—"

No need to ask, though. I found out straightaway.

All of Pu'u o Maui, five hundred feet high and two thousand feet across, crumbled apart and fell into the glowing, spreading crater. From it, a terrific cloud erupted, billowing out like an oncoming sandstorm, alternating between churning moonlit black and burning red.

"That's a pyroclastic flow!" I screamed. "Get to high ground! Get to high ground!"

"We're getting! We're getting!" Zi screamed back.

The cinder storm swept past us, rattling the car windows, plunging us into darkness, then into fearful swirls of cinders and flame. Hot gas poured out of the vents and Yolanda whacked the A/C off. The rattle of gravel below was drowned out by staccato drumming on the roof.

A titanic fragment of debris screamed over us and impacted the hillside. Cinder sprayed out and the jeeps swerved out into the rough hills. Rocks tumbled around the vehicles as they bounced over the rutted hills and we passengers bounced around inside the cabin.

Somehow we found the road, a zigzagging asphalt path climbing up the inside of the crater, but it didn't help. As the cloud roiled up around us, alternately white and roaring, then black and rattling, the road was soon inundated with rocky debris.

Driving blind, Zi struggled to keep it on the road, fishtailing in a cloud of dust that mixed with the clouds so it seemed like the car was swimming through gravel. Light blazed around us, the cloud went dark again—and the headlights of the Range Rover loomed out of the fog.

The Cherokee impacted the Range Rover, throwing us all forward in a blur of bumps and screams. Golden fluid splashed over the inside of the Range Rover, now canted forty-five degrees away from us, and Jewel staggered out of the driver door into the wind.

"Everyone out," I said, kicking the door open, dragging the closest fireweavers with me out of the car, then reaching in and pulling out my stunned companion in the back seat. "Everyone out, and get everyone out of the Range Rover! The gas tanks may blow!"

Zi stumbled out of the car and ran toward the passenger door of the Range Rover. Then I lost him in the roiling clouds. I ran to the passenger door of the Cherokee, pulled out Yolanda, then helped her over to the roadside, where the other fireweavers were climbing atop a rock.

Half-blind, I ran up to Jewel. She was coughing and spitting, eyes squeezed shut against the stinging wind. I seized her and pulled her to me and drew her up onto the rock above the road, holding her tight, as the rattling wind covered us with hot spattering mud.

An enormous thud pummeled my ears.

I drew a breath, then coughed as I inhaled volcanic crap. I tried to breathe through my hand, but a wave of crushing pressure tried to force the air back down my lungs. A second enormous thud rippled across the valley, crackling into the distance like thunder.

Another thudding. A fresh hot wind blasted us on its heels, a renewed sandblasting of razor-sharp particles on near-burning wind. The dented cars creaked and shimmied in the new breeze, and I squeezed Jewel tight, shielding her face from the worst of the gale.

A dark shape crossed the sliver of moon. I looked up. Could it be Pele taking to flight?

But the dark shape whipping overhead was not an entire dragon. It was *just her wing*, sweeping across the heavens, brushing the clouds aside like dust bunnies chased by a leaf blower. Another stupendous downstroke, and for a moment, the whole crater valley was clear.

From Haleakala Crater rose the craggy head of the Dragon Pele, a red and gold crag of rock and metal easily as large as the cinder cone destroyed by her birth. Her snaking neck twisted up with her, followed by the massive body whose throes of rising had destroyed the crater floor. Curved black wings, ridged and rippled like black plains of lava, whipped down around her as the neck craned up and that massive head screamed its birth cry.

It was a fearful sound. It began as a pebble-rattling vibration in the ground, rose into a deep resonance in my gut, then hit audible as her enormous maw opened to the sky. It was the cry of Godzilla, of T-Rex, of a hurricane, rising from the deepness into a trumpeting high-pitched exhilaration that rang my ears as Pele released an absolutely *titanic* gout of flame into the sky.

I flinched from the fire. My eyes watered in its light. My face stung with its heat. The column of dragonfire climbed into the heavens, crackling with thunder, sparking with lightning, illuminating the whole of Haleakala Crater and the breadth of the Pacific as bright as noonday.

As the roiling blast of flame curled into the sky on wings of thunder, the shaggy head inclined downward slightly, a glowing eye seeming to stare straight at us as the two black dragon wings whirled back up into the air at what must have been close to the speed of sound.

Lightning crackled beneath those wings as they cut through the air. My hair stood on end, and green foxfire rippled over the cars as electrical discharge surged out over the landscape. I flinched, but no explosion came—then I gasped, staring up into the sky.

Pele had spread both of her wings wide, an enormous V reaching to the heavens. The inside was not rippled black stoneflesh, but a spectacular rainbow patterns, fractal and wonderful, that simultaneously recalled and shamed every butterfly I had ever seen.

Pele leapt into the sky, wings still spread, forelegs relaxed, hind legs thrusting in titanic earthquake jolts, a snaky tail uncoiling behind her gracefully as she sailed far up into the sky, a white-hot fluid trailing after her, droplets of dragon yolk spattering out over the devastation.

Then the downstroke of those beautiful butterfly wings came, smacking us to the ground with a hurricane force of wind and mana. My ears were squeezed, then popped. My tattoos flared, then went dark. Then Pele flew up into the night.

I stared up after that unbelievable creature, watching her wings beat, trailing twin spirals of magical color behind her as she ascended out of the atmosphere. Jewel had fallen with me, her head on my stomach, and gasped suddenly as Pele trumpeted one last triumph of fire.

Then Pele disappeared into the stars.

62. AFTERMATH

We all stood there, dumbfounded, before the awesome devastation of Haleakala Crater. What had been a vast, sloping valley dotted by cinder cones was now a giant chasm of fire and lava, collapsing in on itself, as roiling black smoke climbed up into the sky.

The collapse stopped just short of our wrecked cars. Not fifty feet behind where the Range Rover had spun about and the Jeep Cherokee had rammed it, the road simply dropped away, its asphalt jutting into the air over the edge of the chasm.

I shuddered. Had the accident happened seconds earlier, the giant sinkhole would have swallowed us whole. Even so . . . we barely survived. The cars were jackknifed together, gasoline seeping from the Cherokee's tank and liquid fire seeping from the Rover's trunk.

Abruptly, the Jeep Cherokee caught fire. We all watched as fire wreathed it, as the gas tank squibbed out in a half-hearted explosion, and then as the Jeep rolled backward toward the ledge, tipped back, slid off . . . and anticlimactically stopped five feet down, lights still on.

Cautiously, I hopped down and limped over to the Range Rover, which was half-impaled on a rock, going nowhere. The danger of electrical fire was over, the gas tank looked sound . . . but the back cargo area glowed . . . where something had splashed out all over it.

I cautiously limped closer. I wasn't just shuddering now—I was shivering, my whole body erupting in aches and pains as the adrenaline left me, and my brain started to feel that perhaps we were safe. I wanted to go lie down . . . but not as much as I wanted to see that glowing liquid.

"Is . . . did it?" Yolanda asked, hobbling up next to me as I peered in. She looked almost as bruised as I felt after the climb. And my ears felt funny, like I'd been to a rock concert without earplugs, and when she spoke, the words seemed to come from far, far away. "Did we—?"

The back cargo area of the Range Rover was splashed with liquid fire. It flowed like milk and glowed like sunrise. Even recreated through the distorted echo of the infinity lens, the mystic power of the dragon created constellations of sparkles dancing over the interior of the Rover.

The back glass was etched in arcane patterns where the magical liquid spattered across it. At points, the hot droplets had penetrated all the way through the glass, running down both the outside and the inside, which was curling with acrid smoke from charred cargo area carpet.

Most of the liquid fire had splashed out of the cauldron, chewing its way through the car, leaking out onto the pavement, oozing into cracks in the asphalt, lost.

But in the dark heart of the cauldron . . . there remained a visible glow.

"Congratulations," I said, grimacing. My throat was unexpectedly raw, and I was again having trouble breathing in the chill night air. "You have your liquid fire."

"We did it," Yolanda said, incredulous. "Princess . . . we did it!"

The fireweavers gathered. Jewel ran forward with a squeal . . . then stopped as she saw me turn toward her. At first, she said nothing. We just stared at each other, scowling and angry. Then, slowly, her face softened, looking me over, seeing my burns and cuts and bruises.

"Oh, Dakota, I'm . . . sorry," she said. I glared—my inner pain was worse, and she looked away. But something worried her, and she asked, "Your dragon really is gone, isn't it? You were the herald, and the dragon flying around was just hatchsign. I was right, wasn't I?"

"You were right," I said. "The spirit of the dragon was on my back."

"If you are the herald, then . . ." she said, looking up. "Where is she going?"

I looked up after Pele, now just a tiny speck in the sky. She had nowhere to go on Earth; she had to be flying into space. How was that even possible? Using her dragon breath like a rocket booster? Using the solar wind, magnetic fields . . . pure magic?

And even then, where would she go? I racked my brains for knowledge of the solar system, and oddly flashed back on my *Close Encounters* moment with the pizza, but not eating pizza with Cinnamon and Vickman—the older memory of me and my mother.

Eating pizza and reading *National Geographic* . . . and then I had it.

"Io," I said. "Pele's going to Io."

"Eye . . . oh?" Jewel said.

"One of Jupiter's moons." I was certain not only that I was right, but also that Pele had told me. I'd felt homesick looking at that pie, not because I had great memories of mom and pizza . . . but because *Pele* was homesick for that image. "Looks like a great big pizza."

"Oh, come on," she said. "Seriously?"

"Seriously," I said. "Crust constantly flexing in Jupiter's gravity, churning with inner heat, covered with sulfur pockmarked with volcanoes. It's the only body in the solar system which approximates Earth's early environment, the only place a dragon could call home—"

"Oh, quit showing off," Jewel said, shaking her head. Then she looked up at me, and her face fell. Her breath caught in her throat. "Oh, God, I've—"

"You've stepped in it, decisively," I said. "Give me your phone."

"Why?"

"So I can call Philip," I said.

Jewel's lower lip trembled. Then she pulled out her phone.

"What are you doing?" Yolanda said, reaching for it. "Don't—"

"Don't interfere," Jewel said sharply, jerking the phone back. "Dakota . . . don't."

"I have to," I said. "I can walk up to the nearest ranger station while the lot of you run like hell, or you can give me your phone and take your medicine."

"What . . . what do you think I should do?"

"Take your medicine," I said.

"You're such a hard woman, Dakota," Jewel said.

"Oh, spare me," I said, shaking my head. But she sounded sincere.

"Dakota," she said, eyes tearing up. "Doesn't what we had mean anything to you?"

Zi laughed roughly, but I kept my eyes on Jewel.

"Everything," I said, "but you said it. It's what we *had*. It's what we had before I knew you were lying to me. Before you kidnapped me. Before you touched my stuff, smearing this awful crap all over me so you could use me in your scheme with no thought of all the hundreds or thousands of people who would have been killed so you could protect a virgin mountaintop. And I *like* virgin mountaintops, but tell me—don't you think you did more damage?"

And I held my hand out toward the glowing crater, the torn-up mountainside, the massive chunks of debris still falling from the sky—and, far in the distance, the lights of the observatory, untouched, because as vast as Pele was, a shield volcano was larger.

"We didn't even get the damn thing," she muttered.

"Good, maybe nobody died." I held out my hand. "Now give me your damn phone."

"Don't do it, Princess," Zi said, stepping between us. "We need to—"

"Shut up and sit down," I said, pointing to a shelf on the rock.

Zi turned on me. "You aren't in charge, Frost. After the wreck you made—"

"All of you *sit the flying fuck down right the fuck now,*" I said, turning on him, pointing at the rock. He blanched, backing up, and I corralled the rest with my arms. "Or I swear to God I will beat the holy living shit out of each and every one of you, one by one or all at once."

"She—she can't get all of us," one of the twins said. "Not if we run—"

I whipped my arm out and shot a coiled vine straight at his chest. It hit him far harder than I meant to—almost like it was fueled by rage for being pinned up so long, though it was probably just an imbalance in the magic from the henna—and he fell back against the cliff.

"Any other takers?" I asked, drawing the vine back to me, then drawing a line in the gravel-covered road with it. "I took you all on and won *without magic.* I'll take you all on again, with the same result. Anyone else want to try round two with a pissed-off dragon herald?"

Zi held up his hands. "No . . . herald."

I looked at the phone. Jewel had left it off. Smart girl. I beeped it on, then waited for signal. At first, I thought we wouldn't get any, but then, improbably, it picked up, two bars. I called Philip. I was a bit surprised I remembered his number.

"Special Agent Philip Davidson," he said, voice straining over what sounded like a leaf blower. I knew what that sound was—one of the Shadowhawk stealth helicopters. Philip was already on his way. Then he continued, "Best magical investigator in the Northeast."

"Stealing my line," I said, laughing. Then I coughed. "Philip, good to hear your voice."

"You too," Philip said warmly. "I know where you are; what's the situation?"

"I've secured the scene," I said firmly, coughing again, staring over at the fireweavers. Jewel looked away from me, and I sighed raggedly. Then I looked over at the glowing back of the Range Rover. "But I may need your help securing some . . . Edgeworld assets."

"Understood," Philip said. "Say no more."

I hung up the phone. Zi stared at me, eyes burning.

"You're going to take it, aren't you?" he said. "Take the liquid fire."

"If you break into my house and fry an egg in my kitchen, it's still your egg."

Zi stared at me, baffled, and I sighed and sat down between Zi and Jewel.

"All of you are going to jail—for kidnapping, for vandalizing a national park, for reckless endangerment of human life," I said, sweeping my hand over the destruction across the valley. "But something wonderful happened—a dragon was born, and liquid fire was made."

"And you're going to take it from us," Jewel said.

"No," I said. "We talked, we dated, we even made love, but you really do *not* know me, Jewel. I practice radical forgiveness. If it weren't for all the people who probably died in this catastrophe, I'd just let you walk away—"

"We survived," Jewel said. "And we were closest—"

"Tsunamis," I said, and she fell silent. "You moved the earth, Jewel. This will rock the whole world. And you can't tell me that you imagine no one was in this park. No camper, no ranger, no poor tourist lost on a late-night drive, no native driving to see relatives—"

"Oh, *God*," Jewel said, putting her head in her hands.

"I can't let you walk away," I said, "but I can't let that fall into the wrong hands."

We stared at the trunk of the Range Rover, and the glowing light filtering out of it.

"The whole world would fight over that," I said. "Not just fireweavers and wizards, but scientists and kings, all desperate for a chance at eternal life or just at a chance to perform a spell that comes along once every dozen generations.

"Heck, the whole world may fight over this crater," I said, "after the U.S. Government begins strip-mining it for all the dragon yolk and dragon's blood—"

"They won't find anything," Zi said bitterly. "It will all burn up—"

"You're thinking old school, of what you could harvest before the Industrial Revolution and all its toys," I said. "They'll find *some* fraction of liquid fire left by the hatching, something people will fight over. Let them fight over it *here*. Let's take the real prize off the table."

"All right," Jewel said. She stood up. "All right." She looked out over the hillside, looked back at the back of the Range Rover, then back at me. "All right, Dakota. But there's no need for everyone to bear the full brunt of this. I'm the princess. I'm the leader. It's all on me."

"Are you sure?" I asked, standing, stepping beside her. "Even if you plea bargain, your accomplices are not going to get off scot-free. It will help things if you take responsibility . . . but are you sure you don't just want to lawyer up and let the courts work this out?"

"Yes, I'm sure," Jewel said. "I never wanted to admit to myself what was necessary to get this done. I have to take responsibility for my actions. But I'm not turning myself over to them, Dakota. I'm turning myself, and my liquid fire, over to you."

I raised an eyebrow.

"I'd never have accepted the rule of any court telling me not to do this," Jewel said bitterly, staring out over the valley. "I told myself it was wrong for Pele's spirit to be lost in the ether, that it was right for us to help her hatch, that it was our right to retake the island.

"But there's no law for this," she said. "I mean, sure, no vandalizing national parks, but, seriously, what if I'd found a true source of liquid fire, or if I'd convinced you of the rightness of my cause? We could have done this in daylight. We could have even gotten a permit.

"The only thing that could have stopped this, maybe, is you," she said, staring up at me. "You, and your 'Magical Security Council.' You would have investigated the hatchsign, put out warnings, taken control of the situation. Stopped it before it got started—"

"How? I can't police the world," I said. "You put too much faith in me—"

"You hatched a dragon, Dakota Frost," Jewel said, extending her hand to the valley. "I believe you can do anything. And I believe you could have, should have, stopped me. Someone, sometime has to be the first person to take it on the chin for your Council. That will be me."

"Are you sure?" I said. "Don't do this for me. This will be hard—"

"Oh, God," she said. "They're not going to let me spin, are they?"

"No," I said quietly. "They won't let you spin. Not fire, anyway."

She stared out over the valley. Her bottom lip trembled. Then she nodded.

I squeezed Jewel tight. The wind picked up, the billowing clouds whipping back and forth—and then a Shadowhawk helicopter appeared, a dark Shamu shape barely visible in the dim moonlight, barely audible against the rumblings of landslides out over the valley.

A spotlight pinned us, and I waved my hand forward, wincing at the sudden light. Soon, three Shadowhawks had settled around us—one on the road above us, one on the hill behind us, and a third still in the air, hovering a few dozen yards back from the Jeep Cherokee.

Philip ran up, eyes widening at my wounds. He saw me holding Jewel, and paused. Jewel and I both turned, and I put one hand on her shoulder. Philip raised an eyebrow, and then, feeling like Judas, I extended my other hand, first to Jewel . . . then to the shattered hillside.

"I'm seizing this location," I said, "on the authority of the Magical Security Council."

Philip froze. "So . . . is that national now?" he said, with a forced laugh.

"Yes. These people are under arrest for performing a hazardous summoning, and the ringleader," I said, placing my hand on Jewel's shoulder, "has turned herself over to me. The damage was beyond their imagining, and she plans to cooperate with our investigation."

Philip stared at her, then at me. "What do you want me to do, Dakota?"

"Arrest them all for reckless endangerment of human life, and possible misuse of magic," I said, motioning him to step toward me. Philip stepped up close to me, and I whispered in his ear, pointing with my free hand, "And prove my trust in you. Secure *that.*"

Philip turned toward the Range Rover and the eerie glow emanating from its trunk. He stepped back slightly, then whirled to look at me. "Is that . . ."

"It is," I said. "And this valley is full of it, which is why I've seized it. There's no telling how much could be recovered, which is why I need you to secure the crater. But that cauldron is the property of the fireweavers, and if you know anything about asset forfeiture—"

"They kidnapped you," Philip said. "Almost certainly it will be seized—"

"And auctioned off by the U.S. Marshal Service? Philip!"

"You really think the DEI is better?" Philip said quietly.

"The DEI may have a bad history, but it's not bad now. Is it?"

Philip didn't answer, just stared off into the distance.

"No," he said at last. "And what choice do we have?"

"Confiscate it, sit on it until I can go get a U-Haul, or . . . pour it out."

Philip looked at me sharply. Then he motioned to an agent, who ran up.

"Miss Frost needs you to *disappear that,*" he said, pointing at the back of the truck. The agent turned, did a double take at the cauldron, then ran off to the Shadowhawk, shouting. Philip looked at me, then turned back to Jewel. "We'll hold it for you until you've paid your debts."

Jewel drew her breath, then nodded.

"I'm ready," she said.

Those beautiful, delicate hands were cuffed behind her back. Then he led her away.

63. Your Chopper is Waiting

I stood on the brink of the disaster, watching an army of people clean up the mess.

They'd moved the command post to a ridge overlooking Haleakala caldera. After a nearly week-long delay, FEMA had finally provided a half dozen modular office trailers, and the DEI had moved them as close as the U.S. Geological Survey team would let us.

Now, I finally had a good overview of the site . . . just as I was leaving.

Across the slopes of the caldera, debris and rock made a fantastic jumble. Below us, the crater that had been Pu'u o Maui had collapsed in on itself, leaving only a steaming rubble that sometimes belched smoke, sometimes belched fire—and sometimes belched pure magic.

But wherever the ground was firm enough to stand, wherever liquid fire had fallen, new life blossomed. In places, the vegetation had burned itself up, but in others, it was a luxurious green carpet, dotted with spiky, orange-gold flowers waving a yard high.

They called it Pele's Protea, and it was too soon to say whether this new species was a simple genetic mutation, or whether in the depths of their magic-twisted cells there was a process that generated liquid fire. Even my new magic-touched eyes couldn't tell me that.

But I wondered whether this was how firecaps had started.

"Miss Frost?" asked a curt voice.

I turned toward this new official, a slightly pudgy Hawaiian with stylish square-rimmed glasses. He didn't have insignia on his coat, and I cursed inwardly. The disaster had become such a jurisdictional *mess*. There was an endless parade of officials from the DEI, the Park Service, FEMA, the National Guard of Hawaii—Army and Air—and even the NOAA, which supplied a whole contingent of serious-looking, well-armed young men and women in blue SWAT-like uniforms to guard the site. I wasn't even aware that the National Oceanic and Atmospheric Administration had a military arm . . . but I was learning. And not just about agency soup.

"I'm sorry," I said, extending my hand. "I don't think we've been introduced—"

"Department of Homeland Security," he said, taking my hand. He looked out over the sweep of the wrecked caldera and the green-gold magical growth, and let out his breath. "Damn. I know we have a whole agency devoted to magic, but I never really believed in it. Until now."

"Kind of hard to keep your head in the sand when the sand's all blown away."

"Yeah," he said. In the glass, I could see his reflection—and his frown. "Ma'am, I've spoken with the MIRCdrakes, the DEI's disaster response action corps. They've recovered a lot of magical equipment. More than would have been needed to hatch the thing—"

"Pele didn't need our help hatching," I said flatly. Of course, I had a very good idea about what he was talking about—the components of Jewel's infinity lens—but staring out at this devastation left me paranoid about talking to anyone about liquid fire.

"Still," he pressed, "are you sure they weren't trying to do anything . . . else—"

"I *am* sure that they were—I was there," I said, turning fully toward him, and his eyes tightened at my healing cuts and bruises. "But if someone was willing to blow up a mountain to do it . . . don't you think that should be need to know?"

"Miss Frost," he said, "my agency needs to know—"

"I know," I said, raising my hands. "Put in a request to the Magical Security Council. We're working out with the DEI just what we can release, and with all due respect, we haven't been introduced. I don't know you're with DHS just because you said so—"

"Steve Baker," he said, pulling out his ID. "I understand."

"Thank you," I said, inspecting it; not that I could spot a fake ID. "I understand that you're trying to find out whether what happened here is an active threat, but we need to control this evidence to do that. Make sure the MIRCdrakes turn everything over to MIRChold—"

"What's that one?" he said, taking his ID back. "*Magical Incident Response Center—*"

"Uhh . . . *Hazardous Objects Logistics Department,* I think," I said, shaking my head.

"Damn alphabet soup," Baker said, staring out over the devastation. "What a mess."

"You're telling me," I said.

"Well," he said, glancing over my fading bruises, "at least we had you there."

"Miss Frost?" asked an agent. I looked over to see a sharp young man from the DEI—the same one Philip had put in charge of the cauldron—standing by the door . . . with a briefcase handcuffed to his arm. "You've been cleared to go—and your chopper is waiting."

"Great," I said, texting Cinnamon to let her know I was on the move—then I stopped, frozen, as the words sank in. *My chopper was waiting.* Jesus. It was just taking me to the airport, to San Francisco, then home to my daughter . . . but still, I wasn't ready for all this.

Finally, I looked up, a forced smile on my face.

"Mr. Baker, it's been a pleasure working with you," I said, extending my hand. "For all of five minutes. I'm, uh, out of cards, but the DEI can get you in touch with the Magical Security Council . . . and, well, the MSC will make sure that you have what you need."

"You're joking, Frost," Baker said, waving at the crater. "We're in the middle of both disaster recovery *and* an investigation, and you're the hinge of both. In all seriousness . . . we *need* you, and not just for your expertise. You can't just leave—"

"You'll find that I can. That wasn't Hawaiian airspace he was talking about—I've been cleared to leave by the US Attorney, and I'm going. When I say things like *I have a twitchy weretiger waiting at home who needs her mother*, I'm just describing the facts—"

"I'm sure," Baker said impatiently, "you can get someone to sit for your daughter—"

"I've been here weeks," I snapped. "I'm not letting it stretch to months—"

"This," Baker said, "is one of the most historic disasters ever—"

I laughed. "We dodged that bullet," I said, thinking of Krakatoa, "but even so . . . the cleanup will be going on for years. And if I let you people have your way, you'll keep me here, staring out of this trailer, until the whole damn valley is cleaned up. Well, no sir. I have a daughter at home, and I am *not* missing her *goddamn birthday—*"

"You're leaving a *dragon hatching,*" Baker said, "for your daughter's *birthday party?*"

"Yes—no; look, it's complicated." I sighed, deciding what to tell him. "Full disclosure—Cinnamon's birthday isn't until October. I'm going back to San Francisco, on business that bears on the dragon's hatching. First, one of the fireweaver's victims is still in the hospital. And second, I need to make sure this"—I waved at the crater—"won't happen again."

Baker's eyes tightened. "How?"

"You'll find out soon enough."

"Damn it, Frost—"

—☙

"There was another group of fireweavers," I said. "Excuse me, my chopper is waiting."

64. Well, I Hope You're Happy

"Well, I hope you're happy," Alex said bitterly, as I climbed the steps of the Valentine Foundation. I stopped as he began to rant, "It got out that I passed you fireweaving knowledge. Jewel's been deposed, I'm going to be censured, if not expelled from the Order—"

"Do you know why I'm here, Alex?" I asked.

"To gloat? To bust my chops? To pick up a fat paycheck made off the backs of—"

I raised an eyebrow. It was almost ten days, but still, everyone I'd met since we'd left Hawaii had asked me about nothing other than the disaster on Mount Haleakala. *What happened on Maui? Were you a witness? And did a dragon really hatch?*

But Alex was all absorbed with his own problems. Maybe they were real problems.

"Here, as in San Francisco?" I said. "For my friend Nyissa. She was horribly burned when the fireweavers kidnapped me. After the doctors in Maui stabilized her condition, the DEI airlifted her back here so the San Francisco vampires could try to save her life."

"The pale, pretty vamp?" he said. "Hit by magical fire? That's horrible. I'm sorry."

"Do you know why I'm here, Alex?" I asked, stopping two steps beneath him. "Here, as in alive? Because of the files you gave me. You helped me crack a mystery, avert a greater disaster, save thousands of lives—and prevent a war which would have split Hawaii off the union. *Relax,* Alex. I am here to pick up a check, and maybe to bust your nuts over that video. But not to gloat, Alex. If you paid a heavy price for me . . . it's just one more thing I owe you."

Alex brought me inside, to the same small conference room. I filled him in on what happened—he was in the Magical Security Council, after all—while he plugged in a laptop and pulled up a video. After I was done briefing him, he showed me the promo videos.

None were as bad as the one that had leaked, but I still got hot under the collar, and Alex took careful notes. At first, I wanted to tell Dennis off in person, but I gathered Alex had decided to insulate me from the rest of the crew as a way of protecting them, and it was a wise move.

My phone buzzed. Earlier I'd texted Cinnamon that I was here; now she texted back: **«gr8 . . . dont kill teh ken doll mom»**

I grinned . . . then thought about what I'd said to Jewel about radical forgiveness. That was my way of life—with her, with the vampire Transomnia, even with Nyissa, who'd threatened me the first time we met and now was one of my closest companions.

All of them, at one time or another, had kidnapped me and threatened my life. All Alex had done was post a slightly unflattering video which would no doubt create great publicity for the series. Alex deserved the same olive branch I'd given to those who'd done me real harm.

"I have one more to show you," Alex said, finishing writing my comments about the last video on a yellow pad. "You may not believe this, but I recorded this before those promos we did. But still, I hope you'll take this as a form of apology—"

"That's all right," I said. "Hey, are all the crew about? And Browning, or Meyer?"

"Y-yes," he said, suspiciously. "Most of them, anyway. What do you have in mind—"

"I'd like to take them all out for beers," I said. "Or dinner, or whatever. My treat. Call it my attempt to bury the hatchet, and not just because we're all going to have to work together. I know I can fly off the handle, and even if I think I've got reasons, it's not fair to them."

Alex stared at me a moment. "All right, Dakota," he said, and hit play.

Alex's image appeared on the screen, up close and approachable, on a bright sunny day with the Golden Gate Bridge over his left shoulder. With what little I'd worked with them so far, I realized how much skill had gone in to make the shot look that good in that bright lighting.

"*Hi, I'm Alex Nicholson, host of* The Exposers," his image said. "*Many of you may know me as Christopher Valentine's protégé. Together, on this show, we've taken a hard line on, as Chris would say, the flim-flammery of our age, exposing mystics for the fakers they were.*

"*Or so we, the staff of* The Exposers *thought, but we were wrong. As many of you may have heard, Christopher Valentine himself has been exposed as a real magician and a criminal, using threats, violence, and even murder to ensure no one ever overcame his Challenges.*

"*Many of you may not have heard that I, his protégé, was almost a victim of his schemes. As his protégé and heir, I've been put in charge of his affairs, and I'm trying to set things right. I've donated Christopher Valentine's estate to his victims' families, but that is not enough.*

"*In this special, we're going to present to you the very last Valentine Challenge, against Dakota Frost. We're going to show, conclusively, that she won; and we're going to break down for you how Christopher planned to prevent her from ever claiming her victory.*

"*I must warn you, some of the material that will be presented is very traumatic, most of all for Ms. Frost, who we thank for agreeing to participate. All proceeds from this special are being donated to charity or to pay what the Valentine Foundation owes Ms. Frost.*

"*So, from the bottom of my heart, thank you for watching. We'll be right back.*"

I stood there, stunned. I hadn't seen his face, but . . . I had heard that voice. Heard genuine pain, genuine sympathy, a genuine desire to make things right. Maybe that was as fake as Christopher Valentine's smile, but it was hard to hear that voice and not believe.

The screen went black. I looked over. Alex had closed his laptop.

"I take it," he said quietly, "you approve."

"You know, Alex," I said, "you're still a ghoul. But—"

"You don't need to say it," he said, though I had no idea how he thought he knew what I was going to say, because I sure as hell didn't. "We have four more tapings, and two scheduled pickups, to finish the damn special. When it's done . . . let's put the damn thing behind us."

I pursed my lips, then nodded.

"The beers thing, it's a good idea," he said. "You don't need to, Dakota. They're crew, you're the talent. You can get away with a lot. They're used to it. But if you feel inclined to smooth some feathers, it will make everyone's lives easier while we . . . what? What?"

I had raised my hand with a wry smile, raising my fingers. "Two things."

Alex leaned back. "Let me guess the first. The advance has to happen."

"You're a great friend, you saved my life, yada yada," I said, "but you've dragged my reputation through the dirt, are making me crawl through the sewer, and *keep welshing on payment.* If the wire transfer hasn't gone through by Friday, we're in court."

"I signed the paperwork today," Alex said. "If it hasn't gone through by tomorrow, I'll sue myself—but, Dakota. You *hatched a dragon*. You're going to be the most famous woman in the world. You'll be a hit. This will end up worth far more than that paltry two million."

"All right," I said, relaxing. There was a chance we could close this thing off after all. "And the other . . . I need to call in a little more on the favor. Call it the gift that keeps on giving. I need to send a message to the fireweavers."

"They won't want to fucking talk to me," he said.

"No, they won't," I said. "And the man I want won't want to be found. But you're damn good, Alex, and your videos are everywhere. Even after this disaster, anything you do, someone will be watching—almost certainly the fireweaver clans, if you're on their shit list."

"Almost certainly," Alex said. "They even said they're watching me—"

"If we just blurt what I want to say out in the open, it creates enormous risk," I said. "But fireweavers can talk without people overhearing, without even people knowing—through the flame symbols that showed up at all of Jewel's attacks. The Fireweaver's Code."

"I don't know it," Alex said.

"I do," I said, pushing a thumb drive over. Alex's eyes went wide, and I smiled. "I coded this on the flight over," I said. "It's not real fire magic, just four solid hours of fumbling with Excel and forty five minutes in Photoshop after I figured out the content of the message—"

"What do you want me to do with it?" Alex said, eyes still wide.

"Put it on *The Exposers's* website," I said, "and it becomes a message the world can see."

65. Walk Across the Bridge

At noon, I strode across the Golden Gate Bridge, the tail of my vestcoat flapping in the strong Pacific wind. An endless stream of cars whooshed by, crowds milled on the bridge, and a cargo ship slid below atop a sheet of water, faintly rippled like dark blue denim.

I marveled at the enormous cables that supported the bridge, at the titanic support columns that loomed above me. Cinnamon had said they were "international orange," painted that way to alert airplanes, and that she was jealous that I was going to go see it.

Me, I was a bit nervous, not because of what I'd planned, but because of the little gap between the East Sidewalk and the road. I'd expected the Bridge to be solid, but instead, I could see through a narrow crevice to catch a glimpse of mist and breakers below.

I'm not afraid of heights, but for some reason, that gave me the willies.

Bicyclists whizzed past. Joggers bopped by. Tourists took pictures—old and young, alone and with family, Midwesterners and Australians, gesticulating Armenians walking past smiling Japanese schoolgirls, talking with a granola San Francisco kid licking a lollipop.

I'd wanted this meeting to be at night, but the sidewalk was closed then.

This would have to do.

I stopped at the center of the bridge and leaned on the rail, staring out over the San Francisco Bay, toward the rising boxes of the city, then toward an island I guessed was Alcatraz. The Bay was pretty. I wondered if I would ever come back here again.

I leaned there a long time, thinking.

Thinking of my lost love. Thinking of her betrayal. Thinking of all else I'd lost.

Thinking of a code. The second half was a time and GPS coordinate, but the first half . . .

```
Bring my ink and dagger to the bridge.
  BRING MYINK ANDDA GGERT OTHEB RIDGE
  RBGNI IMYNK NDDAA GTEGR TOBEH DRIGE
  21543 31245 23451 15324 21543 31245
  DANIE LHILL HILLD ANIEL DANIE LHILL
```

"Sorry I'm late, but you messed up the cipher," said a friendly but guarded voice. "The shuffler for the second stanza should have been HILLD ANIEL, but you scrambled it as LHILL DANIE. It took me quite a while to figure out your mistake. I almost didn't make it."

"Daniel Hill," I said, turning to face the man.

Daniel Hill stood before me, a tough, ripped Hawaiian, skin tanned and weathered, slouching before me in comfortable slacks and a baggy, hooded jacket. He sized me up, eyeing my fading bruises, then he smiled. "Somebody sure kicked the holy living shit out of you."

"I gave far better than I got," I said, sizing him up. I guessed the "dangerous assassin trying to kill my lover" was more likely to be a "reluctant hero with a thankless job"—but that conjecture remained to be proven. Daniel was tough, a bit bigger than Molokii, but nowhere near as muscular. He was slightly wary, and his hands were in his hoodie's oversized front pockets. If he was packing, however, he was in for a shock. I said, "*You* were going to *kill* Pele."

"I swear by the blood of the Christian God that I did not believe Pele was still alive," Daniel said. He took his hands out of his pockets and raised them. "I honestly thought their missionaries killed her when they threw rocks into her egg."

"What?" I said.

"We all had theories what happened to Pele," Daniel said. "The favorite of the Order was that she died. If she really was dead—if all that was down there was a cracked shell filled with burning yolk—then why not harvest it? Why not turn her tragedy into fuel for beauty—"

"*There never was a real Pele,*" I said. "That's just a myth, a metaphor. Or if there was a real Pele, that thing which hatched is not her. Trust me. I carried that thing on my skin for nine months, and it was beautiful and terrible—but it had no memories of anything like humans."

"That only makes my case stronger. You figure out what Jewel wanted to do?"

"Enslave Pele," I said, "and use her to retake Hawai`i for the Hawai`ians."

"Jesus," Daniel said. "I guessed as much. I don't know why she failed—"

"*I'm* why," I said. "I'm the one who thwarted the spell and set Pele free."

Daniel laughed. "So it is true—you really are a screaming egomaniac."

Now I laughed. "Maybe. Let me also credit prayer—and a mountain of dumb luck."

"Well," Daniel said, "thank you, but Jewel still has a lot to answer for."

I turned and fixed him with a glare. He ignored it, staring out over the Bay.

"You will leave her out of this from now on," I said.

"No, we won't," Daniel said, shaking his head. I clearly wasn't getting through to him yet; this would take some work. "This is a fireweaver matter, a matter for the Order. We tried to warn her, but she didn't listen—and you saw what happened. Now she has a lot to answer for—"

"Yes, she has a lot to answer for, but *you* are *done* with her," I said. "Leave her to the MSC. And next time you have a problem with something someone is trying to do, you don't assault them on the street and try to cripple them in front of witnesses. You bring it to *me*."

"Why?" Daniel asked. "Who the hell are you, that we should come to you?"

"Jewel almost won because *you made yourself look like a bad guy!*" I said. "You and I should have been working together from day one, but instead of telling anyone what was really happening, you decided to try to *maim* my *girlfriend* right in front of me!"

Daniel didn't look directly at me—but, to his credit, he wasn't easily deterred.

"I *meant* it. Who the hell are you? Who the hell *were* you?" he said. "*Now* we know you were the herald—but then? Pele's egg was in Hawai`i, that so-called 'princess' Jewel had run to San Francisco. Why would we have turned to you, a tattoo artist from Hicksville, Georgia?"

My nostrils flared. There was that Hicksville again. "OK. So you didn't know. But you know now—you bring it to *me*. I don't care whether you're in Tahiti fighting someone in Timbuktu. From now on, the Edgeworld doesn't police itself alone. You bring it to *me*."

"What, you're going to be judge, jury, and executioner?" Daniel said.

"Oh, hell," I said, turning away. "We're going to need the whole damn thing, aren't we? Courts and police and rules and treaties, not just a roundtable of wankers pretending to be politicians. We're going to need the whole damn thing."

"Only because you say we do. And I say we don't, not even if you were the herald," he said. "Not even if you managed to save Pele after I'd given up hope. You took an enormous risk, Frost. Millions of people could have died. We got lucky. Extremely lucky."

I looked back at him. "Look me in the eye and tell me you wanted to save her."

"I did not *want* to murder the god of my ancestors," Daniel said evenly. "Nor did I have any intention of enslaving one. All I wanted to do was what I thought I had to in order to prevent a disaster—and to keep that little dictator from creating her own personal Godzilla!"

I looked him in the eyes. His lips pursed.

"All right, I admit it," he said. "I wanted to take the opportunity to create more of the fuel I use to spin magic fire. But that was always secondary. If I *just* wanted fuel, Jewel would have given it freely. There would be some bowing and scraping involved—"

"And you're a big enough man to do that?" I asked, and Daniel's eyes tightened. The *text* of my message never mentioned an exchange . . . but the three glyphs at the center of the message *could* be read as *trade liquid fire*. "To let someone else control the source?"

Daniel thought a moment. "Yes, I am," he said. "But . . . look, Frost. I *know* Jewel. You may have dated her, but you really don't know her. Her head is full of bad wires. If she had enslaved Pele . . . she'd have used her to burn all the interlopers off the island."

I sighed.

"That she would have," I said quietly. "All right, Daniel. Let's get to what we're here for."

"Your dagger, and your inks," Daniel said. He stared at me. "I take it you know it's not just *a* dagger. It's a dragon's tooth dagger, and can be used in the spell to crack a dragon's egg—if you have liquid fire. Which I learned is in your firecap ink, thanks to Jewel—"

"You had to have a plant in Jewel's camp," I said, and Daniel smiled at me, curious. "You *had* to. You took my inks to keep them from Jewel, but only she knew about them. Only she, or someone she told—"

"Jewel is never careful," Daniel said. "Always spilling the beans to Molokii in sign language when she thinks no one's looking. But while it's easy to hide signing from someone looking over your shoulder, it's harder if your foe has a telephoto lens."

"So, plain old-fashioned snooping. You found out what I let them say under my nose, to give them privacy," I said, grimacing. "I need to learn to be more nosy. One surreptitious glance at the right time could have ended this months ago."

"What's the phrase?" Daniel said, leaning back against the rail. "Waters under?"

"Something like that," I said. "We are on a bridge."

"Look, if you know what that dagger can do . . . you have to know I can't just give it to you." I glanced at him a for moment, then he shrugged. "Ah . . . I guess we already know what you'd do if a dragon was hatching, don't we, Frost?"

"Proof by demonstration," I said. "My ink and dagger, Daniel."

"You know what the dagger can do. You have to know what it's worth. We have other magical weapons we could use, of course, but we won't readily give them up. When you told me to give them to you, you had to know what I would consider proper payment."

"It's not payment," I said, hands clasped on the rail. "You stole them."

"We're not thieves," Daniel snapped. "Jewel needed liquid fire and mystical weapons to carry out her spell; I tried to keep her from getting any of that, for all the good it did me. When we saw the dagger *with* the inks, naturally we had to take both—"

"You know, the word we use for taking someone else's property," I said, "is stealing—"

"Fine, we stole it," Daniel said. "Fair or not, did you come prepared to trade?"

"Yes," I said, glancing over at him. "Yes, I did."

—

"So you *do* have liquid fire," Daniel said, eyes burning. "What if I just took it?"

66. Stewards of the Secret Flame

I tensed, not moving. Daniel was only a few feet away, in the so-called "kill zone" where you could theoretically deliver a blow before your opponent could retaliate. Not that I wasn't prepared for that, but . . . now was the point where Daniel would show his true colors.

"That doesn't sound like much of a trade," I said cautiously.

"It sounds like you haven't thought this through," he said. "If I took it from you—"

"How?" I asked, staring out over the water. "If you make this a confrontation, I'll throw you over the side—or just push you out into traffic. I may not have the spirit of a dragon on my back anymore, but I have an enormous magical arsenal and I'm an expert martial artist."

Daniel stiffened. "What if I told you the cute couple with the camera—"

"—and the schoolgirls are your plants, ready to pull a gun out of the fake baby stroller?" I said, smirking. "What if I told you I'm willing to jump and pull you with me? I can make a pretty decent parachute out of these vines. You, on the other hand, will hit the water like cement."

"You're far from home," he said, "and this is a dangerous town—"

"Do you know how I got that dagger? One of the vampire lords of San Francisco gave it to me for services rendered," I said, turning toward him, pushing off the rail so I towered over him. "That service was defending Jewel from you."

"Maybe so," Daniel said, "but the vamps can't come out in the day."

"But the fae can," the girl with the lollipop said. The "Japanese" schoolgirls, now clearly just young Hawaiian college students, backed up rapidly from the little fae called Sidhain as she flicked her hair, the glamour coming off, her locks turning white—and her eyes glittering blue.

"Jesus," Daniel said, backing up. "We don't want trouble with the fae—"

I extended my hand. "Then please give me my dagger and inks."

"There's still the matter of trade," Daniel said stubbornly.

"No, there's not," I said. "They're mine, and I want them back. You may have a claim against Jewel, but that's a completely different conversation. I want each of us to walk away from this conversation with what each of us is owed. Now, please, give them to me."

Daniel hesitated, then pulled out a long, narrow case.

"These inks are the signature of your clan . . . so you are their rightful custodian."

I took the case carefully, feeling no mana, getting no signs that it was booby-trapped. Inside, my dragon's tooth dagger rested on blue velvet, with my bottles of ink on either side in small compartments. Sidhain peered in, nodded, then smiled. I closed the case.

"You had a fancy box made?" I asked.

"Consider it icing on the olive branch," Daniel said. "Satisfied?"

"For now," I said, smiling wryly. "I understand that Jewel has been deposed."

"I—" Daniel began, a bit off-put. "Jewel has been . . . removed from office," Daniel said, uneasily staring at the fae girl. "She's no longer the leader of the Order, not while she's in jail and unable to fulfill her ceremonial responsibilities. We've appointed a regent—"

"And that regent is you?" I said.

"Yes," Daniel said. "Not that I wanted it, not that you'd believe it—"

"So you, Fire Prince Daniel Hill, would be the rightful custodian of this."

I withdrew a tiny steel cylinder from my other jacket pocket. I unscrewed its tiny steel top and slowly lifted it, exposing an inner glass cylinder glowing with golden light. Both Daniel and Sidhain gasped. Then I closed the cylinder and slipped it back inside my coat.

"Jesus, Frost! You did have it on you," Daniel said angrily. He stepped up to me, but spoke quietly, urgently. "Frost, you can't go waltzing around with that shit! What if you got mugged? Hit by a car? What if I was a bad guy and had tried to take it from you?"

"You're not a bad guy, then?" I asked. "Now you know . . . you won't try?"

Daniel glanced at Sidhain, then shook his head. "Not even if you didn't have her. We're not thieves or muggers. After Jewel went kazoo, I recruited every fireweaver I could to fight her. You know what we called ourselves? The Fire Safety Squad. We're not the bad guys here—"

"And you say that, with a straight face, after you attacked Union Square?"

"Damn it, Frost, you know what we were trying to stop!" Daniel said. "What do you think would have happened if Jewel had called down hatchsign in Union Square, instead of it being bottled up on your back? Everything we've done was for the greater good—"

"So you're claiming that, all along, you were just trying to stop the bad guys?" I asked. I had already figured as much when Jewel showed her true colors at Haleakala, but I wanted to hear it from him. "So your black pajama squad . . . is actually a police organization?"

"No, I—" Daniel began, then shook his head. "In a way . . . I guess it is."

"Maybe we aren't so different after all," I said. "Look, I can't just hand a canister of liquid fire over to you on a bridge like we're in a bad spy movie. You know what I'd do with it, by demonstration, but I don't know you. We have to build up trust before that happens."

"Before it happens?" Daniel said, looking at me strangely. "You mean—"

"I mean, ultimately . . . I want the Fireweavers' Order to have the liquid fire."

"We want it," Daniel said immediately, "but . . . why even think of giving it to us?"

"Because it's yours—Jewel's, really. Forget for a moment her crazy Hawaiian nativist methods—she knew Pele was hatching, and she knew that could be a world-changing disaster. Everything she did was designed to prevent a dragon's death—or a human catastrophe."

"She should have just let me crack that egg and harvest it," Daniel said.

"Maybe," I said, "and maybe she was a nut-job wannabe dictator—but her plan worked. A dragon was saved. Human life was preserved. And we got a fresh supply of liquid fire. It's the product of her spell, and she deserves it—"

"She deserves," Daniel said hotly, "to go to jail—"

"And she's there now," I said. "And her faction of the Order has a lot to answer for. But unless we do something, the government will step up and confiscate the liquid fire—and I'd rather a bunch of Edgeworlders get it than let the government use it for godknowswhat."

Daniel grimaced.

"You don't know the trouble you're in," I said. "The whole magical world knows your Order performed that spell. And the ones who understand the spell will realize that when Pele hatched, you almost certainly had to make, or harvest, liquid fire from it—"

"You have to know that, if we do get any, we'll never give it up," Daniel said.

"There's not knowing trouble, and then there's asking for trouble," I said. "A whole host of people will come for it. Yes, it's yours, and you shouldn't have to give up your stuff to a robber, but in the end you just want to spin fire. But they don't want to die.

"I've met a lot of ancient wizards over the last few months," I said. "A lot of them are really wise, or sweet, or just plain quirky. But I know how nasty they can get. There's every chance the wizard that tried to murder me wanted the firecap ink in my tattoos."

"I've heard of the spell," Daniel said tightly. "A wizard doesn't even need the ink to give himself a jolt of stolen youth. He just needs to find someone infused with liquid fire, find the right time or place, then be willing to make them bleed . . . when in close contact with them."

I drew a breath. There was a reason that creepy old rapist had done what he'd done to me. A way to use that death and pain to give himself new life. No wonder Valentine had crossed the country raping magically tattooed women—it was his personal Fountain of Youth.

"This," I said, "could get really crazy. We've got to reach out to the wizards, to negotiate with them. You may need to give up some fire, but you'll get something in return. And we've got to preserve some true fire for the future. There are things worth more than spinning fire."

"Is there enough to go around?" Daniel said. "What was that, a milliliter—"

"We got more than a milliliter," I said. "A lot more."

"Jesus," he said. "And it's yours to keep—"

"Did I need it before?" I said, patting my coat. "I have my own source."

"Firecap ink is just an echo of the real thing," Daniel said.

"It's impressive enough. For the Dragon's Noose to activate just from me walking into it, firecap ink's got to be around Fermat level six magic. Of course, from all the things created from the droplets that fell from Pele . . . I'm guessing the real thing's Fermat number is far higher."

Daniel's eyes flashed. "Where do you have the rest?"

"With the Ark of the Covenant," I said.

Daniel looked confused. Then he laughed.

"The DEI has it," he said. "Oh, Frost, you idiot—"

"They would have taken it anyway," I snapped. "But my DEI contact agreed to seize the liquid fire on my personal authority. I've never known how much to trust them, but this is their chance to prove themselves to us. Let's see whether they hold their part of the bargain—"

"You're a fool if you think they will," Daniel said. "But if they do . . . we want it."

"You willing to make reparations?" I said. "Give up a slice to pay for Jewel's crimes? Or are you willing to sue over it? You can't take on the DEI, it won't help to take on me . . . but you can petition the Magical Security Council for the release of your supplies."

"Oh, hell," he said, turning away. He looked back at me, then at Sidhain. "We are going to need the whole damn thing, aren't we? Courts and police and rules and treaties—"

"It's either that, or we go to war," I said.

"That sounds like fun," Sidhain said, licking her lollipop, "but I'm told it's impolite."

"That it is, Sidhain," I said evenly. "Especially when there's a better way."

"All right," Daniel said. "All right. We need the whole damn thing."

"All right," I said quietly. "Care to take a little walk, then?"

I nodded my head toward the northern end of the bridge, then turned and walked off. Daniel and Sidhain wordlessly followed. Cars rushed past as the giant columns of the bridge rose toward us, then fell away behind us. Then we turned into a corner of the parking lot.

Philip and Carnes waited for us, leaning on the trunk of my rental, talking in low tones. They wore similar, far-too-expensive suits, but Carnes's had an odd cut to his jacket and subtle alchemical signs woven into the fabric weave. I wondered if the garment was magical.

"I brought no one," Philip said. "As requested."

"Ha," I said. "You've probably got an airship hidden in your pants—"

"How did you know?" Philip said, mouth quirking up. "We weren't dating that long—"

"Oh, I walked into that," I said. "Special Agent Davidson, Master Wizard Carnes, I believe you already know Sidhain, the Lost Child of the Ford. All of you . . . please meet Fire Prince Daniel Hill. He claims to speak for the

Fireweavers . . . and claims their liquid fire."

"Mr. Hill," Carnes said, extending his hand. "Pleased to . . ."

Daniel stared at his hand doubtfully, then at all of us.

"Who are you all?" he said. "The Mystical Spook Squad?"

"We all," I said, indicating him as well, "are the Stewards of the Secret Flame."

"I can't just release the liquid fire to you," Philip said. "To any of you—no offense, Dakota, but liquid fire is more rare and dangerous than plutonium. But it shouldn't disappear into the MIRChold like the Ark of the Covenant. I'd rather see it in the hands of Edgeworlders—"

"But the question is, who do we give it to?" I said. "Who can we trust with it?"

"Not you," Daniel said. "And not the government, I can tell you that."

"Nor the fae," Sidhain said. "We neither want it . . . nor need it."

"And not you, Daniel," Carnes said. "You attacked my city—"

"I know, I know," Daniel said, raising his hands. He glared at me. "All right, Frost, you were right. I screwed up, and have a lot to answer for. But I can't just join your creepy club. I'm not some dictator like Jewel. I have to run this by the Fireweaver's Council."

"Fair enough," I said. "But a resource of enormous mystical power has been created, and the last thing I want is a war. I—" and I looked off into the air for a moment, then shook my head "—and I just wanted to bring all the . . . stakeholders together. Jesus."

"Stakeholders," Philip said, a wry smile on his face.

"God," Carnes said, putting his face in his palm. "You've already done this too long."

"My job," Philip said, slipping a hand into his pocket, "isn't just to keep America safe from the misuse of magic, but to be an ambassador to the Edgeworld. A mystical version of a beat cop, out in the community, building relationships, creating trust."

He looked at me. "What Dakota's doing in Atlanta . . . I see as the magical community stepping up to police itself, the way the vampires did with the Consulates. Now we have a chance to take it up a level. I'm willing to go to the mat to support this—if you're all in."

"You already have my support," Carnes said. "As for the rest of the Conclave—"

"The fae are inclined to agree with the wizards," Sidhain said.

"You already know where I stand," I said. "Or . . . maybe you don't. To be clear, living in the Edgeworld means breaking the normal law, but I don't care about that. I'm restricting the charter of the Magical Security Council to keeping people safe—"

"Then we'd never get our hands on liquid fire," Daniel said. "It's too dangerous—"

"It all comes down to what people do with it," I said. "Spin fire all you want—but before you use it to cast some greater spell . . . run it by the Magical Security Council. Just don't hoard it. Leave some liquid fire for the rest of us. What do you say, Fire Prince Daniel Hill?"

Daniel considered that a long moment.

"Not like I have a choice," he muttered. "But I agree. We already had to create our own Fire Safety Squad. We should have stopped this before it got started. We should have been working together from the beginning. And working together . . . sure beats a war."

"All right, Dakota Frost," he said. "I'll convince the Fireweavers to do things your way."

67. LIFE IS FIRE

Jewel got seven years in prison . . . and I nearly ended up alongside her.

She was charged with vandalism of a federal park and reckless endangerment of human life . . . all federal crimes, to which she pleaded guilty. And all crimes of which I, technically, was also guilty, when I seized control of the spell and used it to free Pele.

My work securing Haleakala crater didn't help—even though the Hawaii National Guard did their best to seal the crater, and Philip did his best to lock down the whole incident, there was no way to suppress thousands of videos of Pele flying up to space.

So there was no way to stop the US Attorney from investigating how that happened, and as I worked to make sure that any liquid fire in the crater was safely locked down, I was unwittingly building the District of Hawaii's case for reckless endangerment.

No good deed goes unpunished.

But, miraculously, no one died. We blew off the top of a mountain, but no one died. Well, some yahoo got himself killed trying to film the tsunami roiling up onto his hotel, but not from the tsunami—he fell off the roof, while the bathers in the pool survived.

A national park was wrecked, but it had been nearly empty. Dozens of houses collapsed, but everyone in them was already outside watching the eruption. A mammoth chunk of rock from the explosion hit a hotel—but an abandoned one, already scheduled for demolition.

No one died. Miraculously. Apparently, my prayer worked.

So the US Attorney ultimately decided—"by a hair," she told me, "by a hair"—that as a kidnap victim, my actions could be counted as a bizarre form of self-defense, and that even though releasing Pele had enormous repercussions, it was better than another Krakatoa.

Even better, regardless of what I did, I did it in a Federal park, where state authorities had no jurisdiction. The loophole which bit my ass in Atlanta helped me in Hawaii—without a state charge to trigger on, the US Attorney couldn't prosecute a Misuse of Magic charge.

So I went free . . . and the Internet went wild.

In the thousands of videos which were posted to YouTube over the first few days were two innocent-looking videos shot from suspiciously close up—from the ridge overlooking the crater, Science City, where two construction workers had seen Pele taking off.

Then, on day ten, the bombshell hit—a video filmed by a scientist with a telescope hooked up to his camera phone, which had caught most of the initial part of the spell . . . in close enough detail to show the infinity lens, a climbing figure . . . and the interaction of my Dragons.

Now my magic has been seen round the world. It started with the clock I inked for Alex, continuing with photographs during the graffiti fires, and then with my stunt in Union Square. But the YouTube clip, Haleakala Tattoo Dragon Summoning, blew away them all.

They're calling me the Caster at Haleakala now.

And so, Alex assures me, the next season of *The Exposers* will be a hit. I was forced to get an agent just to help me turn down all the offers I've got for interviews and appearances, but soon the agent started, tentatively, to suggest things that I . . . approved of.

I haven't taken a one of them, of course. My gut tells me to fulfill my obligations, then quit. But deep down, I know I've got too much of an exhibitionist streak for that—the publicity has been great for the shop. I don't know what to do . . . or what this will do to my life.

That's not quite true, of course. It's already started doing things to my life. I have to be a little more careful in public; we have a lot more traffic in the shop. But the money pouring in from my inking is nothing compared to that first paycheck . . . when Alex paid up.

This time, I didn't rush out and blow it all. No new house, no new car, not even the new Vectrix motorcycle . . . but I did pour that money into Cinnamon's 529 plan. Hang the gift tax, screw the deductions. Cinnamon now had enough to send her grandchildren to college.

And the publicity, or perhaps the disaster, made the Magical Security Council even more real. After some coaxing, Lord Buckhead did visit the fae in San Francisco, in secret, and gave his blessing to the Northern California Practitioner's Conclave, in a private ceremony.

Apparently, the visit of a small-g god can do more than just smooth fae feathers or unite werekin factions. After Buckhead's visit, the Conclave created its own Security Council, the Magical Supervisor's Board, with Carnes as chair—and Lord Kitana as an uneasy advisor.

With the vampires, the fae and the wizards on my side, even Fire Prince Daniel Hill is playing along. He's agreed to abide by the rules of the San Francisco Magical Supervisor's Board—and to participate as one of my Stewards of the Liquid Fire.

I have no illusions that Daniel and the Fireweavers or Carnes and the Wizarding Guild are playing along willingly; the only reason they haven't tried to seize the fire yet is because Philip is holding the cauldron of fire in a secret location even I don't know.

But we've given each of them the tiniest droplet of liquid fire: a milliliter each, enough for Daniel to renew the fireweaver's supplies, for Devenger to conduct his studies—and for the DEI to assess how dangerous the material is, and whether it should be released at all.

I think it should be, and Philip is backing me up. He's walking a tightrope: he and my fellow Stewards know he's holding the fire, deep in the MIRChold vaults, but his superiors in the DEI think I'm holding the fire in some secret location—giving Philip cover.

When last I extended my trust to the DEI, they betrayed me and destroyed the community that Cinnamon had called home. Now Philip was bending over backward to prove that his organization was one that could earn the Edgeworld's trust.

So far, it's working. The DEI has been following my playbook on how to handle the Haleakala Caldera. They've sealed it off, begun surveying it, begun mining it. It isn't clear what fractions of liquid fire can be salvaged, but with Professor Devenger's help, they're trying.

What Carnes and Devenger and Philip and I—and even Daniel—are worried about, though, is what will happen as this knowledge inevitably leaks out. We're not worried about the immortals anymore; we probably have enough pure fire for one round of spells.

We're worried about people like Jewel.

Daniel calls Jewel a crazy dictator. I wouldn't go that far. She lied to me, but she drew back from the brink. She had some principles at her core—she just really wanted to spin fire. But I think she also wanted to clear off that mountaintop and break Hawaii off the Union.

The Hadean Dragon we now call Pele was the most powerful single organism the human species has ever seen. Her hatching shook the Earth; her launching actually changed its spin, infinitesimally, but measurably—they're going to have to reset every GPS on the planet.

If Jewel had succeeded . . . an army with Pele at its head would have been unstoppable.

And her reality is inescapable. Few people saw her hatch; not everyone believes the YouTube videos. But when Pele hit the edge of airless space, and unfurled her great dragon wings into vast butterfly membranes ten times their original size to catch the solar winds . . .

You can still see her, with a powerful enough telescope.

We now live in a world where almost everyone has seen a real dragon. We live in a world where children everywhere have her rainbow butterfly wings on their T-shirts. And a world where you can see from space the crater left by a magic spell more powerful than an atomic bomb.

So it's not just Cinnamon I'm trying to protect anymore.

Now I'm using everything in my arsenal to push the Magical Security Council farther than ever before—using my magic, my contacts, the publicity, and even politics to try to get people on our side. To establish not just rules—but an early warning system.

Because we can't put liquid fire back in the bottle. Scarcity is only temporary—the Washington Monument has a crown of aluminum because it was so valuable; a few years later, cheap electricity made aluminum so cheap we now use it for disposable food wrapping.

Sooner or later, someone like Devenger will reverse-engineer liquid fire, or figure out how to mass-harvest firecaps, or will invent a completely new source.

We don't know how yet, but we've got to figure out how to stop bad spells, rather than banning magic substances.

Because, sooner or later, someone like Jewel will do something terrible.

I know bad people will use magic for their own evil ends, but I'm not going to give up my own magic or let innocents suffer at their hands anymore. I have to get the power, the resources, the will—and the knowledge—that I need to keep us all safe.

I'm Dakota Frost, skindancer, and magic is my domain—don't screw it up.

ACKNOWLEDGEMENTS

LIQUID FIRE had an unusually long gestation—I started five novels and finished two of them between the time I started it in April of 2008 and the time I sent version 121 to Debra Dixon at Bell Bridge Books in February of 2015.

In that time, I had awesome support from my friends. Many of the crew at the Write to the End writer's group either beta read or helped me work through problems, including Gayle, David, Liza, Betsy, Keiko, Nathan, Ruth, and several others.

My family and friends also helped as well, including my wife Sandi, my mother-in-law Barb, many of my friends in the Edge, including Gordon and Jim, and many of my friends in the Dragon Writers Group back in Atlanta. Thanks to you all.

I also had great research assistance. Keiko O'Leary's linguistic analysis was invaluable to me in keeping Cinnamon sounding like Cinnamon. John Kim, Prosecutor of the County of Maui, helped me understand jurisdictional issues.

Thanks go out to my friends in the Georgia Tech Taido Club, and special thanks to Andy Fossett, a 5th degree black belt who reviewed the Taido scenes in this book. Any Taido mistakes are mine. Any Taido misspellings are Dakota's.

Thanks also to The Crucible of Oakland for providing both wonderful performances and a great space for learning the fire arts, and to Lara Hopwood, the instructor at the Crucible who taught my wife and me to spin fire.

The first major chunk of LIQUID FIRE was written in National Novel Writing Month of 2008, and thanks go to Chris Baty (for creating Nano), Grant Faulkner (for running it), and Ann Arbor (for letting me read clips of LIQUID FIRE on KFJC).

Of the many, many books I read for research, Helen Gaines's CRYPTANALYSIS and Martin Gardner's CODES, CIPHERS AND SECRET WRITING are called out in the text; I also recommend MAUI by Jan TenBruggencate and Douglas Peebles.

LIQUID FIRE is set in the world next door, so thanks to the familiar haunts of Atlanta and to the new haunts of the Bay Area, especially San Francisco's Union Square, Stanford's Bookstore, Palo Alto's Nola, and the much missed Asia de Cuba and Borders. Also thanks to Maui . . . for letting me blow it up. Sorry about the park.

Thanks again to my editor at Bell Bridge, Debra Dixon, who helped me hammer on LIQUID FIRE until it was shorter, tighter and punchier than BLOOD ROCK until, in short, we were both satisfied that you'd be satisfied with it.

Finally, I want to thank you, my readers, for making FROST MOON and BLOOD ROCK a success. I hope you enjoy the continuing adventures of Dakota Frost in LIQUID FIRE.

—the Centaur, February 17, 2015

P.S. Thanks, Big G. You know who you are.

About Anthony Francis

By day, Dr. Anthony G. Francis, Jr. builds intelligent machines and emotional robots; by night, he writes science fiction and draws comic books. He received his PhD from Georgia Tech in 2000 for a thesis applying human memory principles to information retrieval; since then, he's worked on 3D object visualization, search engines, robot pets, military software, police software, and software for the CDC. He cannot confirm or deny that he is currently working on robotics at Google.

Anthony loves exploring the collision of fantasy with reality; in the Skindancer series, he explores what Atlanta, Georgia and the San Francisco Bay Area would be like if populated with vampires, werewolves, wizards, and fae. Anthony spent almost two decades in Atlanta before he and his wife were lured out to San Jose by the Search Engine That Starts With A G. Like Dakota, Anthony dropped out of college chemistry, loves math, and is a brown belt in Taido, but unlike Dakota, he doesn't have a single tattoo.

LIQUID FIRE is the third in the Skindancer urban fantasy series, following FROST MOON and BLOOD ROCK, and Anthony has plans for many more. You can visit Anthony on the web at dresan.com, or learn more about the world of Dakota Frost at dakotafrost.com, or on her Facebook page facebook.com/dakotafrost.

CPSIA information can be obtained at www.ICGtesting.com
Printed in the USA
LVOW06s0743101015

457657LV00002B/325/P